A Year
of Favor

For Charles
and Angela
Thanks for your support!
Julia MacKenna

A YEAR OF FAVOR

A Novel

JULIA MacDONNELL

William Morrow and Company, Inc.
NEW YORK

Library of Congress Cataloging-in-Publication Data

MacDonnell, Julia.
    A year of favor / Julia MacDonnell.
       p.   cm.
    ISBN 0-688-12546-8
    1. Women journalists—New York (N.Y.)—Fiction.   2. Bronx (New York, N.Y.)—Fiction.   I. Title.
PS3563.A29142Y43   1994
813'.54—dc20
                                                     93-11432
                                                     CIP

Printed in the United States of America

First Edition

1 2 3 4 5 6 7 8 9 10

BOOK DESIGN BY GLEN M. EDELSTEIN

In memory of my mother,
Norma Cushing MacDonnell

The author gratefully acknowledges the generous assistance of Dennis R. Chang, Denis Mercier, and translator Lehea Potter Kuphal in the preparation of this manuscript.

PROLOGUE

New York, February 198–

AURORA RODRÍGUEZ WAS MURDERED THE LAST DAY I WORKED THE South Bronx beat. Sometime between midnight and four in the morning, Aurora Rodríguez was beaten and raped and dropped from the rooftop of an abandoned tenement. Her free-fall in the dark ended in a dumpster five stories below. A homeless man, scavenging for food or seeking shelter, found her naked body shortly before dawn.

The day Aurora Rodríguez died, I'd been covering the South Bronx for six years, two months, three weeks, and a day.

You tend to keep track of a fact like this at the *New York Herald-Sun*, the kind of fact with which you chart the trajectory of your career. What this fact told me, which I did not want to hear, was that my career had no trajectory. Somehow my career had lost its trajectory.

For at my newspaper, a newspaper of international stature, beats in the outer boroughs of New York City are considered apprenticeships, places to season reporters and hone their skills before moving them to other, more challenging, more newsworthy places. In fact, my apprenticeship had been the longest anyone could remember, maybe the longest in the history of the paper. Not that I talked about it much or ever actually asked anyone. And I wouldn't go searching through the archives for confirmation.

But time and again I'd been rejected for openings in the national and foreign bureaus, been told I wasn't ready. Recently, after a younger, less experienced metro reporter was sent to Mexico City, a post I coveted, an editor told me I was "too valuable" where I was to reassign. It occurred to me the most valuable thing about me might be my Spanish surname, Guerrera, patrimony of a father who'd disappeared not long after I was born. It was good public relations to have a reporter with a Spanish surname covering the South Bronx.

Long before Aurora Rodríguez was killed, the metro copy desk had begun calling me, but never to my face, the eternal starlet, and I pretended not to know.

"You work the starlet's copy yet, Joe?" "Nah, I like to save the best till last." Chortle. Chortle.

The signs seemed obvious: there was no higher place for me at the *New York Herald-Sun* than a police beat in the Bronx. Still I refused to take the hint. The *Herald-Sun* was one of the world's great newspapers, and I was not about to leave it. Tenacity, the steely hook of my ambition, had gotten me hired in the first place, and it would keep me hanging on no matter what.

The night Aurora Rodríguez was murdered, I didn't have a story. And I hate nights when I don't have a story, nights at my desk, phone silent, when I have nothing to do but diddle with the keyboard of my computer terminal and worry that I'll never get another story.

That particular night—it must have been close to deadline, say around midnight, when other reporters were filing important stories, maybe even front-page stories, and editors were slathering them with praise—I looked beyond the rim of my pod and saw, across the newsroom, in a corner I thought of as the holding pen, a group of shriveled gray retainers, men and women the paper hadn't yet figured out how to get rid of. I saw them listening to police scanners, checking wire service transmissions, writing local obituaries, scurrying around trying to look busy—the ghosts of former reporters whose careers had fizzled out.

I couldn't stop watching them. I looked at them, then at the frantic editors and reporters, and finally at myself. I could actually see how I was going no place, could see how I really was stalled in my career, which was my life. And when I saw this, I felt as if I were standing naked outside, in the frigid wind and snow squalls, not sitting well-dressed in my pod in the newsroom with its sound-absorbing carpets and temperature-controlled air. And I knew I had to get up and get moving, or I might be paralyzed.

I did the only reasonable thing I could have done under the circumstances—I decided to go shopping, shopping for a story.

The ability to develop sources is crucial for reporters, and it happens to be one of my better skills. During my tenure in the South Bronx I'd had the time to work on it, carefully nurturing cops and judges, law clerks, court stenographers and court officers, assistant district attorneys, bail bondsmen, public defenders, secretaries, paralegals, advocates from legal services and the ACLU, welfare case workers, community organizers, clergymen, and bureaucrats and politicians at all levels of borough government.

Once a week or so I would browse through these sources, meandering along East 161st Street to Sheridan Avenue, swinging out to Southern Boulevard, going back in by way of Tremont Avenue, pounding pavements I'd known since birth. Often I would pass, in the shadows of Yankee Stadium, the apartment building where I'd grown up and where my mother still lived.

Sometimes I'd stop and visit her in the fourth-floor walk-up we'd shared until I started working at the *Herald-Sun*. Sometimes we'd drink tea and talk, the Good Mother and Good Daughter following a script. More often something else would happen and we'd go improvisational, creating with no apparent effort yet another episode in the never-ending soap opera of our relationship. Then I'd leave in a hurry, but never fast enough, wondering why, despite my efforts and accomplishments, I couldn't make things better. I felt trapped in a complicated maze.

During those shopping trips to the Bronx, I'd graze among my sources, chat them up, maybe buy them lunch or a drink, finding out directly and/or indirectly what good stuff they might have for me that day. Our contracts were implicit: from time to time, like journalistic sources everywhere, they got back space in the newspaper, and the accompanying feeling of power and importance. Access to the media meant free publicity for themselves and their programs, causes, or ideas. Sometimes they even got a way to carry out, by proxy, their personal vendettas.

Of course, it was too late that night for one of my typical shopping trips. But the moment I'd decided to shop, I'd also known where and how: I would seek out one of my best sources, a man who was very good at what he did, a man who almost always had usable information, a man I always had to see at night. This source had given me several of my best stories—and I'd worked on him long enough to know I could get anything I wanted out of him. Anything he had he would, sooner or later, give me.

Ours was not, however, a standard strain of reporter/source symbiosis. Because my source did not want his name in the paper. He wasn't interested in power, not the usual kind anyway, and he had no causes. He wanted something else. So when I drove up to the Bronx that night I knew I would get something from him and would be giving something too.

The wind was blowing from the northeast, and the weathermen predicted heavy snow. My breath made smoky puffs inside the car. But 42nd Street was incandescent, its crystal lights like strings of morning stars. As I drove eastward across it, I convinced myself I wasn't paralyzed: I was moving forward, going someplace. And as the heater ground away, the frozen feeling left me.

I took the FDR Drive and drove north across the Willis Avenue Bridge, seeing, even in the dark, the murky Harlem River and the railroad freight yards on the river's Bronx bank. Just beyond were Hunts Point and the rows of empty and dilapidated buildings that had housed the neighborhood of Mott Haven not long before. It was a route I could drive sleeping and maybe sometimes did. But that night I wasn't sleeping. That night I was alert, jittery in a hot rush of adrenaline, a news junkie craving a fix and certain she would get one.

I found him at a bar called the Scorpion on Tremont Avenue. Its smoky heat was heaven after the cold wind on the street. Through it, through the boisterous crowd, the rock music hurting my ears, I picked out his shoulders and back as he hunched, elbows on the bar, talking to another detective I recognized. Jukebox rock made thought impossible. Somebody bumped me, blocked my view, and when they moved, he was gone. Then he was beside me, with his arm around me, his holstered .38 pressing into me. He led me to the far end of the bar where it was not as loud and crowded.

What's up, baby? he asked, or something like that, his eyes glittering and distant in the bad light. He held my arm as I slid onto a bar stool, then stood behind me and ordered me a drink. Whenever he leaned over me to get his drink, I felt the gun again. I remembered playing with it, remembered its weight and the metal warming in my hands, remembered how it was always there with us, between us, a part of what we did.

What we did, I liked imagining, was nothing more than trade favors and information, like characters in a film noir. I liked imagining that what we did was harmless, or that we did it for a higher purpose: providing news to the public, news the public had a right to know. This was my fantasy, abetted always by the times and places that we met, by the way he looked and spoke his lines. What I never admitted to myself was that I wasn't always sure about my own role, and that my lines sometimes confused me.

I can't remember most of what we talked about that night anyway. I can't remember most of what I asked, what he told me. Every time I try, I end up confused, thinking of a different night, a different bar. I'm sure I drank quite a bit of Wild Turkey. I'm sure I kept trying to see myself in the mirror that faced the bar. I remember trying, on alternate currents of hilarity and desperation, to find the outline of my face through the clouds of cigarette smoke, trying to reassure myself that I still looked good or that I still existed.

At the same time, I was picking and poking at him. I was tapping for the lode, for facts and information, for dirt about crimes, criminals, or other cops, for a story that might win me a reprieve from the verbal killing field of the metro desk—where my stories about the mundane crimes of the Bronx's dispossessed were hacked to bits, the bones buried on the bottom of page two, section two, under the heading "Metropolitan Briefs."

But at some point as we huddled there together, inside the smoke and music, Wild Turkey thinning out my blood, our film-noir script disintegrated, transformed itself into another kind of script, something darker, more impulsive. I heard him telling me exactly what it was he wanted and how he wanted it. At first I didn't understand. Then he was saying it again, and I was watching him say it in the mirror, his face only half visible through the smoke, and hearing his whispered words, feeling his touch. Something in me erupted with such force that I leaned against him, curled my fingers around his arm to keep from being swept away.

We drove in my car a few blocks to the Galaxy Motel. It's a place with moving colored lights outside, red and pink and orange floodlights glowing up and crisscrossing from between half-dead azaleas. When it's dark enough and you're drunk enough you can stare hard at the moving colored lights for a while and imagine you're in space or about to go there.

That night it was dark enough and no doubt we were drunk enough, but we didn't take the time to stare hard at the lights. Our slow glide into the parking lot set off an otherworldly chorus of dance and song. At the sight of my car, the working girls came at us from the shadows, legs flashing, legs bare below hot pants and miniskirts despite the cold. Their voices, high-pitched and jeering, careened on the cold wind as they converged upon the car, slowed it to a halt. They shrieked and moaned at the sight of me, and when I got out one of them hollered, "What you want tired old white pussy for?" I might have yelled something back, but the others were laughing too hard, and they kept on laughing until the wind or his hand blew back his leather coat and exposed the gun, which silenced them.

Then we were inside and the gun was gleaming on the bed. I began taking off my clothes. The light was a dim yellow, the room full of shadows. I saw my shadow on the wall above the bed—the shadow of me shedding my clothes and letting them fall; the shadow of me readying myself for a role in a different kind of film, a role that wasn't less confusing, but at least had fewer lines.

I can't explain much more about it, our particular ritual. We never talked about ourselves and we didn't talk about not talking. I suppose, now, that it had something to do with being bound and released, with being brought to a dangerous and familiar place where I had no control at all but knew exactly what would happen, a surrender that afterward I tried not to remember.

That night we didn't get far anyway, only far enough for it to hurt when we stopped. What stopped us was a sudden electronic bleat. The high-pitched plaint seemed to be coming from the air, and it halted us as abruptly as if a switch had been thrown, a plug yanked, a generator blown. Then we were motionless, suspended, and all my ganglions were clanging. Bleep bleep bleep, it demanded. Bleep bleep bleep, it insisted. Bleep bleep bleep in a language I didn't understand. Bleep bleep bleep.

He cocked his head above me, listening. His eyes gleamed like a cat's. Almost right away he began to understand. Because he rolled away from me and I was reaching for him, crying no. Bleep, bleep, bleep.

Disconnected and confused, I watched him raking his scalp with his fingers, then lunging off the bed and going after it. Bleep, bleep bleep. He was tearing at the tangled sheets and clothes when I, too, recognized the sound. A beeper. I'd left mine in the car. Fuck, he said, grabbing his from the floor. Fuck. And finally it stopped.

There were no room phones at the Galaxy, so he made his call from a booth outside. The call transformed him into a stranger: sober, wary, and silent. I drove this stranger back to his car at the Scorpion. And I kept on going behind him when he pulled out, following him without an invitation through the vacant streets of the South Bronx. Because I figured that at that time of day in that place I'd take what I could get. The tin-sealed windows of the abandoned tenements, like sad, blind eyes, stared all along the way.

My source stopped at the end of a row of collapsing, burned-out buildings, under a faded billboard for sneakers that read *"La Calle Está Dura."* He got out running, hunched forward into the wind, stumbling once against windblown debris catching at his feet. Through dull gray light I saw him heading for a dumpster in an alley between two buildings.

I pulled up behind two NYPD cruisers, struggled against the wind as I made my way toward the dumpster. In the alley, I couldn't feel the wind. In fact, it was very quiet, though perhaps a dozen men and women were already there—detectives from the Sex Crimes Unit, the Homicide Unit, assorted other laborers for the criminal justice system. They worked without speaking, many of them gathered atop the dumpster. I watched them for a while, and they seemed to be moving very slowly, jotting into their notebooks, placing indiscernible things they were picking up with metal pincers into resealable plastic bags. Nudged more by a sense of duty or professional obligation than by curiosity, I moved closer. I wedged my feet against the dumpster's bottom rim, grabbed its icy metal edge, and hoisted myself up.

She was there within my arm's reach, facedown on a pillow of broken glass, the child whose name turned out to be Aurora. She lay sprawled like a discarded doll on top of broken furniture, burned mattresses, empty liquor bottles, chicken bones, soiled Pampers.

Right away I noted certain details: that her hair was neatly cornrowed, the braids held by red barrettes; that she wore white socks with ruffles at the ankles. Then the forensic photographer began to work and they were illuminated by lightning bolts of icy blue, the bruises that mottled her back and limbs and buttocks like camouflage.

The supernatural light of the photographer's strobe kept flashing, and in it I saw petals of her blood scattered over the debris and how her arms were stretched out above her head, her small fingers curled, as if she'd been trying to grab for something she couldn't quite get hold of.

"Jesus, Lizzie, what in hell . . ." The voice detached me from the dumpster. I stumbled getting down. "What in hell are you doing here?"

It was a detective sergeant named O'Malley, head of the Sex Crimes Unit, and my source's boss. I couldn't seem to answer him. I looked away, saw my source crouched over the body, lifting it, saying something to the photographer. O'Malley grunted, shook his head, walked away. Without meaning to or wanting to I'd given him his answer.

I walked out to the sidewalk and crunched over a frozen puddle. It shattered like a window in a concrete wall, a window looking onto nothing. Then I heard the wail of an ambulance, the ambulance that would take her to the basement morgue of a nearby city hospital. I didn't want to think about that either, was trying not to when O'Malley again showed up beside me. He was holding something, shaking something in my face.

"We found this stuff in there," he rasped, flailing with his other arm toward one of the buildings, its windows sheets of tin. "How old was she? Four or five? Huh? Somebody brought her in there, took their time raping her and beating her, and then dropped her off the roof. Now isn't that a juicy story? Good reading for the public?"

I didn't answer. I watched him, thinking he was not quite in control. I thought maybe he ought to find another line of work.

"Now Lizzie," he went on, stepping so close the things he held brushed my cheek, "thanks to your big, tough boyfriend, you can have the first look at the evidence. Have a real good look at it so you can get it right. Come on now, write it down and maybe you'll get yourself a byline. Write the details in your notebook so you can have yourself a story."

But O'Malley didn't know anything about reporting. He didn't understand the process. O'Malley didn't know reporters don't have to write everything in their notebooks. He didn't understand that reporters remember some things very well without writing them down. And I would always remember exactly what he showed to me that day: a little dress with red hearts on it and a pair of underpants emblazoned with the smiling face of Minnie Mouse.

The Roman goddess of dawn was called Aurora. In Spanish the word means dawn or beginning. It is a name evocative of hope—and perhaps Aurora's mother had some on the day Aurora was born. Every trace of it was gone the day Aurora died.

Her name was María, she was twenty-five, and I found her at the Fox Street Family Shelter, where she'd been living with her children since a fire had destroyed their Grand Concourse apartment. I drove there after waiting several hours at the local precinct to learn the girl's identity and her family's whereabouts. The shelter was actually the gymnasium of a converted elementary school, a vast space filled with cots and cribs and mothers and their children. The high metal-raftered ceiling echoed the din of infants squalling for feedings, the babble of restless children and televisions tuned to *Sesame Street* and *Looney Tunes*. It smelled of sweat and toast and baby poop.

Officials of the shelter had reported Aurora's disappearance the night before. And officials of the shelter had identified the body once it had been brought in to the morgue. Theirs had also been the task of informing Aurora's mother.

I spoke to María maybe an hour later, after arguing with the shelter administrator that the public had a right to know this story. Reluctantly she brought me in and introduced me, hovered in the background. María was rocking to and fro on the edge of a canvas cot. Her black eyes scanned my face, then roved the empty space around it. She wasn't grieving yet. She seemed instead to be lost in a place of dreamy numbness.

"*Soy periodista,*" I said, kneeling on the floor beside her. "*Lo siento mucho.*"

María was dark-skinned, like her daughter, and I wondered what nationality she was, guessed probably Dominican.

"*Mi bebé,*" she whispered, and again she looked away.

But Aurora was not actually her baby. A toddler younger than Aurora was clinging to María's knees, and an infant was curled up in her lap sucking her pinkie. Two older children sat behind her, their arms entwined and wrapped around her, as though to suture the family's newest wound.

I took María's hand, squeezed it until I felt her pulse.

"Soy periodista," I repeated. *"Su historia es muy importante. Quiero contar su historia."*

When María did not respond, I said again, slowly and emphatically, as if to a child, Your story is important. I want to tell your story. She pulled her hand away, shifted the position of the baby she was holding.

"Mi periódico es muy grande," I urged after a minute. *"Podemos contar su historia a mucha gente."*

My newspaper is very large. We can tell your story to many people. I took out my notebook and pen, gestures that seemed to release an audio loop.

"Mi hija. Muerta. Violada. Mi pobrecita. Mi niña bonita. Mi Aurora. Muerta. Violada."

"¿Qué pasó?" I interrupted the hushed, desperate voice, the awful lament. *"Dígame, por favor. Dígame todo."*

The question—What happened?—silenced her, maybe took her someplace she didn't want to go. She shook her head listlessly, moved her gaze across the floor, where frenzied cockroaches feasted on crumbs of Wonder Bread and Oreos. Nearby a plastic trash bag was collapsing from its burden of paper plates and diapers. For a time it hypnotized us, that trash bag, with its slow downward tilt, its imminent collapse.

By then other mothers, other children, were gathering around us, calling out in Spanish various details. Aurora had been watching television in another part of the shelter. Aurora had disobeyed her mother. Aurora was a flirt, a wild and funny child. Aurora had been playing with some older children. Aurora thought she was a teenager. The last time anyone had seen Aurora was about ten o'clock that evening. Then the details ran out. No one could say exactly where she'd been or who she'd been with.

They were very close to us, mothers who looked like children and their children, their voices squeezed high and tight, their eyes bright with the wattage of catastrophe. I turned back to María, who watched us from her distance, her eyes afloat in crescents of fatigue.

"Dígame su historia," I exhorted once again, my voice no more than a whisper. Tell me your story. Again I held her hand, met her eyes, hoping she could read in mine sincerity. And when she finally answered, speaking thoughtfully in fragmented English, I was no longer ready.

"I don't know what happen. I teach my babies, stay by me and you be safe. This all I have to give them. Stay by Mommy. You be safe."

* * *

A snow squall was blowing outside, I couldn't find my gloves, and for a minute with the white flakes whirling all around me, I lost my way, headed back toward the dumpster thinking I was heading back to my car. And when at last I found my car, got into it, I felt somehow lost, didn't know quite what to do or where to go next.

Snow covered the windshield, darkened the inside of the car. The heater blew icy gusts into my face. Of course, I wasn't lost. I knew the territory very well. Still, the shelter had been a foreign place, a colony of helpless women and their children, the kind of women whose stories didn't often interest my editors.

"They're not actually our constituency, Elizabeth," an editor had told me once when I'd tried to pitch a story about the marketing of infant formula to welfare mothers in New York. Our constituency, he didn't need to tell me, consisted of wealthy, well-educated white Manhattanites.

The others, the ones I wrote about, my editors called natives, natives meaning they were indigenous to other, more primitive places—like Africa, say, or the islands of the southern Atlantic or Caribbean. The cities of Eastern Europe, South Africa, China, and the Middle East always got more and better play than Harlem, Bed-Stuy, or the South Bronx.

I had to fight for every inch of space. I was accustomed to my editors' yawns when I came in with a good story, to their constant admonitions that I "boil down" my stories to the "bare bones." I invariably wrote too much and they invariably dismembered what I'd written. Copy editors. I thought of them as august cannibals, languid yet voracious eaters of description and allusion, who calmly carved flesh and muscle off my babies. "Abandon tropes all ye who enter here," read a sign attached to one copy editor's terminal.

Of course, a white girl who'd been savaged in Westchester would automatically make the front page. And a white girl savaged in the northern Bronx would at least make the second front—the first page of the metropolitan section, the best play I ever hoped for. But the story of a black girl savaged in the South Bronx did not have equal news value. This was a fact of my journalistic life, something few reporters would fail to understand. Aurora Rodríguez was the wrong color. I couldn't help pondering this detail as I sat there in my car deciding how to work the story. Aurora Rodríguez was the wrong color. She also had the wrong kind of last name and she'd been murdered in the wrong place. In terms of news values, her story had three strikes against it.

On the other hand, she was the right age. My editors would no doubt find her age "compelling." And she'd been living in a city-run shelter, had in fact been moved into that shelter by city social services officials. Which meant the city bore some of the responsibility for her death, and would be forced to offer an explanation. My editors would like that too. Already my source was tracking down a tip that someone who worked at the shelter had been seen leaving with Aurora. If this tip bore fruit, it would be a major story.

Then another thought emerged on a painful shard of hope: that a wolf pack of neighborhood boys had somehow gotten hold of her. Wolf packs of ghetto youths were getting a very big play that year. And if one of them had gotten to Aurora, I would almost certainly arise from the boneyard of the Metro Briefs. I would make the front page of the newspaper.

The wipers squeaked against the snow, but I was too cold to get out to clear the windshield. Trembling with effort, the wipers cleared twin trapezoids on the glittering screen. The light pouring in was so bright it hurt my eyes, but outside there seemed to be no color. Instead, all the gray snow-touched tenements, the streets and sidewalks, seemed to dance with a weird electric brightness like a TV when the color tube has blown.

I put the car into gear and headed to work along the ice-patched highways. I thought about Aurora, about how to tell her story. I couldn't help thinking that if the story broke right, if my source came through at the right time with something good for me, like an arrest, and if I told the story well, the story would mean something, not just to her family and to me, but to everyone who read it. It would offer a window onto the world of the poor, exposing not only the feminization of poverty, but the infantization of poverty as well. It would tell important truths about how some people had to live.

As I kept driving through sudden blinding gusts of snow that alternated with the awesome brightness—vigilant and fearful of a skid—my head turned big and empty as the sky and Aurora's story got lost among the synapses.

When I pulled into the *Herald-Sun*'s basement garage on 47th Street, everything was shades of gray, still jittering with the weird electric brightness. "Rough night, Lizzie?" somebody asked when I got out of the elevator. The words wrapped around me like an accusation. But when I turned to answer, no one was there. I stopped in the bathroom to make sure my hair was combed and my mouth on straight before I went into the newsroom.

My steps were soundless as I walked across the thick carpet. The walls, floors, and ceilings of the long, windowless room were matching shades of taupe—monochromatic even when my color tube was not blown. The light was soft and even, emanating from hidden suns in an acoustic sky.

The editorial offices of the *New York Herald-Sun* reflected its stature as one of the world's premier news organizations. Expert ergonomists had been consulted in the creation of its electronic newsroom, the ideal working environment. The only sound was the hypnotic humming of computers. You risked becoming a center of attention, which it did not pay to be at the *New York Herald-Sun*, if you spoke above a whisper.

At any moment of the day or night, dozens of reporters would be working in their pods, hidden from each other, while editors, seated in circular or crescent-shaped formations, would be seated silently before their terminals, leaning toward the monitors as if to warm themselves. The newsroom's cool hush and lack of color seemed to feed upon everyone who entered it. Working there I usually felt mute, invisible, and very far from home.

I'd just settled at my desk when I felt a tap on my shoulder. I didn't want to feel it, didn't respond until I felt another tap. I looked up, saw a foreign editor named James McManus standing by my desk. He was shoving horn-rimmed glasses up to his crown. I couldn't remember which part of the world he dealt with, couldn't imagine what he wanted.

"If you've got a minute, Elizabeth, Mr. Van Doorn wants to see you."

His voice was very low, almost a whisper.

"Right away."

There was a scratching sound in his throat that might have been a laugh.

"You know how he is."

But of course I did not know how Van Doorn was, because Van Doorn, managing editor Nathan Van Doorn, had never before asked to see me. Not once in my nine years at the paper had I been inside his office. Of course, I'd met him, chatted with him, at various functions and meetings, but that had been the extent of our relationship.

McManus was a skinny, nervous man, and I hardly knew him either. As I watched him rub his eyelids with his index fingers, I saw my source and me in the dark room at the Galaxy, and I wondered how they'd found out. Such behavior with a source was grounds for automatic termination.

"Let's go," I heard him say, and my heart swelled up into my throat, hammered as if it were trying to get out.

We rode the taupe elevator up to Nathan Van Doorn's taupe office. Sweat dampened my palms. Figuring I'd have to shake his hand, I hid my hands behind my back, wiped them on the railing. Then the doors were sliding open and I was blinking against the bright light pouring through his wall of glass.

Van Doorn's office was on the fifty-third story of a building taller than all those that surrounded it. Wisps of cloud and sparkling snowflakes blew against its windows. He was standing near them, his back to us, surrounded by a jungle of flowering plants, small trees, and vines. He seemed to be surveying a kingdom of purity and peace. But beyond the lacy veil of cloud and snow the sky was heavy and dull as tarnished metal. When he turned, he was holding a long-spouted brass watering can. He didn't look at us, instead leaned into the shiny ficus next to him, sluiced its roots.

"Did you tell her?"

He spoke without expression, face hidden by the ficus, and when he finished, he moved on to other exotic plants preening in the dazzle from his windows.

"No. I thought you ought to."

McManus laughed, but the sound was strangled, as if a wad of paper might be stuck in his throat. McManus and I were standing in front of Van Doorn's marble desk, and we watched him ministering to plants in the silver light. While he worked I quivered at the precipice, glimpsed the abyss beyond it, the black hole where I'd be jobless, stripped of income and status—not even a shriveled gray obituary writer, but instead unemployed. I watched Van Doorn and pretended I wasn't scared. I vowed to not admit a thing, to not give anything away, no emotions, not even any signs of them.

Van Doorn took his time. He let me quake there at the precipice and gaze down into the abyss, while he watered plants, picking off dead leaves and flowers, squishing them. I watched him, certain I'd be crushed like a dead bud, then dropped into the trash. I couldn't help thinking of Aurora, and what had happened to her.

At last Van Doorn placed the watering can on a sparkling étagère in the jungle. He turned to face us, directed his face toward mine, and arranged it into a smile shape, though his eyes did not take part in the arrangement. Then he was coming at me with his hand outstretched, a thick-chested man, his neck above his starched collar as powerful as a pugilist's. His bald pate gleamed in the light, and he was manicured and custom-suited. But I saw the refinements were a thin veneer barely able to contain his aggression, his intelligence.

"Elizabeth," he said. "Elizabeth M. Guerrera from our metropolitan desk."

I took his hand, squeezing hard and fast so he couldn't make me wince. His pinball eyes made a fast circuit from my eyebrows to my ankles, slid back up to my middle, paused somewhere near my belly button. He seemed to examine it through the flowered challis of my skirt before nodding once or twice abruptly, letting go of my hand, walking away.

"We've decided to send you to Central America, Elizabeth. To Bellavista."

The words flew at me, spinning like the snowflakes. Bellavista: an earthquake, an endless civil war, a peaceful solution, a new government. No longer one of the best news places in the world—there were bigger stories elsewhere. But a great news place nonetheless, better than I'd ever dared to hope for. Then I seemed to be spinning too, and I wanted to grab hold of something but I couldn't, couldn't get hold of anything, especially not Van Doorn's words as they hurled me from perdition to salvation.

Bellavista: Alan Hartwell's beat.

"There's a new government in Bellavista, as you know," Van Doorn intoned. "And, uh, what we want is a fresh start down there. New blood. On both sides."

Van Doorn was squinting, sliding one hand over his gleaming crown. He gestured toward a pair of leather chairs before his desk. McManus and I sat down automatically, not an instant too soon. Van Doorn sat behind his own desk, placed his hands flat on top, and cleared his throat.

"And, uh, as you perhaps may know, Hartwell has been reassigned."

Hartwell, the curly-haired wunderkind from Princeton, Nieman Fellow, star player in the annual Pulitzer rumors, Van Doorn's favored little prince. As I no doubt knew, as every journalist in the country no doubt knew, Hartwell had been reassigned. He'd been yanked from Bellavista in a spectacular fall from grace that in itself had made news. And Hartwell had not been reassigned to one of the bigger stories, to Eastern Europe or the Middle East. He'd been sent instead to a suburban bureau in Southern California. But none of that was important. Hartwell didn't matter. I was on my way to Bellavista.

"I've always thought of the South Bronx as a training ground for you, a place to season you and hone your skills. . . ."

The words seemed to be coming from far away, seemed to apply to someone else, and I don't think she understood that all those dark nights in the South Bronx had been part of Van Doorn's strategy for her career.

"I've had my eye on you, Elizabeth." I stared at him, and still he smiled. "You've proved time and again you're a gutsy newswoman, an astute reporter. We believe here at the *Herald-Sun* that Bellavista is a place where you will really shine."

Van Doorn himself was already shining. Light was shimmering on his skull and face and fingernails. But I could hardly see or hear what he was saying.

"We can't let a first-rate journalist like you languish on the city desk. . . ."

The elevator lurched, plunged toward earth, but I seemed to be flying upward, an idea that made me reel, so I grabbed the railing, closed my eyes, felt again how big and empty my head was, like the shell of a huge mollusk. But I also felt elated, exalted. When the elevator doors slid back and I stepped out into the newsroom, I seemed to be emerging from a dream. I felt whole and peaceful as after a long sleep.

When I look back on that moment, the moment I stepped out of the elevator and on into the rest of my life, I see myself transformed. Because when I stepped out, arm in arm with McManus, I was Elizabeth, the foreign correspondent. My smile was brilliant in the cool light of the newsroom's hidden suns. And all the outward clues to my bad night—ratty hair, torn pantyhose, broken fingernail—were miraculously invisible.

Old sad Lizzie, the hungry and unwashed one, late of the Scorpion and Galaxy, probably stayed inside me. But now I didn't feel her, couldn't recognize her. Instead the other me, the gutsy newswoman, the astute reporter, strode through the newsroom with McManus, accepting the congratulations of her colleagues, looking confident and happy.

Surging adrenaline buoyed me all that day, but it also made me giddy, maybe caused amnesia. Because I remember only bits and pieces. I remember meeting with McManus, other editors, the Mexico City bureau chief. I remember going to the personnel department to arrange various papers. I remember talking on the phone to AeroVista, trying to arrange my flight. Then McManus handed me a couple of thick clip files labeled Bellavista and I read about the earthquake that had destroyed the capital, Libertad, and about the long civil war. I read about acts of leftist terrorism, about death squads responsible for the disappearances and murders of thousands of civilians. I read how *los madres de los desaparecidos* were commemorating the missing and the dead with crosses along roadsides where bodies had been found. I read how the Peaceful Solution was making life better for everyone.

Most of the stories had been written by Hartwell. What I didn't read, however—couldn't read, because it wasn't in the file—was the story that had caused his trouble: the report of a military massacre of hundreds of civilians at a place called Aguas Oscuras, a report the State Department insisted was a lie.

"Aguas Oscuras is a conundrum," McManus told me when I asked about the missing clip. "There's no need for you to be concerned with it right now."

So I'd gone to the clip library, found and photocopied Hartwell's story. And maybe it was then, after I'd come back, that the phone on my desk rang and I picked it up without thought, murmured, "Elizabeth Guerrera."

"I love you, baby girl."

"Mum."

"No matter what, I love you, Lizzie. You know I do."

My mother's voice was girlish, breathy. I held my breath, waiting to hear the ice cubes clinking in her highball glass. I couldn't remember what she was talking about, why she was offering this particular oblique apology.

"It's all right, Mum, I know you do." Still I did not remember. "Something's happened, Mummy, something wonderful," I went on, unable to stop. "Here. Today. I've been promoted. I've been made a foreign correspondent. I'm going to Bellavista."

She didn't respond, and as I waited I heard the empty roar in my own head. Then I tried to compose an image of her, my mother, where she was sitting, what she was wearing, the expression on her face. But the tattered bag of my memory yielded only scanty scraps I couldn't piece together.

"You're leaving."

The whispered words rebounded, came back again with gathered force.

"You're leaving me."

"For a couple of years. Maybe more. Oh, I don't mean it that way. I'll be back for visits. But, you know, it's what I've been waiting for all these years, my whole life. It's an opportunity I couldn't—"

"You're all I have." She spoke very slowly with her breathy voice, but what came to me through the wires was the primitive language of her desolation. "And now you're leaving. . . ."

I held the receiver, waiting for more, but the line was hollow, resonating. My exhalations seemed to echo through an abyss, maybe the one I'd seen in Van Doorn's office. I don't know how the connection was broken, if my mother put down the receiver or if I pressed the wrong button by mistake.

I seemed to hear her for a long time after that. But she'd always known my points of entry. She knew how to move in fast, the way she did that day, before I could shut down, close her out. Like a vagabond she'd come in with her rage and sadness to offer a litany of complaints, a long list of my failings. I knew what she was doing, yet she had the power to confuse me, make me guilty. Somehow she held my faith.

"What are the natives stirring up tonight, Lizzie?"

I recognized his voice before I looked up, saw my assignment editor standing by my desk holding a clipboard. I smiled at him, grateful for the interruption.

"You're in the news business and you haven't heard the news?"

He laughed, pulled from his vest pocket the gold watch I'd always thought was a silly affectation. He held it out at arm's length and squinted.

"By my clock you're on the metro desk until after tonight's deadline. I figured you'd want to go out with a bang, a big story. It's your last chance to tell our readers everything you know about the South Bronx."

Of course, that was also my chance to tell him about Aurora, my chance to offer him the story, to get it on the local news budget for the next day's paper. By then I knew the investigation had targeted a neighborhood youth who volunteered at the shelter, and whose whereabouts were currently unknown. But I found as I looked at my assignment editor that I was no longer interested in telling our readers everything I knew about the South Bronx. And though I looked at him, I kept seeing images of the Bronx, like news photos flashing: Yankee Stadium, the criminal courts building, rows of abandoned tenements, the Scorpion, the Galaxy, my mother's place, the Fox Street Family Shelter. Then the images were shrinking and I could see them only from a distance, as in a rearview mirror. I was escaping: I had escaped. I had escaped and I wasn't going back for anything.

"Cut me a break, Jake."

I smiled at my assignment editor and he smiled back, shrugged, and walked away. "What the hell," he called over his shoulder. "What's another Metro Brief?"

Again I glimpsed Aurora, the broken baby in the dumpster. I saw her mottled bruises and her arms stretching up as if she'd been grabbing for something she couldn't quite get hold of. But I also saw that she was someone else's child, a piece in someone else's history, irrelevant to my current circumstances. I didn't need her story anymore.

After that my throat tightened, and my windpipe seemed to contract. I walked out to the water cooler in the hall, pulled down a cone-shaped cup. I pressed the spigot on the big blue bottle, filled the dunce's cap, and drank. I refilled it several times. I walked to the candy machine, bought some spearmint Life Savers, and popped a couple into my mouth to make the bad taste go away.

When I walked back into the newsroom, I saw my coworkers applauding. After a minute of confusion, I understood they were applauding for me. They had gathered, members of the metro staff, the foreign desk, Van Doorn himself, assorted others, at a conference table near the metro copy desk.

There were bottles of champagne and trays of canapés. They called my name, offering congratulations, the rolling murmur a vindication. Well-wishers surrounded me—editors and reporters who hadn't spoken to me for years. I smiled at all of them, shook their hands, accepted the dry lips they brushed against my burning cheeks, and at last I took a glass of champagne.

I'd drunk most of it when I heard the phone on my desk ringing. I listened, couldn't help it, because it kept on ringing like a punishment even as I gulped another glass. I knew it must be him, my source, the sex crimes detective, because he never failed to call me back. I realized he could be calling with the facts, the telling details that would tell Aurora's story.

I held out my glass and somebody refilled it. A froth of bubbles overflowed the glass, spilled down my fingers. I licked them, swallowed the champagne, looked around for more. Because I didn't want to hear his voice or anything he had to say.

PART ONE

Bellavista

CHAPTER ONE

*T*HE SWIMMING POOL AT THE HOTEL LIDO WAS SHAPED EXACTLY like a bean. It filled the hotel's verdant courtyard like a bloated pinto, a fat frijole, one of the cheap, hardy legumes that sustain the peasants of Bellavista. But even when I saw it for the first time, during the steamy languor of siesta, it was obvious the pool's designers had nothing in mind as socially conscious as a monument to surviving *campesinos*. Their driving vision had been more exotic, less definable. For the pool was a dazzling, unnatural azure that danced with blades of steely light as the afternoon sun and an easterly breeze from the Pacific struck it at the same time.

It also wore a thick collar of roses. Fat grandifloras in reds and pinks and yellows billowed toward the water like lengths of bright lace. They stretched and bobbed when riffled by the light wind, offering up their heated perfume. As if by thorns, this perfume clung to the humid air. It had been waiting in my suite when I arrived, had insisted I go out to the gallery to discover its source. I went out, saw the pool, and the elaborate mantel that was broken at each end for a pair of slender ladders. The ladders seemed to invite swimmers, but despite the heat there were none. Only rose petals floated on the surface of the water. One after another they were sucked into the white mouths of the filters.

The Hotel Lido, its name borrowed, for obscure reasons, from an Italian island in the Adriatic, was the first hotel to have been built after the earthquake, and it remained the only first-class hotel in metropolitan Libertad. It provided shelter, comfort, and a base of operations for international journalists and businessmen, agricultural consultants, military advisers.

I'd been given Hartwell's second-story suite—a balconied office that looked down toward Libertad, and a bedroom facing the courtyard and pool. The gallery outside my rooms made a kind of canopy for the terrace restaurant below. From it I could see the restaurant's marble railing, which was aflame with potted flamboyants. Beside the railing was the pool in the landscaped courtyard. Beyond them, *las montañas volcánicas de las Esmeraldas*—the volcanic mountains called the Emeralds— billowed to the sky, offering an opulent display of green.

Above them, a wispy gauze of cirrus overlaid a cerulean sky. A dozen huge black birds hung motionless at the junction of the mountains and sky. Then, as if an unseen hand had suddenly released them, the birds began to plummet one by one.

I watched them fall, saw again the dazzling green of las Esmeraldas. On steep tiers, within their dark earth, they held Bellavista's treasure: coffee, Emerald Mountain coffee, prized throughout the world for nearly two centuries. Most of the fighting had also happened in the mountains. Despite the declared end to the war and the promises of La Solución Pacífica, I was sure las Esmeraldas still held treasure for me, a rich harvest of news stories ripe for me to pick.

The hotel rested on one of the lower slopes, just above the ruined capital. Its pink stucco facade gazed over, majestically ignored, that massive graveyard. I'd seen the hotel on our approach to Cauchimpca International, had wondered what it was, the huge, winged structure alighting like a gawky pink bird on that bright patch of mountainside.

It was rumored that the Hotel Lido had been built with American money sent to aid survivors of the earthquake; that a group of military officers had helped themselves to funds earmarked to build homes for the survivors and had instead built the hotel.

That first day, it was obvious that whoever built the Hotel Lido had worked hard to create within it an island of tranquillity, an anodyne against Bellavista's recent troubled past. The hotel's steel-reinforced cinder-block wings stretched backward, embracing but not entirely encircling the pool and courtyard. In the space between, where the rolling hills seemed to rush toward the hotel's embrace, was a wall of tropical vines and flowers, an intricate tapestry of white and lavender hibiscus, wisteria, red jasmine. It trembled in the light breeze, attracting flocks of small bright birds.

I was wondering how it had grown up there, the floral barrier, when the telltale sparkle of barbed wire and the shine of razor wire coiling through the flowers caught my eye and gave the thing away. The vines and flowers had woven themselves through a high wall of chain link. Lime trees, drooping with their burden of small green fruit, stood sentry all along it.

I stepped back into my room, put on a swimsuit and robe, and walked down to the pool. There were no lounge chairs, so I dropped my robe onto the white-tiled deck and dove into the water. It was warm as a bath, fragrant with the roses, and I was breathless after swimming just a couple of laps. I rolled onto my back, closed my eyes. Soft fingertips caressed my scalp and cheeks, my ribs and thighs and toes. The South Bronx, the newsroom of the *Herald-Sun*, were lifetimes away. Even my problems at the airport seemed evanescent, insubstantial as a dream. I felt rescued, saved.

Heat shimmered like flames behind my eyelids. It had shimmered that way off the tarmac at the airport, creating a field of puddles between me and the arrival building when I'd stepped out of the DC-9. The puddles were mirages, tiny oases in a blacktopped desert, and they'd disappeared as I approached.

"*Bienv nid   a Bel   vist —El Para s   tranqu llo de los trópic s*" read the marquee above the international terminal. The building itself was modern, long and low, neatly landscaped with bright flowers, like a rest stop on an American interstate. But the marquee on its flat roof needed fresh paint and, with its missing letters, seemed to advertise a feature film that had played some time ago.

The building itself failed to fulfill its promise of air conditioning. At first the dim interior looked empty. Then dozens of uniformed men—soldiers, police, customs officials—emerged from the darkness as my eyes adjusted to the light. Some wore holstered handguns. Others carried machetes in elaborate leather scabbards. Many had rifles strapped across their backs as peasant women carry babies. There were enough for a small dress parade. Instead, they roamed the hot space in their well-armed packs, intent upon some mission, however inscrutable to me.

I looked around for passengers from my flight, didn't recognize any. There'd been maybe two dozen of us. Most of the others had been middle-aged men, executives from multinational corporations or State Department employees. In pastel shirts and summer pants, they'd been as neatly uniformed as the armed forces. Instead of weapons, they'd carried attachés. All had somehow disappeared.

I'd spotted the correct baggage claim area and was moving toward it when four uniformed soldiers crossed in front of me and surrounded me, forcing me to stop. The soldiers stood around me, just beyond arm's reach, and slowly eyed me up and down. I eyed them back, half expecting them to demand my watch, the gold chain at my throat. That had happened to me once: young muggers ambushing me as I tried to get into my car, demanding my purse and jewelry. I'd resisted until I'd seen the razor. When I looked into the soldiers' eyes, I saw the eyes of those muggers, dark with compressed violence. I looked away, took a step back. The soldiers backed off too, and began to strut away.

I'd made some progress toward the baggage claim when again I heard a rush of guttural Spanish right behind me. Two words emerged from the babble: *rubia* and *gringa*. The words were very clear, were repeated several times: *La gringa. La rubia.* The blond Yankee. The North American blonde. They sounded like trespasses for which I ought to be held accountable. I turned around, faced three very young men in the black uniforms of the national police. They wore shiny knee-high boots, scabbarded machetes. I couldn't quite meet their eyes, but my glance repelled them anyway. Like the soldiers before them, they about-faced and swaggered off in the opposite direction.

The water had invaded my ears, so I stood, shook my head to get it out, and then began to swim laps, slowly, pacing myself.

I'd been holding up my passport, my work visa, and various other documents by the time I'd reached the customs station. I've always liked the power and prestige that employment with one of the world's great news organizations has given me. I'd assumed that the words "journalist/

periodista" on my visa would permit me to pass quickly and painlessly through customs.

"*Buenos días, señores. ¿Cómo están hoy?*" I'd offered with a gentlewoman's smile, brandishing like talismans my papers.

"*Abre las maletas,*" one custom agent commanded as if I hadn't spoken. He didn't even glance at the papers. Another took them, dropped them in a heap.

I did as I'd been ordered, unlatched and unzipped both suitcases, opened my purse and carry-on. At least six hands upended the bags, dumped out everything. Time seemed to slow down and colors seemed to brighten as I watched all those hands picking through my things— my shirts and skirts, jeans, nighties, stockings, cases of cosmetics, jewelry.

I looked away, and saw, on the wall behind the agents, faded posters in English, French, and Spanish urging tourists to visit Las Playas de la Costa de Plata, Playground of Paradise. While the customs men continued their work, opening and sniffing bottles of cologne and lotion, at least one of which was never returned to my bag, I looked at posters showing idyllic views of sunrises and sunsets over the silver beaches of Bellavista's Pacific coast.

La Costa de Plata: the Silver Coast.

Before the earthquake, the government's *oficina de turismo* had successfully promoted the luxuriant volcanic area as an undiscovered tropical wonderland, a new tourist playground. By offering tax breaks and other incentives, it had convinced some of the best hotel chains to build elaborate resorts there among the mansions and weekend retreats of the families of the oligarchy. Then came the earthquake and the communist insurgency. The Hiltons and Intercontinentals and Ramadas had never opened, or had opened and quickly closed. A Club Med was abandoned halfway through construction. Now all were boarded up, like orphaned tenements in the South Bronx, against Bellavista's continuing catastrophes.

I was musing about doing a news feature on la Costa de Plata when, peripherally, I saw an agent rubbing between his thumb and fingers the crotch of some lace panties. He did it slowly, deliberately, and the others watched him, smirking.

"*¿Qué buscas? ¿El contrabando?*" I was about to ask, but he looked straight at me, met my eyes. His eyes made me think of splotches on a driveway underneath a car, ooze from a broken engine. I looked back at the posters. Then I remembered my documents, began searching for them through the rubble of my stuff. I would show them who I was. If they understood who I was—the new Bellavista correspondent for the *New York Herald-Sun*—they would leave me alone, let me go. As I hunted through the tangled mess, all the agents paused to watch. Yet I found the documents, pulled them out, opened my work visa, and pointed to my own somber face in the photograph. I don't know how long I stood there pointing, how long they stood there watching. Finally I began to understand that the *Herald-Sun* offered no protection, no claim to dignity, in a country with no history of democracy, no free press. Here *la prensa extranjera*, the foreign press, meant exactly what it sounded like: the extraneous press, the external, unessential, irrelevant press.

My heart was racing from my exertions, and I reached for the side of the pool, cursing myself for being so out of condition. I examined the roses till the bright light hurt my eyes, then I slid back into the water, floating on my back. Afterimages of roses, in neon shades, twisted in the dancing flames behind my lids, then disintegrated into an ashen darkness. I felt disembodied, and the world itself seemed about to slip into darkness, when I collided with the pool's edge. I opened my eyes. Beyond the roses, the green edge of las Esmeraldas was a barricade, the sky a blue dome. I could have floated there forever.

I'd been putting away my visa when one of the customs agents began opening a box of tampons. He did this with a series of nods, frowns, and pauses as if he were uncovering an illicit cache. His colleagues moved in, watched as he took one out, held it this way and that, checking it as carefully as one would an explosive. Delicately, he removed its tissue covering, examined that too, finally ejecting the tampon through its cardboard cartridge like a miniature rocket launcher. The others smiled as the tampon's flight was halted by the string stuck in the cardboard. Then the agent held it out at arm's length, tampon dangling down, and he moved it back and forth for everyone to see, as if it were a candle lighting up the darkness.

I was thinking I'd get out of the pool when I noticed a group of men standing near the railing, in front of linen-covered tables. Something shiny in the hand of one of them flashed like a heliograph. The man seemed to be looking my way, and at first I thought he was signaling to me. I watched him, confused, and a second or two passed before I realized my mistake. Embarrassed, I did a surface dive, swam most of the length submerged, then rested again by the ladder at the other end, with my back to them.

I held the ladder sideways, turned just far enough to see them. Most were wearing candy-colored polo shirts and chino pants. They looked American—and could have been military advisers or embassy officials. The man holding the shiny thing was darker than the others, taller by several inches, and he wore white pants and a loose white shirt. He was pointing toward las Esmeraldas, and the others looked where he was gesturing. Several of them nodded.

I slid back into the water and began a sidestroke toward the shallow end, where I loitered in the shadows of the roses for a better look at the man in the guayabera shirt. He looked somehow ascetic in his white clothes, his hair cut so short I could see the outline of his skull. He was clean-shaven, his face long and angular. From my distance, his eyes were lost in the shadows of his prominent brow and cheekbones.

I was wishing I were close enough to see his eyes when he turned, seemed to look right at me. I sank into the water, slid to the bottom of the pool, opened my eyes, touched my way along it. Shafts of sunlight revealed a shimmering film of chemicals. I was remembering some news photographs I'd studied in the *Herald-Sun*'s library when in my mind's eye I saw the man in the guayabera shirt dressed in a military uniform instead. He was General Víctor Rivas Valdez, defense minister of the junta. We had several formal head shots of him. The cutline under one said he'd ordered an immediate end to all violations of citizens' rights by the security forces. He had vowed that the daily lives of civilians would be free of terror.

I burst out of the water, grasped the ladder. The candy-colored men were gone, but he was still there, General Rivas Valdez.

I turned my back to him, swam the length of the pool, hoping he would go away. Then it occurred to me that this was an opportunity. That I ought to get out of the pool and get to work, talk to him, ask him questions. I did another surface dive, swam underwater toward him, emerged when I was out of breath.

The terrace where he stood was higher than the pool, and he'd followed my submarine movements, had accurately predicted the point where I'd emerge. By then, he was leaning forward, his arms draped over the railing. The shiny thing had disappeared and the breeze was lifting dark hair on his forearms. His face was expressionless, his serenity Zenlike.

I figured he did not know who I was, figured that if I spoke Spanish to him, asked him a question, I would catch him off guard, and thereby have the upper hand. I decided to introduce myself, then ask how he planned to keep such a vow, that all citizens' lives would be free of terror. Was keeping such a promise possible?

I moved to the ladder closest to him. Let him watch, I thought, climbing out through streaming water. I'd bought a Norma Kamali swimsuit before I'd left New York and was thinner than I'd been in years. I stood there with my back to him, ran my fingers through my hair, leaned to twist it, squeezing out the water. I bent to pick up my robe from the deck, and I put it on slowly as I turned around. I figured I would dazzle him with my smile.

But I smiled into a void. Because General Víctor Rivas Valdez was no longer there. The place where he had stood was empty. I couldn't even see him walking out through the restaurant. He had simply disappeared. Embarrassment overwhelmed a flash of anger: he'd tricked me. And when I tried to walk away, to walk back to my room, I had trouble getting started, getting my legs to move, as though I'd lost my power.

Sonia Alvinas was slouched against the railing of the gallery upstairs. I didn't recognize or expect her, was surprised to see a skinny camera-laden teenager waiting there, and maybe she was surprised too, for she examined me intently. Her eyes were hidden by dark glasses, but she seemed to be looking me up and down.

"Went for a dip, huh?" She was looking at my swimsuit where the robe had fallen open. Her voice was adolescent, soft, and she spoke slowly, in heavily accented English.

"You're Sonia, my photographer?"

"A photographer. The free-lance photographer who happens, at the moment, to be stringing for the *New York Herald-Sun*."

I was so grateful for her English that I ignored her correction. She took off her sunglasses, maybe trying to get a better look. Her eyes were black ingots, glittering with resentment or disgust. I'd underestimated her age by half a dozen years.

"You're Hartwell's replacement?" Her lip curled, and she began to chew on it.

I nodded, opened my door, and gestured for her to come in. When she moved ahead, I read the back of her T-shirt: "It's Better in the Bahamas."

In fact, the clothes she was wearing that day turned out to be a kind of uniform: yellow T-shirt, baggy pants rolled up at the cuff, and bright pink high-topped sneakers.

Her hair was cut very short, slicked back with oil or water, and gleaming spikes of it stuck up across her scalp in a style favored by street punks in the Bronx. Still, with her full breasts and tiny waist, with her high cheekbones and her finely sculpted features, her femininity was unmistakable. I didn't understand her disguise.

She rushed into my rooms, but slowed down abruptly. She began wandering in a kind of trance, examining the walls, ceiling, and furniture as if trying to place them. Her trousers were cinched with a man's belt so large its tongue flapped out in front of her. She sat on the edge of the bed, untangled herself from the straps and bindings of her gear, then bounded back up off the bed and went into the office, where she began opening and closing file drawers, picking through some dusty papers on the desk, pencils, paper clips, whatever odds and ends Hartwell had left behind. She slipped something into her pocket, then started when she turned and saw me watching.

"Something I left here," she whispered, staring at my knees. I gestured to a chair in the bedroom, and she sat in it, took rolling papers and tobacco from her trouser pocket.

"You worked a lot with Hartwell."

She nodded slightly, but didn't look up or speak. She was shaking tobacco from a red pouch onto a square of rolling paper, concentrating on her task. Two splotches of color replaced the pallor on her cheeks.

"You and Hartwell did a lot of stories together. You took some terrific photographs."

Sonia didn't respond. The index and middle fingers of her right hand were stained from the tobacco. She spun the cigarette quickly, licked its length, lit it with a Zippo she'd fished from her pants pocket.

"What happened at Aguas Oscuras?"

For a minute, I thought she would ignore the question. Her head was tilted back, pressed against the wall. Smoke shot from her nostrils, and she closed her eyes against it. When the smoke cleared, she leaned forward, looked at me.

"Hartwell fucked up."

"What do you mean? How did he fuck up? What did he do?"

"It was what he didn't do." She smiled. One of her front teeth was darker than the others, stained by tobacco or decay. "He didn't take me with him."

She inhaled slowly, gazed at me through the smoke as she exhaled.

"In fact, that was his second mistake."

"What was his first?"

"Going up there."

I smiled. "Really?"

She seemed about to say something, then shrugged, changed her mind.

"No sé, no sé nada," she murmured. I don't know anything.

An inch of ash curled on the end of her cigarette. The ash dropped when she stood, and she ground it into the carpet with her sneaker. Then she went into the office and came back with an ashtray.

Was I going up there, to Aguas Oscuras? she asked, and when I said I didn't know, hadn't decided, she shrugged and smoked and stared, squinting through the puffs of smoke.

"My editors don't want me to bother with it just now."

"Figures," she answered with a shrug. Somehow I'd expected her to want the story, to want to go after it again, and I was disappointed that she showed no interest.

We made plans to meet the next morning for my first assignment, a media event, at the government's Permanent National Emergency Operation a few miles up into the mountains. By then I was wishing she would leave. I could tell she'd already made some negative judgment about me, though I couldn't guess about what. Besides, I wanted to change out of my bathing suit, but not in front of her. I went over to my bags, which were on the bed, thinking I'd start to unpack, thinking that if I did, she might take a hint and go.

"You know, I'm the best," I heard her say after a few minutes, and when I turned to her, she was sitting very straight, staring at me, her eyes hard and bright as onyx. "I know everybody. Everyplace. I'm not afraid of anything. Nothing."

I nodded. I didn't want to challenge her.

As it turned out, Sonia was afraid of many things. As it turned out, Sonia feared everything a woman her age, and of her background, should have feared at that time in Bellavista. Because fear is, after all, a sane response to certain insane situations. But weeks would pass before I learned of Sonia's fears or the reasons for them.

That day, the question of her courage didn't trouble me. It was something else, something I didn't understand, and couldn't quite define.

"I want the Pulitzer," she announced. She darted about the room with her hands near her eyes, shooting pictures with an imaginary camera. "Or some other big prize."

Click. She imitated the closing of the shutter with her mouth, spun an imaginary lens with her nimble fingers, and crouched low in front of me as if to take my picture. Click.

"What other prizes do they have? Do you know? Whatever it is, I want it. I'm going to get it. You'll see."

She flew to another part of the room. Click. She shot me from another angle. She was trying to be funny, but I couldn't laugh.

"That way they'll hire me in New York. Then I can get my mother, and me, out of this godforsaken place. For good."

She threw herself back into the chair, laughed at her own performance. Her laughter was high-pitched, childish. She asked wouldn't I join her for a cold beer downstairs in the bar, and when I said I couldn't, she shook her head vehemently, as if confirming to herself the rejection she'd foretold.

"Okay," she murmured, rubbing her cheek with the back of her hand. She picked up her camera and camera bag and headed for the door. *"Hasta mañana, entonces."*

On her way out she seemed to notice, for the first time, the open suitcases on the bed. She walked over to them, stood staring for a while.

"What's all this shit?" She grabbed a handful of my clothes, which were already a mess from the customs agents, then tossed them aside and snatched something underneath.

"Look at all this fucking stuff. At least fifty fucking pairs of pants. Twenty blouses. Ten bras. Jesus. How many shoes? I can't count all the shoes." It occurred to me that she'd suddenly lost her accent. "How many pairs of shoes does one stinking *gringa* need? And this shit. Powders. Perfume. Body lotions. Hah."

I moved closer.

"I don't have fifty pairs of pants. And I'm not a stinking *gringa*."

"Spoiled *gringa*. Stinking spoiled *gringa*."

She was muttering as if I weren't there. She moved over to the next bag.

"Get your hands off my things."

She didn't seem to hear, began rummaging through the second suitcase with the same crazed energy.

"I'm not a stinking *gringa*, and stop touching my stuff."

She kept going, so I grabbed one of her arms, pushed her shoulder. I tried to take what she was holding, a beige silk slip, but she wouldn't let it go, instead rammed her fist, with the slip, into the space below my ribs.

"Dumb bitch."

I swung at her, but she ducked away, began circling the room, bouncing on her tiptoes like a bantamweight.

"You don't know anything." She threw the slip at me. "I can tell already. You don't know anything. And I bet you're too dumb to know you don't know."

She shook her head. "So of course you couldn't tell how long it's been since I or any of the women in my family, or in my whole neighborhood, have had a pair of stockings or underpants or a bra. Not to mention a pair of shoes. Jesus."

"But look," she said, advancing toward me, grinning and holding her clownish pants far out to each side. "See? I'm luckier than most. My father died and I'm wearing my inheritance."

She did a little Chaplinesque bow, then stared at me. Why didn't she use some of her pay from the *Herald-Sun* to buy herself some decent clothes? I asked. She sputtered that she was paid by assignment, was a day laborer, like the *campesinos*, got no benefits, and hadn't worked for almost a month, not since Hartwell had fucked up.

"So my fashion budget for this season is shot." She pushed back a spike of fallen hair. "And I'm fresh out of deodorant."

She was back by the open suitcases, looking at them without moving. She'd run out of energy abruptly, like a windup toy unwound. She picked up her camera and her bag, sauntered to the door.

"Hasta mañana," she repeated as she left. I went after her, thinking I ought to see her out, try to make up. She was waiting just outside the door.

"What are you doing here, anyway? Why did they send *you* here?"

She asked the questions quickly, one after the other, so close to my face I felt the moist warmth of her breath, could hear the derisive emphasis on the word "you." As though I were a joke. As though she, alone in all the world, understood what type of person ought to be the *Herald-Sun*'s correspondent in Bellavista. And I, in no way, measured up.

Sonia Alvinas didn't wait for answers, didn't want any. I'd known her fifteen minutes, but already knew she'd prefer to leave the hooks of her words swinging in the sultry air, where they might or might not catch me.

They caught me, but I pulled them out. I watched her cameras and camera bag banging against her as she took off, rushing down the stairs, looking fragile enough to disintegrate.

She was halfway down the first flight when she paused and called back without turning around, "By the way, Miss America, nobody swims in the fucking pool. It's just a decoration. For atmosphere. *¿Entiendes?* Not for swimming. Everybody knows."

Then she hurried away.

CHAPTER TWO

SONIA ALVINAS. I WOKE UP WISHING I'D NEVER HAVE TO SEE HER again. Then I rushed off early to pick her up. For as much as I disliked her, I also knew I needed her. I needed her superior knowledge of the country and its language; her understanding of how the press worked in it. She'd accused me of knowing nothing, but I knew enough to realize I wouldn't make it through my first assignment without her help. So there I was, bright and early, searching the Hotel Lido's parking lot for my leased Volvo.

The morning light had bleached the vibrant colors of the mountains and sky, of the vehicles in the lot. They glittered silver-white, their true colors impossible to see from any distance. I walked the lot, row by row, checking license plates.

Periodista: ¡Diga la Verdad!

The first bumper sticker seemed ironic, as if it had been placed there just for me. Journalist: Tell the Truth! But as I went on, searching for my car through the still heat of that bright morning, the righteous admonition, on one vehicle after another, turned into a warning.

Periodista: ¡Diga la Verdad!

Printed against a white background, splattered with drops of red, the red letters of the slogan melted into trickles, as if they were wounded, bleeding. Journalist: Tell the Truth!

I bent to examine one more closely. LOS HIJOS PATRIÓTICOS DE BELLA-VISTA was written in tiny block letters at the bottom. The Patriotic Sons of Bellavista. The name meant nothing to me, but its slogan begged a question that makes most journalists uneasy. What, after all, is *la verdad*? A collection of objective facts? Or something more ambiguous and elusive? Los Hijos Patrióticos evidently had their own ideas, though I couldn't guess what they might be.

"Remember you'll be writing instant history," McManus had told me before I left. "You can't possibly get the whole truth, every fact, about a given situation before a daily deadline. You gather what you can before your deadline and you make damned sure you're accurate. Then you go with what you've got. We don't write in cement. We write on word processors and can change things in an instant."

What I'd be reporting that day wasn't likely to result in any ambiguities of *la verdad*—an event staged by the government for *la prensa internacional*. A media event. It would take place at a dumping ground for those left homeless by the earthquake and civil war. The government had just renamed this vast shantytown—previously called OPEN, the Spanish acronym for Permanent National Emergency Operation—Ciudad de Merced, City of Mercy. Like all good media events, this one was scheduled so that reporters could make deadline for their papers' early editions or for that evening's news broadcasts. Not exactly instant history.

The parking lot was barren and dusty, an antidote to the indolent allure of the hotel's lush interior courtyard. Scouts, Cherokees, and Broncos, pickup trucks and vans appeared to be the vehicles of choice for difficult driving on the country's steep and twisting unpaved roads.

Walking the lot's perimeter, I could see the ruins of Libertad below— destroyed apartment buildings and department stores, the crumbling shells of banks and office buildings. Shattered during the earthquake, they'd been left where they'd fallen, a monument to the thousands who had died, because the country had no money to demolish them or clear them.

Periodista: ¡Diga la Verdad!

The glass on most vehicles in the lot was the color of pewter, a shield against harsh sunlight but also a way of concealing occupants. I put my face to the windshield of a Cherokee beside me, discovered it was nearly an inch thick, bulletproof. A telescope or a machine gun lay beneath a blanket on the backseat.

Periodista: ¡Diga la Verdad!

Two years before, an American free-lance photojournalist had disappeared from the Hotel Lido's parking lot. On assignment for an obscure publication catering to mercenary soldiers, the young man had checked in, drunk a cold beer in the hotel lounge, and gone outside for his rented Toyota, and had never been seen again. The first clue to his disappearance came days later when the car rental agency discovered the yellow Toyota, untouched, in the parking lot.

It was weeks before the young man's editors, and·then his family in Ohio, concluded that he had, in fact, disappeared into the confusing darkness of Bellavista and was not off, incommunicado, reporting in its guerrilla-infested mountains. Some time later, the family showed up in Libertad, was put up at the Hotel Lido, and was informed by the U.S. embassy that it could not guarantee the safety of "uncredentialed" journalists who took on "questionable" assignments for "marginal" publications. Conveniently, during the parents' stay the corpse of a young man the approximate age and size of the journalist was found at a body dump called El Purgatorio. Officials of both governments believed it to be that of the journalist. They theorized that his murder by unknown assailants of the left or right had "no doubt" been a "tragic instance" of mistaken identity. However, since the skull had been crushed and the teeth removed, certain identification was impossible. The parents insisted the horribly disfigured corpse could not possibly be their son. So the toothless body had been left unclaimed and the journalist was still considered missing.

It wasn't yet midmorning, but the cars in the lot had absorbed enough heat to give it back. When I touched one, it burned my hand. I stepped away, saw it was a Toyota, more of a mustard color than yellow. I doubted it was the one rented by the free lance from Ohio, but the sight of it galvanized my paranoia. I felt I was being watched, wondered if I ought to have a gun myself; if a pistol, or a revolver, or maybe one of those tiny submachine guns that can fit into a purse, ought to be standard issue to journalists in Bellavista.

Then I saw the bright pink sneakers jutting out into my path. Sonia was sitting on the bumper of the Volvo, burdened with her cameras. Her elbows were on her knees, her chin in her palms, and a cigarette burned between two of her fingers. Sunglasses hid her eyes, but I knew she'd been watching me. She didn't speak, just nodded. When I nodded back, I couldn't help seeing my own reflection in her glasses.

"Look, I know that I was out of line yesterday," she said, examining her sneaker. "I don't know how it happened. But I, well, I'm sorry. I need this job."

She again looked fragile and very young.

"I wasn't myself either."

I started to offer my hand for a shake, dropped it when I realized she wasn't going to take it.

Sonia didn't explain why she'd come after me that morning instead of waiting for me downtown the way we'd planned. I didn't ask. It would turn into a habit—Sonia finding me, ahead of time, in a place other than the one we'd decided on. As a result, I never knew exactly where she lived, learned nothing about her private life. And once, much later, when it was urgent, essential, for me to find her quickly, I hardly knew where to begin my search.

That first day, Sonia fiddled with the knobs and buttons on the radio, gave up without finding any music. Then she took out her tobacco and papers, rolled and lit a cigarette.

"Where did you learn photojournalism?" I asked, attempting neutral conversation.

"Photojournalism?" she spat back as if she didn't understand.

"News photography. It's a difficult skill. I wondered where you learned it."

"Here and there." She shrugged, exhaled smoke, looked out the window. "Okay, Florida," she amended. "I went to Florida International University."

Her obvious reluctance to talk about herself aroused my curiosity.

"How long ago? When did you graduate?"

"I didn't graduate. My father died so I came home."

"When did he . . ."

"A few years ago," she interrupted, somehow warning me to back off. "The average life expectancy isn't very long in Bellavista."

I was tempted to keep probing the wound of her father's death, but before I could she asked, "Where'd you get a name like Guerrera?" I turned to her but she was staring out the window. "I mean, Guerrera, huh?" She shook her head. "A green-eyed blonde named Guerrera. Jesus."

Despite her accent when I'd met her, she now had complete control of colloquial English, language I assumed she'd learned in Florida.

"I got my name from my father. Where did you get yours?"

A snort of laughter was her answer. After that we didn't talk much. I tried to concentrate on driving, on following her directions. She turned the radio back on, fidgeted with its knobs until she found music, something with a Latin beat. She rolled down the window, smoked, and tapped the door outside in time to the music.

The road to Ciudad de Merced was unsurfaced, deeply rutted. We passed groups of huts and lean-tos that Sonia said were villages. A dense jungle lay just beyond them. Peasants leading burros heaped with fruits and vegetables often passed us on their way down the mountain, and twice we passed ox-drawn wooden wagons on their way up. I thought I saw a gun in Sonia's camera bag, which was open on the floor by her feet. I kept looking into the shadows trying to make it out. When Sonia finished her cigarette, she took it out—it was a small black pistol—and played with it for a few minutes, then dropped it back into the bag.

"Don't worry, Ms. Guerrera," she said, giving me a sidelong glance. "I always keep it loaded."

"You can call me Liz," I said, then realized she was being sarcastic.

The corrugated-tin shacks, the wood-and-tar-paper lean-tos, were crammed together as far as I could see. Ribbons of black smoke fluttered in the air above them, then flattened out, wove themselves into a smoggy blanket that swaddled the barrio. I couldn't see a single tree or shrub. Chain link and barbed wire surrounded Ciudad de Merced, and guard booths flanked the wide gate nearest us. A soldier stepped out of one, waved us to a stop. We showed him our credentials and he waved us on our way.

I followed the narrow and unpaved main street through the center of the barrio. Outside, in the background, a jovial voice, electronically amplified, invited residents to the festivities—to the opening of the underground pipes that would bring drinking water to the barrio for the first time. The scratchy sounds of Latin music played beneath the voice.

At the end of the road, strings of triangular flags, the kind used to decorate gas stations, designated a parking area. A policeman in a riot helmet directed us to a spot. Young men in civilian clothes, bureaucrats from the international press office, greeted us, helped us out, led us to the gaily colored canopies that had been set up to protect *la prensa* and government officials from the scorching sun.

The canopies were striped yellow, green, and black, the colors of Bellavista's flag. Under them, on rows of cloth-covered tables, were punch bowls of sweet drinks, platters of fruit and cheese, cakes and pastry. Peasant women stood around them fanning away flies.

At least two dozen journalists and as many government officials were enjoying the canopies' shade and the free spread. They crowded around the tables, jostling one another. Sonia joined them right away, stuffing her face with ham and avocado sandwiches. She knew most of the reporters and photographers, and began to introduce me. They were from the wire services and an international broadcast news service. I said hello, then tried to move on, wary, as always, of getting trapped inside the journalistic pack. Besides, they seemed to be appraising me, and I didn't want to answer any more questions about Alan Hartwell. About what it felt like to be his replacement, to be the *Herald-Sun*'s new correspondent in Bellavista. I didn't want anyone else to tell me he'd be a tough act to follow.

Outside the canopies, a cordon of soldiers and *policía*, reinforced by a barricade of wooden horses, separated the crowd from the press and government officials. The entire population of OPEN, some fifteen thousand people, seemed to be there. The amplified voice nevertheless urged more to join them.

A platform draped with green, yellow, and black stretched along the space between the crowd and the canopies. Soon government officials would assemble there and the ceremony would begin. It was there, in front of the platform, that I finally saw the object of the ceremony, the "water station." Two pairs of slender faucets, perhaps a yard apart, rose like charmed snakes from the dusty earth. Their tiny copper mouths, about an inch across, were open. Drops of water glistened on their lips. I remembered water fountains in the playgrounds at home, water fountains that were almost always broken. I looked from the faucets to the hot, tense horde pushing up against the barricade. I imagined endless lines of residents waiting to use them, murderous fights breaking out when someone breached the line.

I looked for Sonia, found her still filling up at one of the tables, talking to a couple of other photographers. I told her she ought to get some pictures of the crowd, some pictures of the faucets against the backdrop of the crowd.

"You worry about the words, Miss America," she said, turning back to her companions, whose IDs said Agence France-Press. "I'll worry about the art."

The urge to tear her spiky hair out clump by clump made my fingers twitch. Instead, I turned around and hurried away, as though I had a destination. I composed myself under one of the other canopies. Alone there, I wandered among the tables telling myself I'd call New York and complain about her. Explain that she was obviously, but for no apparent reason, out to get me. I'd ask for permission to hire someone else.

On the tables near me were glossy press packets labeled "La Solución Pacífica." I picked one up, vaguely wondering how much it had cost to put together, who'd paid for it, which public relations firm had done the work. In Spanish and English it detailed the government's "peaceful solution" to the civil war and its national plan for social betterment. I'd read about land reform, a proposed health care system, and a plan to lower unemployment through government-funded public works projects when the sound of a nearby motor distracted me.

A maroon Mercedes had pulled into an isolated area just beyond the canopy. It gleamed despite the dust, surreal in its luxury. I couldn't imagine who it belonged to, or why it had pulled up so close to where I stood, heading away from, not toward, the water ceremony. The windows were tinted glass, so I couldn't see inside. Then the rear window slid down and there, in uniform, was General Rivas Valdez. I waited for him to speak, to acknowledge me. He sat and looked instead. I looked back, but didn't, or couldn't, move away. I wondered if he recognized me as the woman in the pool, and hoped very much he didn't. I don't know how long he watched me and I don't know why. Obviously, he wanted me to know that he was looking, but I didn't get his point. I was feeling somehow trapped when the window suddenly slid shut and the Mercedes took off, disappearing into a cloud of dust, going in the wrong direction.

DRINKING WATER REACHES MERCY CITY

by Elizabeth M. Guerrera
Herald-Sun Staff Writer

LIBERTAD, BELLAVISTA—A tumultuous roar of approval from thousands of waiting peasants greeted the potable water that arrived here yesterday via underground pipes, the first running water to reach this sprawling shantytown since its creation four years ago.

"This is a day many of us thought we would never see," said Luis Miguel Barrera, minister of social welfare, during a ceremony to mark the opening of the water system. "But it is just the first of many days that would have been impossible dreams not long ago."

Electricity, sanitation facilities, paved roads, public transportation, and all other "necessities of a civilized and dignified life" will come to Ciudad de Merced within three years, vowed Barrera, a former professor of political science and a prominent member of the left-of-center Democratic Unification Party.

"We hope this life-giving water proves that our new government intends to serve, rather than oppress you. . . ."

The piping in of water to this community of 15,000 is part of the government's solution to a stubborn communist insurgency. In addition to municipal improvements at many poor barrios like Ciudad de Merced, the government is about to undertake a massive program of land reform that will turn over to peasants vast tracts of farmland now held by the families of the oligarchy.

The turning on of water at Ciudad de Merced comes one week before Congress is scheduled to vote on a $200 million package of aid for this troubled nation. Barrera admitted privately that its timing had "everything" to do with the Congressional vote. "That money is essential to our survival, essential to thwarting the communists," he said.

Aid was cut off in late November to protest what Congress described as "continuing" and "egregious" violations of the human rights of Bellavista's citizens. Last year, some 20,000 civilians are believed to have disappeared or died at the hands of death squads. In holding up its vote on additional aid, Congress demanded proof of an improvement in the human rights situation of civilians here.

In an interview yesterday Barrera said, "The U.S. Congress has asked for proof of the government's good intentions. Giving water to poor people was one of the best proofs we could think of."

CHAPTER THREE

"*I*N A SOCIETY UNFAMILIAR WITH DEMOCRATIC PRINCIPLES, WITH NO HIS-tory of democracy, no understanding of shared power, no experi-ence with even a flawed democratic process, a coup d'état can be a progressive force."

Even on the tape, the ambassador's exhalation was audible. I remem-bered the way it had made his nostrils flare, expelled streams of cigarette smoke. We'd been sitting on a shady terrace outside his office at the embassy, and he'd been staring at a cigarette pack on the table next to him, was shaking another cigarette from it by the time he spoke again.

"The coup here was a progressive force."

In the pause after this sentence, I heard the striking of the match, his quick intake of breath, and his smoky exhalation.

"This junta is moving the country closer to civilian rule, inching it toward democracy."

I was lying on my bed at the hotel, a cassette player on my belly, replaying my conversation with Richard M. Whitaker, the U.S. ambassador to Bellavista. It was just after noon. The sun was bright and I'd closed the shutters on my windows, turned on the ceiling fan.

"What our humanitarian aid program involves, what you could say we, that is the U.S. government, what we're doing here is providing a kind of pacification support. Pacification support. And, uh, the goal of any program of pacification support is to gain the willing endorsement of peasants, that is, the civilian population, for the government's cause. And we believe we can do that. Given the proper support from Congress."

Whitaker was tall and large-boned. His wavy hair was silver, the skin of his face quite pink, and he smelled of good cologne. His nails were manicured, his shoes shined, and his tropical-weight suit sharply creased. But his pale blue eyes were veined with red and slightly popped, making him seem full of tension, about to explode. He also chain-smoked unfiltered cigarettes, stabbing the air with them, and was not particular about where the ashes fell or where he snuffed the butts out.

We talked, or rather he talked, for nearly two hours, and his nasal twang and Boston accent grated so much I had trouble concentrating. I felt myself shrinking in his imposing presence, as if each time he poked the air in front of me with a cigarette I deflated a little, got smaller in my seat. By the time I left him, I felt mauled. It was only afterward, in my room, with his voice disembodied, contained in a box whose buttons I could push, that I began to hear what he'd been saying.

"Our training and equipping of Bellavista's armed forces has a single tight focus from which we never deviate: developing their professionalism, their discipline. Our task is to assist them in their mission of maintaining peace here with the least possible amount of force."

The U.S. embassy, previously housed in a walled complex of rosy granite in the center of the city, had for decades been considered the single most powerful institution in all of Bellavista, scaffold of successive military governments, constant target of leftist guerrillas and terrorists with undelineated affiliations.

The complex had withstood the firebombs and grenades of generations of guerrillas and terrorists, but the assault of El Gran Temblor, the great earthquake, had reduced it to rubble in moments. Downtown Libertad burned that day in an ersatz twilight created by an impenetrable nimbus of smoke and pulverized concrete. But student radicals had found one another through the darkness, chaos, and collapse; had managed to gather in celebration before the demolished nerve center of Yankee power and influence.

Their victory celebration turned out to be premature. For a squat concrete fortress had emerged with almost magical speed from the tall golden grass around the airport. Close to downtown Libertad, but not easily accessible, the new embassy complex had so far proved impregnable. The terrace upon which Whitaker and I had met faced a landscaped courtyard filled with flowering shrubs and vines. Raucous tropical birds fluttered among them.

Now and then the screech of a departing jet had interrupted us, and faintly, but steadily, we heard students shooting at the nearby Academia Militar. My audiotape reduced the sounds to a muffled atmospheric hum.

"See, the first thing this Rivas Valdez did was to order an end to all violations of citizens' rights by members of the armed services. And he vowed to severely punish any officer found guilty of such violations. It was a seminal moment in the history of Bellavista."

"What makes it seminal? What's so great about it?"

"What's so great about it?"

His raspy laugh ended with a violent cough.

"If you don't know the answer to that question, you don't know anything about Bellavista."

He chuckled softly, or cleared his throat again.

"What's so great is that for the first time in the history of the republic, two hundred goddam years, a very powerful agent of the government has publicly acknowledged that all citizens have rights, that civil rights aren't only for the wealthy."

"He's wealthy, isn't he? Rivas Valdez?"

There was silence on the tape, but I remembered Whitaker's smile.

"Who knows? Perhaps personal wealth makes him incorruptible."

Our talk was off-the-record, what Whitaker called a "backgrounder," so I hadn't taken any notes. I couldn't use anything he said, even without attribution. He'd agreed, however, to being taped. And because he'd been "so hard" on Hartwell, since he'd given Hartwell "such a bad rap," Whitaker said he owed it to the *Herald-Sun* to help me get started on "the right foot," to be "candid" and "forthright" with me, perhaps to go so far as to give me a "leg up," an "edge" against the competition.

Of course, he'd had no choice, he quickly added. He'd been forced into the Aguas Oscuras investigation, forced to make public his findings. The truth demanded to be told. Bad apples had to be plucked out of the basket. Every profession had them, the foreign service, even journalism. Bad apples had to go.

Before launching into his candid, forthright discussion of the situation in Bellavista, Whitaker said it might be "valuable" if he shared with me his insights into "Hartwell's problem." In Whitaker's view, Hartwell's problem was that he'd gotten "carried away" by his emotions. He had been a "real go-getter," a "fine reporter," but he'd gotten "flummoxed" in the heat of his battle to tell the truth. Anger and outrage had skewed his vision, had robbed him of his objectivity. Whitaker hoped the same thing would not happen to a promising young journalist like me.

He fixed me with his eyes. His translucent blue irises were like ice chips floating on pink water, but he was beaming with what I took to be his version of a paternal smile. I arranged my face into a suitable daughterly response.

One indication of Hartwell's "spin away from the center," a hint of what was to come later in his coverage of the massacre at Aguas Oscuras, was his series on life in a "liberated zone," datelined from "behind the lines" at a guerrilla base in one of the remote mountain provinces. Hartwell had been the first and only journalist to penetrate the labyrinthine Mateo Omaño National Liberation Front, to establish such a trust with certain of its factions that he'd been allowed to live and travel with them for a time. He'd reported on their establishment of health clinics and schools, on their care and feeding of poor children, and on their humane treatment of prisoners of war.

More to Whitaker's point, Hartwell had also reported that in more than two weeks with the guerrillas, he had not seen a single Soviet weapon, a single Cuban adviser.

"But tell me, Miss Guerrera, do you think some damn fool guerrilla is going to blow away a captured soldier in front of a *gringo* reporter? Do you think he's going to haul out his AK-47, his Kalashnikov? Do you think they're stupid enough to parade their Cuban advisers for North American journalists to see? Do you?"

He'd jabbed the air near my cheek with his index and middle fingers, a burning cigarette held tightly in between them.

"I'm not saying Hartwell lied or deliberately deceived the public. He was duped. As for Aguas Oscuras, well, *el frente* found a witness for him and he bought her story. But he bought her story because he'd lost his objectivity. He couldn't see the truth because it didn't jibe with his ideology. And he passed his misperceptions on to the public."

Whitaker's insights into Hartwell's problem segued into a rant about the failings of the press in general.

Was I old enough to realize, he asked, that the exact thing had happened in Vietnam: the entire press corps, reporters, photographers, broadcast journalists, editors, passing on misperceptions? Did I realize the misperceptions stymied, in the end destroyed, the United States' mission in South Vietnam? Did I understand the same thing could happen in Bellavista?

Whitaker spoke from a "position of personal experience" because he had been assigned to the Saigon embassy from 1967 to 1971. And press accounts to the contrary, the U.S. government, and more particularly the State Department and the Pentagon, had learned some very important lessons in Vietnam.

What they'd learned, said Whitaker, was that the "misbegotten" hearts-and-mind program, the "ill-fated" pacification plan, the "obtuse and unwieldy" land reform program attempted in South Vietnam with American assistance, had been neither misbegotten nor ill-fated nor obtuse until the press had made them that way and until Congress bought the story.

A peaceful solution to South Vietnam's difficulties had been thwarted because there'd been no money, no manpower, to implement land reform. And there was no support from Congress because Congress simply didn't understand "what in hell" was going on.

"Now if you people only told the truth here, we'd get our money, get our support. And if we got those things, we'd win. Which means we'd halt the spread of communism in the Western Hemisphere."

Whitaker lit yet another cigarette before telling me about a misperception "even more insidious than the idea that American programs don't work." The "promotion" of this particular misperception by members of the press had made it "almost impossible" to "hold the line" against communism in Bellavista.

The misperception was that the government itself was ruthless and bloodthirsty in its maintenance of the oligarchy; that the government itself was responsible for the disappearances and deaths of thousands of civilians, political activists, and clergymen, for the terror in the countryside.

"It's not the government but the fringe extremists who've been wreaking the havoc. It started four years ago when the Cocos and American plates slammed together with this horrific force somewhere out there underneath the Pacific, releasing, what, more than a century of grinding tensions."

Sitting with him in the fragrant warmth of the embassy terrace, I'd been mesmerized by the sight of his big pink hands slamming together, mimicking the collision of the tectonic plates, the fingers of each hand crashing into, then somehow intertwining with the fingers of the other; he vibrated the new formation so intensely, in imitation of the quake, that his jowls vibrated too.

"The aftershocks rippled landward, five or six hundred miles an hour, bored into the soft earth beneath Libertad, reduced the place to rubble in a few minutes. Bam!"

He'd slammed a fist into a palm, then held out both hands in what might have been a gesture of supplication.

"The capital, the heart of the goddam country, the center itself, disappeared in an instant."

He declaimed then about the years of strife and terror that led to the toppling of the dictator and his replacement with a group of military officers and civilians—the self-proclaimed junta of reform and reconciliation.

"What the coup gave us," Whitaker finally said, his voice quivering with urgency, "was the chance to grab hold of an elusive center. Abracadabra. Now you see it, now you don't. Well, we grabbed that center. And now we've got it like this."

Whitaker had shaken a big fist at me.

"You'd better believe it, girl. Now the center's holding."

TERRORIST BOMBS DESTROY MAJOR CITY BUSINESSES

by Elizabeth M. Guerrera
Herald-Sun Staff Writer

LIBERTAD, BELLAVISTA—A series of explosions early yesterday ignited a conflagration here that gutted major banks, department stores, and office buildings, throwing the center of this capital city into chaos. There were no known casualties in the wind-driven fire, which caused an estimated $40 million in damage, government officials said.

According to a defense ministry statement, time bombs had been placed in the multistoried headquarters of both Banco Castellano and Banco Vista, which occupy the opposite ends of a large commercial block. The bombs exploded within minutes of each other shortly after 3 a.m. The resulting fire, said the statement, apparently activated other smaller bombs in buildings along the block.

"There's little doubt that this is the work of terrorists," said U.S. Ambassador Richard M. Whitaker. He called the bombings "a crippling blow to this nation's effort to get back on its feet."

The devastated commercial block was one of very few to have been rebuilt after the earthquake four years ago which demolished the center of the city and took at least 13,000 lives.

Yesterday, known radicals of the political right and left were arrested for questioning, according to the defense ministry. The government is offering a cash reward of $25,000 for information leading to the successful prosecution of the guilty parties.

An estimated 1,700 people were left without work because of the fire, said government officials.

CHAPTER FOUR

A TALL AMERICAN STOOD OUTSIDE MY DOOR, SQUINTING INTO THE dusk of my suite, one fist held up to knock again.

"The center's holding, huh?" she asked and dropped her hand. In the other, rolled up like a club, was a newspaper, and even at a glance I recognized its typeface as the *New York Herald-Sun*'s.

"He's not here, is he?" Her voice was soft and hoarse. "Whitaker, I mean?" She peered into the shadows of my room, then switched her gaze to my T-shirt and blue jeans. I held up the cassette for her.

"Abracadabra. Now you hear him. Now you don't."

She nodded, but didn't smile, instead looked at me as if she was trying to figure something out.

"You're Elizabeth Guerrera?"

I said yes, and she nodded again. Her face was splattered with freckles, and her red hair flounced around it like a spray of crinkled wires.

"I'm Mary Healy." She demanded that I meet her eyes. Hers were palest gray, thinly fringed with colorless lashes, limpid pools in a kinetic body. I dropped mine, saw her proffered hand, took it. It was large and strong, and as I wondered what she did, how she'd grown hands like that, she said she ran a health clinic at Nuestra Señora del Refugio, a big church in Libertad, and another up at OPEN, the place now called Ciudad de Merced.

She knew him, Whitaker, she went on, taking back her hand, raking it through her hair. She'd spoken to Whitaker many times, she said, the last time when he'd suggested she might be better off elsewhere employed. Somewhere, say, beyond the borders of Bellavista. But that had been before the coup, before the junta of reform and reconciliation had taken power.

The truth, the question of truth, had prompted her to seek me out, she said, and as she did, she unfolded the newspaper, grasped it by its top edge so I couldn't miss Sonia's page-three photograph of barefoot urchins dancing in the water of Ciudad de Merced, a picture by then more than a week old. My story ran beside it, the closest I'd come in years to the front page of the paper. She jabbed my byline with her finger.

"The government spews out claptrap and you people lap it up."

She wasn't the first to tell me, I remarked, but she paid no attention. She said her anger wasn't personal, wasn't directed specifically at me at all. Except my Hispanic surname made her think I might be tied ancestrally to the Third World, and might, therefore, care personally about what was going on in it.

She glanced into my eyes, searched for affirmation, but I couldn't give her any.

"I'm not talking just about you, anyway," she went on, struggling to fold up the newspaper. I took it, did it for her. "I'm talking about the whole *prensa norteamericana* with its self-importance, its so-called objective reporting, its liberal views."

She made the harsh, throaty sound I would later recognize as laughter. A copper crucifix glinted against the chambray of her shirt.

"Not one story that's come out of here—not even what's-his-name's, your predecessor's, yes, Hartwell's, which came the closest—not one story has ever hit upon the truth, has ever told what's at stake."

She stepped backward, took hold of the vine-covered railing that edged the gallery, looked out toward the pool.

"What's at stake?" I interjected, smiling at her back. "Everybody knows what's at stake. The peasants want power. They want land."

"Ahh!"

My words had somehow pained her, but she didn't turn around, interrupted when I tried to ask if she wanted to come in.

"You see, you call them peasants too. All the media call them peasants without ever thinking about what the word means. Think about it, huh? Can you have peasants without lords and masters? No! The term's relational."

She snatched a flower from the vine beside her, remained there with her back to me.

"I'd like to make you understand something," she went on. "You and every other North American who comes down here and turns overnight into an instant expert on Latin America."

She was standing with her feet wide apart looking straight ahead, a markswoman expert at hitting targets behind her back.

"The indigenous people of Bellavista were transformed into peasants just a few hundred years ago, after the Europeans showed up and began stealing their land, destroying their faith and culture, murdering them."

She gripped the railing, leaned out over it, a thin, big-boned woman whose faded blue jeans stopped short of her ankles. She wore ancient leather sandals. The jeans were bell-bottoms, relics from the sixties.

"You call them peasants, and when you do, you're accepting their subjugation. Calling them peasants is a way of taking part in the master-slave structure."

She turned around, holding a floppy red flower with a yellow calix. She began tearing it to small pieces, dropping the pieces and watching them fall.

Wasn't it kind of a joke, really, she asked me, intent upon her task, that they'd named the new airport Cauchimpca after the Indians' volcano goddess, considering they'd destroyed the religion, the language, from which the word had come?

They? Who were they? I asked when she paused for breath. The oligarchs, she answered, the nine families of the oligarchy known simply as La Nueve. And, of course, the military. La Nueve and the military made up the power structure of Bellavista.

The truth was, their culture had produced not a single hero, not one person respectable enough to name any public structure after. And so they were stuck, had to borrow a name from the Indians.

She laughed the raw laugh, tossed the stripped stem over the railing.

"I heard what he said," she told me then, her pale eyes fixed on mine. "What Whitaker told you. I was standing outside, and I heard that part about extremists coming up out of the cracks in the earth after the earthquake. Well, what's really crazy is that the earthquake did release a tremendous force. The spiritual energy of *los indígenos*. Of all the poor in Bellavista."

"Spiritual energy?"

She nodded, smiled again. Her teeth looked perfect. I couldn't help thinking they were the product of expert and very expensive dental work.

"The belief that everything happens for a reason," she said. "That everything is part of God's plan. The divine plan. It's pure teleology."

She was quiet for a moment, and I watched her. For that moment she looked tranquil, but somehow alert, as if she were straining to hear a far-off whisper. The look was familiar but displaced until I remembered the beatific faces of some homeless women in Manhattan. Then I felt afraid for her.

"Why don't you come with me now?" Again I felt afraid, not for her, but for myself. The feeling made no sense, and I shook it off, realized she might be a good source, that I might get at least one good story from her. "I mean, I can't exactly show you the Divine Plan. Or the spiritual energy. But I can show you other things, more obvious phenomena, that might help you figure out what's going on."

I went to change, but she said she couldn't wait. She had a patient in the early stages of labor, and had to get right back to her clinic. "Anyway," she added, laughing her odd laugh, "it's not an occasion you need to dress for."

Her blue Dodge Ram was parked in the middle of the hotel's landscaped front drive, in a space clearly marked Prohibido Estacionarse. No Parking. The van was dented front and rear, rusted at its edges, and covered with mud and dust. A host of crisply uniformed hotel employees were chattering and twittering around it, examining it with wonder and consternation, as if it were a giant fossil just discovered in their midst.

Tranquilos, be calm, Mary commanded, wading into them, shooing them away with her big hands. The men obeyed, jumping quickly back, uttering not a sound as she climbed regally into the van, turned on the ignition. I followed, climbed in beside her once she'd opened the door on my side. She pulled out with a screech, paying no attention at all to the hotelmen, who were forced to jump out of her way.

Then we were off, following the same route that Sonia and I had taken the week before. She drove very fast, but didn't bother with her seat belt. I strapped myself in, gripped the dash to keep steady in the seat. She kept slamming into the sharp curves so the van fishtailed time and again, threatening a skid into disaster. Whenever we approached a rut or gully, she'd accelerate, so the van was airborne over it, bounced and shimmied when we landed.

"I'm a midwife, I already told you," she said at one point, although she hadn't. She squinted into the fierce light, brushing away my questions with one hand. "I'm a midwife and a missionary, but I'm not with any religious order. So I guess you could call me a free lance. A free-lance evangelist who is bringing Good News to the poor of Bellavista."

She turned to me and grinned.

"Something else we have in common: we both deal with news. But mine's better than yours." She laughed, but I didn't think her joke was funny.

I pressed her to tell me about herself. What interested me, and what she seemed unaware of, was the clash between her queenly carriage and her shabby clothes, her cultured speech and her extreme ideas. Her bell-bottoms and sandals, the hand-wrought copper crucifix on its leather cord, were artifacts of another age. Yet I knew somehow that she'd been born into money, that hers was a higher social class than mine. Evident in her posture and her gestures, in her voice and language, was an ineffable attitude, a kind of confidence, that only the wealthy can afford. It came as no surprise, later, when I learned she'd been a debutante; that she was the rebellious middle daughter of Connecticut socialites whose Roman Catholicism had always marked them as outsiders.

That day she insisted her personal history was irrelevant. What mattered, she said, was the history of *los indígenos*, the indigenous people of this fecund volcanic land.

To understand what was going on now, she told me, I had to know that most of the poor were Taupil Indians, scattered and deracinated descendants of the Mayas, who had inhabited the region for thousands of years before the time of Christ. I had to know that for eons, within their tribal communities, the Taupils had worshiped the earth as a goddess, had called her Tocinanatzil, the word in their lost language meaning "mother of us all."

I had to know that in worshiping her, they'd understood all natural occurrences, the changes of the seasons, storms, eruptions of volcanos, as part of her divine plan.

"Then came the Europeans," she declared, letting go of the steering wheel, holding both hands, palms up, above it. "The conquerors and their priests, missionaries. Raping women, banning the Taupils' language, outlawing their religion, murdering as heretics their prophets . . ."

She paused as we entered a shadowy tunnel of overhanging branches. We bored through it, plunged on through the sunlight of a dusty clearing where raucous children, chickens, and dogs swirled out of our path, blurred inside billows of dust.

Through succeeding generations, she said, the Taupils' culture had been obliterated. Only one myth had been passed on through the generations, and that myth had been the radix of their hope: that their own souls, their divine spirits, had remained inviolate, had escaped the Conquest by burrowing deep into the earth, to a special place within the molten heart of Tocinanatzil, where they'd survived in her protection.

We skidded close to the edge of a gorge, and I must have made a noise, because Mary glanced at me, tapped a black metal box on the seat between us.

"Consecrated hosts," she said. "I bring them to eucharistic ministers in some of the small villages."

Her role in the deliverance of the Body and Blood of Christ, she went on to say, gave her a "special dispensation" against disaster. I watched her, waiting for a punch line that didn't come. And maybe while I watched her, looking so serious and so serene, I began to recognize her spirituality, began to understand that she felt a visceral connection with God, with a loving and all-powerful source of life, a God I knew nothing about.

Her spirituality confused me, and I guess I was profoundly skeptical, because it was expressed in Roman Catholicism, the dark, punishing religion of my childhood, the faith of my mother's suffering and fear.

"You see, Elizabeth, it was the earthquake," she went on, "the horror of the earthquake, that forced the Taupils to confront their lost faith, to think about their place in the divine plan. They saw El Gran Temblor as a long-awaited settling of scores: Tocinanatzil taking her revenge on the conquerors for their rape of her; for their growth of export crops, like coffee and sugar, to enrich themselves while her children, the children of the Taupils, starved and died before their time."

During the earthquake, she said, they believed that their captive souls had at last been released. They believed, she said, that the earth had opened up to release their souls, and that their souls, like white birds, *espíritus santos*, had flown out of her, giving them, once again, the power to control their own lives.

"Now, instead of collaborating in their own oppression, they've become the catalysts of their own liberation."

"But how does it work?"

What I wanted was the political connection, something I could turn into a story. Somewhere along the line, I figured, the Taupils' spiritual energy must intersect with the struggle for social justice, with the revolution. It was there that my story would begin.

"Oh, there's no explaining it." Mary Healy brushed away my question with her hand. "Not in any words I know."

"Sounds mysterious," I remarked, irritated, and she agreed that it was mysterious, one of the great mysteries of human life.

"Even when there was no running water at OPEN, we drank from living water and were never thirsty—"

The biblical diction annoyed me, and I cut her off, said anything that powerful, that mysterious, was probably subversive. My remark lacked the tone of irony I'd intended for it, but she laughed anyway, the raw, staccato laugh that punctuated so much of what she said. Whatever else it might be, she agreed, the spiritual energy of the poor was indeed subversive, a genuine threat to a "sinful status quo," for it fueled the people's liberation struggle and God had given them an unlimited supply.

She had misunderstood me, but glancing at her tranquil face, I decided not to tell her. What I told her, instead, was that ideas about teleology, divine plans, and spiritual energy were too difficult, too complex. I'd never be able to sell them to my editors or use them in a news story.

"My editors," I told her, "like clear-cut stories, written in simple language. You know, stories with a lot of facts and no ambiguities."

"You mean they like simple-minded stories written in simple-minded language. That's why all of you keep missing the point."

We were quiet after that, and soon Ciudad de Merced's vast grid of shacks and huts, shrouded by smoke from hundreds of cooking fires, grew visible beyond the crest of an upcoming hill. Mary slowed down as we passed the army barracks outside the barrio's main gate, and stopped briefly for the sentries at the gate, who glanced at our documents and waved us on our way.

We drove through the stifling, abandoned streets on what Mary called a quick tour of the dumping ground. And she told me as she drove that what the poor of Bellavista wanted more than anything was to free themselves from the bondages of sin. Sin? I didn't try to hide my disappointment. Yes, sin, she answered, because deadly, mortal sin permeated all aspects of life in Bellavista. Sin in Bellavista was inescapable, was as ubiquitous as oxygen.

"What's sin?" I asked reflexively, regretting that I'd gone with her, doubting that anything she told me could ever be shaped into a story for the *New York Herald-Sun.* "Is sin really an operative concept in the late twentieth century?"

She threw her head back laughing, but quickly stopped, braked the van in the center of a narrow street, turned to look at me. "Is sin an operative concept?"

She frowned until the lines around her eyes and forehead created an intricate pattern, and I wondered how old she was.

"Open your eyes, girl," she said. "See how people here have to live. Then you tell me."

She put the van back into gear and moved forward slowly, and a hot, fetid breeze blew in and swathed my face. If I wanted evidence of sin, she said, she had evidence that could fill volumes. After all, as a nurse and a midwife, she was working on the front lines. And in her seven years in Bellavista, she'd attended the births of about six thousand infants. Fewer than fifteen hundred had survived in good health into childhood. Nearly one-third had died before their first birthdays, mostly from preventable gastrointestinal ailments. Half of the survivors were now brain-damaged, retarded, as the result of malnutrition.

Virtually all the survivors continued to suffer chronic hunger, chronic diarrhea, she said. And it was needless suffering.

"You're describing social conditions. Which are the result of complex political and economic forces."

Again she stopped, turned to look at me.

"I'm describing evil at work in the world."

I looked away, because her eyes were full of compassion or sorrow.

Not much later, we arrived at the water station, the barren clearing where the water ceremony had taken place. Instead of bright canopies, there were mountains of fly-infested refuse. The smell of shit gagged me. Dilapidated huts edged the water station. They'd been decorated with debris from the water ceremony: strings of triangular flags and the banner that read *Bienvenido a la Ciudad de Merced*.

Mary parked, jumped out, and I went after her. Two faucets lay broken on the ground, and a rusty trickle ran from one of the remaining two. Several chickens and a scruffy dog were playing in the mud. Mary stopped abruptly, reached for one of the remaining faucets, turned it on, cupping her hands to catch a stream of brownish water.

"Care for a taste of OPEN's unlimited supply of potable running water?" She offered me her cupped hands. The water stained her fingers as it dribbled out between them.

I was ready to go back to Libertad, to the Hotel Lido. I'd seen as much as I wanted to see. I wanted a hot shower and a drink. I wanted to play my tapes, transcribe them. But Mary said she had an errand at her clinic that would only take a minute.

On the way, we paused at a garden of small crosses, many adorned with plastic flowers and statues of the Virgin. It was a children's cemetery, she said, then pointed to its far side, where a convoy of tanker trucks was parked, one behind the other.

"See, over there are *las capitalistas*. They're the ones the water project was supposed to put out of business." She stretched her arm far out her window. "You want to know about sin? Those devils sell drinking water to poor people, people who earn one or two dollars a day, for fifty cents a bottle."

"Who are they?" I resented her attitude, her self-righteousness.

"The usual conspiracy of thieves—military officers, the *policía*. The trucks are conveniently borrowed from the government, and they fill up at the purification plant in Libertad." Within the next hour or so, she said, scores of women would be lining up there to buy their water. "Yes," she said as she drove on, "we're surrounded by sinners here in Bellavista."

"Who . . . ?" I began to ask, but she interrupted me.

"We know exactly who they are."

She smiled the gentle, well-bred smile that so conflicted with her words. Beyond the wild hair, crucifix, and faded denim, I glimpsed an aging debutante, the socialite I knew was lurking there.

"The wives of Bellavista's wealthy sun themselves on the terraces of

Miami condominiums," she went on, and I couldn't help imagining her doing the same. "They sip Perrier and nibble caviar, while mothers here can't feed their kids. You know, the flight of capital. They left and took all the money with them."

She pulled up in front of a square adobe building two or three times the size of those surrounding it. She was already around to my side, opening the back door, when I got out, saw its handwritten sign: *El Centro de Salud Familiar. No se niega servicios a quien no puede pagar.*

Family Health Center. Services are not denied to those who cannot pay.

"You know, we won't take anything that's been paid for by the U.S. government no matter how desperate we are," she said as she reached for a carton, handed it to me.

The carton was stamped with the initials of the World Health Organization. Beneath them in English were the words "Oral Rehydration Therapy Kits, for use with sterile water only."

"With one hand the U.S. sends down crates of paper diapers, some powdered milk to ease its guilt." Mary headed for the center carrying a basket of oranges. "With the other, it arms our oppressors with automatic rifles, submachine guns, and grenades." She laughed her odd laugh, kept walking. "Uncle Sam throws surplus Flintstone vitamins at our children while training our oppressors in state-of-the-art techniques of murder."

The mewling of babies, the cries of small children, the coos of mothers greeted us before my eyes adjusted to the darkness and I made them out, the women and their offspring, huddled on the earthen floor, along the walls, standing near openings that served as windows. I couldn't help remembering the Fox Street Family Shelter where I'd interviewed Aurora's mother. It was an electrified version of this place, a sanctuary of powerless Third World mothers and their children.

Mary walked in front of me, put down the basket of oranges and told everyone to take what they wanted. The waiting women embraced her, kissed her, called her Sor María—Sister Mary—and she turned to tell me she was not a nun, was not a member of any religious order.

She took me by the arm, ushered me into another room.

"My manager," she said as a Taupil with silver braids came through a doorway toward us, her hands held out in greeting.

Mary introduced her as Tía Amparo, said she herself had trained Amparo as a midwife and nurse. "She doesn't have a license, but she's as good as anyone I know." The woman took both my hands in hers, led us into another room filled with cots, a physician's examination table, rudimentary medical equipment. A thin barefoot girl with matted black hair was sitting on the table. A naked infant was whimpering and thrashing in her arms.

"*Ya no tengo leche,*" the girl was crying. "*Ella tiene mucha hambre porque no tengo leche.*"

My milk is gone. She's hungry because I have no milk.

Mary took the baby, laid her on the table, took her pulse and temperature, then handed her to Tía Amparo, who placed her in a plastic tub filled with brownish water.

As the infant cried and thrashed in the water, Mary explained in Spanish to the girl that her baby was not hungry, but was very sick, would die if she did not receive help soon.

No, the girl insisted. Her baby was only hungry because she, the mother, had no milk left and no way to buy formula. Mary nodded, didn't argue, asked the girl her name and age. She responded that her name and her baby's name was Milagros, which Mary said meant a miracle, or a divine occurrence. Milagros thought she herself was fifteen—but she could neither read nor write and did not know how old her baby was.

Mary repeated that the baby had a dangerous infection that had nothing to do with hunger. Then she said she wanted to take the baby to Libertad, where she would give her intravenous feedings, medications to bring down the fever and fight the infection. Milagros should come too, she said, because she could eat well, nurse the infant herself, pump her breasts with an electric gadget to increase her milk supply.

While they talked, Tía Amparo diapered the baby, wrapped her in a cotton blanket, then held the infant as Mary inserted a medicine dropper into her mouth. The baby vomited, expelling milky saliva, heaving violently. Mary held her forward so she wouldn't choke on her vomit, murmured something until the retching stopped.

"*El bebé se está muriendo,*" Tía Amparo repeated softly. The baby was dying because she'd had the diarrhea and vomiting since the day before, had taken no liquids, and her high fever went on unabated.

"*¡Sí, sí!*" the mother shrieked suddenly, jumping off the examination table. "*Nuestro señor se quiere llevar mi preciosa.*"

Milagros ran to her baby, blessed her with the sign of the cross, kissed her toes, then blessed herself.

"*Nuestro señor se quiere llevar mi preciosa,*" she repeated, flinging herself to her knees. Our Lord wants to take my precious one to heaven.

Mary handed the baby to Tía Amparo, who began to clean her once again. She watched the mother for several minutes, then lifted her by one armpit to her feet. The girl quieted, flinching against her touch.

"Our Lord does not want to take your precious baby to heaven," Mary told her in Spanish. "Our Lord wants you to fight so your baby will live. God wants you and your baby to be healthy, strong enough to fight the oppression that causes these unnecessary ailments."

Tía Amparo gave Milagros back her infant, put her arm around the two of them, told her the baby would need her mother's milk when she got better, that it was the best food she could have.

"Our Lord wants my baby," Milagros said again, crying louder.

"Well, I'm not going to let Him have your baby."

Milagros started at Mary's harsh tone, stepped backward as Mary snatched the infant from her. Mary clasped the howling infant, said there was no time to waste, that she was leaving for Libertad. Was Milagros going to stay or go? she asked, but Milagros couldn't answer. She seemed paralyzed looking up at Mary, who loomed above her. Mary didn't blink, instead gazed down at Milagros with powerful pale eyes.

"This country's full of mothers who've lost children," she said in English, her eyes still on Milagros. "Somebody, the landlords or the priests, brainwashes them with the fantasy that it's a special blessing when the Lord takes their child."

Mary let Tía Amparo take the baby, watched Amparo give the baby to the mother and whisper something to her.

"The death of a child puts holes in their souls that never close back up again," Mary went on. "Makes them feel helpless, which is just what those in power want. Nothing empowers these women faster than saving their own children, nursing their young, bringing them to health with the milk of their own bodies."

I looked at the frail girl and the pathetic baby she cradled like a rag doll. The girl's tears had cleared wriggling tracks in the film of dirt on her cheeks. Milagros seemed barely capable of caring for herself. I couldn't help wondering what hope there was for the two of them and if their future held anything but misery. I couldn't help thinking that Milagros might be better off without the burden of an infant; that it might be better to let nature take its course. But then they quieted, mother and daughter, and Tía Amparo was moving them toward the door.

"No tengo nada que comer. No tengo nada," I heard Milagros say as she went by. I have no food. I have nothing. And it seemed true, for they had nothing to bring with them, no one to tell where they were going.

In moments we were flying down the wide border street of Ciudad de Merced, but we hadn't gone far when Milagros, the mother, was wailing once again, pounding on the front seat, crying that she was afraid, couldn't go to Libertad because it was a city of death, the place the earth had opened, would open once again, and besides the Lord wanted her baby and she was going to give her baby to the Lord.

Mary said nothing, braked sharply, turned onto one of the nameless streets that led into the heart of OPEN. She frowned into the windshield as mother wailed and infant howled. She drove through a blur of animals and people, by then awakened from siesta, who were forced to scramble out of our path. She stopped when we reached the children's cemetery, opened the back door, pulled out the weeping Milagros and her baby, dragged them toward the crosses.

I went after them, saw, on the far side of the cemetery, queues of women with plastic jugs, waiting to buy water from the trucks. Close to us, in the shade of a scraggly jacaranda, three shirtless, barefoot men were sleeping.

I had trouble hearing, trouble translating for myself Mary's words, but she seemed to be asking if Milagros wanted her daughter's eternal rest to begin there.

"Do you think perpetual light is going to shine upon her in this place?" she asked, or something like that.

The Milagroses wailed as Mary held them tightly with one arm, shouting to be heard above their noise.

"Do you want to be one of them next week?"

She pointed to some black spots among the crosses, still sacks of cloth, which, as I watched them, turned into kneeling women dressed in black, mourning mothers, faceless as they crouched over their children's graves. When Milagros did not answer, Mary grabbed the squalling infant once again, held her up, face to face with her mother. The baby opened her brown eyes, bright and liquid from the fever, recognized her mother's eyes, and quieted. She broke into a toothless grin, began swatting the air with both arms in a clumsy but unmistakable effort to reach her mother.

"Do you want to let her die?" Mary asked.

Milagros was quiet for a moment, then the baby's flailing arms knocked something away, and she collapsed, sobbing, against her baby and Mary Healy. Mary held them both, stroked Milagros's tangled hair. After a moment, she led them back to the van.

"Come on," she said to me. "We've got to get this baby back. And I've got to get back myself, because another's on its way."

Then we were speeding along the road that would lead us out of
Ciudad de Merced.

"Isn't it a contradiction," I asked before we'd gone far, "that you're
trying to save these people with the same religion that was used to
oppress them, to destroy their culture?"

Mary laughed as though I'd cracked a joke, told me I had it all wrong.

"Ours is a Galilean church, not a Roman church," she said. "There's
a crucial difference. We deal in love and community, not power."

I'd never heard of it, her Galilean church, but she went on before I
could ask her anything about it.

"Who says I'm trying to save these people anyway? I'll be lucky if I
save myself."

"But you are, aren't you?"

"No." She shook her head emphatically. "They're going to save
themselves. They'll find their own way to salvation. No *gringa*, no out-
sider, is ever going to lead them there."

Ours was the only motor vehicle on the road, and everyone seemed
to recognize it. Mothers tending children, fruit peddlers, others selling
tortillas, stopped what they were doing, stepped to the roadside to wave,
to call *"¡Hola!"* and *"¿Cómo estás, Sor María?"* Mary grinned and waved
to each of them.

If I loved God, or thought I did, if I believed in the Gospel, or thought
I did, she told me through it all, then I had to love the helpless,
abandoned people of Bellavista with an active liberating love.

Is that what you do? I asked her. Love them with an active liberating
love?

"You see, the Kingdom is coming," she went on as if I hadn't spoken.
"Because what's at stake is the humanity of the poor. That means the
struggle's deeper, more important, than anyone in the media has figured
out yet. It started in a completely different place and every one of you
has missed it."

She braked again, and a pair of toothless, shirtless boys appeared
grinning at her window. She reached into the back seat and gave them
small packs of crackers, and they took off laughing.

"The skirmishes all of you write about, your tallies of victories and
losses, don't matter. The events you're all so obsessed with mean almost
nothing at all. The rise or fall of communism is irrelevant. Because a
spiritual process has been set into motion. The poor have begun taking
part in the process of their own liberation."

She slowed as we reached the guard post at the gates, waved out the window to the sentries there.

"That's why it's a laugh when you reporters write that the civil disorder, or the revolution, or whatever, has ended." The sentries nodded, turned to watch as we drove on. "They haven't ended with this junta of so-called reform and reconciliation." She glanced at the guards, then back at me, and smiled her expensive smile. "I'd stake my life on it."

Then, as she picked up speed on our descent to the Hotel Lido, I heard the sweet voice of a child singing to another child, her own, words of a lullaby I didn't understand.

MASSIVE AID APPROVED FOR BELLAVISTA
from the Associated Press

WASHINGTON, D.C.—The Senate yesterday approved a $200 million package of military and economic aid for Bellavista after weeks of wrangling about this troubled nation's human rights violations.

The Senate's approval by a vote of 64–31 follows last week's endorsement of the aid package by the House of Representatives. It brings to $650 million the amount of aid sent to the Massachusetts-sized country in the past three years and to $350 million the amount sent during the past fiscal year.

Late last year, Congress began withholding aid to Bellavista because of what it said were egregious violations of the human rights of civilians by the military and security forces. An estimated 800 citizens each month were dying or disappearing at the hands of right-wing death squads.

At that time, Americas Watch, a private organization monitoring human rights in the Western Hemisphere, stated that these violations of human rights were not "aberrations" but were, rather, "selectively directed by the armed forces against those perceived to be opposing the nation's political and economic system."

By stopping the flow of aid, Congress said it was attempting to end the torture and murder of the government's political opponents by members of its armed forces.

In urging Congress to support the new aid package, the President called Bellavista "a crucial U.S. ally."

CHAPTER FIVE

I'D STRUGGLED WITH HARTWELL'S STORY SINCE THE DAY I'D BEEN promoted, reading it so often that the paper had become thin and frayed. Almost every time I looked at it, I remembered McManus's words: "Aguas Oscuras is a riddle, a conundrum. Of course, it must be dealt with . . . and it will be. But not by you. And not right now." One month into my assignment in Bellavista, when the story was almost three months old, I picked it up again and read:

WITNESS: SOLDIERS MASSACRE CIVILIANS AT VIRGIN'S SHRINE

by Alan Hartwell
Herald-Sun Correspondent

AGUAS OSCURAS, BELLAVISTA—The population of this mountain community and religious shrine has been exterminated and the village itself burned to ash in one of the worst civilian massacres of this country's long and bloody civil war.

Uniformed troops are responsible for the carnage two weeks ago in which more than 700 women and children are believed to have been murdered, said a village woman who survived the massacre by hiding in a cave.

Other peasants who live in nearby hamlets have confirmed many parts of the woman's story. However, they said they are afraid to be quoted.

A government spokesman yesterday denied that such a massacre had occurred. He said the villagers themselves may have abandoned their homes as fighting intensified between government soldiers and guerrillas in the nearby mountains.

He also challenged the witness to identify herself. If she had evidence of actual murders or of military involvement in them, he vowed, the "rogue soldiers" would be brought to justice. The Indian survivor remains in hiding.

Before going into hiding, she gave this account:

Sometime after midnight, soldiers in the camouflage uniforms of Bellavista's army drove jeeps and armored vehicles into the center of the village, debarked, and began running up and down the streets. They banged on doors with their rifle butts, shouting "Where are the Marxists?" and "Death to the Marxist vermin!"

Among the marauders were several American military advisers. They stayed near their jeep about 100 feet from the shrine of the Madonna of Aguas Oscuras, which occupies a hillock at the edge of a spring-fed mountain pool. The American soldiers later disappeared while Bellavistan soldiers emptied dwellings, shoving and kicking occupants and lining them up along the roadside.

The soldiers separated infants and children from their mothers. They called the youngsters *subversivos del futuro*—subversives of the future—and fired on them as their mothers watched. Afterward, they opened fire on the mothers and old people.

At last the soldiers began dousing corpses and village buildings, mostly mud and straw huts, with gasoline and setting them ablaze.

Ten days after the attack, during Christmas week, which is usually a time of celebration here, the ground of Aguas Oscuras was barren. There were no villagers about and no buildings were left standing. A cornerstone here and there indicated where dwellings, a one-room schoolhouse, and a health clinic may have stood. The air was thick with the smell of fire. Wet ground bore the tracks of heavy equipment, and it appeared that much of the earth had already been turned over, both bodies and debris removed. Countless vultures circled overhead.

The demise of Aguas Oscuras represents an especially bitter twist in a civil war that has claimed some 43,000 lives. For decades, the village has been considered sacred. Succeeding generations of its peasants have witnessed apparitions of a black-haired Virgin, in rose-colored robes and a beaded belt, rising out of the natural pool for which Aguas Oscuras, meaning Dark Waters, is named. This Madonna of the Dark Waters appears, say peasants, to reaffirm Christ's message that the poor are to inherit the earth. She is the object of worship throughout the country.

It has long been believed that the Mateo Omaño National Liberation Front maintained an important base here. The Mateo Omaño National Liberation Front, widely known by its Spanish acronym, FMOLN, is an alliance of at least a dozen Marxist groups. It is named for a farm laborer who was executed after leading a rebellion against landowners in 1939.

The Aguas Oscuras slaughter came to light after the witness sought refuge with missionaries at a nearby parish. Several days later, a missionary contacted this reporter.

In recent weeks, the government-controlled newspaper *Las Noticias* and the government-controlled radio station have carried accounts of government victories in the rural mountain provinces above Libertad. Gen. Víctor Rivas Valdez, commanding officer for those regions, has been quoted as stating that the communists have been defeated in most of the territories above the capital. These lands, site of the nation's prime plantations before civil strife erupted in the wake of an earthquake four years ago, have been secured by the government once again, according to *Las Noticias*. There is no opposition newspaper.

Neither *Las Noticias* nor the government-run radio station has reported the recent events at Aguas Oscuras. Except for the poor peasants of the remote hamlets surrounding it, residents of Bellavista remain ignorant of the slaughter.

In the past four years, the government of Bellavista has received nearly $600 million in U.S. aid. Its government is currently supported with $1.5 million a day from the United States.

According to Congressional sources, 60 North American military advisers, members of the U.S. Army Special Forces, or Green Berets, are currently working with Bellavista's military.

According to sources, at least 20 U.S. advisers are assigned to companies in Tato Ina province, which includes Aguas Oscuras. This region has been the site of heavy fighting in recent months.

Last night the Pentagon declined to confirm the presence of Green Berets in Tato Ina. The Pentagon denied the involvement of any U.S. soldiers in the incident at Aguas Oscuras, which is located in a dense hilly forest 45 miles northeast of Libertad.

The grotto of the Virgin, with its backdrop of enormous cedars, dominates the village. It remained intact last week despite the devastation all around it. A statue of the Virgin, in rose-colored robes and beaded belt, stood with her arms extended out above the water as she has as long as anyone can remember. Her feet were strewn with withered flowers left by pilgrims some time ago.

Accounts of apparitions of the Madonna of the Dark Waters first began to circulate in the 1940s. Fervent peasants were quoted as saying the Virgin hovered above the pool urging women who wanted children to bathe there, to pray to her, and they would be fulfilled.

The survivor says she saw the massacre from a concealed place in the grotto. It was illuminated by what she called *una luz sobrenatural*, a supernatural light, that likely came from illumination flares fired by the attackers. Just before dawn, during a brief drenching rain, she said she made her way out of the cave, then through the forest to a nearby hamlet.

The crucial thing to understand about Hartwell's story was that it ignored the *Herald-Sun*'s rigid rules for sourcing. It defied the unbreakable editorial rule that at least two named sources confirm such controversial information. Hartwell had used a single anonymous source to accuse a foreign government, a U.S. ally, of mass murder.

At the time, however, Hartwell was considered the best and brightest of the *Herald-Sun*'s young reporters. And he hadn't done his story in a vacuum. The massacre story had, obviously, made it all the way through the *Herald-Sun*'s rigorous editorial process. Obviously a top editor—either McManus or someone higher up—had signed off on it. Which meant that Hartwell had other information he did not include in the story, information that convinced the editors of its accuracy. Or it meant their trust in him was complete.

But that trust was shaken, then shattered, in the storm of protest that greeted the story's publication. First, a group of congressmen accused Hartwell and the *Herald-Sun* of aiding and abetting the FMOLN, a story that was picked up by the wire services and several major city dailies. At the same time, the Pentagon denied the presence of U.S. advisers anywhere near Aguas Oscuras and denounced both Hartwell's reporting and the *Herald-Sun* itself. Then two newsweeklies reported that the Secretary of State had called Nathan Van Doorn to discuss the *Herald-Sun*'s coverage of Latin America.

The whole story might have died down except that the government of Bellavista quickly conceded that a massacre had, in fact, occurred at Aguas Oscuras. It insisted, however, that a new terrorist organization called Estrella Luminosa—"Shining Star"—was responsible for the carnage.

In a press conference held to discuss the emergence of Estrella Luminosa, government officials suggested that Hartwell had been duped by the terrorists. It also revised down to 187 its estimate of those who had been killed and called Hartwell's original death toll "grossly overstated."

While Hartwell's war coverage was turning into as big a story as the war itself, the State Department announced that a probe of the site by U.S. military criminologists was underway. Two weeks later, Whitaker himself released the report. Not surprisingly, it stated that evidence "tended to support" the recent contention of the Bellavista government that terrorists of the Brigada Estrella Luminosa, or Shining Star Brigade, were responsible for the devastation.

"I examined every inch of that ground myself," Whitaker told reporters. "I saw nothing to indicate crimes by either government."

The day Whitaker released this report, Hartwell was recalled from Bellavista and reassigned to the San Diego bureau. Bellavista's defense ministry announced that a reward of $10,000 was being offered for information leading to the arrest of anyone involved in the Aguas Oscuras incident. However, efforts to locate the witness came to nothing. Despite promises of protection from both governments, she did not come forward to identify herself.

At some point I decided to go straight to the source, or at least as close to the source as I could get. I decided to call Hartwell. I thought I might persuade him to tell me who the witness was or where I might start to search for her. His reputation and his career were at stake—and it seemed to me that I could help him while reporting a great story. I figured there was no harm in trying. It took me several days to connect with the San Diego bureau. Whoever answered—a reporter or an editorial assistant—said Hartwell wasn't there. He said that, in fact, Hartwell no longer worked for the *New York Herald-Sun*. He had no idea where Hartwell might be found.

CHAPTER SIX

H E SAID THE ENEMY WAS ELUSIVE. HE WAS TOO, SEATED BEHIND A
utilitarian desk in his office at the Comandancia Militar Central. He watched his own hands instead of me while he spoke,
speaking perfect English that was softly inflected with the Spanish I'd
expected him to speak. He fidgeted somehow indolently with objects
on his desk—a rubber band, a letter opener, the buttons of his telephone—while telling me how the armed forces of Bellavista had finally
contained a stubborn and destructive communist insurgency.

"The enemy was difficult, sometimes impossible, to identify," he said,
intent upon the rubber band he was entwining among his fingers. His
hands were large but well shaped, the fingers long and tapered, ringless,
the nails better manicured than mine.

"But now, according to our intelligence, we have cleared and we are holding virtually all of our urban areas and our most important mountain territories."

Wound around his fingers, the rubber band pulled his palms together in a gesture of prayer. He raised his hands to his chin, rested them there for a moment. A gold Piaget twinkled in the nest of dark hair on his wrist.

"But the fighting isn't over."

"Pockets of resistance remain. Here and there."

In fact, he said, those "pockets of resistance" had been declared free-fire zones. He leaned far back in his leather chair and clasped his hands behind his head, and the short sleeves of his shirt slipped back to show the blue-veined flexors of his upper arms, the shadowy hollows of his armpits.

"Free-fire zones?"

"Minor areas of turbulence. In a country that was fully engaged in war one year ago."

Then Rivas Valdez let his chair drop forward, turned, and caught me in his gaze, and for an instant I felt as if I were trapped in the lights of an onrushing vehicle. He looked and I looked back. At first his eyes seemed pure gold, but deeply set and shadowed with fatigue. Then, as we stared, I began to make them out, the shimmering alloys, shards of yellow, green, and brown which, just before he looked away, went dark and vitriolic.

The general had already earned the reputation, among the press corps, of being difficult and inaccessible. My own requests for a meeting had been rebuffed several times when, by letter, an aide informed me that the general would meet with me the following day at the Comandancia Militar Central. Its massive gates slid back to admit my car at exactly eleven, the scheduled hour of our appointment.

La comandancia, a sprawling steel-and-concrete fortress, had been erected amid the ruins of Libertad, next to the plaza of the old city. Built with $30 million or $40 million or $50 million in American aid, depending upon whom you asked, this temporary seat of government was hexagonal, crowned by glass guard towers, ringed by an eight-foot concrete barricade that was itself encrusted with spikes, electrical barbed wire, and an angled net of chain link.

Outside, edging the plaza, then circling around to back roads still lined with the rubble of the quake, the barricade was reinforced by armored personnel carriers—Commando Scouts mounted with loud-speakers, riot hoses, machine guns, grenade launchers, recoilless rifles. Foot soldiers ceaselessly patrolled this perimeter.

General Rivas Valdez's second-story office was, however, Spartan, its cinder-block walls unadorned but for a large map of Bellavista. Like the newsroom of the *Herald-Sun*, it was monochromatic, but instead of taupe, the walls were grayish-green, the desk and chairs a darker shade of the same color. On the desk was a large and very modern console telephone with buttons for perhaps a dozen lines.

Rivas Valdez was austere in the plain uniform I'd seen him in before, and once I'd gotten through the layers of security surrounding him, once I'd been led by a laconic soldier through a cinder-block maze that ended in a reception area outside his office, an area manned by a teeming colony of soldiers, I felt I'd survived a hazardous journey, had crossed a volatile border, and now required time to get my bearings. But he was behind his desk, gazing into some abyss beyond my face, waiting for my questions. And from a straight-backed metal chair beside his desk, I found the questions, and I got them off in spite of his restlessness, his apparent boredom.

"What about Estrella Luminosa?"

"Estrella Luminosa? What about it?"

He got up, walked to the row of windows that faced the bustling yard, then lounged against the narrow sill, his arms crossed on his chest.

"How much of a threat is Estrella Luminosa? What do you know about it? There was that bombing last week. Whitaker said . . ."

My questions trailed off as he gazed at me across the sun-filled room.

"What we are after now is the communist infrastructure that has supported *el frente*, and terrorist organizations like Estrella Luminosa."

"Infrastructure?"

"The network of dedicated cadres that remains intact in certain areas of Bellavista. It must be dismantled."

He stood, turned to look out the window.

"It is these cadres, perhaps not immediately recognizable as subver-sives, who support the remnants of the FMOLN, the Estrella Luminosa. Somehow they endow these subversive organizations with tremendous resiliency, with the ability to regenerate themselves and to thus engage the government in a prolonged, exhausting struggle."

Then he turned to look directly at me. "I'm curious about your surname," he said, interrupting himself so abruptly I wasn't sure I'd heard him. He left the windows, advanced toward me, backlit, his hands in the side pockets of his trousers.

"The Spanish word for female soldier, woman warrior, instead of the much more common Guerrero, meaning fighter or soldier."

How had I come by it? he wanted to know. By way of some centuries-old, long-forgotten familial aberration? Or had I changed the *o* to an *a* myself and was I one of them, one of those North American feminists who were always making noise, always in the news, always trying to export their struggle for so-called liberation?

Of course, I'd always known what my Spanish surname meant, but I'd neither considered its connotations nor drawn any inferences from it. My mother joked about it sometimes. I almost never did. To me it was a group of sounds without significance, donated by an absent father in an act bereft of meaning. The general's question confounded me. I couldn't think of anything to say.

"What about it?"

He took his chair, adjusted it to face mine, slid into it, stretched his long legs out in front so his feet came perilously close to mine, which were crossed at the ankle, tucked behind one chair leg.

"Well, the name came from my father, but I don't know much about my paternal family."

I pushed out the sentence quickly, looking at my notebook, which was in my lap. I was thinking I ought to open it, look through it for more of the questions I'd prepared.

"Your father was Spanish?"

"By way of Mexico City. But the name's a joke, really. It's all he ever gave me. He disappeared before I was a year old."

"Disappeared?"

His tone was sharp, and when I looked up, I saw he'd misunderstood me.

"Not the way men disappear in Bellavista. He went to church one Sunday morning and didn't come back. Maybe it was the Gospel. 'Leave everything you have and follow me.' "

"Men no longer disappear in Bellavista. And your name is not a joke, only ironic considering your appearance."

"Because I don't look like a soldier?"

"You don't look Spanish. Irish would have been my guess."

"Well, the joke is that the name makes me, technically, the member of a minority group—"

A quiet buzz interrupted the beginning of my tired story, the saga of my government-funded graduate school education, my difficult ascension at the *Herald-Sun* via its minority training programs. He picked up the telephone, turned away, spoke so rapidly I didn't understand a word. He apologized for the interruption after hanging up.

By then I was standing, thinking I would leave, although I still had many questions. But he was standing, too, telling me I could not, must not go, that he planned to take me to lunch a short way up into the mountains. He walked around his desk, gestured to the map, said there was a fine restaurant there where we could discuss Bellavista in more comfortable surroundings, and it would please him very much if I would consent to go.

Now I realize I should have declined his invitation. I should have ended the interview and left, the moment he seized control by questioning me. I should have asserted myself by saying no to lunch. If I'd left then, I think I could have maintained control of our relationship. But I didn't assert myself. Instead for reasons I still cannot explain, I went along with him as if I had no choice.

We'd no sooner left his office than tingling bare skin inside my elbow signaled his touch, and looking down I saw his fingers there, saw they did not belong. I moved away so he couldn't touch me again as we made our way through windowless corridors, stairwells, and tunnels to the outside. And as we went I heard myself telling him, as if he'd pressed a talking button when he touched me, how the dean of the Columbia Graduate School of Journalism had been chagrined the first time he'd met me, a minority recruit, and seen the face that went along with the Hispanic surname. And how certain editors at my newspaper, to this day, seemed to think I was a fraud, a fake ethnic, because of the minority program through which I'd been hired. And I was truly grateful when he at last pushed open a heavy metal door that brought us into molten sunlight, for it somehow switched the talking button off. It stopped me before I told him that I often felt I'd gotten into graduate school by mistake, and my job through a bureaucratic error. Before I explained my fear of being found out and turned in; of losing both my M.S. and my job in a stupendous fall from grace, a fall that would plunge me back to the bottom of the working class.

I heard the purring of the big sedan before I saw it there in front of us. A burly soldier appeared, held the door for me. Half blinded, I entered the shadowy interior. Then the interior got even darker, as if a scud had blown across the sun, and he was there beside me, legs stretched out in front of him, hands on his thighs, his body heat palpable in the icy air conditioning.

The big car rolled forward, moving slowly through the yard, a sea of soldiers parting so we could pass. Through tinted windows I saw them at attention, saluting as we passed. Rivas Valdez leaned forward, scanned the hordes through half-closed eyes, and when he'd seen enough he sat back, staring straight ahead.

The sedan, a BMW, picked up speed as soon as we left *la comandancia*. We zoomed past Nuestra Señora del Refugio, and the cathedral's crucifix, shadowed on the plaza, flashed by like a billboard you don't have time to read. The BMW swayed voluptuously on the wide stretch of paved road that sloped gently out of Libertad. Plush cushions invited me to settle in, and I accepted. Then he took something from his pocket, and I heard him fidgeting, stole a glance, saw his toy, a heavy gold key ring with no keys attached. His initials, VRV, were shaped on it by diamonds, the letters blurred by refracted light. His middle finger was in the ring, and he was flicking the initialed part with his thumb, enclosing the whole thing in his palm, then flipping it back out again.

It must have been this key ring, signaling like a heliograph, I realized, that had caught my eye that first day at the hotel. I looked up, saw him watching me, and wondered if he was remembering that day too. By then he was holding his hand out, palm down so the key ring dangled, firing off darts of light. Then he slid it off his finger, held it curled up in his palm, where it glittered, determined to make its point.

"My wife had this made for me in Miami," he murmured, watching me with his metallic eyes. "She sent it to me for my birthday, my forty-fourth."

This personal revelation embarrassed me, as I believe he intended it to. I turned to look out my window. "Does she vacation there?"

"I suppose you could say that. I suppose you could say my wife and children, and the wives and children of the other families, those you in the media call La Nueve, have been on vacation for several years now. Some are in Caracas, some in Guatamala City, some in Miami. I thought you reporters made it your business to find out such things. Don't you?" I turned to him but didn't answer. He was looking out his window.

Then he rapped the front seat twice, impatiently, and classical music burst from speakers behind our heads, flooded the sedan. After a moment, I recognized Beethoven's Fifth Piano Concerto.

The wide paved road soon gave way to a lane of twisting gravel. But the cushions didn't loosen their embrace, absorbed even the harshest jolts. With the air conditioning and stereophonic Beethoven, we were sealed away from the world, were gliding through it in a gleaming ship.

Yet that world couldn't be denied. For around every bend, ragged mothers and children were standing at the roadsides, where they'd hazard being struck by flying stones, to wave, and watch in wonder as we passed. Sometimes excited children would leap into our path and mothers would snatch them back an instant before the fatal collision. But the gleaming ship never slowed and never swerved.

Its windows were thick and tinted, probably bulletproof. Through them the passing scene was a video documentary of Third World poverty—see the toddlers with the distended bellies, the spiky orange hair of near-starvation, and frantic infants gnawing at their mothers' shriveled tits—a documentary with the wrong sound track, a sound track so inappropriate it was either very funny or a symptom of psychosis. But I couldn't laugh, and didn't want to think about the other possibility. So I pressed my cheek against the glass to watch gravel spinning up from underneath the tires.

I felt the car slow to stop, and I turned, saw his window sliding down. Moist air invaded as he gestured toward the ruins of a plantation. The charred shell of the great house was antebellum with its crumbling veranda, its ragged cloak of vines and flowers.

Communism, like a noxious weed, had strangled all the coffee plants, like those there on the slopes, he said, his arm extended out into the world, his wristwatch blinking in the light. It had happened throughout the country, and the sustenance of Bellavista had been destroyed.

He brought his arm back in, rapped the chrome frame of the window. The glass slid back into place, and the car surged forward. Then he turned to me with his accusatory look.

"Unlike you—that is, the United States—we have no natural resources, no industries. Coffee is all we have."

He sank back into the seat, dropped his voice, which attached itself to the humming of the motor and droned along with it.

Yes, the fields had been made sterile for a time, a disastrous time, but now the strangling roots of communism had been removed from the earth of the great plantations. Some poison roots remained—hidden in the towns and cities, clinging to the barren soil of the northern mountains—but the destructive weed was gone from the plantations and the hills were safe for planting once again.

*   *   *

As we pulled into the parking area of the chalet-style restaurant, fat pellets of water began to splash against the windshield. I jumped out the moment the car stopped. The rain was slow and gentle, the sun shone through it, and the mountains shimmered with plumes of refracted light as if they'd been salted with tiny prisms.

They were beside me in an instant, the driver holding an umbrella and Rivas Valdez admonishing me about getting wet. I insisted I wouldn't melt, then we were inside, seated by an enormous window at a round table covered with rose damask. Trembling against our window, their faces pressed into the glass, were wild roses and hibiscus, shiny from the rain. And right away I tried to ask him questions, to ask about land reform and the attitudes of the oligarchs. But he evaded all my questions, sometimes glancing out the window, sometimes around the restaurant, more often gazing at some point beyond my shoulder.

A waiter in knickers and an Alpine jacket made a great show of uncorking a bottle of wine and pouring it. Some time after that, with the wine racing through my empty stomach and filling up my head, I understood that the general had ordered the entire meal in advance, for it was served to us, course by course, soup, seafood cocktails, salad, steak, without his ever speaking to the waiters. He almost never raised a finger, never even seemed to look at them, yet they appeared the instant they were needed to serve or clear.

Right away it occurred to me that I was violating the *Herald-Sun's* code of ethics by accepting the meal. But I couldn't seem to bring this up. So I drank my wine thinking I would simply pay for the meal myself, at least my half. No one ever brought a bill.

During the silences I looked at the flowers and wondered why I was there with him. If he wouldn't answer questions or give me information, there seemed to be no point.

Then, after we'd been served the seafood cocktails, he murmured, "Alan Hartwell's problem was that he was too ambitious." I looked at him, thinking I'd missed an important part of the conversation. He speared a snowy hunk of lobster, brought it to his mouth.

"Alan Hartwell's problem? Who says he had a problem?"

He shrugged, went back to his shrimp and lobster, which he finished without speaking. I drank the wine, Château Something, which was dry and wonderful. I considered the phrase "Alan Hartwell's problem." Ambassador Whitaker had also used it: Alan Hartwell's problem. Then a paragraph from Hartwell's Aguas Oscuras story floated into my mind: "The soldiers separated infants and children from their mothers. They called the youngsters *subversivos del futuro* and fired on them as their mothers watched. Afterward, they opened fire on the mothers and old people."

We were served tenderloins, and the general went on to say that Hartwell had come to Bellavista determined to make an international reputation. Maneuvering through the meat without once putting down his fork or knife or changing them from hand to hand, he said that Hartwell, in the course of foraging the countryside for stories, had become addicted to his own glory, addicted to seeing his byline on the front page.

I watched him, befuddled by his purpose. But by then, the wine had relieved me of the burden of responding, of being intelligent. I looked out the window, past the flowers, saw the view was from a dream, a place so beautiful you didn't believe you'd ever get there. Beyond the flowers pressed against our window, the lambent slopes of las Esmeraldas tumbled an incalculable distance down to the Pacific. The ocean itself was bright turquoise, but I glimpsed it only intermittently through a veil of silver mist.

Why don't you examine closely the body of Hartwell's reportage? he suggested. If I did, he said, I would notice its leftist bias, would no doubt conclude, as he, Rivas Valdez, had, and as many other knowledgeable officials had, including members of my own country's State Department, that Hartwell had been the guerrillas' most important propaganda tool.

I managed a glance into his eyes. The pupils had contracted into pinpoints, and he pricked me with them to make me pay attention. Still I couldn't think of anything to say, no adequate defense of Hartwell or of my own profession. And maybe then I realized that some of the borders between me and the rest of the world, my scalp and lips and toes and fingertips, were numbing up, turning indistinct. I couldn't tell exactly where they were even when I was looking at them. So I stopped looking at them, looked back out the window, where las Esmeraldas played a symphony in green.

Then he gestured toward my plate, asked what was wrong with my steak. Looking down, I saw it sitting in a puddle of bloody juice. Nothing was wrong, I told him, and he asked if I preferred to eat something else, a veal chop, or perhaps some broiled fish, and when I answered no, he asked did I suffer from the North American obsession with thinness. He didn't wait for my answer, instead told me I shouldn't drink so much on a nearly empty stomach.

In fact, I was drinking more than my share—first white to go with the seafood, then red to accompany the meat. I was embarrassed that he'd noticed, but each time I put my glass down a waiter appeared to fill it up again. The wines were the best I'd ever tasted. I couldn't imagine that such a remote restaurant actually stocked them. When I said this, Rivas Valdez met my eyes for a fleeting instant, said of course it didn't, that he'd had one of his men deliver them that morning.

Then he reapplied himself to the tenderloin and Alan Hartwell, saying that Hartwell had made so many people angry that he'd jeopardized his own well-being.

Of course, the best journalists, in their pursuit of truth, had often put their lives in danger. I could have given a dozen examples. But I wasn't thinking of them, was, rather, almost overwhelmed by the idea that Rivas Valdez did not find anything amiss about a place where you risked your personal well-being by making certain people angry. Then I understood what we were doing at the restaurant: he was trying to scare me.

"So that's what this meal is, huh? An elaborate threat? Why didn't you just tell me to watch my step? Or have one of your bullies do it for you?"

I was sneering like a Bronx waitress, but I only made him smile.

What he'd wanted to do during the luncheon, he said, his voice low and urgent, was to explain carefully the government's view of the international press and its presence in Bellavista. I should know, he said, that the government had an obligation to monitor outgoing press reports. All nations did so, he went on, but this was an especially critical time for Bellavista. It was essential that the truth be told.

"*Periodista: ¡Diga la Verdad!*"

"That's correct," he said, oblivious to any ambiguities. "Journalist, tell the truth. Of course, that is your obligation, to tell the truth. It's what you've been trained to do. And you would not have been sent here unless you were able to do it."

A waiter cleared away our plates, and another presented cups of strong black coffee, a decanter of liqueur, a pair of tiny goblets. The general himself poured the liqueur, told me it was made from Emerald Mountain coffee, was one of Bellavista's most delightful secrets. He slid a goblet across the table toward me till it collided with my fingertips and I rediscovered where they were. The liqueur was very sweet, but it blazed a trail into my belly, went off there like an artillery projectile.

After that, as we sipped our coffee and liqueur, Rivas Valdez himself spent some time looking out the window, leaving me to think about my training and about the search for truth. While he pondered the view, acting as if I weren't there, I began thinking or feeling that maybe, after all, I wasn't, or that I shouldn't be.

When we left, the ground was spongy under my feet and the car seemed very far away. When we finally reached it, the driver held the door for me, and I let him help me in. I glimpsed myself mirrored in its dark flank, and it registered somewhere in my head that our gleaming ship, filmed with dust when we'd debarked, was gleaming once again. And when this registered, I said to myself, "See, you're not drunk." And what I wanted above all was to get back to the hotel and very far away from General Víctor Rivas Valdez.

But when we reached the end of the restaurant's winding drive, the chauffeur turned the wrong way, headed higher up the mountain.

"I am going to show you something," Rivas Valdez said as the BMW rocketed up the slope. "I'm certain you will find it interesting."

Music, something by Stravinsky, erupted from the speakers, gushed over us. My ears popped, the angle of our ascent snatched away my breath, and my heart began to rear and gallop as if it were trying to get out.

Then the terror of having misplaced my borders hit, for the music, dissonances clashing, seemed to be savaging its way through me. I tried to focus on externals, to concentrate on the scenery, thinking this would keep me from panicking. But when I glanced out the window, the angle was so steep, the drop beside it so sheer, I couldn't bear to look ahead or back. As from a distance, I watched my own chest heaving, and I gasped for breath, but the effort was futile. No air was getting in. Black specks began dancing at the edges of my vision. I put my head back on the seat and closed them, thinking I'd be better off without sight. The music screeched around me, so I opened my eyes, leaned forward. I grabbed the front seat, feeling the way I sometimes did at night, struggling out of sleep against the sensation of falling backward into nothingness.

"Señorita Guerrera, are you well?"

His was a voice out of a whirlwind. My head snapped toward him before I knew it shouldn't. He was in the shadows, but his eyes on me were shiny, metallic. He tugged his lower lip, stared. Then his hand invaded the space between us, and in it was a square of white cloth, a handkerchief. Seeing it, I felt the moisture at my temples, the tiny trickle down my cheek. But I couldn't take the handkerchief, because I knew my hands were trembling and I wouldn't let him see. The white linen leaped to my face and it swabbed my upper lip, my cheeks, before I saw him folding it back up, carefully, to preserve his specimen. He put the handkerchief back into his pocket.

"Le Sacre du Printemps?" I asked to prove I could talk, although the words came out so soft the proof was doubtful.

"Yes. Do you like it?"

"I wouldn't call it easy listening."

"I asked you if you liked it."

"Sounds like annihilation."

"But do you like it?"

"It's not one of my favorites."

He nodded, watching me as if I couldn't see him, and the Stravinsky roiled on. But the crisis, whatever it had been, had passed. I could breathe, felt sober, and when I did look out the window, the road seemed to have at least a shoulder, some margin for error. The vegetation began to thin out until only scrub pines lined the road. Finally the driver stopped, pulled off the road against some scraggly pines, into a space just big enough for one car. I evaded the driver's assistance getting out, breathed deeply of the moist air, which smelled of pine and flowers.

"This way," I heard Rivas Valdez say. I located him beyond the back of the BMW, hands on his hips, his eyes directed toward my feet as I made my way across sandy, root-tangled ground. I'd nearly reached him when he turned, walked farther among the pines, disappeared, and called to me. I followed, and he repeated the procedure at least twice more so it became an eerie game, one I knew he'd win, and he did, for when at last I got to him, perhaps fifty yards from the car, the world fell away below his feet, the mountain dropped off, and I gasped to see the misty greens and blues of Bellavista lavishly arrayed in the vast hollow far below us. Miles away were the ruins of Libertad, *la comandancia* a black dot at their center. Beyond them was the rippling Pacific, which stretched to the horizon. The air seemed thinner, cooler than before.

"Look. Down over there is Tantauncapa," he was saying, gesturing toward a distant volcano spewing smoke into the sky.

His outstretched arm was the foreground, and I could hardly see beyond it. I thought of taking hold of it, of wrapping it around me, as if by doing so I could keep myself from falling into the sumptuous abyss of Bellavista.

Instead I stepped back, switched my eyes from the panorama to the turf closer to our feet. We were standing side by side, a footstep from the cliff's edge, our shadows falling over it. I leaned to look over, saw not the unrelieved drop I'd imagined, but one of perhaps only eight feet. Then the slope angled outward very slightly and continued in a series of steep, ridged tiers until it ended an impossible distance away in a tangled forest valley.

The tier closest to us was covered with tiny shrubs, flowering vines, patches of green grass over rusty earth. It took me several minutes to realize it must be the slope I'd read about so often and seen in so many news photographs, strewn with maggoty corpses, the victims of the death squads; to realize that this must be the infamous body dump of Bellavista called El Purgatorio.

I supposed it was what the general had brought me to see: El Purgatorio no longer existed. The body dump had been cleaned up. I inched closer to the edge, imagining wives and mothers reclaiming there their dead, news photographers scavenging for pictures. I wondered how many had made the trip and what the trips had cost them. Then the rusty earth and flowering vines were heaving up toward me and I felt the euphoria of a free-fall. I was giving myself up to it when one hand caught me between the ribs and another encircled my arm like a steel band. He pulled me up, pulled me back so forcefully the buckle of his belt jabbed into my spine.

"I wasn't going to fall. You made me."

He stepped backward, pulled me back with him, his chest heaving against my back. I heard another shriek.

"You made me slip, it's your fault. You pushed me."

I didn't recognize the pinched screech, but the words seemed true, that his touch had pushed me over, had not prevented me from falling.

I was facing him, immobilized by his hands around my upper arms. His chest rose like a blank wall inches from my face. I saw his throat, and then his face, which was very far away. He was watching from his distance, looking down with mineral eyes, and his eyes were radiating pale light as if a generator had just kicked on behind them.

I shoved him away, or he let go. I ran back to the car. Through the scraggly pines I heard tinny strains of Stravinsky, a cacophony of percussion instruments and strings. I went after the music, let its increasing volume guide me. My upper arms were reddened from his grip, burning where he'd held me. I rubbed and rubbed them as I ran, but I couldn't make the feeling go away.

GOV'T BAN ON DISSENT EXTENDED
by Elizabeth M. Guerrera
Herald-Sun Staff Writer

LIBERTAD, BELLAVISTA—A public order law that bans all forms of opposition to the government has been extended indefinitely, the ministry of defense confirmed yesterday, dashing widespread hopes that the new junta would ease severe governmental restrictions on public debate here.

A spokesman for Tutela Legal, the human rights office of the archdiocese here, said, "The citizens of Bellavista are still stripped of basic human rights."

Executives of Tutela Legal alerted the media to the fact that the Law for the Defense and Guarantee of Public Order remained in effect. Instituted one year ago by Luis Obando-Reyes, during his final bloody months as dictator, the law was scheduled to be rescinded last month.

"This temporary measure will allow the government to respond effectively to renewed terrorist activity in the capital and to a resurgence of communist organizing in the countryside," said a statement released yesterday by the ministry of defense.

The *ley de orden* makes illegal all expression of opinion and the dissemination of any information "through word of mouth, through writing, or through any other means that would tend to destroy the social order."

It also outlaws strikes and public meetings except those conducted by governmental agencies.

In addition, the law suspends normal judicial procedures in cases of alleged offenses against the public order. Those arrested have neither the right to legal counsel nor the right to public trial.

The law has decimated the country's trade unions and its reformist organizations, such as those associated with the Roman Catholic Church and various educational institutions. Its rigid rules for censorship succeeded in silencing the opposition press some time ago.

Yesterday, U.S. Ambassador Richard M. Whitaker said: "All governments have the right, and the obligation, to use any legal means to maintain domestic order, to halt terrorism, and to protect their sovereignty."

Questioned about the obvious potential for serious human rights violations, he said: "You've got to make a distinction between our standards of human rights and what we can impose on others.

"I don't think we have either the right or the duty to impose our standards on countries that may not be ready for them."

CHAPTER SEVEN

*I*T STARTED IN THE AFTERNOON, THE ACHING IN MY GROIN, THROBBING warning of misery to come, of the pain that would curl me into a fetal ball and leave me helpless on my bed until I began to bleed, when it would go away.

Outside the air was still and hot. I was feverish myself, had taken to my bed for siesta, the quotidian torpor that lasted till late afternoon. Hoping to doze off, I'd turned on the ceiling fan and radio, closed the shutters on my windows. Yet sunlight leaking in around them begged me to look at shadows it was throwing on the walls. The shadows danced with the spinning fan, hinting at something just beyond the reach of memory.

My hands, fingertips touching, were resting on my abdomen, just above the pubic bone. And I could feel, or imagined I could feel, my ovaries swollen, almost bursting. I pressed and poked, searched for the source of my extraordinary pain—even though I already knew there was none, no specific cause any physician had yet been able to discover.

"It's in my head, that's what you mean?" I'd asked the last one, but he hadn't answered, had said instead I ought to learn to live with it. I can't remember his face at all, just his words: "It's yours, this pain, part of your life. You've got to find a way to accommodate it, or better yet, to transcend it."

Over the years, through trial and error, I'd found ways to accommodate, to transcend. I'd take off from work, and as the pain invaded one end of me, I'd wash down Percodans with Wild Turkey at the other. In a sense, this transcendence was authentic, for it didn't so much kill the pain as make it seem to be happening to someone else, someone far below, far away from me. I'd watch her wandering, half in and half out of her body for a day or two, until the bleeding started, and then she'd be okay. She'd feel somehow reborn in her own blood.

But that afternoon at the Hotel Lido, I didn't have any Percodans, hadn't yet bought the bourbon. What I did have was a deadline, and a story to complete before it.

Luis Miguel Barrera, Bellavista's minister of social welfare, will run for president in next year's general election, the first free election to be held here in more than a century.

"My primary goal as president would be the permanent dismantling of an unwieldy and unjust oligarchy," said Barrera during a press conference here today. "The voices of the people must be heard."

Scion of a wealthy banking family, Barrera, 36, is the first member of the military and civilian junta to announce his candidacy.

I always made my deadlines, and I would make that one too, would telex my story to New York with time to spare, but first I tried to rest. I closed my eyes and watched afterimages of shadows dancing, watched them for long time, feeling lighter and lighter till I was almost weightless, which was how I wanted to feel, and the premenstrual ache evolved into a diffuse glow. In it, I saw an egg of mine, a gamete with essential ancestral information, escape its prison, begin its journey to the Place of Conception. And watching from a distance, I knew it was not a trip to Nowhere, for I could see, unobstructed, the dark looping tunnels it would pass through, and the warm, open chamber of my womb.

I could feel hands on my belly, stroking and caressing, the hands of my mother, the hands of a lover, then my own hands, warm and moist, and finally still, pressed flat against my belly, and the radiant eyes of my own fingertips probed the darkness, told me what I had to know, that everything was ripe, everything was ready: I would conceive. Then I was drifting farther from myself, was floating through an interstellar darkness, unafraid, feeling whole and tranquil, because I was conceiving, I knew I was conceiving, and as I drifted, I recited like a schoolgirl: "For to conceive means not only to become pregnant, gravid with unborn progeny, but also to originate, to cause to begin, to imagine, to apprehend by reason or imagination."

My voice was young and very sweet. I heard it, listened carefully, and accepted joyfully the retrieval of something lost, given up for good. I spoke slowly, then saw, without surprise, the words turn into stars when they left my mouth. Somehow I'd known this would happen, had known, too, that the stars contained another message if only I could find it through the dazzle. Without blinking, I watched the stars streaking through the black sky, colliding with one another, giving off showers of sparks. I was still peering into the brightness, searching for the message, when an electrical disturbance buzzed through my drowse, exploded the stars into glittering dots and blew them back into the darkness. Beneath the whirring of the ceiling fan, I recognized static from the radio. The government-owned station had stopped broadcasting *la música suave de la siesta*.

I opened my eyes and sat up, struggling for clear vision through a glistening rain of disintegrating thoughts. Then a group of whole words, complete with punctuation marks, flitted past, and I glimpsed them before they, too, blew away: I have conceived, therefore I am (not barren).

By dusk I'd showered, had dressed in a sleeveless cotton dress, and was sitting at my desk working on my story. From my window, as I typed, I could see the outline of Libertad. Beyond the city, an orange sun had all but melted into the ocean. The sky was streaked purple, red and pink.

In declaring his candidacy, Barrera, founder of the leftist Democratic Unification Party, also called for amnesty for members of the Mateo Omaño National Liberation Front, the rebel army. He proposed immediate negotiations with the remaining insurgents, who are said to maintain bases along the country's northern border near Costa Negra.

"We can negotiate an end to this disastrous conflict," Barrera told reporters. "Negotiations would demonstrate our government's commitment to hearing the voices of many people."

Barrera, who holds advanced degrees in political science from the University of Notre Dame in Indiana, has long been considered an advocate of the country's poor and disenfranchised. A professor of political science at the University of Bellavista until it was closed by the army three years ago, Barrera designed such key parts of La Solución Pacífica as the planned mother-child health care and nutrition project.

I could see tiny lights flickering in the ruins, knew they were the flashlights and kerosene lamps of *los sobrevivientes*, the survivors of the earthquake, who had fashioned homes out of the collapsed shells of banks, stores, and apartment buildings. Not far from them, the lights of *la comandancia* glowed steadily. Soon the massive searchlight on its highest turret would begin its nocturnal revolutions, eye of a Cyclops, peering through the city until dawn.

The lights made me think of Mary Healy, and I wondered which of them came from Nuestra Señora del Refugio, wondered if she was there, and if so, what she might be doing. I considered paying her a visit once I'd filed the story, then almost immediately decided against it. In a while the premenstrual pain would slither deeper into my belly, coil there, throbbing and fattening, until it burst. It was an invariable progression, inevitable as tides, the phases of the moon, and I had to finish the story, go back to bed, before it happened.

Barrera's amnesty proposal has sparked controversy within the junta, whose other members, including Gen. Víctor Rivas Valdez, minister of defense, have accused him of playing into the hands of the communists.

"We consider it both immoral and a threat to our national integrity to negotiate with terrorists," said Rivas Valdez in a statement released today by the ministry of defense.

Then the phone was ringing.

"I'm so scared, baby girl."

My mother's voice was soft and tentative, but her words were distinct, not slurred, and this surprised me. I heard, or thought I heard, the ice cubes clinking in her highball glass.

"I'm so afraid, baby, all the time. You don't know how much. I can't sleep."

I imagined my mother in her chair by the front window of our fourth-floor walk-up in the Bronx.

"I've tried so many times to get you to move," I told her, trying not to feel my guilt. "I would have bought you that little co-op in Riverdale. You said you didn't want it. Don't tell me you're scared now when I'm a couple thousand miles away."

"Not scared for myself, damm it," she said, her voice barely audible, as though she'd dropped the receiver. "I'm not thinking about myself. It's you. I saw your story yesterday."

My story yesterday had not been yesterday for me, had occurred at least three days earlier. Two civilians had been killed, trampled to death, perhaps two dozen injured, during a demonstration in Libertad. Thousands of survivors had marched on *la comandancia* to demand an end to their designation as illegal squatters.

Soldiers had ordered the crowd to disperse, and when it held its ground, they'd encircled it, begun firing water cannons and tear gas into it. The crowd panicked, mistaking the exploding tear-gas canisters for live shells. Rivas Valdez had immediately ordered the soldiers back, had also ordered military ambulances and medics to attend to the injured. Then, from a sound truck outside *la comandancia*, he'd promised to establish civilian grievance committees and to end corruption and random violence in the security forces.

Within two hours, trailers loaded with North American surplus rice and beans and dried milk were parked along the plaza. Packets of the goods were given free to all families who registered their addresses and the names of their family members with the ministry of social welfare.

"It's all so violent, so confusing," my mother was saying. I tried to interrupt, to tell her what had happened was actually cause for hope, was not at all personally dangerous to me. She wasn't listening.

"Nobody knows what it means. I ask my friends. Nobody knows. And you're right there, in the middle of it. Day after day. Sixty-three of them so far. I can't stand to think about it. About what you're doing there."

"Don't read the newspaper."

"I have to read the newspaper. It's like getting a letter. It's how I know you're alive."

I heard the ice cubes clink and what must have been the sound of her swallowing. I was holding the phone in my lap, pressed against my belly, and the coiling wire to the receiver spilled out like an umbilical.

"I'm working on a story, Mum. I've got a deadline."

"You don't have time to talk to me." I didn't answer, and in a minute she went on anyway. "Well, it's Saturday night. You used to come on Sundays. That's what I miss. Our Sundays."

"I miss them too."

"Remember brunch on City Island?"

"I remember. Easter, eggs Benedict."

"Mother's Day. Last Mother's Day. I had a mushroom omelette."

I couldn't think of a reply, and in the pause, I heard her breathing. The breaths were short, shallow, very fast.

"What's wrong, Mum?"

"I can't sleep nights thinking I could lose you. Lose you in a war that doesn't make sense to anyone I know."

"Why are you doing this to me?" I kept the rage out of my voice, managed to sound as distant as I was. "You know I'm working, I've got to work, and still you're doing this to me."

The sound of her breathing stopped, and I imagined she was holding her breath, swallowing hard, trying not to cry.

"You're everything," she said at last. "Everything."

Then I heard the familiar click and the roaring of the open wire. She'd hung up, cut the cord. I put the phone back onto the desk, but her voice and image stayed with me.

"I couldn't sleep last night, all this past week, because you're really leaving. It's finally happening."

We were at the airport, drinking coffee in the departure lounge, before my flight was called. She was wearing a navy suit and a red blouse. She'd had her hair done and a manicure to see me off. Still I couldn't look at her, watched instead my own hand, which was flat, palm down, on the Formica tabletop. Then she put hers on top of it, pressed down hard so I couldn't pull mine away. Our hands were nearly identical, the exact same size and shape, but her skin was shiny, almost transparent.

"You're really leaving me."

I couldn't answer, never did, and I later walked the long, empty corridor to my departure gate without once looking back. I didn't look because I didn't want the memory of her standing there with brimming eyes. I couldn't bear to see her smiling and waving and trying not to cry. I couldn't afford to think about what the goodbye was costing her, about what she'd do when she left the airport. So I went on by myself, without turning around, figuring if I could make it through the gleaming, silent corridor to the plane, I'd have it made, have the chance to make something of myself.

A waiter in a green cutaway jacket delivered the bottle of bourbon not long after I'd returned to my room. I'd turned on the paddle fan, but not the lights, and I didn't like the way he looked at me, the way he looked around to see if I had company. If I'd already been drinking, I probably would have told him to mind his business, to fuck off. But I hadn't been drinking, so I settled for shoving a large tip into his hand, U.S. dollars.

Of course, I could have brought the bottle up myself, but when I'd gone to the lounge to buy it, the entire press corps, what was left of it in Bellavista, seemed to be crammed around the adjacent tables, and I didn't want them to see, to know what I was doing.

One of them, a Reuters correspondent, had stood and called to me. He held out a chair, gestured to it, so I was forced to walk over to murmur my thanks but no thanks. I was beat, I said, and on my way to bed. Then I noticed Sonia sitting in the shadows, smiling and smoking, her hair spiked diabolically around her face.

"Miss America, you look paler than usual tonight, like you've seen a ghost or something." She exhaled a stream of cigarette smoke, and her black eyes glittered through it. "You're one white girl who's really white."

Several of the others grinned at her remark.

"My name happens to be Guerrera, not America, and I haven't seen any ghosts." I immediately regretted my retort: I'd promised myself to avoid the trap of talking to her. Yet I went on. "I just happen to be dead. I mean really tired. And if you're not too busy, maybe you could send off the photos for the Barrera story."

She smirked, shrugged. I knew, and she knew I knew, that she'd already sent the photos. She said nothing, instead mashed out her cigarette.

"Miss America says she's dead," she muttered, then looked up at me. "Maybe the ghost you saw was your own."

"Fuck you too," I said, heard them laughing as I walked away. I wondered what the joke was.

After that I couldn't wait to get to my room, to get away from them, from everyone. I was tired of talking, writing, using words. What I wanted was to turn myself into a mute, capable of hearing sounds, not words. Then I'd play wordless music very loudly and let it take me out of time.

I was thinking of César Franck, or Handel, was going through my cassettes trying to decide, when the waiter knocked. I filled my glass with bourbon, drank enough to get a good blaze going. My belly throbbed with cramps, and the bourbon helped to numb it right away.

I chose Handel's *Water Music*, thinking it would complement the watery shadows on my walls, thinking it would soothe me. But even when I drank some more, and turned the tape player to full volume, I remained jangled, and the fevered restlessness hung on.

Earlier I had telexed my story to New York from the desk in the lobby. When I went downstairs, the lobby had been bustling with patrons of the restaurant, lounge, and discotheque. The light was soft, and the scents of tobacco smoke and expensive colognes hung in the air. The atmosphere was cosmopolitan, festive, and I had a momentary urge to join the festivities, to change into something pretty and treat myself to dinner in the restaurant. But I wasn't hungry, the telex beckoned from a cubicle at one end of the front desk, and my deadline was perilously near. So I went ahead and filed my story.

I'd finished my transmission, was standing waiting for the sign-off from New York, when I saw Rivas Valdez on the far side of the lobby. He was surrounded by his men, but was tallest by a head, which made me wonder if it was a requirement to work for him, the shorter stature that permitted him to gaze about majestically, his view never obstructed. Then our eyes collided and I realized he'd been watching me—watching me look him over. He didn't look away, and so I did, humiliated, remembering without wanting to my drunken slip at El Purgatorio.

I turned back to the telex, prayed for the sign-off, was about to leave without it when I heard his voice, turned involuntarily to see him and his group passing near me on their way into the restaurant. He was talking to one of the men, but his eyes flickered over my body, moved to my face, met mine, and lingered.

"Señorita Guerrera, buenas noches."

He stopped in front of me, and by the time his courteous greeting reached me, my right hand was gently clasped in his. It was a gracious gesture, one of urbane civility.

"¿La señorita está bien esta noche?"

The señorita is well tonight? It was a standard inquiry, cast in the third person because the second person, you, would have been too intimate, too familiar. Yet the question, spoken so pointedly in Spanish, which we had not spoken together, seemed freighted with ambiguities, and I couldn't answer right away. He waited, watching me with feral eyes, eyes that betrayed all of his refinements. He raised my hand a little. For an instant I was afraid he'd kiss the back of it, like a knight. He smiled, as though he'd seen my thoughts, released my hand.

"*Estoy bien, gracias. ¿Y usted?*" I managed to say, but couldn't pronounce either his title or his name. He nodded, said he was glad that I was well, murmured other courtesies. Then he moved on with his entourage and I rushed out of the lobby, as though I had someplace to go.

I must have decided at that moment to visit Mary Healy, because I remember the offers of assistance from the hotelmen to get my car from the lot, remember ignoring them. Then I was gliding down the Avenida Independencia in the dark, and finally circling the plaza.

The plaza was lit by torches on poles stuck into the ground. Peddlers, beggars, prostitutes thronged there in the fiery light. Pairs of soldiers and *policía* walked among them. At one end, an old man played a guitar and a group of younger men stood around him singing. At the other, teenagers danced to American rock-and-roll blaring from a boom box.

I drove around and around but couldn't seem to find a place to park, couldn't seem to stop or get out of the car. Twice I got stuck behind troop carriers leaving *la comandancia*, embarking upon unknown missions. Once a group of orphans converged upon my car, some standing right in front of it, some pounding on the windows. I had to give them money so they'd move on, go away.

I saw the army jeeps parked in front of El Centro de Cambio y Creatividad—Mary Healy's health clinic—on my second or third circuit; noticed, too, the bright lights in the brick house and the trailers. But the scene had seemed somehow unreal, like a stage set, and I kept on driving. I'd driven around several more times when I saw soldiers, maybe half a dozen, climbing into the only remaining jeep. They drove away, and I followed at a distance, saw the jeep turn into *la comandancia*.

Of course, the soldiers could as easily, maybe more easily, have walked—because *la comandancia* was straight across the plaza from Nuestra Señora del Refugio. But as I drove behind them, it was obvious the jeep, with its peculiar whine, and the recoilless rifle mounted on its backside, delivered a more resonant message than foot soldiers ever could.

It wasn't until I was back in my room at the hotel and had drunk enough Wild Turkey to be getting transcendental that I began to wonder why I hadn't gone back to El Centro de Cambio y Creatividad to find out what had happened, what the soldiers' visit meant. It was not until I was drunk, and could no longer identify my own pain, that I began to wonder why I'd driven straight back to the hotel once the jeep had gone into *la comandancia*. Only then did I see the woman who looked like me, the foreign correspondent, driving away, not bothering to find out if there was a story, not even to find out if Mary Healy or anyone else at the clinic was in trouble. From my distance I understood, but only vaguely, that pain coiling up between her legs had forced her back. Still I knew the correspondent had made a mistake. So I stood up clumsily, made my way over to my desk, picked up the phone, asked the operator to dial the number of Nuestra Señora.

"*¿Quién?*" The voice was young and sweet. "*¿Quién?*"

Who? Who is it? I couldn't answer, couldn't think of a single word to say. She said hers once more—"*¿Quién?*"—before I hung up, went back to the bed, poured another glass of bourbon.

I rewound the tape, Handel's *Water Music*, restarted it, lay down. Rivas Valdez came to me then and I saw him, felt him, holding my hand. But though I saw him clearly, I couldn't tell if he was giving me something or taking something away.

After that I saw myself driving around the plaza, going around in circles. When I closed my eyes, I could feel myself swirling, spinning, pirouetting, and the sensation reminded me how, every month, I ended up in the same place, helpless on my bed. Knowing I always ended up in the same place made me understand that I was, in fact, going in circles, going nowhere in my life, spiraling through time.

I opened my eyes, again saw moonlight splashing shadows through the room. The fan seemed to be pushing them, and the walls and ceilings danced with shades of gray and black and white which seemed electronic, incandescent. I watched them for a time, until I visualized the other place, the one I couldn't quite remember in the afternoon.

That room had been small and warm and dark, but the light given off by the ultrasonic monitor had splashed like moonlight on the walls and ceiling. There, a humming cephalopod, an ultrasonic monitor, had beamed down upon me, efficient and indifferent. Its multiple arms had been attached to my bare belly, sunk into a transparent slime through which I could feel them gently sucking. The eye each rubber tentacle contained penetrated skin and muscle, threw back onto the monitor images of its discoveries, the murky secrets of my body. The images leaped and swirled in shades of gray, jumped with each beat of my heart, danced to the rhythm of my pulse. I watched them, awed by the frantic vitality of what was going on inside me. I couldn't see the doctors, they were someplace behind me, but I could hear their gentle exhalations beneath the humming of the cephalopod. If I shut my eyes, the machine seemed to be breathing. Then a human finger touched the screen, traced a dark thing within the pulsing mass of ultrasonic waves, and a voice was saying very softly, more to the other doctors than to me, "See, there, it's very small, almost inverted, a shape that tends to be inconsistent with female reproductive capacity. . . ."

I could barely make it out under his finger, a feathery black spot within the grays, the shriveled place, my womb.

Maybe then, or maybe sometime later, the *Water Music* stopped, and another sound was coming at me very loudly, whirling toward me through the shadows. Maybe the sound woke me up, or maybe a dream created itself around the sound, and I was hurrying out to meet the rescue chopper before I knew I was awake. But it turned before I got there: the rescue chopper left without me. I was standing in the middle of my room, arms outstretched, watching the paddle fan going around and around.

CHAPTER EIGHT

ARY HEALY, STANDING WITH HER BACK TO ME, WAS IN A TINY office crowded with a desk and bookshelves, odd pieces of medical equipment, and crates of medical supplies. She wore a white lab coat, her wild hair a mist around its shoulders. She turned abruptly, held aloft a bunch of surgical gloves whose fingers flopped over her fist like wilted flowers in a nosegay.

"All too small," she said in Spanish to a girl I recognized as Milagros, the young mother from OPEN whose baby had been dying. "See if you can find me some that fit."

Milagros, now sleek and clean, with a haircut and new clothes, nodded and hurried away. Then Mary looked at me, and her gaze chilled me just a little. She seemed thinner, paler, as if something had drained out of her in the three weeks or so since I'd seen her.

"They arrested one of the women who work here last night," she said. "Our cook. A widow in her sixties."

"They?"

"One of the goon squads. Soldiers. Who else?"

She began to trace something on the desktop with her index finger.

"Why?" I waited for her to invite me to sit down. She didn't and instead kept tracing with her finger and watching what she traced.

"It's what the goon squads do. They arrest people, jail them at undisclosed locations for indeterminate lengths of time. They don't even have to say why. You know that. You wrote about it."

She looked up at me, her glance accusatory, as though I'd created the public order law when I reported on it.

"Is she still being held? Have they stated the charges?"

Her spurt of hoarse laughter told me my questions were absurd.

"No, they haven't charged her. But I happen to know what she's guilty of." She began tracing again. "And I also happen to know that she is guilty. So I don't expect to see her anytime soon."

She looked at me, demanded my next question.

"What did she do?"

"She prayed. She prayed with other poor people. She's guilty of organizing prayer groups. We call them base communities. She's guilty of helping poor people find strength in one another and in the Gospel."

"That's a crime?"

"You're the one who wrote about the *ley de orden*. Don't you understand it?"

I'd been standing in the doorway, and her sarcasm turned me around, bumped me against the doorframe.

"For your information, Elizabeth," she called, and her defeated tone slowly turned me back, "the soldiers are within the law when they barge in here with machetes and M-16s, terrify the children. They're within the law when they fondle women here and search my files." She paused and watched me, her eyes points of light in the dull room. "They're within the law when they hit pregnant women in the belly with their guns and call them factories for subversives. But it's a crime for the women who live here to meet and talk about their lives. It's a crime for us to pray together."

"I wish I'd been here. I wish I'd seen it."

"Why?"

"I could have written a firsthand account."

"Which would have given your career a boost, right?"

Mary chuckled, gestured to a chair near her desk, and I moved toward it.

"Unfortunately, *las fuerzas armadas* don't put on such shows for reporters." She took a seat behind her desk. "Not reporters for big *yanqui* papers anyway."

"Tell me about it on the record." I was taking out my notebook. "I can try to track down your cook, get a response from the defense ministry. I can write the story, anyway."

She looked at my notebook, seemed to consider the ramifications of the story.

"I want to keep doing what I'm doing for a while longer," she said at last. "These women need me. I'm the only one who can do it."

"What exactly do you do?" Even then I believed her work was essentially political, but wondered if she knew it, wondered what she'd tell me.

"I help poor women discover their own spiritual strength, their ability to heal and be healed." She spoke without hesitation—it was a line she'd thought about, rehearsed.

"You don't deal only with the spirit."

She grinned, picked up a small wooden Madonna from her desk, looked at it as she spoke. I tried to take notes. "No, we also do a lot of body work," she said. "Body and spirit are deeply intertwined. So I teach women about the reproductive cycle, about caring for their own bodies and caring for their young. Basic health care and hygiene. They can't begin to control their lives until they have some control over their bodies."

She rolled the Madonna between her palms. "In fact, I happen to believe in reproductive freedom for all women." She glanced up at me. "Which pits me directly against the Roman Church, not to mention the government of Bellavista." She placed the Madonna back on the desk, near her telephone. "Luckily for me, neither abortion nor birth control is an important issue here. Because we have death control in Bellavista. Death control makes birth control and abortion on demand pretty much irrelevant."

I smiled, but sensed she was trying to sidetrack me.

"When we were up at OPEN you told Milagros you would teach her about the oppression that causes unnecessary ailments like the one that almost killed her daughter. Do you do that? Teach poor women about oppression?"

"In Hebrew, the Old Testament defines at least five categories of poor people. Did you know that?" She squinted at me as if trying to get me into focus. "In English and Spanish we use the single word 'poor,' *pobre,* meaning, above all, economically deprived. But in the language of the Bible there were separate words for paupers, the physically weak, the unsatisfied, the persecuted, and finally the abased or humiliated whose very misery makes it impossible for them to assert themselves."

I looked at her, while trying at the same time to jot her words into my notebook.

"Like the Eskimos with snow—don't they have a dozen words for it?—the ancient Hebrews understood all the subtle nuances of poverty." She frowned, repeated that I ought to think about what I meant when I talked about "the poor."

"Scripture asserts repeatedly that God hears the cries of the poor. What He hears are all different kinds of cries from all the world's unfortunates. Not just the economically deprived."

"So you teach poor women about oppression?"

"We talk about the root causes of poverty and ignorance. We talk about institutionalized violence and injustice."

"The government considers you subversive."

She shrugged.

"I've been here for a long time." She pulled out a desk drawer, rummaged through it, slammed it shut without removing anything. "At first, when I began to feed the hungry, clothe the naked, give free health care to the poor, everybody loved me. I was the wonderful Sister Mary. I even got invited to the embassy." She paused, leaned toward me, her hands flat on the desk. "As soon as I asked why the poor had no food or clothes or health care, and as soon as those I treated began to ask that question for themselves, well, all of a sudden I turned into a subversive."

"How could my story hurt?"

She laughed her ragged laugh, looked at me in wonder. Emotion, maybe anger, flushed her cheeks and turned her pale eyes blue.

"It would enrage the government, the military. It's exactly the kind of attention we don't need. Not right now, anyway."

"The story might embarrass them so much they'd release your cook."

"Maybe. But there'd also be long-term repercussions for the rest of us. More harassment." She raked her fingers through her hair, gestured toward the ceiling. "Half the women here used to sell themselves out there on the plaza. Sometimes the soldiers still come here looking for it. They're too dumb to figure out it's not for sale anymore. And we don't give anything away." She smiled without mirth. "Of course, they want to take it anyway."

She stopped abruptly, seemed embarrassed by her vehemence.

"I haven't finished my work here yet," she said after a minute. "I'm not ready to go home."

"Where's home?"

She hesitated, then offered her answer—Greenwich. Greenwich, Connecticut—like a challenge. Greenwich. Nestled on the wooded shore of Long Island Sound, one of the country's wealthiest towns, the very heart and soul of old money in America. A jolt of exultation struck me: Sister Mary came from money. I was right. But instead of picking up her challenge, I asked what she was going to do about her cook.

"I spent more than half the night at *la comandancia* trying to get her out. I didn't succeed, but because I went there, let them know I'm watching, I don't think they'll 'disappear' her for good. Meanwhile, however, I'm not going to put an international spotlight on the army and its human rights violations."

"What about you? Aren't you afraid?"

"Even the goon squads wouldn't be stupid enough to hurt a *gringa* while Uncle Sam is giving them more than a million bucks a day."

Milagros reappeared and handed a package of surgical gloves to Mary, whispering that something or someone was ready.

"Bueno." Mary clapped once. "Come on," she said to me, heading for the door behind Milagros. "Now you can see firsthand what we're really all about."

She stopped and grabbed the girl by the shoulders, spun her around to face me, clasping her in an awkward hug.

"Hey, wait a minute," she said. "Did you recognize Milagros? Isn't she beautiful? And her baby, well, she's turned into a fat little princess. That's what her mother did for her."

Again I complimented the girl on her rapid transformation, but she eyed me sullenly. Mary touched her cheek and let her go.

"If you want to know about my work here at El Centro de Cambio y Creatividad," she said, her arm entwining mine, "take a look at Milagros. That's what I mean by healing and being healed. That's what I do."

Her hand, clasping mine, felt feverish as she took me with her along an unlit corridor. It smelled of incense, reminiscent of ancient Catholic rituals. A low groan from somewhere nearby startled me and touched off an intense urge to flee, but Mary carried me along on the energy of her determination.

"Childbirth," she whispered, her eyes luminous. "It's another miracle. I've attended thousands and it still blows me away."

A muffled shriek galvanized my urge to run. I heard another cry, a soothing answer, a barely distinguishable laugh or moan.

"Come on," she urged, still holding me in her hot grip, pushing through another door, taking me along. "It's a privilege to witness."

We entered a warm, narrow room.

"*¿Cómo estás, Silvia?*" Mary called to a woman who lay on a sheet-draped cot in the middle. All I could see was a tangle of black hair, a mountain of a belly, peaks of knees beyond it. Mary gestured for me to join her by the woman, who half smiled, half grimaced up at Mary. Her face was slick with sweat. She tried to sit up, but fell back as if pinioned by the weight of her great belly. Mary took her hand, leaned down to stroke her cheek, whispered something. Silvia nodded, gripped Mary's arm with both of hers, groaned as a contraction grabbed at her midsection and rippled through her swollen body.

"*Está casi lista.*"

She is almost ready.

The cool voice emanated from beyond the mountain of Silvia's belly. Then its owner peeked out from her hiding place, a low stool between the woman's legs.

"*¡Mira!*" said this beautiful young girl, smiling up at Mary.

"Alba, one of my apprentices," Mary murmured, moving to the foot of the cot, thrusting the sheets aside, gesturing once more for me to join her. "This is a very special delivery, her first."

Alba, maybe seventeen, had the caramel skin and prominent high cheekbones of an Indian. Gleaming plaits of black hair ran behind her ears, disappeared under the collar of her lab coat. She was pressing her gloved hands against the insides of Silvia's thighs, waiting for Mary's opinion.

"Check her dilation once more," Mary said in Spanish, and peripherally, I saw Alba's fingers disappear into the woman's body. I watched Alba's face instead. Even as she worked she seemed serene, absolutely sure of what she was doing. Her face was covered with a sheen of perspiration, her cheeks rosy underneath. I heard Mary telling me that Alba had been selling herself for pennies before she'd ever menstruated. When Mary had found her outside the clinic, several years earlier, she'd been near death, hemorrhaging from a self-induced abortion.

Milagros came back into the room, helped Mary scrub and put on gloves. After that, the incipient birth demanded all of their attention, and I watched them mesmerized; watched Mary and her young apprentices offer comfort and emotional support along with skilled midwifery. By then Silvia was crying constantly and thrashing against the pain, but Milagros and Mary kept soothing her with soft words and caresses.

At some point, Mary told Silvia to ask Jesus to keep her from getting lost in the pain. She pointed to the crucifix on the wall, and Silvia's dazed eyes found it. "Remember what Christ did for us," she said. "Pray and He'll help you through this. We won't let you get lost in the pain."

Mary took a low stool at the foot of the delivery table next to Alba, while Milagros climbed onto the side rungs of the bed and leaned across it, demanding that Silvia breathe along with her. Milagros held Silvia's hands and began to blow short, sharp breaths out through her mouth, and Silvia soon began to do the same. For a time, the pair offered a duet of huffs and puffs, which were increasingly interrupted by Silvia's whimpering whenever a contraction hit. Soon the contractions struck one after the other and there was hardly any time for the funny huffings and puffings.

Once Silvia screamed, but she quieted immediately as Alba called her name, told her that the top of the baby's head was visible, that it was ready to be born.

I couldn't help stealing a look at that almost unrecognizable place between Silvia's legs. In the frame of Alba's gloved hands was a barely discernible patch of scalp. Another contraction struck, Silvia moaned, and the patch grew larger, asserting itself with spurts of blood and water.

By then, Silvia was grasping Milagros by her wrists, clutching at her each time a contraction struck. She was crying out *"¡No más!"*—no more—and the force of her mad clutching seemed certain to topple tiny Milagros, who stood braced and quivering against the birthing bed.

Mary joined Milagros, and soon the two of them were holding Silvia around her back and by each leg. With each contraction, they heaved her to a sitting position and squeezed her torso toward her legs—as though this would help Silvia push her baby out. I don't know how many times they did this—so many both of them were wet with sweat. I took turns watching them and watching Alba, who was massaging Silvia's upper thighs, her vulva and perineum, which Mary said would keep the baby from tearing her as it thrust into the world.

Through the women's grunts and moans and murmurs, through the sweat and blood, the event suddenly seemed sacred. Mary's prophecy had come true: I felt I was a privileged witness. It wasn't only the birth itself, but also the transformation of Milagros and the efforts of a midwife who was barely old enough to be a mother. The three of them—Mary, Alba, and Milagros—worked in an efficient, wordless intimacy, and Silvia trusted them completely.

Then I saw myself, sitting on the sidelines: Elizabeth M. Guerrera, reporter, impartial observer. Yes, I was a good journalist—irrelevant to them and to everything that was going on.

Suddenly a purple, wrinkled creature, streaked with white goo, was inching out into Alba's hands. What began to emerge didn't look exactly human, with its closed and swollen eyes, flattened nose, battered cheeks, and tiny bud of a mouth. Silvia bellowed joyfully once the head was through. The rest of the baby slid out in a huge gush of blood and water that showered Alba and flooded the sterile cloths beneath her feet. The baby arrived curled up, its limbs bent up tight like a frog's. All of us were leaning in and stretching to see the same thing, its genitals, which would foretell so much about its future.

Alba, childish in her excitement, grabbed the baby by its feet, stood and held it high.

"*El niño,*" she cried, as the purple hose of the umbilical uncoiled between mother and child and thrashed in the air like a snake. The baby began to wail.

"A boy," Mary murmured. I saw the infant's purple knob of a penis and swollen scrotum. The baby howled mightily, and his mother, too, was crying, blessing herself, whispering a prayer.

Alba sat back down. She cut the umbilical cord and handed the baby to Mary, who carried him to the sink, tied the umbilical, and washed him while Alba delivered the placenta. As soon as she had, Silvia raised herself up on an elbow, called to Mary, her voice hoarsened by her own screams. "*Dame mi niño, por favor. Dame mi precioso.*"

Give me my precious baby.

"In a minute," Mary told her, laughing. "I'm still cleaning him."

"No," Silvia cried with her arms outstretched. "*Ahora. Lo quiero ver ahora mismo.*"

Mary brought her the baby. Silvia took him with a happy cry, cradled him on her belly. He quieted as she began to caress his body. She covered him with kisses.

"You know, the prognosis for these babies isn't very good."

Mary was standing beside me watching Silvia while Alba and Milagros cleaned up the bloody mess. "Most of the time, like half the people in this country, Silvia's too poor to buy food. And she certainly doesn't have land to grow it on."

Silvia was holding her baby very close, rocking him and crooning to him, laughing and whispering as if no one else were in the room.

"That's what I meant by death control: not enough food and no access to health care."

Silvia rested the baby on her legs and opened her cotton gown. Her breasts were swollen, embroidered with stretch marks, webbed with blue veins. She began to rub one nipple along the baby's cheek, cooing her encouragement. The baby turned toward it, rooting like a blind beast, his mouth opening and closing, opening and closing. In a moment, though he could not see, he found what he was after. His mouth closed over the nipple and then he knew exactly what to do, how to suck, and once he began, his wrinkled face contorting with the effort, he squirmed and thrashed in pure delight.

"These women have so much courage," Mary said as we watched. "They're surrounded by death, and their deepest yearning is to give life."

She went over to Silvia, put an arm around her. *"Tú eres muy valiente, Silvia,"* she said. *"Ahora tienes un hijo fuerte y sano también."*

Silvia smiled and nodded, still watching her child. The baby's sucking seemed to have transformed her. Her cheeks had flushed and her eyes brightened, so that even in the poor light she seemed to glow.

"Muchas gracias, Sor María," she whispered, gazing with wet eyes at her baby. *"Muchísimas gracias para todo. Estoy muy contenta."*

Everyone was quiet, so quiet the sounds of the baby's lusty sucking filled the room. Alba and Milagros stopped what they were doing, cocked their heads, and listened for a moment before they recognized the sound. They looked at one another and began to laugh. They paused once in their laughter, and the sucking grew louder, more furious.

"Hay Dios mío," cried Silvia. *"¡Mi teta!"*

She made a face, touched the breast below his cheek in mock agony. The women laughed again, laughed long and loud, until tears ran down their faces.

ACCIDENTAL BLAST KILLS TERRORISTS
by Elizabeth M. Guerrera
Herald-Sun Staff Writer

LIBERTAD, BELLAVISTA—Four suspected terrorists were killed yesterday when explosives they were handling detonated near the sprawling settlement of Ciudad de Merced.

Government officials said the blast destroyed the alleged terrorists' van, a car, and a small house. It ignited the surrounding forest and left a large crater in a clearing about 100 yards from a main road.

The identities of the dead were unknown last night.

Authorities said the house was a known retreat for leftist rebels of the Mateo Omaño National Liberation Front (FMOLN).

Defense ministry officials speculated that the terrorists were removing explosives from the van and carrying them into the house when the explosives accidentally detonated.

Defense Minister Víctor Rivas Valdez said charred notebooks that detailed plans for a bombing campaign against government targets were retrieved from the house along with shortwave radios, walkie-talkies, and explosive materials. The general theorized that the terrorists' intended target was a military barracks outside the gates of Ciudad de Merced, about two miles from where the explosion occurred. He said evidence gleaned from the site indicated two of the dead men had intended to drive the explosives-laden van into the barracks in a suicide bombing similar to one which destroyed a Marine barracks in Beirut several years ago.

In the past, the FMOLN has often used explosives in its armed campaign to overthrow the government. Three times in recent years it has bombed military barracks, destroying the facilities and wounding many soldiers. However, its typical targets have been bridges, power stations and power lines, shipping docks, railroad tracks, and the plantations of the oligarchy.

CHAPTER NINE

H E WAS DRIVING VERY FAST, HURTLING UP STEEP GRAVEL ROADS, past abandoned plantations, through villages of adobe huts and scraggly, dried-up *milpas*. Even the military roadblocks, three, maybe four of them, failed to impede us. The Cherokee would screech to a halt and his emergence from it would transform the surly soldiers into sculptures of respect and discipline.

I'd watch this from the inside, from behind dark glass, where I was invisible. The soldiers would stand at attention, and he'd inspect them until the only movement was tears of sweat trickling down their cheeks. Then he'd slide back behind the wheel and we'd be off, pushing forward, leaving everything behind.

A cold wind was blowing from the air conditioner, abrading the bare skin of my face and arms, as it hummed beneath piano concerti by Mozart and Ravel. And the submachine gun he'd dropped into the space between our leather bucket seats kept shifting and skidding on the sharp turns of the road. I wondered how it worked, if a sudden movement, a bump or swerve, might accidentally set it off.

I curled into the corner of my seat, away from the cold wind and the gun. Caught in a surge of dread, I tried rolling down the window, was struggling with the knob when I heard him say the vehicle was armored with about a ton of steel, that its bulletproof windows were immobile. In Spanish he told me to be still, and he said my name, Elisabet. It stung like a dart, paralyzing me.

When we were almost there, the road withered into blackish ruts and the forest became so dense we seemed to be driving through a green tunnel. Then we burst into a clearing domed with a lustrous cobalt sky. The clearing was a plateau, and las Esmeraldas rose steeply just beyond it, disappearing into silver mist. We sped toward them through swaying high grass. The grass was sunlit, yellowing, and it swirled around like golden water. The plateau wasn't large, appeared longer than it was wide, and we'd nearly reached the mountains when I noticed the lake, the body of dark water for which the place had been named. It shimmered like a massive bronze disk dropped in the grass. Gigantic cedars and conifers marked its far shore. Their reflections undulated on its surface.

I thought the water was our destination, but he veered suddenly away, swooped into and back out of a ravine, and again accelerated. We jounced off in the opposite direction. Suddenly he clutched, shook the gearshift, reversed the Cherokee, and circled back another way. I wondered what was going on, but didn't ask. He muttered Spanish expletives I didn't understand.

Then a blurred arc of color in the side mirror caught my eye. "Look," I demanded, pointing to a rainbow above the water. At once we were rushing toward it. The arcs of green and pink and gold grew more distinct, then something else, something darker, began emerging through the streams of color. It was a woman with her arms outstretched. She wore a rose-colored dress and a beaded belt sparkled at her waist. I realized she must be *la virgen*, the Madonna of Aguas Oscuras.

"*Ya ella viene,*" he said. Finally she comes—as if she'd been late for their appointment. The Madonna hovered above the placid water, entreating us with her arms. I got out of the car, ran toward her.

* * *

After Luis Miguel Barrera declared himself a presidential candidate, my editors assigned a profile of General Rivas Valdez, which they planned to feature in the Sunday magazine. Rivas Valdez was, they suggested, a progressive and charismatic military strongman not unlike the late General Omar Torrijos Herrera of Panama. My editors speculated that like Torrijos, Rivas Valdez was capable of developing a populist coalition strong enough to support the state's implementation of essential social reforms. Yet his virulent anticommunism would bind him to the center, they said. Because of his ties to the United States, my editors believed he was unlikely to sponsor Torrijos's brand of nationalism, with its vehement anti-Americanism.

Through an aide, the general had agreed to a series of interviews. I was also to accompany him through a typical workday. I'd gone to *la comandancia* that morning expecting to attend a meeting of the junta and afterward to observe U.S. Army personnel training Bellavistan pilots at the airport.

Instead, the general had escorted me out to the Cherokee, which was parked in a remote, abandoned part of the yard. The vehicle was black, and sunlight danced on its hood. I kept expecting his burly chauffeur to appear, to whisk us off into the day, but it was Rivas Valdez himself who opened the door for me. Then he was behind the wheel dropping onto the console between our seats a gun, an Ingram MAC-10 fitted with a sound suppressor. I recognized the MAC-10 right away—the firearm of choice among drug thugs in the Bronx.

"Where shall we go today, Señorita Guerrera?" he asked, half-smiling, as though mine were a social call, not a professional appointment. The interior was cool, dimmed by the tinted glass. His eyes were feline, depthless, a place for getting lost in. I looked away.

"Where shall I take you?" he repeated from across the chasm of the seats. "Have you thought about it? Hmm?"

"Cauchimpca? Or maybe the Academia Militar?"

I'm positive I said those words, but he didn't respond. Just then his movements, or the chill, released the scent of his soap or cologne. It was a subtle musk, and I held my breath against its lure, resisted the impulse to move closer, to fill my lungs with it. He was leaning over the gun, fidgeting with part of it I couldn't see.

"I will take you anyplace you want to go, Señorita Guerrera," he said, still playing with the gun. "Where do you want to go?"

His words were deliberately ambiguous. Their insistent chords tightened around my throat, making it hard to answer.

"*La periodista astuta* is confused?"

The wise journalist, the astute reporter.

He glanced up, watched me intently while chewing on his lower lip. Again I looked away.

"Why would I be confused?" I smiled at my own hands. "I want to go to Aguas Oscuras."

"Yes," he said, putting the Cherokee into gear, "you must see Aguas Oscuras."

Gushing adrenaline eddied as I stared up at the Madonna's sightless marble eyes, her pitted plaster skin. My mad rush to her had abruptly ended once the rainbow disappeared and revealed a statue, not an apparition, a statue attached to an outcropping of stone over the water. Yet my few moments of absolute belief had stunned me, and left me giddy and uncertain. I didn't know if I was going to laugh or cry. Then he was there beside me, and I wanted to run, but his hand encircled my upper arm, preventing me.

"My God," I whispered, and he answered, "No, *su madre*," his mother, which detonated my wild laughter. I tried to stifle it, hiccuped in the effort. I put my face into my hands to hide my flush of shame, to muzzle other crazy noises.

"Exquisite, isn't it? The illusion?"

I couldn't answer, tried to nod, was shaken by another spasm when his grip tightened on my arm and the weight of his arm fell against my back. He pretended not to notice, moved me closer to the grotto, pointing toward it with the MAC-10, which he was holding in his other hand.

"Of course, like many beautiful things, the illusion is fragile, elusive. It is apparent only at certain times, from certain angles. I had not seen it myself for years, and I worried for a time, there in the field, that I couldn't make it happen for you."

The shrine occupied the crest of a small hill maybe six feet higher than the ground we stood on, and steep narrow stone steps led up to it. The outcropping, strewn with withered flowers, was like an altar. The statue had been angled there so it gazed out across the plateau. From the rocks beneath it, water cascaded into the pond, sent up sprays of water in which, I realized, the sunlight was refracted. He gestured toward the waterfall.

"An underground mountain stream feeds the pond," he said. "It is extremely cold, condenses here, in the warmer air——"

"Where it refracts the sunlight," I interrupted him.

Again, the Virgin's beribboned robe shifted in the breeze. It had been crudely sewn from coarse fabric, was faded and dirty.

"The way the wind shifted her dress made it seem she was moving," I heard myself explaining. When he didn't answer, I glanced up at him, found him staring at me as if he knew something about me I didn't know myself. And I might have asked what he was thinking of, but he moved off and took me along, heading for the hillock.

"Did you know," he asked as we climbed the weedy slope, "that the Taupils' goddess of childbirth and healing, Tato Ina, reigned here for perhaps five hundred years before the Madonna succeeded in deposing her?"

I didn't know if I knew or not, didn't try to answer.

"Did you know Tato Ina also wore a rose-colored dress and an intricate sash of beads and shells?"

We stopped directly behind the crumbling Madonna. From the new angle she was diminutive. Her crown of withered roses had slipped precariously to one side of her head. Except for the color of her hair and eyes, she was identical to the Madonna at Holy Redeemer in the Bronx, beneath which my mother lit weekly votive candles, knelt to pray. Identical, too, was the black plaster serpent protruding from her feet.

"Because of her similarity to Tato Ina, the Vatican has denied the authenticity of the Virgin of Aguas Oscuras. The Roman Catholic hierarchy believes the Taupils, in their fervid Mariolatry, or greed, somehow confused Tato Ina and God's mother."

Rivas Valdez reached out to straighten the Madonna's crown, but the roses disintegrated, and a snow of broken petals flew past.

"However, as you must know, the visitations by the Madonna of Aguas Oscuras continued despite the ruling of the Vatican. And, of course, as you must also know, the village prospered."

All I could tell, from where we stood, was that there was no longer any village. Its demise was indisputable. Again I felt like laughing— because there was no village, prosperous or otherwise, no villagers to witness any visitations. I swallowed hard, managed to smother the outburst. But I failed to make my point and didn't even ask when the village's prosperity had ended.

I looked over the clearing, saw its golden carpet marred by curlicues of crushed grass where we'd driven. Then I saw a pair of dark ruts, parallel and gently curving, that cut diagonally across it, wriggling off into the mountains like twin serpents. I thought they must have been the main street of Aguas Oscuras, the only obvious clue to the village's existence.

Something brushed my skirt, made me jump. He was standing very close to me, had accidentally bumped me when shifting the gun from one hand to the other.

"You seem very nervous, Elisabet." He wasn't looking at me, was balancing the gun across his palm with his fingers on the trigger.

"I'm not nervous. I'm just a little jumpy."

I hugged myself as I watched him. I expected him to say more, but he didn't. His wristwatch flashed frantically, but his fingers on the trigger remained absolutely still.

After a moment, he tucked the gun under his arm and we walked back down to where large rocks and boulders were heaped beside the water. We walked along the curving shore until the rocks gave way to rusty sand. He crouched down, dropped the gun onto the sand, put his hands into the water. When I crouched beside him, he let the water run through his fingers, showing me its color, dark reddish brown, the color of old blood.

Again I thought about the massacre. I couldn't help imagining that its blood had drenched the earth around the lake and seeped into the water. But I didn't bring this up. Instead I put my hands into the water, swirled them this way and that. Sunlight caught startling glints of red and orange.

"Like a sunset," I said.

"The Taupils have a different idea. According to their lore, the pool is fathomless at its center, leads into the womb of Tocinanatzil, the great earth mother."

He picked up a flat stone, rubbed it between his fingers.

"They believe the water is tinged with her menstrual blood, and somehow this convinced them that bathing in the water can make barren women fertile."

He skipped the stone across the water. It ricocheted three times before it disappeared.

"For peasant women, infertility is the worst of scourges, an unbearable affliction." He stood, shook the water off his hands, rubbed them together. "So it is not surprising that they discovered, or, rather, created, a form of healing which, if nothing else, gave them hope."

I stood, wiped my hands on my dress, wanting, suddenly and urgently, to go back to Libertad.

"But, in fact," he added, gesturing out toward the cedars on the far shore, "it is a phenol from the trees, tannin, that leaches into the water, staining it. The dark water is only cedar water, very soft and pure despite the color. It is not uncommon. And many believe it has some curative properties even if it cannot make barren women fertile."

He stooped to retrieve the MAC-10, took my elbow, headed us toward the ruts of the old road. I went along with him, and sometimes I glanced at him, caught him scanning the trees, or turning lazily to look behind us. The gun had a wrist strap, but he held it by its handle, struck his thigh with the barrel as we walked. The sound was faint but metronomic. The road was lined with gullies whose depth varied, and once, where the ditch was shallow, we shifted course, began meandering through the meadow. I stepped over several large stones, or, rather, concrete blocks set into the earth. Perhaps they'd been the cornerstones of buildings. Behind the shrine, not far from the water, we discovered a place where the grass was soft and new, shin-high. The bright green was splotched here and there by chicory and dandelions, and with red and purple wildflowers whose name I didn't know. I also found a place where the earth was mounded into an oval, although the mound was hidden by the grass until I was on top of it. I was tracing it with my footsteps when he said something I didn't quite hear.

"What?" I asked, looking up. I think I'd been smiling, but the way he looked made me stop. Again, in Spanish, he muttered something I didn't understand. Then he about-faced and walked away. In a while I followed.

He'd walked around the hillock to the stone steps of the shrine. He dropped the gun onto the altar and leaned against the steps. He plucked out a blade of long grass and pulled it between his lips. Just above him, the limpid Virgin smiled.

Feeling that he'd dismissed me, or that I'd done something wrong, I wandered over to one of the large rocks by the water, found a flat one, and sat on it. The rock was hot from the sun. Perspiration tickled my upper lip, glistened on my palms. I didn't know what I'd done wrong. Again I had the urge to flee, but there was no place to go, no way to get anyplace on my own. Then it occurred to me that we were at the end of something, Rivas Valdez and I, but not quite at the beginning of something else. We were stuck in the airless space between what has been and what will be. As I sat there on the rock, watching sunlight dance on the water, I believed we would be stuck there forever.

I was wrong. I hadn't heard a sound when his shadow fell across me. I saw his hand put the gun onto the rock beside me. His fingertips caressed my throat. The voltage of his first touch rippled through me. When it passed, I felt him stroking my cheek, very gently. The MAC-10, its black barrel pointing to the water, was inches from my fingers. I thought of picking up the gun and blowing both of us away. I was thinking if the sound suppressor worked, no one would even hear. My hand had barely twitched before his hand was over mine and the gun was locked between his upper arm and rib cage. He smiled inexplicably. Sunlight bounded off his face. He didn't seem real at all.

"Come, Elisabet," he said. I looked into his eyes, which were dark and bottomless as the water. "Let's go to la Costa de Plata, shall we?"

So we left for la Costa de Plata. We drove by way of a winding coastal road edged on one side by the water, on the other by the jungle. The road was carved from a cliff high above the Pacific but flattened as we sped along. I saw, for what must have been miles, the pale ribbon of gravel curving downward to the flat place where it shoved aside the jungle, pulled the ocean toward the black sand of the beaches.

The air was warm and moist, and it pressed against me, like the mountains rising up behind us. I had no idea what our destination was, couldn't ask, or even think about it. He didn't speak. I didn't look at him.

As we traveled, low gray clouds blew in from the water, darkened and intensified all the blues and greens, and I was certain it would rain. Almost immediately, the midday sun burned through the clouds, made lambent patches in the jungle, on the water. The patches kept growing bigger, until, after a while, the clouds had burned up or blown away, and everything was throbbing brightly again.

Just before we reached the coastal plain, I began to see the estates, the mansions of the wealthy, and the half-built and abandoned hotels of the previous government's ill-fated tourist project. He turned off the coast road, followed the secluded drive to one of the hotels. He turned to me, smiling so I saw his gold teeth, and as I looked away he said he wanted to show me how an international consortium of businessmen had invested in the future of Bellavista.

I met Colombians, Peruvians, and a group of North Americans who, with revolvers holstered at their hips or stuck into the waistbands of their pants, were supervising crews of construction workers in hard hats. He may have introduced me by my first name. I don't remember if he mentioned my profession.

We made several stops, during which Rivas Valdez abandoned the MAC-10, replaced it with a silver pistol shoved into his waistband. He'd take my arm just above the elbow, at a pulse point, so I felt the throbbing of my own blood every time he held me.

The North Americans, he said, were from Miami. They were very tanned, and taciturn; they eyed me strangely, mumbled something I didn't understand, turned and walked away. Their response made Rivas Valdez grin, which I also didn't understand. I didn't understand much of anything, certainly not his rapid, seemingly heated conversations with the Colombians and Peruvians. And even though I heard saws and hammers, viewed piles of lumber, wallboard, and brick, along with construction workers, the scenario would not come together for me.

All the hotels had lonely beaches hidden from the road by coconut palms, lime trees, and pines. We spent time walking around them. The sand of the Silver Coast was not, however, silver. It was dark gray speckled with black, and when I ran it through my fingers, the black spots stuck to them. Volcanic ash, Rivas Valdez said.

He showed me that work had been completed on marinas for a couple of the hotels. There were docks for pleasure craft and sleek cabin cruisers docked at some of them.

I suppose I should have wondered what kind of boats would dock there, at those particular hotels, at that particular time, and why; wondered about their cargo, their possible destinations. But I wasn't wondering. I was confused and panicky. I felt like a hostage, not knowing what I was doing there or what was coming next.

"Please, please take me back," I asked at one point. I'd grasped his forearm, clutched it until my nails broke his skin. With his hand he covered mine, entwined each of his fingers around mine, and plucked them, one by one, from his flesh. He held my hand as we looked at the scratches on his forearm, the shadowy crescents where my nails had been.

"*¿A dónde?*" he asked. Where to? I couldn't answer. Later, when I was sure I couldn't stand any more, when I would have had to scream for help or run away, we were back inside the Cherokee, driving up the coast road, turning onto another secluded drive that soon brought us to a walled estate.

The walls were stone, interrupted by high iron gates with a gatehouse out in front. As we approached, a man ran out of the gatehouse, pulled open the gates. Beyond a long, curving drive and vast green lawn was a large stone house with a columned veranda. The lawn was glistening with small geysers, sprays of water that shot straight up, fell arcing to the right, pushed by the breeze, and I watched them for several minutes before I understood they were the jets of an in-ground sprinkler system.

A peacock ambled toward us, its head bobbing as it bore its regal burden of tail feathers through the sprinklers. Rivas Valdez braked, and the peacock sidled up to the car. His elegant crest twinkled, and he puffed his brilliant chest while fanning his iridescent tail. The eyes of his feathers flashed and winked.

Then we rushed across the veranda and into the house, which was full of light, dazzling, like the waterfall at Aguas Oscuras. The tile floor of the foyer glistened like water, and sunlight reflecting off the ocean poured through a wall of windows at its far end. There were paintings in gold frames, a gleaming grand piano, a broad, curving pale oak staircase. He had me by the hand, led me up the stairs.

The room he brought me to was cool, shadowy, and ornate, done in the colors of the peacock. When he'd opened its door, there was a soft roar, and I thought the noise was in my head until I saw French doors opening onto the ocean.

He brought me over to the bed, which was a canopied four-poster, mahogany, elaborately carved, the posts high and pointed. It seemed to fill the room.

"Take off your dress," he said, and when I hesitated, he reached for the dress himself. I stepped back, began to take it off, slowly, and I let him watch while I watched him. His eyes seemed radiant as they scanned me, and I felt their heat around me like a cloud.

He reached out, stroked my cheeks with the fingertips of both hands, slid his fingers from my face to my neck and throat and breasts. When he reached my waist he pushed me back, gently, until I was resting on the silky bed amid great downy pillows and he was there beside me. I reached for the buttons of his shirt, again smelled his exotic scent, wanted to find its source. He brushed my hands away, encircled both wrists in one hand, pinioned my arms above my head in one of his hands, slid the other over my breasts to my belly, where, with his fingertips, he traced concentric circles around my navel, then on the skin below it. He moved his hand back to my breasts, caressed them, traced one nipple, then the other, brushed his fingers over them, watching for signs of impact, signs of change, and my nipples tightened up, obliged him.

The way he held me made my shoulder sockets ache. I tried to pull away but recoiled against the spokes of pain shooting through them. What he was doing with his other hand finally dulled the discomfort, lulled me away from it. He paused exactly when I did not want him to, the moment his languid but persistent motions lured me from anxiety to desire. His grip on my wrists loosened, and I smiled, believing I'd been released. But when I tried to reach for him, he manacled me once more, clamped his thumb and fingers tightly around both my wrists, restrained my upper body with very little effort. We were still for several moments, watched each other through the watery light, his eyes a submarine illumination marking off my course. Watching them, I sensed the rhythms of our exhalations, which were out of time, his deep and steady, mine short and shallow, and I tried to slow my breathing down.

My legs were bent, thighs pressed together. With his free hand, he began to stroke one knee, so gently the movement made me shiver. He was touching me with his index and middle fingers. His pinkie and ring finger were curled against his palm, covered by his thumb, the gesture of a benediction. Holding his fingers that way, he slid them to the soft flesh inside my knee, pressed against it.

"Let me see you. I want to see you."

The words splashed over me without sense. I was naked and he could already see me.

"Let me see."

He spread his hand out, pressed it against the inside of my thigh.

"I want to see you. You want me to."

The words were indistinct, as if they were coming from the ocean, and his hand, my legs, blurred, as if we were underwater.

"I know you want me to see you."

I began to understand, and, through the watery shadows, I saw my thighs moving, opening indolently but without hesitation, and his hand descending into the place between them. He began an expert exploration of the hidden places. He took his time, moved very slowly, watched his own work, watched without expression the changes wrought by his skillful fingerplay. Now and then he moved his eyes to mine, looked at my face, and I tried to turn away, because I felt mine crumbling, knew it must be disfigured by lust and shame.

Once I closed my eyes, but then the heat between my legs swelled through the rest of me, almost overwhelmed me, and I wanted it to overwhelm me, but not like that. I didn't want to come that way. I opened my eyes, tried to think of something else, failed, managed finally to control a helpless cry, but not my incipient thrust against his fingers. He must have sensed its wild amperage, for he stopped what he was doing, partially withdrew his fingers, and a noise came out of my throat, raw and awful, not swallowed up or even gentled by the ocean. It rippled across his face like a gust over still water. His eyes, inches from mine, were glittering signals from the darkness, and he kept them aimed at me while, transfixed, I quivered on his fingers. He watched until his gaze sucked tears out of my eyes. Then, with very little effort, as if it didn't matter one way or the other, he moved his fingers in me once again, pushed me into the orgasm. He whispered something when he did—*Elisabeta, la guerrera, sin vergüenza*—and it echoed like a child's taunt. *Elisabeta, la guerrera, sin vergüenza.*

Elizabeth, the fighter, the warrior, you are shameless.

When I opened my eyes, he was gone. I sat up, heard water running somewhere nearby, imagined him washing his hands, rinsing away the feel and scent of me. And I wished I could rinse away my disgrace, wash myself away. I hated him, wanted to escape, to not ever see him or think about the day again. I got up, but my knees were weak and I couldn't see my dress, couldn't remember where I'd dropped it. I sat back on the bed, curled up, put my face into my hands. I stroked my face, thinking I might rearrange it, somehow put it back into its former shape.

Then I heard the sound of skin sliding over silk, but it made no sense until I felt teeth on my spine, his tongue pressing the bones. He was kissing my back and ribs and waist, and his arms like constrictors were wrapping all around me.

CHAPTER TEN

*I*T WAS ALMOST LIGHT BY THE TIME THEY BROUGHT US TO THE GUER-
rillas, who were laid out on the beach in the shadows of the fishing
boats. The guerrillas were covered with a dark green tarpaulin,
which a pair of Bellavistan soldiers pulled back with a snap and flourish
as if presenting prizes on a game show. A plague of black flies buzzed
out from underneath, heralding the stench of decaying human flesh. The
press corps watched in silence.

"Maybe it looks like an ambush, but it was not an ambush," the
lieutenant colonel was telling us. "The guerrillas walked into us. They
fired first. They tried to blow us out."

The guerrillas were small and very young. They wore shorts or jeans,
old shirts and rubber sandals. The T-shirt of one said in big red letters,
"Coke Is It!"

Some of their bellies had been blown open, and it looked as if the bloody entrails had spilled out, then been shoved back into the cavities. Others had neat head and chest wounds. The eyes of many were still open, and they stared up at us in supplication, though we managed to ignore them. The camera lights began to flash, washing color from the bodies. The guerrillas were electrified for a moment, then subsided into death.

The ambassador and the lieutenant colonel were motioning us onward, to a black hole in the jungle made by the guerrillas' hand grenades.

"Their move was suicidal," I heard the lieutenant colonel say. "Obviously, they did not know what was out there."

He kept on talking, but I'd lost interest. I'd seen enough of the broken trees, spent shells, and blood where the firefight had taken place. I held back as the others moved on. I slipped back to the bodies, impelled to purgatory by a question I couldn't formulate, an inchoate thought that seemed to clog my throat along with the corpses' sickening smell.

The tarp was still folded back along the row of feet. I walked along it. Hoping to dislodge the question, I began to count the number of head wounds, the number of back and chest wounds, began entering the figures into my notebook.

I thought I noticed something right away, something I'd learned about when I was covering drug murders in the South Bronx. There were peculiar blackish smudges around some of the wounds. I got onto my knees and looked at them through the shadows of the fishing boats, wondering if the runic markings could be dirt, and at last I began to think they must be an illusion, the tincture of my paranoia, not powder burns. Because to get a powder burn you'd have to be shot at point-blank range, and you would not be shot at point-blank range during a firefight. Unless you shot yourself.

"Would you mind moving so we can get some shots?"

I turned, looked up to see a television reporter's electronic smile. His cameraman and producer were beside him, looking down with smiles of lesser wattage.

"Fuck off," I told them, offering my own version of the smile, watching for a moment their puzzlement at my failure to speak the code, to acquiesce. Then, as the news team walked away, with one of them muttering something about a hostile bitch, the question was dislodged, formed itself around the buttocks of a guerrilla who was lying facedown within my arm's reach. I moved toward the body, raised it at the shoulder.

It shouldn't have surprised me, yet it did surprise me, the tawny face of the teenage girl whose pants had been put on backward. The fly-front zipper on her backside had registered its subliminal message when I'd first looked at the bodies. I did not know what it meant.

Her hair was short. Her earrings were tiny golden crosses. One rested on her neck just below the lobe. Above that ear was a neat hole. I held her face in both hands, raised it. Her head was heavy as a stone. Above the other ear was a swelling like a fist, veined and mottled, and her facial skin and scalp were pulled taut over it like a balloon about to pop. I stared at the swollen mass until I saw inside, saw the bullet floating there in a bloody stew of brain and hair and broken bone. I wondered what had stopped its exit.

Before the soldiers came back, I found three more women, all face-down, genderless in their ragged clothes. One's belly was ripped open. There was a clean hole under the breasts of another. The third's skull had been partially blown off when the bullet entering above the right ear, had blasted out above the left.

The shirts of two were undone, and their exposed breasts were contused, a term my South Bronx source would use, and the word made me think of him. I knew if he were there, the sex crimes detective, he'd be able to find all the clues and decipher them. He'd know how to figure out what had happened. I was wondering if I could myself when I felt the rifle against my temple where the first woman had the swelling like a fist. A soldier was telling me in accented English, "Don't touch," and when I looked up, I saw another soldier pointing an M-16 at me from the other side. Beyond them was the television news team. Each of its members wore an electronic smile until the soldiers motioned them away with the rifles, then stooped to pull up the tarp, sealing away all answers to all questions.

I stood up through a hail of black and silver spots, stumbled off in search of my equilibrium and couldn't seem to find it. The air was torpid, and the gulf itself was listless, shrunken back into itself. The tidal reek made it difficult to breathe. The path ahead was fogged with gnats. I searched for the others, although I did not really want to find them, didn't want to join them. I couldn't help remembering the day before, the night before, the ride up to the gulf. All the bits and pieces kept getting mixed up, kept intruding into my present, so that time seemed to have stopped working. I couldn't tell what mattered and what didn't.

I wanted to find a shady spot to sit down in, a place to hide and rest. I was thinking if I did, I might find the old professor who'd been with me on the ride up in the chopper. His voice, like that of a good father, had come to me in a moment of great need to tell me what I had to know.

"Every story has its own necessities, facts and details which must be included if the story is to be fully told," he had said, and I kept clinging to this rope of words, somehow reassured that I knew what had to be done and how to do it.

His voice had come to me that morning as rotors on the helicopter's head and tail began scything through the predawn sky. But the minute I'd discovered him, Sonia interrupted.

"Would you look at that?" she'd said, jabbing me with an elbow, as we ascended, shuddering. She pulled me toward her window. Below, the city's lights were beginning to twinkle after a night-long breakdown at the Libertad power station. We could see them lighting up on a vast grid as power surged through the wires. There were maybe thirty of us on board, and the others were looking too, shouting their approval of the electronic age, applauding civilization's new dawn.

"When all the lights are on, there will be a black hole in the center," Sonia announced, standing up, tapping on the window to make them pay attention, and shouting to be heard above the rotors. "I happen to live in the black hole, otherwise known as *la colonia de los sobrevivientes.*"

"Viva la colonia de los sobrevivientes," someone called out.

When I'd picked her up, that black hole had been invisible. But she'd been watching for me somewhere and had run out, waving down my car, at an intersection of nameless streets. She was wearing an enormous hooded sweatshirt which concealed her cameras. The hood was draped like a friar's robe around her shoulders, and the shirt itself fell so far past her knees I'd thought, for a moment, some crazy monk was after me.

"I bet you guys think you had it rough last night at the Hotel Lido," she yelled. "You couldn't see your pretty faces in the bathroom mirror. Well, you ought to try living where there's never any power."

Her laughter was echoed by softer laughter. We'd all been drinking together in the hotel bar just hours before, and our state of liquored bonhomie was tenuous, but holding.

"Hey, Sonia, who'd you mug to get the sweatshirt?" shouted a reporter named Jack Travis I'd once worked with in New York.

I'd seen the logo of the *New York Herald-Sun* on the back and remembered they'd been given out, a couple of years before, to members of the paper's charity softball team.

"Hartwell," Travis called, answering his own question. "She stole poor Hartwell's sweatshirt. He's been grief-stricken ever since. Not to mention cold."

"No way," Sonia answered, sticking out her chest, smoothing the sweatshirt, so we could see the outline of her breasts. "It was a gift. The man gave it to me." She laughed again. "You know I'm just a poor native girl. And Hartwell is a man of compassion."

"Look where it got him," someone remarked, and then there was silence. The roar of the helicopter, or thoughts of Hartwell, overwhelmed our bonhomie. Minutes later, with her face nestled in the shirt's big sleeve, Sonia was asleep.

The chopper's noise made it hard for me to think or even see. When I looked around, the rest of them seemed colorless. Their faces were gray shadows, their bodies rimmed with light. Some were staring into space, but many, like Sonia, had managed to fall asleep. I envied their repose. Through it I saw Rivas Valdez racing to la Costa de Plata, impregnable within himself, and me beside him with no refuge.

I'd even slept without repose, and the high-pitched chirring of the insects outside had drawn me out of restless sleep. The sound had been prolonged, apocalyptic, first around me, then within me, and I'd come to consciousness irrational, afraid I'd lost my skin.

My room was very hot, the sheet drenched, my body slick with sweat. The ceiling fan had stopped. My night light was out. I sat up, hurting all over, as if I'd fallen down a flight of stairs. I looked through my shutters at moonlight showering the hotel's darkened grounds, felt something oozing out of me, wondered if I weren't broken and leaking vital fluids. Then I remembered, and I touched the trickle of his semen.

Beside me, Sonia's mouth had fallen open and she'd begun to snore. I watched her for a while, then closed my own eyes, tried to conjure the old professor and make him talk to me some more.

The U.S. Army helicopter had not yet reached el Golfo de Virtud, the perilous chasm between Costa Negra and Bellavista's northwestern coast. But, with the hallucinogenic power that sometimes comes after a night of no rest, I saw the waters of the gulf, black and swirling. And as I watched them, the professor's craggy face emerged.

"Your first task as a reporter is to understand the necessities of your story," he intoned, and I fell back into a smoky seminar room in the Journalism Building at 116th Street and Broadway.

"This understanding is an essential navigational tool that will permit you to maneuver through the treacherous waters of newsgathering.

"It guides not only the questions you will ask your sources, but also your very observations, what you will see and hear, what you will think, while out on assignment."

"What did you do with General Rivas Valdez?"

Sonia's whispered question shattered my reverie. I turned to look at her, not understanding.

"You remember, our illustrious defense minister. Vic the Prick. You were reporting on your profile yesterday. How did you pass the time?"

"Oh," I said at last. "We went around. You know. To a couple of places. Aguas Oscuras. La Costa de Plata."

"Yeah?" She examined me with her smoky eyes. "He lives there, in la Costa de Plata."

"Does he?"

"In one of those mansions out there."

"Well, we didn't drop by for tea," I hastened to tell her. "We went out to see that tourist project, you know, where they're building all the hotels."

"Oh, that CIA thing."

"What do you mean, that CIA thing?"

"I don't know. Just some shit you hear around. It doesn't make sense. What would the CIA want with those hotels?"

I didn't have an answer, forgot the question as she went on to say she'd wanted to ask about Rivas Valdez the night before, in the hotel bar, but hadn't because so many other reporters, "our competition," had been there, and it never paid to let anyone else know what you were working on. She wanted me to know that she was "loyal" to me, to "our team," even if I didn't like her.

Of course I liked her, I interrupted, respected her work, too, but she paid no attention.

"What made me curious," she whispered, leaning close, peering into my eyes, "was that you were such a mess when you got back last night. You know, frizzled, not your usual well-groomed self."

"You mean frazzled?"

"Yeah, I guess so. Frizzled. Frazzled. Your hair looked like you'd stuck your finger in a socket. No lipstick. So what happened? Did he hit on you? I bet you're just his type."

She grinned.

"What do you mean, 'his type'?" I asked without thought. "What makes you think a journalist could ever be his type?" I laughed myself, then went on. "As for the man's ideas about gender, well, they're retrograde. I'd place them somewhere in the fifth century, the early Dark Ages. I mean, I think he's really a throwback, you know, medieval, and that's a generous assessment. . . ."

I was shaking my head, stopped talking when I realized I might be overdoing it.

"It was just a funny idea I had, that's all," Sonia said, still watching me.

"Well, since you brought it up, I never worry about the way I look when I'm on assignment. Yesterday was a very long day, which is no doubt why I looked frizzled. I mean frazzled."

"You look a little tacky this morning, too." She picked at my jeans.

"Just trying to fit in."

She watched me for a while, and finally settled back into her sweatshirt and her snooze. I settled back myself, closed my eyes, and began to search for my professor. "Without understanding what you need," I heard him say, "you risk drowning in the maelstrom of information and misinformation, of facts and suppositions, into which you plunge each time you go after a story."

Then the chopper plummeted. The news horde relinquished its repose even before we had settled onto the shore. Sonia and I were swept up in the rush toward the door, then pushed into the balmy dark. Whitaker was coming toward us, grinning, and waving a big hand in greeting.

"We brought you up here so every one of you could see for yourself what's going on. So there would be no distortions, no mistakes."

He was shouting to be heard above the rotors, gesturing wildly as if to amplify his words, and the red glow of his cigarette swooped and darted through the shadows like an aberrant firefly. He was dressed like a soldier, in camouflage fatigues, and the jungle swallowed up his body, released his great white head, which hovered moonlike above the ranks of reporters and photographers who stood in front of me.

"The United States government can't stress enough the importance of this discovery," he went on, shouting, and repeating the statement at least twice more at the request of broadcast news teams, which were having trouble getting sound bites. At last he turned to lead us off into the jungle, along a narrow path, to an encampment of the Special Forces Mobile Training Team. The encampment consisted of several small tents, a pair of wooden lean-tos. The burly lieutenant colonel, wearing his distinctive green beret at a jaunty angle, walked out of one of them. Whitaker introduced him as a commander of the U.S. Military Group in Bellavista.

"What the lieutenant colonel is about to show you," said Whitaker, gesturing toward the other man, "is proof positive that Costa Negra has permitted its territory to be used as a transfer point for the shipment of arms and ammunition to the leftist terrorists of Bellavista."

His statement provoked a clamorous chorus from the press corps, but its calculated drama was deflated when a television reporter asked him to reposition himself and then repeat it. The U.S. envoy stood where he was bidden, smoothed back his silver hair, smiled, then rearranged his face into a more suitable frown and reproduced the statement word for word.

I was far back in the pack, saw Sonia slithering among the television newsies to get her stills. Then the lieutenant colonel, reading from a piece of wrinkled paper, which he kept shifting to catch the light, announced that the previous morning, at approximately 0700 hours, a team of Green Beret advisers, on a training mission in the coastal jungle with a group of Bellavistan soldiers, had encountered a heavily armed unit of *el frente*. The Bellavistan trainees had engaged the guerrillas in combat. Both sides exchanged heavy fire. Within an hour, the guerrillas had been vanquished. The training team and the soldiers had subsequently discovered that the guerrillas' boats, nondescript fishing boats common in the villages around Virtud, were loaded with Soviet and Chinese weapons apparently bound for a guerrilla base camp deeper in the country.

"*¡Qué bastardo estúpido!*" Sonia muttered, coming up beside me, lighting a cigarette. I saw she'd bought a pack, wasn't rolling them that morning. Her coal eyes smoldered. She exhaled a thick stream of smoke in the direction of a blond male with a microphone. In the midst of the lieutenant colonel's statement, he was offering his videocamera a surreal display of dental work.

"Dumb bastard," she repeated. "Did you see him trying to trip me up in all his goddam wires?"

"He probably didn't see you."

"I know he didn't see me," she fumed. "That's the point. I'm standing right there shooting and he comes up behind me, knocks me out of the way, almost steps on me. He didn't see me because he's blinded by his self-absorption."

"At least it wasn't personal."

"Those TV guys are fucking ignorant."

"But powerful in their way, very powerful."

"I wouldn't know. The reception's lousy in my neighborhood."

By then, the ambassador and the lieutenant colonel were leading us out of the jungle back toward the gulf. Half a dozen camouflage jeeps were silhouetted against the black water and the lightening sky. A soldier stood beside each one motioning us on board.

"Top of the morning to you, Lizzie."

The voice belonged to Travis, a tall, freckled Irishman with thinning red hair. He'd settled in beside me, and he grabbed my knee and shook it.

"Hell of a morning so far," he said as the jeep, driven by the soldier, bounced off along the beach.

I looked around, saw that Sonia and I had become detached, but I knew many of the others in the jeep, had been with them in the hotel bar. I'd been coming back from la Costa de Plata when I'd seen the newly arrived swarm packed inside la oficina de la Prensa Internacional just off the lobby. Most had just come to Bellavista to cover the start of land reform the following week. I'd recognized the embassy's press attaché and many of the reporters and photographers. They'd been speaking in their code, which I didn't understand and didn't want to. As I walked by, someone reached out and grabbed me, hugged me, said Liz Guerrera, great to see you. I saw Travis, whom I hadn't seen for years and hadn't wanted to. He was smiling just inches from my face. He pulled me into the press office, where I began to understand phrases like "major news" and "evidence the insurgency is not indigenous." I heard plans being made for the press corps to fly out of Cauchimpca before dawn. Then I was enfolded into the swarm, and I found myself being carried off to La Jaula d'Oro, a bar around the corner from the press office. There we all drank ourselves into hilarity, then into near hysteria, talking about the war, the new government, the ambassador, and La Solución Pacífica.

The jeeps were open, with crash bars over the top, but there was hardly any breeze even as we sped along the beach. Sweat began to creep along my scalp, and I was wishing I'd brought along dark glasses.

"Hey, you never answered me last night," I heard Travis say, and I turned to smile at him. "You just disappeared. I turned around and you were gone. Up in smoke."

"What question was that?" I asked, remembering it exactly. I saw my shoelace was undone and bent over to tie it.

"About how it feels to have what you always wanted."

"Oh, that question." I worked on the lace. "It's a dumb question, Jack. I mean, what do you want me to say? Everything's coming up roses? Anyway, you already know, don't you?"

I pointed out that he was the Mexico City bureau chief of a large Texas daily.

He shrugged, said he'd just been curious, curious about whether or not he could get a direct answer out of me on anything, curious about whether or not I was as evasive, as secretive, as I used to be.

"I think you're still the title holder," he said, stifling a yawn. I laughed.

"I'm glad the curiosity isn't killing you."

"The hangover's what's killing me."

In fact, in the grayish light, everyone looked the worse for wear. The night before, in the candlelight of the bar, they'd seemed to glisten and their mood had been euphoric. Sitting alone with my bourbon watching them, I'd thought the euphoria was based on their conviction that there was real news, breaking news, to cover, not just the carefully orchestrated canned news of land reform's initiation.

I half-listened to them while telling myself that everything was okay and I was okay, too—but the mantra didn't work. Rivas Valdez kept intruding, ruining my concentration. He kept coming to me with such force that I felt his hands were actually on me even when he wasn't there. Then Travis pulled out the chair beside me and slid into it, bringing with him unwanted memories of another afternoon, a drunken interlude that, I assured myself, meant nothing because we'd just been bored and killing time. I hadn't seen him since.

"You've had some great stories since you've been here, Lizzie, huh?' he'd asked. He placed a drink in front of me, was sipping at his own, and I couldn't help but think of the long liquid lunch we'd shared in a bar near Madison Square Garden before going to the hotel. It had happened during a break in the Democratic National Convention, which we'd been covering as our respective newspapers' fifth- or sixth-string backup reporters, assigned to the Hispanic Women's Caucus.

There's no such thing as a small story, only small reporters, we kept joking all through lunch, knowing that our assignments wouldn't yield more than an inch or two of copy. The joke got funnier as we got drunker.

"So tell me, Lizzie," he'd said at La Jaula d'Oro, leaning so close I smelled his aftershave, "how does it feel to have what you always wanted?"

I asked him what he meant. He laughed.

"That you're a foreign correspondent. What else? Wasn't that the goal at the end of the fast track you were running on?"

"Fast track? After six years in the South Bronx?"

The violent bumping of the jeep brought me back into the present. I don't know how long I'd been looking at him, but he was rubbing his chin, apologizing.

"I know, I know. I'm in dire need of a shave. But my trusty Remington refuses to do its job when it's deprived of juice."

"Not unlike its owner," somebody remarked.

"Isn't that one of the Ten Commandments of Journalism 101?" another reporter asked. "Never rely on electrical appliances when reporting in the Third World?"

Then someone was promising him his very own Bic Disposable, and we were ushered out of the jeeps, and led toward the fishing boats where Bellavistan soldiers would pull back the dark green tarp.

There was something on my hands, blood and something else I'd picked up from the bodies. I felt it, smelled it, as I headed along the path toward the others, whom I could see not far ahead. On my left, through the tangled vines and branches, I could also see the water, silvery and misted at the horizon. I cut back toward it, thinking I would wash my hands. Wet sand sucked at my sneakers as I crossed the beach. I couldn't see the sun, but it was shining on the water. I scanned the water for a long time, trying to concentrate on the story, trying to remember what to do next.

"What in hell are you doing?" I heard Sonia shouting. I turned to see her running toward me across the beach. "At least you could fucking answer. You're missing everything."

I quickly stooped to rinse my hands, then held them up to show her what a good girl I was.

"I had to wash my hands."

"Wash your hands?"

She was breathless, seemed harnessed by her cameras.

"That's great. Clean hands are important. I thought maybe you were collecting shells, or making sand castles."

She was shaking her head, her face crinkled in disgust.

"You know, Miss America, world news continues breaking even when your lily-white hands are soiled."

She was hunting through the sweatshirt pockets for a cigarette, snorted when she lit it and exhaled. I stood up.

"I got some blood, and other, more disgusting stuff on them when I was picking through the corpses."

"When you were picking through the corpses?"

"I went back to get a better look. Four of them were women."

"No shit?"

"You hadn't noticed anything?"

She was shaking her head no. She stamped her feet, and punched her body with her fists until her sleeves unrolled.

"I can't believe I missed it. Those fucks. They must have been hiding them on purpose. What are you going to do?"

"I'm going to get Whitaker alone and ask him about it."

She nodded vehemently.

"I bet nobody else noticed. But maybe I picked up something. You know, something might show up on the contact sheets. Won't it be great if we're the only ones who get it?

She was hooting with delight as we made our way back to the fishing boats. The crates of weapons had been opened, and were displayed so the beach looked like an open-air gun and ammo market. Wasn't it some fucking coincidence, anyway, Sonia asked as we walked, that these gun-running guerrillas had been found the very day the press corps arrived in town to cover the start of land reform? She was right, it was some coincidence, but I didn't want to think about that. Just ahead, the ambassador and the lieutenant colonel were behind the crates of weapons, gesturing like merchants, and reporters were clustered in front like shoppers examining the goods.

"It was them or us," the lieutenant colonel was saying. "I defended myself. The other advisers were well within their rights to do the same."

"But how do you know the boats came from Costa Negra?" Travis asked.

"They didn't fall out of the sky," the lieutenant colonel answered to a burst of laughter. "They ended up here by mistake. We've known for months the guerrillas have been running guns this way. They've just always managed to elude us."

"This gulf is treacherous," contributed Whitaker, gesturing toward the water. "We figure they ran aground here during the night, that they were somehow shunted off course by a fierce current. The only wonder is that it hasn't happened before this."

The arsenal on display immediately exhausted my knowledge of armaments. But as I walked around it, I could see most of the crates were filled with M-16s. I was about to ask about them when someone else did.

"I was hoping one of you would pick up on that," Whitaker answered. He stooped to pull a couple of rifles from one of the crates. With one in each hand, he stood and shook them into the air. I could hear the whizz and click of cameras. "American-made rifles, the best money can buy, direct from Saigon. That is, Ho Chi Minh City."

He dropped one rifle, pointed to the serial numbers on the other.

"We've already checked through State," he said. "These guns were among those left behind in Saigon during the evacuation."

Someone asked what it meant, and the ambassador had his answer ready.

"There is no longer any doubt." He brandished the M-16s again, fixing us with his protruding eyes. "A savvy and experienced communist arms shipment network is helping Bellavista's leftists in their attempts to overthrow this country's government." He began to pace behind the arsenal. "Do you know what kind of hell these weapons could create?" He tried to make eye contact with each of us as he moved along the boxes of grenades and antitank weapons. "Do you know what these weapons could do to this country? We are talking chaos. Absolute chaos."

"Did you take any prisoners?" I asked in the silence following his proclamation. Whitaker turned to the lieutenant colonel, who was looking us over in search of the questioner. I saw he hadn't found me.

"No, we didn't take any prisoners," the lieutenant colonel said at last. "One or two of the guerrillas might have escaped into the jungle, but we don't think so. They fought to the death. It was their choice."

Then the ambassador and the lieutenant colonel were leading us back toward the jeeps, and I worked my way through the horde. I finally managed to squeeze myself between them.

"What about those women?"

I whispered so no one else would hear.

"What about them, Lizzie?"

Whitaker stopped walking and smiled down at me from his great height.

"They were facedown. All of them. And neither you nor the lieutenant colonel made any mention of them."

"Oho," he bellowed, grinning. "You think we were trying to hide something? That's what you think, isn't it?"

He didn't wait for an answer, instead addressed the lieutenant colonel, said, "That must be what she thinks."

The lieutenant colonel nodded.

"Well, you're dead wrong, Lizzie, my dear girl. There's no nefarious plot here. After all, you had no trouble finding them, did you?"

"Why didn't you say anything about it?"

It was a dumb question. The ambassador merely smiled as the lieutenant colonel spoke.

"We did not consider it a significant detail."

I turned to him. He was smiling too.

The others had clustered up behind us, and I could sense their interest. They'd picked up the scent of something going on. Whitaker turned to face them. Like a tour guide, he held up one arm.

"Lizzie here, being the astute reporter that she is, brought up a question that I think is worth clarifying."

He was smiling benignly, and most of the journalists were smiling too, colluding in his benevolence, as he robbed me, gave away my story.

"Lizzie pointed out, as most of you no doubt noticed, that several of the casualties were girls, that is, women, ahh, female guerrillas. Four of them."

The murmurs of surprise were audible, but Whitaker pretended not to hear them. By then, all of them knew what he was doing to me, but they didn't mind a bit, since he wasn't doing it to them.

"I assumed, perhaps wrongly, since none of you asked about them, that you didn't have questions. Now, just so you'll know nobody's trying to conceal anything, I'm asking you point-blank: Do you have any questions?"

"The mighty Green Berets are out here killing women?" Travis called out.

"Wait a minute, wait a darned minute," Whitaker shouted, again waving his hand, which held a burning cigarette.

"We're not talking about some innocent peasant girls here. We're talking about well-armed, well-trained commandos. In fact, I don't believe anyone on our side knew women were involved until after the shooting had stopped."

"That's correct," said the lieutenant colonel. "We didn't do a sex check before we started to defend ourselves."

I heard another burst of laughter, decided to play another card.

"Two of the women had head wounds. They'd each been shot once above the ear. At what looked to me like point-blank range. How do you explain that?"

"May I?" the lieutenant colonel asked the envoy, who nodded the affirmative as smoke spewed out of his nostrils.

"When we found them, they were dead, so we can't say for sure what happened. The two you're referring to had taken up a position in the trees just beyond the beach. With most of their *compañeros* dead, and with no way to get to the ammunition on the boats, they must have known their situation was hopeless. It looks as if they shot one another. To avoid being taken prisoner."

"It's what *el frente* teaches them to do," interrupted Whitaker. "You could say they were good soldiers."

A cacophony of questions and answers followed, but I paid no attention, kept on walking toward the jeeps. As I went I jettisoned images that begged more questions: the bruised breasts of the women and their blue jeans put on backward. I let them go because I decided they were irrelevant to my story. When we were in the jeeps, driving back to the helicopter, Sonia sat beside me and berated me for not waiting until we got back to Libertad, and away from the others, to ask Whitaker my questions. She called me stupid for the way I'd asked my question and said Hartwell would never have been such an ass. Travis, on my other side, thanked me profusely for saving his. He began to argue with Sonia that I really was an astute reporter despite my chronic paranoia, my compulsion to be secretive.

The chopper's rotors were bending back the trees and sending up a squall of leaves as we climbed into the air. I found a window seat, curled into the corner, closed my eyes, and found my old professor waiting.

"If you don't know what you're looking for, you won't know how to find it." His voice vibrated with derision. "Which means you'll never make it as a journalist." He stood at the end of the seminar table, the knuckles of both hands pressed against the top. He scanned the room with laser eyes, and I didn't look away, but I could tell he didn't see me; that he didn't know who I might be. "What we're after is the truth. Our job is to make meaning out of chaos." Then a wide grin split his face, and he disappeared. The professor left me to contemplate a blank space at the seminar table as the chopper circled out over the gulf and headed back to Libertad.

U.S. ADVISERS IN FIREFIGHT; 14 REBELS KILLED

by Elizabeth M. Guerrera
Herald-Sun Staff Writer

LIBERTAD, BELLAVISTA—Crates of Chinese-, Soviet-, and American-made weapons, apparently destined for a clandestine base camp of the Mateo Omaño National Liberation Front (FMOLN) were confiscated from two boats grounded off the Gulf of Virtud after their crews of FMOLN guerrillas were defeated there in an early-morning encounter with government soldiers and their U.S. Army advisers.

Fourteen guerrillas, including four women, died during the brief firefight yesterday. Their boats had run aground in Virtud during a night crossing from Costa Negra, according to American officials.

U.S. Ambassador Richard M. Whitaker called the recovered weapons "proof positive that Costa Negra has permitted its territory to be used as a transfer point for the shipment of arms and ammunition to the leftist terrorists of Bellavista."

The government of Costa Negra immediately denied the charge, citing its neutrality in the four-year-old civil conflict here which has claimed an estimated 43,000 lives.

Among the seized weapons were a variety of hand-held arms and grenades as well as Soviet-made antitank weapons. However, the majority were American-made M-16 rifles. U.S. officials confirmed last night that the M-16s were identified through their serial numbers as having been among those left behind during the U.S. evacuation of Vietnam in 1975.

According to defense minister Gen. Víctor Rivas Valdez, the FMOLN has been attempting, in recent weeks, to stockpile weapons for another offensive in the rural countryside. He called the seizure of the weapons at Virtud a critical blow to that effort.

By preventing the buildup of arms and the distribution of supplies, he said, the government intends to rout remaining units of the FMOLN and achieve a lasting victory.

"Without arms and supplies there can be no rebel army," Rivas Valdez said.

CHAPTER ELEVEN

*T*HE WINDOWLESS ROOM WAS WARM AND DARK, LIT BY A SMALL LAN-
tern and a candle. The light flitted around a circle of men,
women, and children who were kneeling or sitting on the
earthen floor. An infant whimpered, and a woman on the far side of
the circle adjusted her shawl to place the baby at her breast.

"Jesus did not say blessed are the white-skinned, the wealthy, or the
well-educated," said a wizened Taupil with the broad, calloused hands
of a *campesino*. "Jesus said blessed are the humble, the meek, the poor."

His voice was deep and rich, at odds with his small stature. His words
evoked murmurs of agreement, prayerful responses.

"For many years now, the wealthy in Bellavista have been spreading
death to protect their riches, their privileges," he went on, and I strug-

gled to understand his accent, the occasional odd word of his dialect. "We can see this in the suffering and destruction all around us, in the murders of our brothers and sisters."

I was sitting near Mary, crouched over my pocket tape recorder, which I'd hidden under my bag. Mary whispered that his name was Chepe Alvarria, that he was a delegate of The Word, a kind of lay minister.

On my other side knelt Tía Amparo, the woman with silver braids I'd met on my first visit. She knelt close to me, kept smiling at me. I smiled back, hoping she didn't see my recorder.

"What is money anyway but a symbol of the earth's fruits and of the work of human hands?" Alvarria asked.

It was quiet when Mary's voice cut through the room.

"God created money, or permitted its creation, as a means of making easier the distribution of goods and services among all people." Her eyes were incandescent with her passion. "That's all money is. But what's happened here is that the greedy have taken everything. They're using money to thwart God's plan of justice and equality."

Her eyes darted, making contact with the others.

"The poor feel their poverty like shackles and chains, but the rich, though enslaved by their possessions, feel almost nothing. The weight of their possessions numbs them."

Our eyes met for an instant, but she looked away, receded into the bright folds of her poncho and bowed her head.

She'd awakened me just hours after I'd returned from el Golfo de Virtud.

"How did you get in?" I'd complained once I understood she was real, not some awful apparition. She gestured toward the door and its flimsy knob.

"Great security," she said. "I hardly even shook it." She sat beside me on the bed, pulled the copper crucifix out of her poncho, said that she was indeed trying to awaken me, to offer me a spiritual opportunity, if only I had the courage to accept it.

"Shit," I muttered, getting up and heading for the bathroom.

She followed me, said she believed that I was searching for something, maybe something spiritual. A great story is all I'm after, I told her. And even as I sat to pee she went on talking, standing in the doorway, telling me how Bellavista's base communities had ended their collaboration with the dominators, the hierarchical church that was allied with power and oppression. Those in the base communities, she said, relied upon and trusted only the truth and power of the Gospel.

I finished, stood at the sink to brush my teeth, and she moved in right behind me, aimed her words into my ear. They rushed to me on sweet vapors of alcohol. The whiskey smell surprised me even as it made me think of my mother. I wondered if Mary was a secret drunk, a lush. I made a mental note to watch her.

The Gospel, she was saying, is an invitation to conversion and salvation. It tells how to move from captivity to liberation, from darkness into light.

I glimpsed her in the mirror. She was gazing at me with that look she shared with women who live in cartons on the sidewalks of Manhattan.

"The spirit of the Lord is upon me because He has anointed me." I stopped what I was doing. "He has sent me to bring good news to the poor, recovery of sight to the blind, healing to the brokenhearted . . ."

She was quoting Scripture. Later I confirmed the passage was from Isaiah and was repeated in Luke as Christ's declaration of His mission.

"He has sent me to proclaim liberty to the captives, to set free the oppressed, to announce a year of favor from the Lord, and a day of vindication by our God—"

"A year of favor?"

"A time of reconciliation, a time of grace. It's here now. Come with me and you'll see."

And so I'd gone, so deprived of sleep I felt as fragile as blown glass. A woman named Luz and her two young daughters were waiting for us downstairs in the lobby. To the consternation of the bellmen, they were standing near the front door. All three were barefoot and wore threadbare flowered dresses, ribbons in their hair. Next to them were Mary's medical bag, the metal box of consecrated hosts, and two paper bags that contained Luz's wordly goods.

While I drove them to Mary's Centro de Salud Familiar at OPEN, Mary sat beside me, talking nonstop, while Luz and her daughters dozed in the back. The rich and powerful could meet whenever the hell they wanted, Mary said softly. There were no laws against their Hijos Patrióticos, their coffee growers' associations, their women's clubs for social betterment and so-called charity, their paramilitary groups.

There were only laws against meeting to pray. Defying that law, keeping their base community together, Mary said, was a form of passive resistance, of civil disobedience, which was a legitimate nonviolent tool in the struggle for social justice.

What about the consequences? I asked, and she replied that the wealthy and powerful could not be saved until they stopped oppressing the poor. She paused, and I glanced at her, saw her fingers tapping the metal box in her lap. "The light shines in the darkness," she said, "and the darkness has never put it out."

The clinic was stifling. My silent translations kept lagging a word or two behind whoever happened to be speaking, so the meeting seemed like a badly dubbed foreign film. I kept thinking I'd missed an essential word or phrase.

"Our society is riven by demons, the demons of greed and power, the demons of arrogance," Alvarria said. "But an even more insidious demon is the demon of passivity."

He paused, and the prayer circle seemed to lean toward him.

"Now we must admit it to ourselves. It was not only the rapacious greed of the rich and powerful that put us into our deplorable condition. It was also our own passivity."

Many nodded, blessed themselves, whispered their agreement.

"We must begin to cry out about our suffering," Amparo interjected. "Only our cries will awaken the wealthy to the Gospel's demands."

"We have a God-given right to pray together, to raise our voices," Alvarria went on. "No junta, no worldly generals, can take that away from us."

"The public order law is intolerable," said Mary. "But we can't forget that opposition to Christ, in His time, was also powerful and evil. This made Christ's fidelity to His Father very painful and full of conflict. Like ours."

"Sometimes I am afraid," said a woman in a brown shawl. "I think about what they, the soldiers, would do to us if they found us meeting."

Several in the circle nodded.

"Then I think about Christ at Calvary, what He endured for us," the woman continued, "and I remember that the unjust government is using terror to cut us off from God our Father. It makes me less afraid."

"When you leave fear behind, you are free," said an old man next to Tía Amparo. "When you release yourself from terror, they can't hurt you anymore."

"Christ did not want to suffer," said Alvarria. "He didn't want to die before His time any more than we do. Yet, because He was faithful to His Father, to God's will, He bore the powerful evil force of those who opposed Him."

Then Tía Amparo tugged on my hand, which she'd taken into both of hers, and spoke directly to me.

"The government says we are communists. That's why we're not allowed to pray together."

She looked at the others with a sly smile, was greeted with soft laughter.

"Well, it's true." She nodded. "We are communists, very radical and subversive. We could overthrow this government, the whole lopsided system, without ever firing a gun." She leaned closer to me. "Because ours is a communism of the spirit, more powerful than any weapons the death-dealing North Americans give to our oppressors."

"May I tell you my experience of your communism?" asked an unfamiliar voice. I looked around, found, not far along the circle, the woman Luz.

"Por favor," several voices chorused. Luz was kneeling on her calves, holding the toddler, who was asleep. The older girl knelt beside her.

"My belly was big with pregnancy and my time was growing near when Sor María found me and my daughters making our way to Libertad." She looked across the circle to Mary.

"We had been living near one of the big plantations, in a shed nobody used. My husband had worked there before he disappeared. Others said he had been killed, but I believed he would come back."

Luz seemed very shy, but her voice was clear and steady.

"My husband did not return. Only the soldiers kept coming around." She paused, looked at the floor. "They helped now and then with cornmeal, rice, some beans. But you know they wanted something for it. When I grew fat with the baby, I was frightened. They didn't want me that way. And I was afraid of what would happen, what they would do to us, to my girls."

She looked up, her face bright in the candlelight. "So we left, looking for the road to the city. For many days we were lost. We had no food. Sor María found us sleeping by the road. She brought us to Our Lady of Refuge. First thing, she bathed us. She helped wash away the dirt of that time, how many months I don't know. We all thought we had new skin."

Luz laughed softly, took the hands of both her daughters. She examined their hands before covering them with her own.

"By then, my baby did not stir. I would put my hands on my belly thinking the child was peaceful, resting, getting ready to come. But Sor María knew right away. She told me I was too weak, too ill, to give life to a child. He had withered in my womb. She and Alba, they stayed with me through that long night of his birth, which was not a birth at all."

Again Luz gazed at Mary.

"They helped me in the days afterward when I felt full of death. They helped me see things I could not see before, that, by taking my son, unstained by the pain of this world, the Lord was making me ready for other tasks."

She bowed her head.

"They helped you to find God?" Amparo asked.

Luz nodded yes.

"He showed Himself to me as a God who wants me to work hard to make a better life for my daughters and for their sons and daughters."

Chepe asked how she planned to do that. Luz replied that Mary had trained her as a *sanitaria*. Now she was on her way to a village near Aguas Oscuras, where she would visit women in their homes to teach them about the importance of washing hands and boiling water. She'd also learned oral rehydration therapy. She would teach this to mothers to help them prevent the dehydration of diarrhea in their children.

"Your name means light," Chepe said when she had finished. "Now, truly, you have become a woman of light."

He turned to me. "John in his Gospel speaks of children of light, but there are no children of light in Bellavista," he said. "Life here is too hard, too dangerous. You grow up fast or die."

"But surely," Amparo interrupted, "those who live the Gospel, like Luz and Sor María, are people of light."

Soon after that, Tía Amparo and Chepe Alvarria began preparing for Communion. They opened Mary's black box and brought out a pottery ciborium full of hosts, a flask of wine, and a chalice. They spread an embroidered cloth upon the floor.

All rose to their knees, and took one another's hands. Somehow I ended up on my knees, too. Mary held one of my hands and an old man the other. I wanted to go, yet hesitated, thinking it would be rude to interrupt their sacrament.

Amparo filled the chalice with wine, and placed it and the ciborium in front of Chepe, who held his hands above them, whispered the words of the consecration.

"Through the sacrament of the Eucharist, the death and resurrection of His Son Jesus Christ, God the Father reveals His deep communion in our sorrow and His promise of salvation," Chepe prayed.

I managed, gently, to pull my hands away, and Mary turned to me. I pointed to my watch, whispered that I had to get back before curfew.

She nodded, reached into her medical bag for something, then stood to walk me out. Before we reached the door, she put her arm around me and handed me a flashlight.

"You might need this. If not for light, then maybe for a weapon." She laughed and switched it on, and its beam lit up the road several yards ahead of us. I switched it off.

"The one who walks in darkness does not know where he is going," she said softly. "Believe in the light, then, while you have it."

"I know what you're trying to do," I told her then, meaning that she was trying to gain my sympathy, to enlist me in her cause.

"Oh, you're right, Lizzie," she said. "I'm trying to make you a woman of light." I heard a muted version of her odd laugh as I walked into the dark.

CATHOLICS TO DEFY PUBLIC ORDER LAW

by Elizabeth M. Guerrera
Herald-Sun Staff Writer

LIBERTAD, BELLAVISTA—Thousands of Roman Catholics, members of prayer groups called basic Christian communities, say they will defy this troubled country's public order law by continuing to meet to pray together and talk about the Gospel.

"The state is trying to destroy our faith communities," said a leader of the Colectivo Nacional de las Comunidades Cristianas. "Our defiance is part of a long Christian tradition of passive resistance to unjust laws."

So far more than 200 of the groups, known here by the acronym CEB, from the Spanish for "basic ecclesiastical community," have declared their intention to continue meeting, said the leader, who spoke on the condition that he not be named.

"We believe it is our God-given right to talk about the Word of God," he said.

The public order law, which makes illegal virtually all forms of opposition to the government, was extended for an indefinite period last month.

Ordinarily, the law would not prevent religious gatherings, said a Bellavistan official. However, he said, the CEBs encourage social activism by seeking solutions to what they call the institutionalized injustice of the government.

Said Defense Minister Víctor Rivas Valdez, "We don't object to prayer. We object to perverting prayer into a plan to overthrow the government."

The archbishop of Libertad, the Rev. Juan Miguel Figueroa, released this statement:

"In some cases, by no means all, they [the CEBs] have gone from evangelization to politicization. Some foreign missionaries are using religion to stir up our people. They are inciting them to rebel against the government. We must remember that Christ was a man of peace, and that His message was never political."

CEB members say the word "basic" indicates their groups' return to basic Scriptural teachings and their rejection of the trappings and rituals of the traditional Catholic Church.

"By relying on the Bible," said a CEB member, "we are criticizing the church of power, compromise, and conservatism. We do not have holy water or votive candles or novenas."

CHAPTER TWELVE

*T*HE MEMBERS OF THE JUNTA WERE SEATED SIDE BY SIDE ON A DAIS behind a table draped with Bellavista's colors—black, green, and yellow. Microphones rose like charmed snakes before each of their faces. Within reach of each man's hands were cut-glass pitchers of water, gleaming tumblers.

It was the first time I'd seen them all together, the first time they'd met together for a press conference. It was a gesture obviously designed to counteract the growing number of jokes about the two-man junta made up of political opposites, Barrera and Rivas Valdez, jokes about a two-headed monster eating itself alive.

Hiding myself inside a mass of reporters and photographers, I moved past them: first, Barrera, the presidential candidate; then Carlos Castillo

Montt, a Harvard-trained physician and political moderate who was said to have successfully negotiated with military officers for Barrera's admission to the junta; National Guard colonel Ignacio Molina, head of the security forces, and a Rivas Valdez ally; retired army general Guillermo José Salvador; and finally Rivas Valdez himself, resplendent in a black dress uniform.

I hadn't seen him since our interlude at la Costa de Plata, the week before. Just looking back at that experience felt life-threatening—so I pretended that it hadn't happened and went on with my life. But the sight of him, and his penetrating gaze in my direction, shoved me back into the peacock-colored room. I might have gotten lost there, but someone grabbed my shoulder.

"Better get packing, Lizzie," said Jack Travis, who was behind me. "The way those thugs are looking at you, your visa is about to be revoked." He chuckled to himself.

The junta members had been looking down at us as we filed past. Their glances seemed to linger on me, but I would have thought it was my paranoia if Travis hadn't spoken.

"Maybe they'll just kidnap you and torture you to find out who your sources are," he added.

"The CEB story was no big deal," I told him, and I hadn't thought it was until after it had broken. Then he and several others, assigned to do a follow-up, had started picking at me for my sources. Whitaker himself had called to say perhaps I'd like to talk to him again about my strategy for covering Bellavista.

"It breached the government's control of information," said Travis. "Which means it was dangerous."

"To whom?"

"Your sources." He grinned. "And possibly to you."

I shrugged.

"They don't scare me. Those thugs."

"Maybe they should."

They did not scare me, but maybe they did scare Mary Healy, for she'd called me when the story broke and she'd sounded frantic. My story had made their lives even more difficult, she'd said, had made all of them so vulnerable. What had she expected? I'd asked, but she didn't answer, called the story "cold," and "devoid of human interest." Yes, the story was accurate, she'd conceded, but it had failed to present a true picture of the people's struggle, their suffering, the injustice of the government. I said I couldn't be their advocate; that I was bound, professionally, to be objective. She replied that objectivity favored power.

"You've given credence to their lies," she'd said and hung up. I hadn't told her that I'd been stopped by *policía* at OPEN, just after I'd left her, and that they'd confiscated my notebook and tape recorder. She hadn't given me a chance.

I wanted to sit somewhere out of Rivas Valdez's sightlines, wanted to sit where I could see him but he could not see me. Instead, I found myself being guided by Travis into a seat close to the front, diagonally across from the general, whose eyes met mine for an instant when Travis took my arm.

"*Bienvenidos*, welcome," Luis Miguel Barrera was saying as we settled into our seats. The news conference had been called, he said, in honor of the day Bellavista was to leave "its feudal past behind and leap into its democratic future."

To celebrate what everyone was calling a seminal event, we'd already been served, in another room, an enormous breakfast on tables set with crystal and silver, fragrant with great bouquets of roses. Whitaker and several aides had been on hand to brief us, and we'd each received a glossy full-color information packet about land reform and its history in the Third World. Later, we would witness the creation of the first peasant cooperative. But first we were to meet the members of the junta, to have complete access to them, so that all of our questions could be accurately answered.

The first question to be answered, however, begged another one, the question of what exactly we were celebrating. For the number of land parcels to be transferred to the peasants had been reduced from seventy-five to one. Barrera was asked to repeat the statement, and when he did, there was scattered laughter followed by silence.

In fact, Barrera went on, La Nueve, the nine families of the oligarchy, were "fighting with feral tenacity" the loss of their lands.

"Feral tenacity?" Rivas Valdez interrupted, his unamplified voice carrying easily throughout the room. He smiled at Barrera from the opposite end of the table. "Is that not an exaggeration, Señor Barrera? After all, the fight has been verbal, not martial."

Barrera flushed, nodded, and went on.

"Let us say there has been an avalanche of opposition, which has made the paperwork, the processing of the deeds, the title transfers, extremely slow and difficult. In addition, the matter of compensation has not been settled."

"Compensation to whom?" somebody asked.

"The current landowners, the landowning families."

"Haven't they been compensated enough over the past couple of centuries?" Travis asked, going on to remark that they'd made hundreds of millions, maybe billions, cheating their workers, letting the poor starve.

General Salvador was leaning toward Rivas Valdez, asking in Spanish what the questioning reporter's name was, the whispered inquiry inadvertently broadcast by the opened microphone. A bespectacled interpreter, who had appeared at the far end of the dais, began to translate, as if the question had been intended for Travis all along. Travis stood, gave his name, the name of his newspaper. Rivas Valdez leaned to whisper something to Salvador, then turned to bestow upon Travis a radiant smile.

"Señor Travis, in answer to your question about whether the landowners have been, as you put it, compensated enough, there seems to be some disagreement about what they should be given and who should give it to them."

"But, sir," continued Travis, "do you support their lobbying efforts in Washington?"

"Lobbying efforts?"

"As you must know, the families have hired lobbyists to work Congress. They want to be paid market-value prices, in American dollars, for their land. Because it was the Americans who made land reform a criteria for aid. Do you support the lobby?"

"The government has offered the landowners long-term bonds. What they have done in response to our offer I cannot say."

"Their lobbying is a private effort," Barrera interrupted, trying to bring the conference's attention back to himself, succeeding when his mike gave off a painful high-pitched shriek.

"The junta takes no official position on anything the landowners might be doing," he added. "Theirs is a private effort."

Travis nodded and sat down.

"When will the *ley de orden* be rescinded?" I stood to ask, unable to resist the urge to look at Rivas Valdez. He smiled.

"Tell me, Elisabet," he chided, "what does the *ley de orden* have to do with land reform?"

"Elisabet," others voices softly mimicked, Travis and Sonia, maybe someone else. The echo of the name he'd spoken so deliberately distracted me, and my answer was cut off in a barrage of other questions. How many political prisoners were being held? When would the disappeared be accounted for? When would members of the death squads be brought to justice?

By then Rivas Valdez was sitting back, smoothing out the fabric of the tablecloth in front of him, while Salvador and Molina argued with each other. Montt was nodding, drinking a glass of water, as Barrera talked to him. Then Barrera grabbed his microphone, said the questions were important ones, needed answers, that the junta could not look to the future without acknowledging the past.

"What kinds of answers shall we give them, Señor Barrera?" the general asked, his soft voice silencing the gathering. "What do you propose?"

The interpreter looked at him in consternation, decided against a translation.

"Here is my proposition," Barrera said in English, gesturing toward Rivas Valdez with his microphone. "And I will stake my political future on it. I am appointing myself a commission of one to find the answers to some of these questions. Until there are some answers, the legitimacy of our government remains in doubt. What I am promising is the release of political prisoners and an accounting of the disappeared."

Like morning stars, strobe lights began breaking through the gloom, anointing Barrera with their special radiance. The general pushed back his chair to watch, and I watched him as journalists surged toward Barrera, watched him watching with a face that said nothing at all. One hand disappeared from the table, returned holding something that caught the light, a shiny thing he flicked between his fingers, captured in his palm and then let go. It was the diamond key ring, the one that held no keys. He turned to me and seemed to know that I'd be watching. Our eyes collided, and he grew tenser, more alert. Then his face relaxed and opened. It opened enough for me to see that he had no trouble looking back—and that he was, at that moment, remembering.

Then we were herded out of the hotel. We were driven up through the mountains, past Aguas Oscuras, to the sprawling Rivera plantation, driven in a pair of brand-new air-conditioned buses paid for by U.S. taxpayers in a package of so-called humanitarian aid.

LAND REFORM: PEASANTS TAKE PLANTATION AS AGRICULTURAL CO-OP BEGINS

by Elizabeth M. Guerrera
Herald-Sun Staff Writer

LIBERTAD, BELLAVISTA—The economic grip of this troubled country's oligarchy loosened yesterday when title to a 2,700-acre coffee plantation, one of the oligarchy's richest, was transferred to a cooperative of farm laborers, descendants of indigenous Indians, whose families have been landless since the Conquest.

The creation of the Cooperativo Nuevo de Jerusalem marked the start of a sweeping land redistribution program here that promises, within the next two years, to take from private owners more than half of the country's arable farm land and turn it over to cooperatives made up of peasants who have, for generations, worked as seasonal farm laborers.

"We are leaving behind our feudal past and leaping toward our democratic future," said Minister of Social Welfare Luis Miguel Barrera.

During an early-morning ceremony at the vast *finca*, owned for a century by the Rivera family, Barrera said agricultural reform "will close the gap between rich and poor. It will nourish our most precious resource, which is the spirit of our people."

Said U.S. Ambassador Richard M. Whitaker, "The equitable distribution of

land will help Bellavista find the political center which has eluded it for more than a century."

Agrarian reform is the linchpin of the military and civilian junta's so-called Peaceful Solution, an elaborate plan for social improvements designed to end a stubborn civil war. The fighting has so far claimed more than 43,000 lives.

The most extensive land redistribution program yet attempted in Latin America, the plan will virtually divest the La Nueve, the nine families of the oligarchy, of their most productive lands, according to a State Department official who helped to design it.

"We're taking from the rich and giving to the poor," said the official, who spoke on the condition that he not be named. "It's the beginning of the end for them."

The families of the oligarchy, descendants of the original Spanish conquistadors and more recent European immigrants, make up less than 2 percent of the population, but own more than half of this Massachusetts-sized country's arable farmland. They earn well over 50 percent of its income.

They created their vast *fincas* by annexing the Indians' tribal lands over the course of several generations. According to the State Department official, the oligarchy developed the army, the national guard, and the national police to enforce its annexations. The Indians, driven off their traditional lands, were forced to work as seasonal laborers on the plantations, he said.

Bellavista's annual per capita income of $800 is one of the lowest in the world, second in the Western Hemisphere only to Haiti's.

Yet the per capita income figure is deceptive, the official said, because it averages the oligarchs' multimillion-dollar incomes with those of the majority of peasant laborers who earn less than $100 a year.

Land reform, said Barrera, "will ease some of the inequities created by our painful history."

Yesterday, cooperative leader Plácido Arriega knelt with the other peasant laborers, called *campesinos*, in a dusty clearing not far from the plantation's lush tiers of coffee plants. Beneath cloudless skies, in brilliant sunshine, he quoted a passage from the Book of Isaiah which gives the cooperative its name.

"I am making a new earth and new heavens," Arriega said with his arms raised high above his head. "The events of the past will be completely forgotten. Be glad and rejoice in what is created. The new Jerusalem will be full of joy and her people will be happy."

Then he and the other farm laborers, whose tribes have lived in these mountains since before the time of Christ, bent to kiss the earth.

"Land is everything," one of them cried, breaking the silence that had fallen upon the huge crowd of peasants, government officials, soldiers, and reporters. "When we work our land we find God. We also find communion with our sisters and our brothers who are the children of God."

The speedy initiation of land reform, only five months after dictator Luis Obando-Reyes was ousted in a coup, came largely at the behest of the U.S. government.

Congress had threatened to withhold financial aid to this devastated country unless "significant improvement" in the human rights of Bellavista's citizens could be documented, and until "significant progress" had been made toward allowing citizens a voice in their own government. Land reform, several Congressional committees suggested, was one way the junta could demonstrate its commitment to social change.

Agricultural experts, working through the State Department's Agency for International Development (AID), devised the three-phased plan. They were also the architects of the so-called hearts-and-minds program in South Vietnam.

Whitaker described North American involvement in the program as "assertive diplomacy" that is offering the citizens of Bellavista a "viable and very positive alternative to Marxist revolution."

During the first phase of the three-part reform plan, the country's largest plantations, those of 1,200 acres or more, will be turned into cooperatives, owned and managed by the peasants who previously labored on them. Some 250 large cooperatives are expected to be created during this first phase. If successful, the land redistribution effort will benefit more than one million people, roughly half of the rural population, according to government figures.

Originally the titles to 75 properties were scheduled to be transferred today, but only the Rivera plantation was turned over. This happened, said Barrera, because "an avalanche" of opposition made the processing of the deed transfers almost impossible, and because of the country's huge balance-of-payments deficit.

At present, the nation does not have enough currency to buy supplies like seed, insecticide, and fertilizer for the coming year's crops. International creditors are reluctant to make loans to Bellavista because of continuing guerrilla violence.

So far, the United States has given nearly $60 million to the program. It has also bought agricultural equipment, seed, fertilizer, and insecticides. Through AID, a score of agricultural advisers are working here.

Despite its apparent benefits, land reform is a target of criticism by both the left and right and both predict its quick demise.

The Mateo Omaño National Liberation Front, the largest rebel organization, has charged that the redistribution plan will create a conservative class of rural capitalists but will exclude more than half of the country's agricultural workers. The plan, the FMOLN said, would thereby exacerbate the country's dire social problems.

The association of landowning families charges that the cooperatives will be identical to the communist farm collectives of rural China.

Whitaker laughed when asked if the cooperatives would resemble Chinese collectives.

"Designed by the United States and funded with our tax dollars?" he asked. "That's a good one."

CHAPTER THIRTEEN

"Once He gets started on you, once He gets into you, He doesn't ever finish," Mary Healy said, then leaned toward me so her face brightened in the candlelight. "He's back at you again and again. And every time He's at you, He's more difficult and more demanding than the time before."

We were eating filets mignons and drinking Pinot Noir on the terrace of the Hotel Lido. What had brought her to me that evening was a crude cartoon she'd found nailed to the front door of her clinic. It showed a woman with a spray of crinkly hair being raped by a soldier and strangled with the chain of her crucifix. Lined up behind him were several other soldiers, holding like weapons their grotesquely large penises. "This is a house of communist whores," was written above the drawing. "Death to All Who Enter Here. Try it and see!"

Mary's palm covered the drawing, which lay folded on the tablecloth between us. Its discovery that morning, she told me, had given her a rush of pure terror—and the almost overwhelming urge to buy her airline ticket home. Staying on in the face of her own fear was one of the awful demands that He, Jesus Christ, was making of her.

"Without faith, I'd be . . ." She shook her head, unable to complete her thought.

"Why don't you just leave? Do something else. Be a midwife in the South Bronx."

"Because I love these women." Her voice betrayed her passion. "You know, Alba. Milagros. Luz. So many others you haven't met. I love them."

She paused to drink some wine, went on. "I love them in a way they never have been loved. Which means I value their minds and their hearts. I understand how fragile and how precarious they are."

She picked up her fork and probed her steak until she found a tender spot. Then she cut out a neat triangle and popped it into her mouth.

When she'd called to tell me about the drawing, I asked to see her at the clinic. I wanted to interview some of the women, turn the incident into a story, although the drawing itself was too obscene to publish. Mary said such a story would further enrage the military; would make everyone at her health center more vulnerable. She agreed to meet me later in the hotel lobby, but only if I promised not to write about the drawing.

I had my own reasons for wanting to see her, my own rush of terror to tell her about, even though it put me in a quandary. After the prayer meeting at OPEN, I'd been grabbed from behind as I put the key in my car door. I was shoved against the car. A pistol pressed my temple while a hand groped between my legs. *"Documentos!"* a voice demanded as I glimpsed the shiny black boots of the *policía.* Two of them had been waiting for me. While one grabbed my purse, notebook, and tape recorder, the other rubbed my crotch, felt my breasts under my shirt. They were dragging me toward their jeep when another police jeep screeched to a stop beside us. A brass-encrusted officer jumped out. In the exchange of guttural Spanish that followed, I understood I'd been rescued, and the phrase that rescued me was this: *la puta de Rivas Valdez.* The brass-encrusted one was telling the others to let me go because I was Rivas Valdez's whore.

They turned to look at me, and I looked back—my vibrant fear replaced with excruciating relief. I couldn't help imagining myself the way they must have seen me, haloed by the headlights: *la rubia, la norteamericana de Rivas Valdez,* untouchable, and maybe dangerous.

"Give me back my things," I demanded, stepping closer and putting out my hand. The brass-encrusted one gave me my purse and notebook, but clasped my recorder to his breast.

"I have my orders," he said, and turned away.

I had every intention of telling Mary Healy about it that night over dinner. It would be easier, I figured, once we'd had some wine. The worst part would be telling her I'd surreptitiously taped the meeting. But she was agitated when she showed up, flushed as she shoved the drawing into my hand.

Bring it to the embassy, I urged her, arguing that the embassy was supposed to help protect U.S. citizens. But she reminded me that Whitaker had already suggested she leave the country. He'd already advised her that he couldn't guarantee her safety.

The lobby had been bustling with patrons of the restaurant and bar. The light was golden, the atmosphere benevolent.

"Let me buy you dinner," I said, but she shook her head no, said she had meetings to attend, a baby to deliver. "I'll put it on my expense account," I insisted. "Tell yourself it's work so you won't feel guilty. I'm interviewing you for a story." She laughed and said the smell of grilled beef from the restaurant was so delicious she could have wept.

"Have steak," I encouraged. "A big juicy hunk of rare meat. And bread and butter and potatoes. You know, a fat Yankee meal. A cholesterol pig-out. And we'll have wine. Get drunk if you want."

She nodded yes, smiling like a child.

"You don't really have to starve, anyway, do you?" I asked while we waited for our table. "You're rich, aren't you?"

"Rich?" Her face turned pink.

"Wealthy. Aren't you wealthy?"

"The past is irrelevant as far as I'm concerned. I've left all that behind."

"Oh, Mary, you can tell me," I kidded. "I won't tell anybody else." She smiled and shrugged.

"Okay, my family is . . . sure, I suppose you could say I'm rich. But it's not my fault." She laughed. "My father's a retired lawyer who was awfully good at making money. It means a lot to him. I grew up on an estate, a fairly lavish one. Had horses, attended private schools. My coming out must have cost thousands. But I never cared about any of it. I always felt that Daddy was trying to buy me off." Everything her father had given her, she said, she used to support her clinics. "Believe me, it drives him crazy."

"So what's the starvation thing about?" I asked. "Is it a sin to eat well?"

"When women and children all around you are starving? I think it is." It was a choice she'd made years before, she said, to live a life of voluntary poverty.

Then a maître d' appeared and escorted us to our table. He held out our chairs, handed us large silk-covered menus. Mary laughed softly, said she did not want to see any choices, that she'd be incapable of making one. I ordered for both of us.

"Anyway, I'm often fasting," she said once the waiter left. "The denial of the appetites, the mortification of the sensuality, really helps in Bellavista."

"The mortification of the sensuality?"

The phrase reminded me of schoolbook stories of the lives of saints who flagellated themselves and offered up their suffering, who sought torture and martyrdom, to demonstrate their love of Christ.

"You deny your earthly appetites until they wither," she said with her odd, beatific look. "Without nourishment, the senses die. Only then can the soul be released from its bondage to the body."

"Why release the soul?" I was watching her intently, alert for any trace of irony.

"So it can rise up, connect with God. That's how you achieve oneness. With Him, I mean."

"I thought that only happened when you died."

She was shaking her head no when a waiter appeared beside me, uncorked our wine, poured a taste into my glass. When I'd tried it, he filled Mary's goblet, then my own.

"It can happen when you're living," she murmured after sipping it. "But not if your senses are always at war with your spirit."

She paused, and the two of us looked around the terrace. Perhaps two dozen elegantly coiffed and bejeweled patrons sat here and there at linen-covered tables beneath a star-filled sky. Their rings, necklaces, and bracelets glittered in the candlelight. Attending them, and us, were waiters in white cutaways who hovered in the shadows, watching and anticipating our needs.

"It's nuts to be talking like this here," she exclaimed, but she went right on. "What I mean is that your soul gets trapped. By your body's desires. Then it's always in torment. So you can't achieve that oneness."

Her hair was coppery in the light, her pale eyes luminous. She smiled, then took a seeded roll from the basket on the table. She broke it in two, slathered it with butter, and took a healthy bite.

"In today's skirmish with the spirit," she said through her mouthful, "my senses won."

"I suppose sex is one of the earthly appetites."

Her hand flew to her mouth, and I thought she might be choking. She looked away, as the color deepened in her cheeks.

"I suppose."

"Are you . . ."

"Celibacy is an important option," she interrupted. "It's an ascetic choice that brings you close to God."

She swallowed wine, kept her eyes on the glass. She savored it, lowering her eyelids. I watched her for a time, and as I did, I heard music from the electric organ in the lounge. It was playing "The Girl from Ipanema."

What I'd been going to ask, what I wanted to know, was if she was a virgin. I wondered if she'd ever made love with anyone, ever had an orgasm. The questions were simple, but I couldn't get them out. Then I wondered, despising my dirty journalistic mind, if she was sexually involved with Alba or Luz or any of the other women at the center. Before I could fully consider this possibility, she leaned forward, placed her fingers over mine.

"It causes so much loneliness," she said. "It's really awful sometimes."

It was hard to meet her eyes. I was rescued from the effort by the waiter, who served us plump shrimp in ice-filled crystal bowls. She squeezed lemon onto the shrimp, speared one with a tiny fork.

"Why does the mortification of sensuality help so much in Bellavista?"

"Because there's so much evil here. It's lurking everywhere." She looked at me with wonder—as if my stupidity confounded her. "That's why, if you're an activist, you must have faith. You have to be an activist and a mystic at the same time. Otherwise you're just rumbling around in darkness. Like the death squads."

"But He keeps making these demands on you."

"Does He ever." She drank more wine, explained that she had, in fact, left Bellavista for good, just after the Aguas Oscuras massacre, when repression against the church escalated. Many priests, catechists, and Delegates of The Word had been disappeared or killed.

"The terror was indescribable. It got to me. So I went home."

The waiter presented our meals. Mary gasped over her steak, exclaimed that it could feed a family for a week. She dropped her utensils, pushed away the plate while gazing at the filet, which was wrapped in bacon, topped with broiled mushrooms. The waiter stepped forward, reached for the offending plate, but she gestured him away. Finally, laughing nervously, she picked up her fork and knife, began cutting into the meat, cutting faster as she went along, chewing and swallowing voraciously, but neatly and gracefully, a starving debutante.

Maybe it was then, when she was chewing bites of steak, and explaining what had happened to her once she'd gone home, that I noticed waiters preparing a long table at the far edge of the terrace, the table I'd seen Rivas Valdez at before. It occurred to me that he might be coming, that I might see him. The idea careened through my mind until my fingers twitched.

"My parents are old, well into their seventies. So I thought they might need me at home," she was saying. "But my parents don't need me. They have each other." She smiled. "And I have no one else. I mean, besides the women here at the center. My whole time at home I felt ripped to shreds. Because I'd abandoned them."

The waiter arrived with more wine, and she waited until he'd uncorked it and poured for us.

"I saw it very clearly Christmas Day, after dinner, when they, Mom and Daddy, went outside to walk around their garden. I was sitting in the dining room, watching them through the bay window. Everything was dead, cut back, the rose bushes covered in burlap against winterkill. But the two of them walked around, holding hands and smiling, like the place was full of blooming flowers.

"The light was so bright and they were so frail I thought I saw right through them. And in this awesome light, I also seemed to see how worthless my own life was. The feeling of despair was overwhelming." She paused long enough for me to wonder if she was stuck in her bad memory. "Well, I can't explain what happened after that. Somehow I hit bottom, and afterward I felt a tremendous surge of energy. New energy. Like it was coming to me from the light. And I knew I had to get back here."

I nodded.

"Maybe it was just an alternative to suicide. Who knows? But it felt like conversion."

"Conversion?"

"When He's asking you to do something you're afraid to do, but you go ahead and do it anyway."

Again I nodded without understanding. She smiled at me.

"Saint Peter experienced his conversion in a boat on the Sea of Galilee. Mine happened in a dining room in Greenwich."

The waiters had placed flower arrangments on the long table and were lighting candles there.

"I felt it so strongly when I got off the plane," she continued. "Walking down those steps, inhaling the smell of Bellavista, which is like noplace else on earth. Leaded gas and flowers. And the air as heavy as a shawl." The waiter took her plate. "I knew then that I'd passed through a threshold. He'd opened up a door for me and I'd managed to walk through it. Now everything is different."

"How so?"

"I can't really explain. But I'm here now. I'm here for the duration."

"Things are better, aren't they, with the junta?"

As I asked her this, or maybe just before or just afterward, Rivas Valdez and his entourage were ushered to the table. There was a momentary hush, a lull in conversations, service, as he and his companions were seated. With him were two other members of the junta, several diplomats, and his bodyguards. One took a seat, alone, at a table behind him. The other, the husky chauffeur, began patrolling, very casually, along the far edge of the terrace.

"Things are better now with the junta," I heard her say as I watched them being seated. I couldn't tell if it was a statement or a question. All the men were dressed in lightweight trousers and jackets, but Rivas Valdez stood out in a pale beige suit. He sat at the head of the table, gestured toward the sommelier, and when the man appeared instantaneously beside him, he ordered rapidly.

Against the fashion of his country, where male vanity revealed itself in thick shocks of hair and sideburns, luxuriant mustaches and beards, Rivas Valdez was clean-shaven, his hair clipped very short. And in a place where wealthy men used their necks and fingers to display their riches, Rivas Valdez wore only a wristwatch. His personal style set him apart from the men in his party, the other men in the restaurant, defined him as somehow austere, self-controlled. I watched his ringless fingers slice through the air as he spoke. I couldn't help remembering his hands on me. I remembered what he felt like and what he whispered, and the memories rushed at me, stabbed me with desire. Mary turned toward where I was looking.

"Speak of the devil," she said, then slouched over the table, as if the sight of him had wounded her. I reached for her hand, but she recovered in an instant, sat up regally once more.

"When I got back here, Lizzie, that's when they told me about *las matanzas navideñas*." Her voice was soft, but urgent.

"The Christmas massacres?"

"Aguas Oscuras wasn't the only bloodbath," she said. "Maybe it was just a practice run. Because on Christmas Eve, and into Christmas morning, soldiers went into dozens of remote villages in the mountains, places that had hidden and helped guerrillas, places that had no contact with the outside world. They surprised people at their masses and feasts. Nobody knows how many."

"That's impossible," I said. "Christmas was after the coup, after the junta took power."

"Rivas Valdez," she said. "Víctor the Terrible. He's the one. They say he's the one who ordered it."

As we gazed at each other, I thought I heard him laughing. When I moved my eyes to look at him, he was smiling, his teeth gleaming in the candlelight.

"Aguas Oscuras wasn't unique," she said, her voice seeming to come from someplace far away. "The only problem there was that somebody survived."

I turned to her, compelled by a flash of intuition.

"You're the one, aren't you?" I asked. "You're the missionary who brought the witness to Alan Hartwell."

The color went out of her face, but she stared hard at me as if trying to figure something out. "The vision still has its time," she said. "It presses on toward fulfillment."

"What's that supposed to mean?" I said, irritated.

"Someday the story will be told."

"When?"

"When the time comes," she said, and she glanced again toward Rivas Valdez. He was leaning forward, talking rapidly, motioning with his hands. The other men were hunched toward him, intent upon his words. It occurred to me that we ought to leave, that it wouldn't do either of us any good if he saw us together. I told the waiter we'd have coffee and a liqueur in the lounge. There, I thought, Mary might tell me more about Aguas Oscuras. She didn't, and I decided not to press her. Instead she talked about her clinics. When we left she seemed a little drunk, and I was afraid to let her drive home alone. I walked her to the parking lot and drove behind her to Nuestra Señora del Refugio.

As I followed her into the city, *la comandancia* glowed in the distance. The revolving light on its highest turret slashed through the sky. When Mary parked in front of the clinic, I saw that it illuminated, on each rotation, the crucifix on top of the cathedral. As I pulled up behind her, waiting for her to let herself in, I watched Christ on the cross revealed in stark light for a second. Then Mary was running back to my car. I rolled down the window.

"I forgot to tell you something. Maybe the most important thing." She leaned through the open window, her fingers curled along its edge. "Love and faith are dangerous. They pull you out of all your hiding places. They take you places you don't want to go."

She touched my cheek and took off again. She was closing the clinic door behind herself when I remembered the confiscated tape.

CHAPTER FOURTEEN

A SCENTED WIND BLEW IN FROM THE PACIFIC, LIFTING SHEER CUR-tains at the windows. They billowed like dancers' veils, not quite in time to the chamber music that suffused the golden room. The complex melody sounded so clear, so perfect, that I wouldn't have been surprised, when the chauffeur opened the oak doors, if an ensemble of musicians had been sitting there.

He was, however, alone, in a gold wing chair, facing the open windows. The room was lit by candles. Shadows flickered on brocade walls, on oil paintings in gilded frames. He turned sharply at the sound of the opening door, rose, and walked to me. He took my hands and led me into the room. The chauffeur left without a word.

We walked to the open French doors. Candles spilled shimmering arcs of light outside. I glimpsed a dark expanse of lawn, a seawall at its edge. He held my hands and watched the light play across my face. His face was fierce but his eyes were reverential, a look that thrilled and scared me. Seeing him that way made me feel I'd lost my balance and needed to grab hold of something to keep from falling. But there was nothing to grab hold of except his hands, which were already holding mine. He let them go and stepped back. He ran his fingertips across my forehead, down my cheeks to my neck and throat. Again his touch felt like a benediction, but it also made me weak. I sank back against the doorjamb, held it with my hands. We watched each other without moving. I was wondering if I had time to escape when he shifted his attention to my hair, which was pulled to one side and clasped in a tortoiseshell barrette. He unclasped the barrette, tossed it onto a nearby table. My hair fell across my cheek. He touched it.

"It was so good of you to come, Elisabet," he said, and then he walked away.

I almost laughed but couldn't. And I could have asked, but didn't, if I'd had any choice about coming. I could have asked what would have happened to me if I'd run, or screamed, instead of soundlessly acquiescing when the unfamiliar car had blocked my path across the hotel's parking lot and the strange man had gotten out to open its back door.

I'd watched calmly as it happened. I was returning to the hotel after leaving Mary. I was locking my car when the other car pulled up. A man I'd never seen before emerged. I recognized the bulge of a shoulder-holstered gun as he reached to open the car's rear door. I also saw that the parking lot was abandoned, dark but for the sedan's glowing lights. In the illumination of the sedan's interior light, I saw a silver pistol glinting on the dashboard and recognized the hulking driver. I climbed into the backseat.

Rivas Valdez had gone into the shadows on the far side of the room. The volume of the music dropped abruptly, and the ocean's resonance seemed to fill the room. Now and then a few notes from the strings or woodwinds would emerge from this soft roar. He returned holding an iced drink, which he put into my hand. I didn't think to ask how he'd known what I wanted, my preference for bourbon, for that particular bourbon. He gestured to a wing chair which was identical to his, angled toward it, also facing the windows and the ocean. I shook my head no, because I felt soldered to the doorjamb and safe that way. The breeze was blowing past me, tugging at my white skirt so it swayed around my legs like the gauzy curtains. He watched me from his chair, his legs stretched out in front of him. I couldn't help basking in his gaze even though its heat was dangerous. I felt it inflame my skin and penetrate my bones. I thought of Mary's crazy words at the restaurant—that the vision was pressing toward fulfillment. I didn't understand her mysticism, but standing in the doorway, with Rivas Valdez watching, I could feel myself sliding toward something, or being pulled toward something, that I wouldn't be able to control or stop.

I was trying to stop that slide, or stave off what was coming, when I broke the silence with a question.

"What were *las matanzas navideñas?*"

"Las matanzas navideñas?" He put his drink down on the table next to his chair. "Is that what *la comadrona* was telling you over dinner? Hmmm? About some Christmas massacres?"

His soft words brought her to me, *la comadrona*, the midwife, Mary Healy. I saw her in the open window of my car, the smoky sky around her like a halo. She stayed there for a moment, warned me of betrayal.

"Not her," I lied. "Everybody in the press corps. It's what all the reporters are saying. That soldiers went into villages, dozens of them, on Christmas Eve and Christmas morning. That they killed indiscriminately, wiping out whole villages."

Still he watched me, but the heat diminished, as if a cloud had blown across the sun. He knew nothing of any Christmas massacres, he said. Of course, the army had conducted a series of cordon-and-search operations in suspected enemy strongholds in December. But hadn't he told me all about it during our first interview? Didn't I remember?

As he spoke, I moved into the room, pressured by an urgency I didn't understand, but also feeling weightless, as insubstantial as the curtains. On a table, I saw my barrette, unclasped and abandoned. I went over to it, feeling a pang, as though it were important. I wanted to put it back into my hair, but couldn't seem to pick it up. Instead I placed my drink beside it.

"Cordon-and-search operations?"

"Troops seal off a designated area. Then they search it."

His gentle tone turned me around. His expression surprised me, and I moved closer for a better look. Irritation and amusement came into focus, but also desire—and desire was, by far, the strongest of the three. It smoldered in his eyes, hot but with no flame.

"Seal off?"

He watched some part of me, maybe my skirt, as I drifted to him.

"Soldiers put up roadblocks. They take up positions on the area's perimeter. They prevent anyone from entering or leaving."

I stopped just out of his arm's reach, feeling detached from everything except his gaze—as if I would float away if he stopped looking at me. But I knew he wouldn't, and the knowledge made me strong.

"What do they search?"

"Various structures. And, of course, the population." He reached for the fringed end of the sash I wore looped around my waist. "Soldiers must sift through the population for weapons and supplies. And for members of the communist infrastructure." He pulled me closer with the sash. "Our goal was to isolate and contain the guerrillas, then to clear and hold our territories. So that pacification could begin." When he released the sash, our legs touched, and I was tilted precariously over him.

"What about the civilians, the noncombatants?" I put my hands on his chair arms to keep from toppling.

Didn't I know what a free-fire zone was? he asked. He began to stroke the neckline of my dress, gathering its soft cotton in his fingers. Didn't I understand the point of designating free-fire zones? Didn't I know anything about war?

He let me go when he was finished, and I stood, turned my back to him. "Tell me about war," I said. I took one step, then felt the tugging at my waist. I turned to see the slender bridge of my sash vibrating between us. He pulled harder and it came undone, slithering to the floor.

The government had evacuated all civilians from the combat areas, he repeated, reaching out for me and pulling me into the space between his legs. Those who'd chosen to remain could not be considered civilians. They were subversives, enemies of the people.

"On Christmas morning?"

"Is that what *la comadrona* said?"

The soft words seemed to caress me as he reached again into the neckline of my dress. I thought he was searching for its opening, which was right there, in the buttons at his fingers, though he didn't seem to see it.

"Local commanders had moved at times they considered auspicious. One or two operations may have occurred on Christmas Eve or Christmas morning." I watched him fingering the fabric, but resisted the urge to help him. "After all," he went on, "the element of surprise is a legitimate military tool whose skillful use can mean the difference between success and failure."

He tugged against the neckline. The bodice made no sound as it gave way, only the buttons clattered to the floor and rolled away. He frowned at the satin of my bra, but quickly saw it had no straps, and he slid it down, brushed aside the sleeves so they fell around my elbows.

"That is how one fights a war, Señorita Guerrera," he said, and I felt my breasts in his hands, the nipples hard against his palms. "We are fighting a war, aren't we?"

CHAPTER FIFTEEN

ARISTOCRATIC GENERAL HELPS LEAD TROUBLED REPUBLIC TOWARD A DEMOCRATIC FUTURE

by Elizabeth M. Guerrera
Herald-Sun Staff Writer

LIBERTAD, BELLAVISTA—Not long ago, in the airy, sunlit dining room of the U.S. embassy here, Defense Minister Víctor Rivas Valdez demonstrated yet again that he is a man who knows exactly what he wants as well as how to get it.

What he wanted that day was sup-port—from an elite gathering of diplomats, military officers, oligarchs, and North American consultants—for creating "strategic villages" in scores of this devastated country's remote mountain hamlets.

"The communists have been exploiting

the extreme poverty and isolation of these villages," said Rivas Valdez as waiters prepared to serve Emerald Mountain coffee in china cups embossed with the American eagle. "Obviously we—that is, the government—must offer something better than the communists. And perhaps, after all, we owe them something better."

His listeners, who'd lunched on gazpacho, grilled snapper, and mango sorbet, were quietly attentive, although, during four years of a stubborn insurgency, they've probably considered dozens of such plans.

They were seated casually at round tables, and many had joined their host, Ambassador Richard M. Whitaker, in an after-meal cigarette.

Rivas Valdez, who, in a linen suit, looked more like a diplomat than a military man, explained that citizens of each strategic village would be employed to build schools, health clinics, roads, and irrigation systems. They would also be trained in rudimentary military techniques and organized into civil self-defense patrols monitored by local commanders.

The benefits of strategic villages would be twofold, the general said. They would provide a mechanism for controlling poor peasants of the rural highlands while at the same time making their lives better.

"An attitude of resolve on your part, a commitment to these strategic villages," he concluded, "will help insure future peace and freedom for all citizens of Bellavista."

By the time the ambassador's power lunch dispersed, not an hour later, the general had exactly what he wanted: permission to begin creating strategic villages. In a nation unencumbered by the voice of the people—there is no functioning congress, no national assembly—such decisions are not uncommon. But this particular decision seems to illustrate an emerging fact about power in Bellavista: when Rivas Valdez talks, people listen. Very important people listen.

According to the U.S. envoy, they ought to.

For it is Rivas Valdez, Whitaker insists, who has transformed Bellavista's military from a "corrupt, ragtag gang of stumblebums" into an "efficient and remorseless fighting force." The change, says Whitaker, has enabled the government to take the initiative in its war with communist guerrillas and to "finally put the rebels on the run."

More important, the ambassador believes Rivas Valdez has staked out a centrist position on the junta. His centrist position, says Whitaker, recognizes the need for drastic social reforms, but would carry them out within a context of governmental stability. It has, he believes, "opened a door onto a viable alternative" to the dictatorships that have ruled here for more than a century, and to the violent leftists who have been intent upon overthrowing them.

"Now that the door's open," said Whitaker, "we've got to help people see the benefits of what's on the other side."

It has long been axiomatic among members of the press corps that the U.S.

ambassador is the single most powerful individual in Bellavista. Recently, an embassy official, describing Whitaker's role in the establishment of the military and civilian junta, said, "He created this government with a felt-tip pen on a yellow legal pad."

The remark visibly rankles the general, whose aquiline features do not often reveal what he might be thinking or feeling.

"The days of United States hegemony are coming to a close," he said during a recent, and rare, interview in his stark cinder-block office at la Comandancia Militar Central. "In spite of our current need for North American aid, for your technical expertise, we are fully capable of determining our own course and of looking after our own interests."

Tall, lithe, and surprisingly soft-spoken, Rivas Valdez shuns the trappings of military power and seems to rely on a blend of personal charisma, intelligence, and prodigious energy to inspire his men. He works in a simple khaki uniform, adorned only by a line of gold stars on the pocket flap, and he works long hours every day. He is as likely to address a foot soldier as the man's commanding officer, and is as interested in the kind of rations carried by soldiers in the field as in devising movement strategies for battalions of those soldiers.

"He's a fanatical detail man," says a lieutenant colonel with the U.S. Military Group here. "And he's got the brains and experience to fit all the little details together so this incredibly complex machine keeps on rolling without squeaks or glitches."

Another American adviser credits Rivas Valdez with drastically reducing, if not ending, corruption in the officer corps, and with bringing the "intractable and incompetent commanders into line."

"They'd all carved out their fiefdoms in the countryside, and they ruled like little emperors," said the adviser. "It was a century-old tradition. Now he's the only emperor, but it seems to be okay. I guess he speaks their language. They respect him."

That respect, agreed North American and Bellavistan officers, was earned through courage. "He is the most fearless man I've ever known," said a captain who was with Rivas Valdez during several operations.

Colonel Ignacio Molina, a member of the junta and head of the nation's security forces, said Rivas Valdez never asks a soldier to do something he would not do himself.

During the December offensive, said Molina, "he led the most dangerous operations and put himself into the riskiest positions. This is how he earned the fidelity of the troops."

"At first I thought he was reckless," said an American. "But what it is is that he absolutely lacks any sense of personal danger."

Rivas Valdez, 44, declines to answer questions about his private life, and little is known beyond what is available in the library of news clippings maintained by the conservative newspaper *Las Noticias.*

He graduated from a private military school in the United States and was a political science major at Catholic University in Washington, D.C., for two years before he dropped out and returned home. He subsequently graduated from the Academia Militar here and went on to receive additional officer's training at Fort Bragg and then with the U.S. Southern Command in Panama.

Some twenty years ago, he married Esther Hoff, one of several daughters of Guillermo Hoff. Their three teenage children currently attend school in the United States.

The general's father, Reinaldo, was a painter and a dilettante who is said to have squandered the family fortune in a series of bad investments. After selling off most of the family's land to pay off his debts, he made, in the 1960s, a substantial contribution to the Universidad de Bellavista, which named its library after him. The army his son now commands closed the university, and the Reinaldo Rivas Library, several years ago.

The general's father-in-law, Guillermo Hoff, is reputed to be one of the nation's wealthiest men. He is a newcomer to the oligarchy who emigrated with his parents from Germany in the 1930s. According to local legend, the Hoffs, who apparently changed their name shortly before or after emigrating, bought their way into the oligarchy by purchasing the floundering plantations of the older families. Hoff is now believed to control nearly one-quarter of the coffee industry here. Repeated efforts to interview him were unavailing.

The defense minister's older brother, Raúl, married another Hoff. The merger of the Rivas and Hoff clans, of the poor but venerated old family with the wealthy newcomers, is said to be typical of how the oligarchy has consolidated its power and revitalized itself through succeeding generations.

The story, despite its romantic aspects, does not have a fairy-tale ending. Raúl, the father of four, was kidnapped by guerrillas early in the insurgency. Guillermo Hoff paid the demanded ransom of $3 million, but the mutilated and bullet-ridden body of Raúl Rivas Valdez, then 41, was left outside the gate of the Rivas estate in la Costa de Plata. The corpse was wrapped in the flag of Bellavista.

Reinaldo Rivas died of a heart ailment not long afterward. Many other members of the family have left the country.

Many Bellavistans are now convinced that the guerrillas kidnapped Raúl by mistake; that Víctor, known even then as an aggressive and ambitious army officer, was their true target. Many say the error is evidence of the profound incompetence of the Mateo Omaño National Liberation Front (FMOLN), the Marxist alliance that was believed to be responsible for the murder. The outcome of the civil conflict would have been much different, they assert, had the guerrillas murdered the younger Rivas Valdez.

The defense minister declines to comment on such suggestions or on anything else about his private life.

"Does the señorita have any other questions I might answer?" he responds, with invincible courtesy, to a series of inquiries about his family and his private life.

The government claims to have driven the rebels back into northeastern Ixtapanga, where, according to Rivas Valdez, they continue to be supported not only by "a deeply woven civilian infrastructure" but also by the government of Costa Negra.

At least 10 free-fire zones have been designated there, in the difficult terrain of the Bellavistan border at the Río Luciente. Civilians have been evacuated from the area, says the defense ministry, and are forbidden to travel in the zones where ground combat, as well as air strikes and artillery bombardments, are being carried out indiscriminately.

The designation of the free-fire zones, said Rivas Valdez, was a device for separating civilians from guerrillas. By isolating the rebels, he said, the government intends to keep them from recruiting and training new guerrillas or planning for the future.

"Without the collusion of the populace, the communists would have neither sanctuaries nor food," he says. "Without civilian support, there could be no rebel army."

The evacuees, who may number up to 27,000, will be permitted to return to their homes once the area is safe, he said. Most are being provided for in government-run refugee centers and in camps run by the International Red Cross.

Questioned about persistent reports of noncombatant casualties in the military operation zones, Rivas Valdez said, "There are no civilians in those areas, only subversives, enemies of the people."

As the general and his entourage approached La Joya on horseback, the horses' hooves kicked up a mist of dust that billowed up into the vast sky.

Among them were soldiers, embassy officials, workers from the Agency for International Development (AID), and a reporter and photographer. The general, astride a sleek palomino mare, had taken the lead, next to the commander of the local garrison, where he rode with the easy authority of a skilled horseman.

Then two barefoot boys with rifles, who were patrolling the path that led into the village, stopped abruptly at the sight of soldiers. One jerked into a exaggerated salute. The other took off running but stopped when his partner called out to him. The boy then about-faced and arranged himself into the same slapstick salute.

The boys, who looked about 12, watched Rivas Valdez paralyzed, not moving even as he cantered close to them.

"Would you take off if guerrillas tried to come here?" the general asked the boy who ran.

The boy shook his head no. "I would shoot the guerrillas," he answered.

Rivas Valdez nodded and asked the boys where their hats and boots were. When they said they had none, he turned to look over the young soldiers who were riding behind him. He said something to the local commander, who in turn gestured to a pair of spiffy, straight-backed soldiers. The soldiers slowly dismounted and, with obvious reluctance, removed their dashing, wide-brimmed camouflage hats. They brought them to the boys of the civilian self-defense patrol. Meanwhile, the local commander had produced pencil and paper and was outlining the boys' feet. He promised the general that the boots would be delivered within the week.

Then, with the civil defense patrolmen grinning in their oversized sombreros, the general and his party trotted into La Joya.

The village, whose name in Spanish means The Jewel, consists of a few dilapidated huts huddled on a ridge below mist-enshrouded peaks. The nearest source of water is a well more than a mile away. The yards around the huts are bereft of grass or shrubs. The subsistence crops of villagers were destroyed during recent fighting. A fog of dust seems always to hang in the thin, cool air.

Like so many other of the country's mountain hamlets, La Joya has no electricity, no sanitation facilities, and no communication system other than word of mouth. It is inaccessible by motor vehicle, difficult to reach even on horseback. The Indians who live here travel by foot and have virtually no contact with the outside world.

Yet La Joya, whose environs provided sanctuaries for the FMOLN not long ago, has become a strategic village.

Now, in addition to its civil self-defense patrol, it has a commitment from the government to spend tens of thousands of dollars here on a new well, an irrigation system, and livestock for a cooperative farm. It also has the junta's promise to employ every villager in agricultural endeavors intended to bring La Joya into Bellavista's economic mainstream.

Shortly after the general's party arrived, the erratic shrieks and thumps of a distant air bombardment echoed through the mountains. Several children began wailing and running for their mothers, who scanned the sky impassively. At first it was empty, then three aircraft appeared. Rivas Valdez identified them as Dragonflies. They appeared as small and harmless as the insect they were named for. Then they circled around and disappeared, and the sounds of a bombardment began again.

"The guerrillas controlled La Joya not two months ago," the general said, gesturing toward the mountains. "Now we will maintain our presence here, but will also demonstrate that the government is not an enemy."

An AID worker conducted a tour of AID's tents, which were filled with agricultural equipment and cartons of supplies. In front of one of them, a Bellavistan, under contract to AID, was explaining the irrigation system to a dozen villagers.

While men toiled on nearby slopes to build the system, most females were absorbed in their eternal task of grinding corn for tortillas and tending to children.

It was difficult to gauge the villagers' response to its designation as a strategic village. Several turned away from a reporter's questions. Others shrugged and said, *"Vamos a ver"*—We'll see.

Several young women, who were returning from the well with jugs of water on their heads, were reluctant to talk, and expressed fear of the camera.

"There are no troubles here," whispered one. "We are not political." All of them hurried away.

What role the strategic villages will play in Bellavista's future and whether the rebels will finally be vanquished remain open questions. Even if the government prevails, what will happen afterward is another question. So seems the future of the general.

Throughout Bellavista's modern history, military strongmen who have, like him, controlled the armed forces have simply declared themselves head of state. And they have used the considerable means at their disposal to ensure the security of their own rules.

Despite its professed dedication to freedom and democracy, the United States has never been unwilling to support such dictators as long as they protected U.S. interests.

Rivas Valdez waved his hand impatiently when reminded of this history and questioned again about his future.

"The authoritarian epoch is over," he said. "Today, the people must have a voice, a mechanism for expressing opinions and exerting control over their own lives."

Then he stroked the mare's neck, tugged against the reins, and galloped off into the sunshine.

REBELS ATTACK AIR BASE; U.S. AIRCRAFT DAMAGED

by Elizabeth M. Guerrera
Herald-Sun Staff Writer

LIBERTAD, BELLAVISTA—Communist rebels attacked this country's largest air base yesterday, damaging a score of American warplanes and helicopters in a post-midnight barrage of armor-piercing rockets, grenades, and machine-gun fire.

North American investigators, are looking into the possibility that rebel infiltrators into the ranks of Bellavista's air force may have aided the attack by setting off dynamite charges inside some of the planes and helicopters, said a spokesman for the U.S. embassy here.

Defense Minister Víctor Rivas Valdez termed such a possibility absurd. He denied that major damage had occurred and said soldiers had quickly routed the guerrillas.

A civilian employee of the air base, who spoke on the condition that he not be named, said as many as 20 aircraft, including a dozen Cessna Dragonflies and eight or nine helicopters, "were at least half-wrecked."

"They weren't completely destroyed," said the employee, who claimed to be a witness, "but I doubt they will be flying for a long time."

In addition, said the civilian, a half-dozen soldiers appeared to have been injured and were taken from the air base in ambulances.

Rivas Valdez declined to comment on the civilian's assertion.

CHAPTER SIXTEEN

"SALVATION HAPPENS HERE ON EARTH," MARY SAID INSTEAD OF GREETING
me the next time I saw her. "You know that, don't you?"

It was early morning when I found her in the yard outside
Nuestra Señora del Refugio. She was surrounded by ragged women and
their children, supervising them as they streamed out of her Dodge van,
a small bus, an ancient pickup truck. She didn't look at me, asked her
question as if she'd been waiting for the chance, then turned and charged
into the stream.

"What's that supposed to mean?" I asked when I caught up with her.
The morning light exposed complex webs around her eyes, the silver in
her hair. I didn't care whether she answered me, but found myself
following her to the back of the truck, where she took by the arms a

white-haired woman dressed in black. She helped the woman onto the dusty ground. The woman held a rosary, muttered prayers as Mary moved her. Then Alba appeared, took the woman by the arm, led her across the yard into the center.

"That you can save yourself, right here and now."

She turned to look at me for the first time. Something metallic glinted in her eyes. Self-righteousness, I thought.

"It depends on what you do or don't do during your life." She stared at me, or, rather, through me. "On the choices that you make."

I turned away, regretted my decision to try to see her, to try to explain. I was about to leave when I saw Milagros and other women from the center helping more new arrivals.

"Who are they?"

I gestured toward the women and children, who seemed scared and lost.

"Refugees." She waded deeper into the stream. "Exiles in their own country." They'd been forced out of their homes, out of Sangre de Cristo, other smaller villages up north, she told me as I followed her. Some were sharecroppers forced off their land by owners intent upon thwarting land reform. If landowners don't have sharecroppers to whom they can give title to the land, she went on, they get to keep it. Others had fled from free-fire zones.

I searched the scene for color, for points of interest, points of light, but there was no color, no light—only shades of black and brown, dark hair and skin and eyes, faded clothing, against the looming backdrop of the cathedral.

"You really ought to take a run up there yourself, find out for yourself what's going on." She tried skewering me with a glance. "I mean, if you're such a great reporter, shouldn't you see things firsthand?"

"Easier said than done." I felt compelled to defend myself. "We can't travel without special credentials from the defense ministry, which they're currently refusing to issue."

Her crucifix was tangled in the stethoscope around her neck. She wove her fingers through the tangle, pulled it out, frowned over the crowd.

"These are a messianic people," she said, then took my arm, moved us toward the cathedral. "Encouraged by their faith, they've started on their pilgrimmage, their march toward salvation."

"Sounds Maoist," I joked, and she stopped abruptly, squeezed my arm.

"It's not communist." Her pale eyes bored through me. "It's not political at all. Anyone who thinks that is crazy. Plain wrong."

She stopped, interrupted by the weeping of a woman who clasped impassive children to her sides. Her husband had disappeared, the woman said. Now she'd left home with their children, thinking she could save them, but she realized that she'd never see her man again. Mary consoled her for a moment, pointed to the doorway of the brick house. She told her to go in, to get some soup and milk for the children. Then she smiled at me.

"It's something I've been thinking about a lot lately. Salvation, I mean." A spasm of dry coughs seized her, and she hunched forward until it passed. "I'm certain the only place it could happen is here, now." Her eyes were reddened, watery from coughing. "Where else, when else, could it happen?"

I thought the question was rhetorical, but she repeated it, where else could salvation happen, and its sharp point jabbed me, demanded a response. I glanced into her eyes, looked away, heard myself saying, "I suppose if salvation actually happens, it must take place on earth."

"No ifs," she said. "It happens."

Again she turned her back to me, crouched down, enfolded in her arms a filthy barefoot toddler who was crying for its mother.

"You don't know me, you don't know anything about me," I told her as she lifted the child above her head, began calling for its mother. "But you're judging me. You must think you're God Almighty——"

"I know everything I need to know," she cut me off, then repeated my name, Elizabeth, Elizabeth, in a singsong voice as a frantic girl emerged from the crowd and reached up to claim the child. A sleeping infant was tied to her chest inside a red-striped cloth.

"What are you going to do about it?"

The young mother moved away, scolding her child. I felt Mary close beside me, but wouldn't turn to look at her.

"These women have so many children," I remarked, looking them over, trying to count them. I figured each female of childbearing age had reproduced herself three or four times.

"Babies are their only means of production, their only wealth. They've never had your opportunities, your choices."

Her words were bright with condescension, and they repelled me. I started to walk away.

"What about Chepe Alvarria?"

The whispered question stopped me.

"What about him?" I turned around.

"They cut out his tongue because he was a delegate of The Word, and they cut off his penis because he refused to be a dominator. He believed in the equality of men and women——"

"I saw the body," I interrupted. I watched dust settle on my sandals, remembering the slashes and the burn marks on his back and thighs and arms, his thumbs tied behind his back with his own shoelaces. Almost a week before, his body had been found propped up against the jacaranda tree in the children's cemetery at Ciudad de Merced. It had been laid out on a pallet in his family's one-room hut by the time Mary had brought me to see him.

"El Frente claimed responsibility," I went on, kicking the ground so the dust billowed. "They said he was *una oreja*, an informant for the government."

"But it's not true. Everybody knows it isn't true." She coughed, stepped back from the dust cloud. "Chepe was a revolutionary, but only of the spirit. He was bringing God's word to the illiterate. That's why the soldiers tortured him and mutilated him."

"You don't know who did it."

"It wasn't the FMOLN."

"How do you know?"

I turned, saw her pale skin fired by self-righteousness.

"Because *el frente* kills cleanly. And they always warn their victims. They give them a chance to change their ways, to save themselves. They don't torture. They don't mutilate."

"They're such nice *muchachos*, those guerrillas. They don't torture. They just assassinate."

Again I started off, and again she stopped me.

"Listen, girl." Her command was interrupted by another spasm of coughs. "Maybe you think it's a fine distinction," she went on once it had passed, "but it's not. There's a world of moral difference between a bullet to the heart and having bits and pieces of your body hacked off by machetes while you're still alive."

"Murder's murder," I replied. When I looked at her, drops of water were spilling from her eyes, sliding down her cheeks. My shoulders moved in an involuntary shrug.

"My editors didn't think it was a story, okay? They didn't think it was a story that our readers could relate to."

It was what I'd gone to tell her, why I'd sought her out that morning.

But the explanation shattered as it struck her, smote by her mighty indignation. She didn't move, stared with no expression. I met her eyes for a millisecond, then looked around, saw we'd become separated from the others, stood close to each other, but apart from them. For an instant, I saw us from the outside, two tall, fair-haired *gringas* arguing in English, arguing about the butcheries, and their news value, of a war that had little to do with either one of us. Then I saw the others watching.

"I mean my editors said it was an isolated incident," I explained. "They said there was no way to verify what had happened, or even if his death had anything to do with the base communities. There was no way to find the truth."

"You know what the truth is, don't you?"

"Of course I don't know what the truth is. I couldn't verify a single fact about who killed him or why."

"Chepe's death, his murder, is not a story, but the life of Víctor Rivas Valdez is?"

"Rivas Valdez is a public figure of international stature. He makes, he's already made, history."

"Chepe was a martyr, a saint."

"I don't control what's printed. My editors decide what news is. I only gather it."

"Hah!" Her ragged bark released the smell of alcohol, and it chilled me as it pitched me back into a dim apartment in the Bronx and the soft arms of my mother. "You don't only gather it like fucking berries you toss into a basket."

"You've been drinking," I accused.

"For medicinal purposes only." She grinned. "For my chronic bronchitis, my pharyngitis."

I started to walk away.

"You help choose the stories that get printed," I heard her cry. I saw Alba floating toward us, then she paused and hovered at the edge of the crowd. "You're the one who's on the front lines, who decides what's worth writing about. You figure out what's important and tell your editors. You sell them your stories."

I took another step away but heard her move behind me. She grabbed my arms, pulled me back.

"Víctor Rivas Valdez is a man who knows exactly what he wants as well as how to get it . . . the most powerful man in Bellavista." The hands around my arms were powerful as a man's, and they shook me while the whispered words, twined with sarcasm, bound and trapped me. "When Rivas Valdez talks, people listen. Very important people listen."

She laughed a wild squawk of laughter, said he wasn't really the most powerful, that there was one more powerful than he, one who was helping Bellavista's poor find life's healing, reconciling forces. I found my strength, broke her grip, pushed her away.

"You're drunk. And crazy."

"The wicked man in his pride hunts down the poor," she went on as if I hadn't spoken, her words tight with contempt. "Arrogant as he is, he scorns the Lord and leaves no place for God in all his schemes."

"You're nuts. *Loca.*"

Still she kept on, her face pink with excitement.

"His mouth is full of lies and violence. Mischief and trouble lurk under his tongue."

"*Loca,*" I shouted, turning to the women around us, pointing to her. "*Ten cuidado, mujeres. La comadrona, la gringa, es loca y emborrachada.*"

She's crazy and drunk.

I rushed through the yard, heading for my car. I stumbled once and was halted by stragglers who materialized before me. I heard Mary calling brightly, "The tenth psalm, Elizabeth. Seems to speak to our situation, doesn't it?"

The letter, addressed in a flamboyant red scrawl, sat propped against my desk lamp the whole time I worked on the story. On the chair beside the desk, not far from the lamp and letter, sat the green gift box with its filmy tissue. The white fabric of the gift inside protruded like a surrender flag.

The story itself was a gift of sorts, an inexplicable gift, and, as it turned out, an unintended one, but it didn't matter to me why or how I'd gotten it. I'd immediately recognized its value and had grabbed it eagerly, perhaps too eagerly. I didn't care about that either. I'd felt feverish all afternoon on the phone to Washington and New York; exhilarated because I knew I was the only one who had the story; high as I watched myself finesse a privately made chance remark about M-16s being shipped to Bellavista into a front-page story. Even my New York editors were impressed. They told me something I already knew, that the story provided a rare glimpse into the world of international arms deals, a window onto hidden State Department machinations.

The desk man at the hotel had hailed me, then handed me the letter and the box when I'd passed through the lobby on my way back from seeing Mary. Right away, I saw the letter's sealed edge was torn and smudged. I figured it had been opened and read, legally, under the state of siege. I'd never seen Mary's handwriting, but I somehow knew that the big flourished letters must be hers. Again I was seared by a hot flash of anger at the idea that she was after me and that I'd never get away from her.

The gift box, however, was mysterious. It was neatly taped, redolent of an exotic, vaguely familiar perfume, a scent which made my heart pump faster even though I couldn't remember where or when I'd smelled it.

I was hardly through the doors to my room when I had opened it, seen its contents, and tossed it away. The white dress fell, billowing out over the gift box as it tumbled to the floor. Then I was on my knees, examining with my fingertips its fine details, the tiny handsewn pleats and intricate embroidery of the dress. I knew what it was, a replacement for the one of mine he'd torn. And I was thinking that it was so much finer than my old one that the two did not belong in the same closet. I was appalled that I'd even consider putting the dress into my closet, so I stuffed it back into the box and carried it into the office. Only later, when I was working on the story, the other gift from the same source, did I see the hem beckoning like a white surrender flag.

Sometimes, working on the story, I'd glance at the little flag, and sometimes at the red scrawl of the letter, and tell them both to fuck off—out loud like a lunatic. I'd tell them they couldn't stop me from doing my job, which was to tell the story.

But afterward, when I'd finished it, and when all the words had been transformed into electrical impulses for the trip through wire to New York, and adrenaline was still rushing through my body with such force I could hear the ringing in my ears, and I was drinking bourbon to try to stop it, thoughts of the dress and letter overpowered me. After a while I went back into the office to touch the hem again. I tugged more out of the box, wanting to put it on. I wanted to see myself in it, and wanted him to see me. It was in the effort to resist that I grabbed Mary's letter and went back to my bed.

"How long, O Lord?" it began. "I cry for help, but you do not listen! I cry out to you, 'Violence!' but you do not intervene. Why do you let me see ruin? Why must I look at misery? Destruction and violence are before me: there is strife and clamorous discord.

"Then the Lord answered me and said: Write down the vision clearly upon the tablets, so that one can read it readily. For the vision still has its time, presses on to fulfillment, and will not disappoint. If it delays, wait for it; it will surely come, it will not be late."

The biblical citation was smudged, impossible to read. Just below it were these words, a passage from John's Gospel:

"I am telling you the truth: when you were young you used to get ready and go anywhere you wanted to; but when you are old, you will stretch out your hands and someone else will tie you up and take you where you do not want to go."

I read the letter several times, knowing she'd written it and mailed it before our encounter, probably before Chepe Alvarria had been killed. In it she seemed to be asking me to tell her version of the story, to write her "vision on the tablet." The second passage seemed to predict that I would somehow be compelled to join her cause. Both ideas angered me, even more than her attitude that morning.

It occurred to me that I ought to tell her story; ought to write about what she was doing, maybe in a profile. That would fix her. Yes, such a story, as she knew, would no doubt have devastating consequences. Yet her ideas and activities were certainly fair game for a reporter. She couldn't stop me from writing about her.

I don't know how long I sat there thinking about how to tell her story and enjoying an imagined revenge for the difficulty she'd caused me. Maybe I had another drink or two and listened to a long tape of Ravel before I heard the soft knock on my door. I glanced at the clock, saw it was nearly curfew. When I opened the door, Mary herself rushed through. She didn't seem quite real.

"This isn't a social call," she said, suddenly hesitant, distant. Confronted with her pure eyes, her piety, my vengeful feelings curdled into hot shame. I looked away, afraid she'd know what I'd been thinking. I gestured toward my unmade bed, and she walked over to it, but didn't sit. She glanced at the bottle of Wild Turkey and then at me. I thought of offering her a drink, immediately decided against it. She held up a blue-and-green plastic bag imprinted with the logo of Banco Vista.

"You'll never guess what's in here."

She was right—I couldn't even think about it. Because she kept watching me, judging and assessing, in a way that made me want to crawl under the bed to hide.

Mary upended the bag so its contents banged and clanked onto the bed. Two dozen steel cylinders slammed into one another, then rolled into folds of bedclothes. I picked one up, thought I recognized it from a book on American-made armaments. It was a 40mm high-explosive projectile. When fired from its launcher, it could shear off a human head even if it didn't detonate.

"It's a grenade."

"I figured they were some kind of bullet," she said. She started to laugh, but the laugh stuck in her throat. I looked at her, remembering how I'd called her crazy. At that moment, she seemed absolutely sane.

"I guess you could say they're big bullets," I told her. "But they don't explode by themselves. They have to be fired out of launchers that are attached to M-16s. I think Colt manufactures them."

"We found them under our pillows."

"What do you mean?"

"Just now. We were putting the children, some of the babies, to bed, and we found these things, these metal phalluses, under the pillows. Like a tooth fairy with a very weird sense of humor had paid us a visit."

"How do you think they got there?"

She shrugged.

"Every one of us got one. Even the babies."

She began pushing the grenades around with her index finger. I looked at them, thinking that what she was telling me could not be true, that she must be making it up.

"Do you think if women designed ammunition it would still be shaped this way?"

Her question made me laugh, but I saw how serious she was.

"I think the shape has to do with aerodynamics, not sexual politics."

She held one up and turned it all around.

"But it looks exactly like one, doesn't it?" she asked. "Like a steel prick."

It did, but by then it had occurred to me that Mary herself might have gotten the grenades, that she might be making up the story to win sympathy, get publicity. My idea made little sense, but it also relieved me of the necessity of immediately pursuing the ramifications of the incident.

"Why don't you ask your friend Rivas Valdez what's going on with this junta of so-called reform and reconciliation?"

The question was deliberately insinuating, and I turned away.

"What do you mean, my friend?"

"You have access to him. You're one of the few who does. I think he ought to comment on this. On the record."

Again she moved the grenades around with her fingers. They made a soft, metallic clank. I was trying to imagine the story, trying to imagine asking him. I couldn't.

"Do you think it goes up that high?"

She looked at me dumbfounded.

"Cut the shit, Lizzie. Not only does it go up that high, it goes sideways, straight across to the State Department. To the U.S. embassy. You know it. You have to know it."

She looked at me some more, maybe saw my disbelief, or my paralysis. Gradually her expression changed until she seemed to see me as a stranger. As though our encounter were the result of a profoundly embarrassing instance of mistaken identity. She began packing up the grenades, putting them back into the bag from Banco Vista. When she was finished, she picked up the bag and walked out of my room.

COLT RIFLES SOLD TO JUNTA
by Elizabeth M. Guerrera
Herald-Sun Staff Writer

LIBERTAD, BELLAVISTA—Nearly $14 million in American arms were sold to this troubled country's military and shipped here last week with State Department approval. Now a group of U.S. senators is calling this commercial transaction "a back-door approach" to arming a foreign government involved in human rights violations and an attempt by the State Department to sidestep the required Congressional review of such arms shipments.

"State blindsided us," said Sen. John P. Mulligan, D.-Mass., of the $13.9 million weapons sale, which was licensed by the State Department several weeks ago.

"They [the State Department] found a loophole in Congress's Foreign Military Sales Program and used it to provide lethal weaponry on a massive scale to a questionable government."

The sale, which involved 20,000 M-16 rifles manufactured by Colt Industries, "would have generated tremendous controversy" if considered by Congress, he said. Mulligan predicted that the request would have been denied.

"I think that's what the American people would have wanted," said the lawmaker.

Mulligan, a member of the Senate's Appropriations Subcommittee on Foreign

Operations, said during a telephone interview yesterday that he and 15 other lawmakers have signed a letter to the Secretary of State expressing outrage over what he called "an alarming effort to thwart the wishes" of Congress.

According to Stephen Howell, a New York representative for Colt Industries, the M-16s were shipped to Libertad late last week.

"What we did was perfectly legal," said Howell. "We are in business to sell arms."

Commercial arms sales to Bellavista and many other countries require Congressional approval only if they exceed $14 million. However, all arms sales require an export license that must be approved by the State Department.

"There was absolutely no attempt to deceive Congress," said a State Department official involved in Central American policy. He conceded, however, that the $13.9 million in sales was so close to the $14 million threshold that "I suppose it might appear that way."

"Everything was totally aboveboard," said the official. "Nobody was trying to get through any loopholes."

The official said it was against State Department policy to publicize its commercial arms deals. However, he said, the State Department "would have been glad" to brief Congress about the deal had such a request been made. He said that the department's munitions control section

approved the export license, and Colt Industries had shipped the arms, "before anyone expressed the slightest interest in what was going on."

Sen. Mulligan responded that Congress did not know what was going on—and therefore could express no interest. He pointed out that in a recent $200 million aid package for Bellavista, Congress had severely restricted weaponry because of what it said were continuing questions about the armed forces' attitude toward civilians.

"They wanted 32,000 [M-16s]," said Mulligan. "We gave them 7,000. We wanted them to know we have standards of behavior they must adhere to. Why would they clean up their act if they can get any weapon they want?"

Colt Industries' Howell declined to say whether the junta was currently negotiating for more guns. The public, said Howell, "doesn't necessarily" have a right to know about such "private deals."

However, the State Department official involved in Central American policy confirmed that Colt had begun the application process for another license.

"There is nothing to indicate that this export license should be denied," said the State Department official.

On the contrary, he said, its approval and the expeditious shipment of the arms was "in keeping with the U.S. policy of support" for the government of Bellavista.

CHAPTER SEVENTEEN

*I*T WAS JUST AFTER NIGHTFALL, AND THE GILDED ROOM WAS BLURRED by shadows. No candles had been lit, no lamps switched on, so the light was gray instead of gold, sullen. I couldn't tell where the walls began or the floor ended. He was wearing white, a white shirt rolled at the cuffs, casual white trousers. Wear white at night, I thought when I saw him standing with his back to me on the far side of the room.

"I never suspected you were such a treacherous bitch, Elisabet," he said without turning around. "I never guessed. And I consider myself an astute judge of character."

When at last he turned to face me, I saw he held the *Herald-Sun*, the edition with the M-16 story on the front page. He made sure I saw the newspaper, then tossed it onto a table. I couldn't tell if he was angry.

"Treacherous," he said again, softly, as he sauntered toward me. The word sounded like an endearment, except by then he was looking at my jeans, sweatshirt, and sneakers. His eyes went ashy and his mouth twisted as if he'd tasted something rank.

"I've showered, I'm clean," I announced.

He stopped not far from where I stood by the oak doors and stretched out his arm so his fingertips grazed my cheek. He would have to watch himself now, wouldn't he? he asked. Watch every word for fear that it would be verified and amplified into news for publication in the North American press? He dropped his hand and stepped back, as though to keep his distance.

Of course, the M-16 story had been harmless, he continued, had, in fact, been quite amusing—yet another act in a *yanqui* political comedy that seemed to have no end. Still, it had been a betrayal.

I went to him, put my hands on his chest, warmed them in his startling body heat for a moment, then slid them down his sides until they met his belt.

"I couldn't resist," I told him, curling my fingers around the braided leather. "It was too good to pass up." I tilted back my head to see his face, glimpsed parts of the merciless terrain, the ridge of nose, jutting precipice of chin and vining carotid. "Besides," I added, fingering the buckle, "I thought you wanted me to have it."

He brushed my hands away, stepped back laughing, a curious rustle, like dry leaves being kicked through.

"Is that what you thought?"

He was smiling, but his amusement was quickly consumed by something else, an enkindled restlessness. He examined my clothes while chewing on his lip.

"You didn't like the dress."

What dress, I began to ask, then remembered, protested that of course I'd liked it.

"It didn't fit?"

"It fit," I lied, remembering how much I'd wanted to put it on.

"But you didn't wear it."

I turned away because I didn't have an explanation. I tried saying something about the other reporters at the hotel talking, noticing. I turned around and was thinking of going back out the doors when he grabbed my waistband from behind.

"Elisabet, darling, your masquerade as a common laborer is ludicrous," he said. "You can't hide what you are."

He pulled me close so I felt the tension of his body all along my spine. I didn't ask him what I was.

"You shouldn't wear these things," he said, massaging my buttocks. "They don't become you."

His complaint might have made me laugh except the movement of his hand reminded me of something and I responded with my own.

"One of your thugs at OPEN did the same thing to me, what you're doing now. One of your uniformed bully boys at Ciudad de Merced."

His fingers stopped at the knobbed intersection of seams.

"What do you mean?"

The words were whispered close to my ear, and the exhalation that propelled them lightly brushed my cheek.

"The *policía* at OPEN groped me just the way you're groping me. Do they teach the technique at the police academy? Or maybe at the military school?"

He turned me to face him, and his eyes were flickering with yellow light, like smoky windows on a furnace.

"What are you talking about?"

"You know. They stopped me," I said, lowering my eyes to his throat. "While one of them was looking at my papers, the other one grabbed my ass and felt between my legs. Is that part of the new armed forces code of conduct?"

"Is that all he did?"

"He put his hand under my shirt and touched my breasts."

"What else?"

"Nothing else."

His hands around my upper arms tightened, and he shook me just a little. "Nothing?" His eyes had darkened, but I saw the embers smoldering. He slid one hand around my neck, entwined his fingers in my hair. "What else happened?"

"He stopped because his commander showed up and told him to."

"That was all? They let you go?"

His fingers yanked my hair, pulled out the answer.

"The head thug said I was your whore. I heard him. *La puta de Rivas Valdez* is what he said."

He jerked back my head and held it there, encircled my throat with his other hand. He stroked my neck, somehow warning me he could break it, although he didn't speak. He only stared, his eyes incendiary but without warmth. The air between us seemed to throb and shimmer, and there was not enough of it. Then he let me go, pushed me away, combed his fingers through his clipped hair.

"You've been drinking."

I laughed, a giddy froth of sound I hardly recognized.

"You were drinking," he repeated. It was a question, one he wanted answered.

"With the others, at the hotel," I explained. "You know, the other reporters. I couldn't not. It's just something that's done. Thank God it's Friday, and all that."

"Thank God it's Friday," he repeated, mystified. He left me, crossed the room into the shadows, where I saw him making drinks. He gestured to one of the gold wing chairs, but I didn't take it. Instead I wandered to the windows. They were open, but the curtains had been tied back. The gusting oceanic air was insistent, irritating.

In fact, I regretted having talked to the others. They'd all been eating sandwiches, drinking beer, and watching a boxing match from the United States when I walked into the bar.

"Quiet, quiet, here she comes," Jack Travis said in an exaggerated stage whisper. Then he grinned, said they hadn't been really talking about me, it was just a joke. But when I looked around the table, nobody was smiling. He made a place for me beside him, then went on about how I owned the Bellavista story. I had sources to the left, sources to the right, sources in the middle. His cheeks were flushed, his eyes bright from the beer. A reporter's only as good as her sources, I said, half joking, when someone said it didn't hurt to be on a first-name basis with the minister of defense.

"Who's on a first-name basis?"

I looked around the tables, saw Sonia grinning in her corner, was about to speak again when I was interrupted by another accusation.

"When you do PR for the ministry of defense, they do tend to return your phone calls."

"Who's doing PR? I broke news in that profile," I said loudly, turning in a futile search for my accuser. "Nobody, not one of you, knew anything about strategic villages until my profile ran. Then every major paper in the country assigned a follow-up."

No one spoke. I looked at them and saw envy in their faces. I remembered all the times I'd played catch-up, finessing day-old news into something fresh for our paper.

"Tough luck about the M-16 story, huh?"

I shouldn't have said it, but couldn't stop myself. I immediately wished

I hadn't when Travis, in a whisper, admonished me about rubbing it in. He said he hoped success wouldn't make me arrogant.

"Hey, it's only a game, right?" Sonia said after a moment. "You have to give a little to get a little. Every journalist does it." She smiled, holding the nub of a hand-rolled cigarette. "Of course, there's one important question you always have to answer for yourself." She spoke slowly, looked around to make sure her audience was listening. "Is what you're getting back worth what you're giving?"

Her eyes turned into black probes for an instant, made painful contact with mine. Then her face, like a magician's, disappeared in smoke as she mashed out her cigarette.

"That's true," said Travis, motioning to the waiter to bring another round. "Maybe he is a good source, but the profile glamorized him. It was accurate and informative, but somehow bankrupt. I mean morally. He came across as this icon of power. Might makes right. Like what he's doing here is acceptable as long as he has this veneer of civility." Travis picked up a frosty pilsner glass, swallowed beer. "But that's typical *Herald-Sun*, isn't it?" he said. "Puff up the mighty and ignore the weak."

He was still shaking his head when the others began to plan a softball game with the embassy staff for that weekend. I declined an invitation to play, also declined Travis's invitation to go out later. I saw it was time to drive to the airport, where I would meet the chauffeur. I was walking out of the bar when I heard Jack's voice, then Sonia's.

"I guess Lizzie doesn't play softball. Maybe she doesn't like team sports anymore."

"Did she before? I figured she's always preferred more intimate types of games."

Then there was laughter, but I couldn't tell whose it was.

The lip of the glass was icy against mine, the liquor hot in my mouth. I'd come for solace, refuge, and thought he should give me some. Instead, he put his hand around mine on the glass and took the glass away. He said I shouldn't drink so fast.

"Why did you give it to me if you didn't want me to have it?"

He seemed not to hear the question, and he left me standing empty-handed, before I turned my back on him and walked over to the doors. I thought I'd walk outside to the water, but the screen door was locked and I couldn't find the latch. There were no stars or moon, but the sky glowed with a strange yellow light.

"Nightglow," I heard him say, turned to see him stretched out in the wing chair. He seemed to be looking at his hands, which were resting on his thighs.

"Is it going to storm?"

He shook his head no. He said the eerie light resulted from a reaction of gases caused by solar radiation in the upper atmosphere.

"It portends nothing," he said after a while. He sipped his drink, put it down, drummed his fingers on the chair's arm.

I spied my glass on the table next to him, walked over to retrieve it, snatched it up, began to drink while he wasn't looking. I watched him ignore me and felt the blades of his repudiation cut me. Then I was on my knees in front of him, rubbing my hands along his thighs. I'm so sorry, Víctor, I said. I could change. Please let me. Because I could make you happy, Víctor. I know I could, if only you would let me. Give me another chance. As I pleaded, I watched his eyes change, go dark but with a distant, yellow glow, so you couldn't tell where the light was coming from or what it meant.

Then we were upstairs in the peacock-colored room and it seemed magical that the change of clothes was already there, arrayed across the bed, a revelation of his desire and his need: the scarlet dress, lacy underthings, and high-heeled sandals. He put one arm around me, picked up the red dress, touched my cheek with it. Put it on, he said, so I can see how beautiful you are.

I got away from him, found myself before the enormous gilt mirror of the dresser. I stood there thinking I should learn something about periods and styles of furniture—because then I'd know more about how he lived. I couldn't tell if the dresser and mirror were French or Spanish or Italian; from the seventeenth or eighteenth or nineteenth century or none of the above. Then he was behind me, embracing me, kissing my neck and whispering between the kisses that I was beautiful and he wanted me to let him see how beautiful I was, that he knew I wanted to. I watched him in the mirror help me out of my shirt and bra, watched him caress my breasts, my nipples. He moved his hands to my jeans, pulled down the zipper. I slid out of them in a way that made me think of pupas, chrysalises. Only my metamorphosis was interrupted long before I had the dress on. He came to me and reached for me, his face distorted by desire. He lifted me and kissed me. I tried to resist him and my own body's clamor, but he compressed me in his arms, made me breathless with his tongue. His body pressed hard against me, and his penis swelled between us, an imperative. He whispered something, maybe *la puta de Rivas Valdez*, as he pushed me down and I slid down, slid to my knees. I clasped the pylons of his legs, discovered tremors in the pylons. My scalp burned from his fingers entangled in my hair and it somehow made me think of praying, but even when it hurt I didn't stop.

"Darling Elisabet, whatever possessed you to wear those clothes?" We were back downstairs, sitting at a table perfumed by roses floating in a crystal bowl. The table was covered with lace, set with china in an Oriental pattern, ornate silver.

"Have you been indoctrinated into the women's liberation struggle during your visits to El Centro de Cambio y Creatividad?"

I looked around and tried to get my bearings, but the lavish room disappeared into shadow, seemed dimensionless. The walls were covered with dark brocade, and the draperies were of a matching velvet. The only light source was a pair of candles burning on the table close to us. The huge chandelier above the table was unlit.

"Hmm?" he prodded, reaching over to touch my throat. Upstairs he'd adorned it with a gold chain set with gems I hoped were fake. "Or were you trying to imitate her, *la comadrona*?"

He moved his hand, ran his fingertips along the thin strap of the dress, which displayed my body through its silky knit and made it accessible, available.

"Women's liberation?" I asked. The term was so outmoded it almost made me laugh.

"The feminist revolution she is trying to import from your country."

He took his hand away, leaned back, while a servant uncorked a bottle of white wine, poured it into our glasses. The wine was fruity, delicate, the glass so fragile I was afraid it would shatter between my lips.

"Isn't it based on the idea that men and women are equal in all things?" he asked once the servant had departed. "That they are exactly the same except for their reproductive equipment? Isn't that the idea?"

I shrugged, a gesture he interpreted as assent. He leaned closer.

"The midwife tells these peasant women that they're equal to their men," he said. "But you know that, don't you? You know what is going on there. You have gone there often enough, haven't you?" He touched the décolletage of the dress. "So you must know that she is teaching them they can control their lives once they control their bodies." He swept his fingers back and forth inside its soft curve. "But women cannot control their bodies, can they, Elisabet?" He took away his hand, and my nipples pushed against the fabric. "Aren't their bodies constantly betraying them?"

He glanced at me, as if he'd proved his point about betrayal. I looked into his eyes, thinking he ought to be warned against placing so much significance on the apparent betrayals of erectile tissue. But I decided not to tell him.

Still I felt compelled to correct him about Mary Healy, to tell him that Mary Healy was not trying to launch a feminist revolution; that, in fact, her ideas were broader, more comprehensive, that her goals had little to do with gender.

"She's personally a feminist, but El Centro de Cambio y Creatividad isn't about women's liberation. It's about faith, about spiritual liberation."

"Spiritual liberation?" He leaned back, picked up his glass, swirled the wine in it, drank. "Tell me about spiritual liberation."

"It means a change in your way of thinking so radical it frees you." I picked up my own glass and emptied it, watched him pour me more. "She's helping these women to free themselves from the self-defeating patterns of their history."

"Self-defeating patterns?"

He seemed to lose interest in my words. He reached over and slipped a strap off my shoulder.

"She's teaching the Gospel, really," I went on, determined to make my point. He looked me over as if I were a sculpture and he the artist, pleased, for the moment, with his work. He smoothed my hair back from my shoulder, rested his fingers there.

"I mean, she's using it to challenge their traditional ways of thinking. Like finding proof in the Gospel that God doesn't want these women to be so poor and miserable."

He reached into the dress, cupped my breast, rubbed the nipple with his thumb. I looked away. Shadows all around made it seem as though we were floating in the dark.

"The point is to open up their minds, that's the liberation part."

The motion of his thumb sent hot little impulses rippling through my belly to my groin, but I didn't move. I wanted him to pay attention, wanted him to hear me.

"Is that her point?"

"Yes." I turned to look at him. "So that they won't be passive collaborators in their own oppression anymore."

I wasn't sure he heard me. He seemed enchanted by me or by my breast. I said his name, Víctor, and he let it go, rearranged the dress so I was covered once again. He took my hand, brought it to his lips, kissed my fingertips.

"The Center for Change and Creativity is about faith," I repeated. "It's about a prophetic faith, which has almost nothing to do with traditional Catholicism, less to do with communism."

"Prophetic faith?"

He held my wrist, traced the blue veins with a finger, watched me from beneath his lowered lids.

"These women have a vision of the future, of the Kingdom, the Promised Land, which they believe was prophesied in Scripture. It's a place where their children will have food, health care, education. A place where everyone will live in dignity."

"Obviously, darling, this promised land is here on earth. Isn't it here, in Bellavista?"

"Obviously, their faith critiques the way things are here. They want to change the existing order. They . . ."

I picked up my glass and drank, saw him watching me. He didn't smile or speak. Maybe that's why I heard my own words for a long time. Around us, the black space seemed like a betrayal. I felt myself falling through it and heard my own words echoing.

"Your skin is lovely." He caressed the inside of my arm. "So fine and delicate."

"It's spiritual," I heard myself say. "It's just words. All they do is talk."

"You shouldn't ever sun yourself," he went on, ignoring me. "Bright sunlight would damage your skin so quickly. Don't ever sunbathe. Promise me."

I don't know what happened right after that, what we said to each other. I only know that Mary disappeared. She was swallowed up in the black space. Afterward, we sat there for such a long time that the borders between me and the rest of the world began to blur, and my fine, delicate skin began to feel as flimsy as the red dress.

During the time we sat there, I don't think he ever stopped touching me. He always had a hand on me, on my hip, rib, throat, or shoulder. It felt as if he were reaching into me, not staying on the surface, until, at last, whatever place he touched seemed to become intense, a focus of heat and energy. I wondered if when he took his hand away I would be weakened, maybe lifeless.

Music, Liszt rhapsodies, Beethoven symphonies, played softly in the background, but I couldn't locate the speakers, so the music seemed to have no source. The servant, too, seemed to come from noplace. Some time or other, it began to seem like another movie with an absurdly dramatic soundtrack: the servant appearing in his dark suit to uncork wine, pour it into our glasses, sometimes changing the glasses; the servant appearing with oysters, shrimp, salad, bread, cheeses, fruit; the servant appearing without speaking, clearing plates away. I couldn't tell where he was coming from or where he went, but the rhythm of his appearances and departures reflected perfectly our needs, or, I should say, Rivas Valdez's needs, because I wasn't hungry. Yet Rivas Valdez made me eat. He fed me from a silver fork, his fingers putting the choicest morsels to my lips, coaxing until I took them, chewed and swallowed. Once he gave me fruit, melon or pineapple, his fingers dripping with the juice, and he held them to my lips until I licked the juice away.

The air was warm and very sweet, sultry, but now and then, cooler, pungent air would blow in from the water. The house, he told me at some point, belonged to his brother, or would have had his brother lived. It was nearly two hundred years old, the last remnant of the Rivas family fortune. He told me he'd grown up there, but hadn't lived there after marrying. Rather, he'd lived with his family in a town house in Libertad, a home now emptied of its treasures and boarded up against Bellavista's continuing disasters. He lamented the loss of certain treasures. He seemed amused, and in that context it was amusing, when I repeated something Mary had said, that the weight of their possessions numb the rich.

"She says the poor feel their poverty like shackles and chains but that the rich feel almost nothing."

"Do you think it's true?"

"I wouldn't know."

"Would you like to?" he asked as his hand fell into my lap. Mary emerged then from the black space, and she stayed there, a spirit from the dark, prodding me to say more.

"She says the cries of the poor will awaken the wealthy to the demands of the Gospel."

The soft fabric of my skirt gave way to his fingers.

"The cries of the poor?"

"Do you ever hear them, Víctor, the cries of the poor?"

"*Pobrecita,*" he answered, and leaned over to kiss me.

*   *   *

Later, not much later, we were upstairs in the peacock-colored chamber and I'd taken off my clothes for him, undressing for him the way he wanted me to. And now I think what happened after that might not have happened if we'd gone upstairs immediately, as soon as he said *"Pobrecita"* and leaned over to kiss me. If we had left the table right then, I think the rest of the night would have turned out better. But we didn't go upstairs then, because he stopped kissing me abruptly. He pulled away from me as though he'd just remembered something urgent.

"Elisabet, *mi amor*, tell me why you've never married, never had children."

I couldn't speak.

"Why?" His face was close to mine and his eyes so strange that I thought if I blew out the candles, they'd glow like a cat's.

"Women here are grandmothers by the time they're in their early thirties. Your age," he went on softly. "It is a source of pride, evidence of their fecundity, their femaleness."

I leaned away from him, saw my snifter of liqueur on the table not far from me. I picked it up, finished it in one gulp, concentrating on the Beethoven.

"Elisabet, why didn't you marry?"

"Why didn't I marry?"

I repeated his question, confounded out of my stupor by the verb tense, the simple past, which seemed to foreclose on any possibility that I would ever marry, something I had not yet considered.

"I'm sure you haven't lacked for opportunities."

I saw the decanter of liqueur and reached for it, but he got it first, moved it away from me.

"I was too busy working. I had to work."

"You don't have to work. You could stop."

Something in his tone made me avoid his eyes.

"No, I can't stop. I have to work. My mother isn't well. I support her."

"Don't you want children? You could have them anyway. That seems to be quite the Yankee fashion these days, isn't it? Unmarried women having children. After all, isn't motherhood the natural fulfillment of a woman?"

"How would I know?"

I laughed, reached across the table to pick a rose out of the bowl. I saw its thorns had been clipped off; there were pale spots on the green stem where they'd been.

"Can a woman be fulfilled without children?"

He took my chin into his hand, turned me to face him. He took the rose out of my hand and said a woman must experience a particular satisfaction through the achievement of her gender's life-giving potential, mustn't she? He dropped the rose back into the bowl, watched me for a response I couldn't give.

I looked away, wishing he'd stop talking. I looked up and saw myself, tiny and far away, reflected in the brass globe of the chandelier. Rather, I saw a woman in a red dress who must have been me, although she was not at all familiar. She was broadened and flattened in the globe, with a moon face, a fish mouth, and big doughy breasts. I gazed at her floating there above the table, blurred. I wondered who she was and what she was doing. I was still looking into the globe when I saw his arm slide across the table. His hand opened very slowly, closed around the arm of the woman in the red dress.

"By the way," he asked, "what form of contraception do you use? I've been remiss not asking you before."

I managed to look at him, took in his burnished skin, the gleaming white teeth embellished here and there by gold. We smiled at each other. I was about to reassure him, to tell him I took birth-control pills, when he went on.

"I know you don't use a diaphragm, a cervical cap, those little sponges, or an IUD. You don't use the pill. So what, my love, could it be? Something we haven't heard of yet in our poor underdeveloped country?"

He'd made a rhyme, and I was going to point it out to him. Then I wondered how he knew I didn't use the pill, my alibi, but decided not to ask. I realized I didn't want an answer. His hand slid up to my throat and out to my chin, which he squeezed between his fingers. Still he smiled.

"What is the solution to this mystery, darling Elisabet?"

He turned my face this way and that as though to see it better. I watched him watching, feeling flames licking at my face.

"An accidental conception would be disastrous, wouldn't it? Isn't it something we should avoid very carefully?"

His eyes attached themselves to me like the electronic eyes of the ultrasonic monitor, but there wasn't any hum, no sound at all as they penetrated skin, muscle, and bone to find the feathery black spot, the shriveled place. Against the pain of his search, drops of sweat sprang from my pores. Soon after I felt them, he ran his fingers across my chin, my upper lip, wiping them away. He looked at his moist fingers.

"Did something happen to you? Some accident?" He picked up his liqueur, frowned as he sipped. "Or were you born that way?"

What way? I almost asked but didn't. I looked around the table, looked for something, I didn't know what. I kept thinking there must be something to take hold of, something that would make his words go away. I picked up a fork and dropped it, poked my fingers through the lace cloth, toyed with the crystal stem of the liqueur glass. I raised it to my mouth, thinking the liqueur might wash away the blockage in my throat. I was surprised to see my glass was empty.

"It's not important," I heard him say at last. "You don't have to answer." When I looked at him, his face was luminous, suffused with what I thought was joy. He took my hand, kissed it. "It's a flaw that makes you perfect," he said after a time. "What an exquisite irony."

Later, upstairs, there wasn't any music, only the rhapsodic thrashing of the ocean. But by the time we got there, he'd lost his luminous veneer. He was restless, and he paced the room speaking Spanish, which confused me and turned him into a stranger. He kept calling me *mi muñequita*, my little doll, as though he'd forgotten my name or forgotten who I was. I was afraid he had. This fear billowed around me, and I felt endangered, as though I had, or would soon, lose myself. I watched him rove the room, but couldn't guess what he was after.

At last he sat in a chair with a very high back, carved arms, clawed feet. He slouched into it, low on his spine, his legs apart, his head to one side. His laser eyes were cool and penetrating as I struggled out of the red dress. I found myself shivering even though the room was warm. I thought I must be in a ritual, a ceremony whose significance I didn't understand. Sometimes I glimpsed myself in the mirror, more often I watched him watching. He seemed to be looking through me, an idea that unnerved me. And he seemed to see that I was maimed, mutilated. I could actually see what he was thinking: that I was a joke, a sexual mutant, a woman incapable of achieving her gender's life-giving potential.

My flaw must have made him angry, because he was an angry stranger when he came to me and kissed me, cool and mechanical as he stroked my fragile skin, touched me between my legs. He touched me there until he'd stroked my craving, and then he stopped. He held my face in his hands and gazed at me. I told him what I wanted, whispered what I wanted him to do.

"Whore," he answered, and he dug his fingers into my cheeks, pulled to lacerate me. I heard the ocean, wished it would flood the room, sweep me away. I was trapped between him and the bed while ruts of flame consumed my face. It was hard to look at him, but finally I managed. He looked back, kept his eyes on mine as his fingers dug into the soft skin of my throat just above my breastbone. When he raked his hand down my chest, his manicured nails scratched like claws. When I tried to pull away, he slapped my face, then caught me on the rebound with his other hand. I would have fallen except he grabbed my arms, held them behind me. I followed his eyes to my chest, where red welts tracked his fingers' path. "You are a perfect whore, you know," he said. "Spayed, the way a whore should be."

By then my body was vibrating and I couldn't find a way to stop it. I kept hearing a siren, a high-pitched siren in my head that seemed to signal hazards befallen someone else. "What was it you said you wanted?" he asked. I shook my head no because I couldn't answer. "Tell me what you want," he demanded, and again I couldn't answer. He reached for something on the bedside table, the diamond-studded key ring. It glittered in the light, and I thought it was the diamonds. But when he held it closer, I saw the blade, silver, with a fine edge like a scalpel. His hand was absolutely still when he lowered it, put the blade against my throat. "Now, what did you say you wanted, whore?" he repeated. He made me say it again, what I'd said before. He lowered the blade, made a small slit in my breast. Blood trickled out. We watched the red drops tremble there, near the nipple that would never flow with milk. Then he cursed, muttering words I didn't understand. He threw the key ring across the room. I heard its muted thud but didn't see where it landed. He embraced me, pushing me onto the bed. He kissed my hair, my face, my stomach. I felt his urgency, his heat, though the siren did not stop. Maybe I was crying, because my nose was running, and I was sniffling to stop it, but couldn't. I cried the whole time he held me, telling me that I was lovely, beautiful, and that he was so sorry for what he'd just done, for what he'd said. Somehow he ended up holding my foot. He stroked the sole, the blue veins near my ankle. He kept saying my name, Elisabet. He kept telling me he hadn't meant what he said; that he hadn't meant to hurt me, not like that. He hoped his cruelty hadn't ruined everything. For he'd wanted to do something special, and he would, still, if I let him. He wanted, he said, to take me to a place I'd never been before, a place where I would find myself, where he would give me the gift of myself. *Coraje.* Courage, he said. Did I have the courage to go there, to find out who I was?

His words were soft and puffy. They sounded far away, and I was having trouble concentrating, having trouble holding the words together long enough to understand them. They seemed to gather above us like a cloud, but I couldn't find the sense of them. Then I glanced at his face and saw his eyes were radiating light. The light seemed to be flooding all around me. I began to feel its warmth, the rapture. He supposed it was a matter of faith, not prophetic faith, but a purer sort, faith in him. Trust. Could I give myself to him?

There was something on the bed close to his thigh, dark cords, coiled like shiny serpents. I didn't know what they were, couldn't seem to get them into focus. What I kept watching was my foot and his fingers massaging it. I began to understand what he was saying. I must have understood what he was saying, because I heard myself telling him I didn't want to be hurt, that I hated pain.

What do you know about pain? he asked me. How do you know what pain is? How? he repeated, and his exhalation softly enveloped me. I didn't have an answer.

By then both of us were looking at my foot, watching it intently, as if, at any moment, my foot might manifest a meaning. It remained mute for a long time, so long I decided it belonged to someone else, the once-familiar foot with its ridge of callus along the metatarsal. Finally, this foot arched against his fingers, pointed like a dancer's as it pressed into his groin. The dark cord flashed, uncoiling, and he began to take me where I did not want to go.

U.S. EMBASSY ATTACKED; TERRORISTS ESCAPE

by Elizabeth M. Guerrera
Herald-Sun Staff Writer

LIBERTAD, BELLAVISTA—Leftist terrorists commandeered a fleet of city buses here yesterday and drove them through this devastated capital firing machine guns and rocket-propelled grenades at police stations, government offices, and the Central Military Command building. The orgy of violence injured dozens and caused an estimated $2 million in damage before the terrorists disappeared, leaving the city workday at a standstill.

The U.S. embassy complex, located on the outskirts of the city, was also fired upon by unknown assailants in a city bus, said an embassy spokesman.

According to a government official, several remote military barracks and police stations were also firebombed. Despite extensive damage to government buildings, there were no known injuries during those early-morning attacks, he said.

Defense Minister Víctor Rivas Valdez called the incidents "a coordinated and well-executed terrorist strategy" intended to "create chaos and undermine confidence in the government."

Said U.S. Ambassador Richard M. Whitaker, "The attack seems symbolic, a warning that these terrorists are capable of organizing and executing large-scale operations, and of causing serious physical injuries if they choose to."

At the embassy, said Whitaker, Marine guards returned fire from the bus, which immediately turned and drove back toward the city.

Whatever the terrorists were firing, he said, "bounced off this place like BBs off the side of a rhinoceros."

No group has so far claimed responsibility.

CHAPTER EIGHTEEN

ONIA ALVINAS'S BLACK EYES SOMETIMES SEEMED FLAT AND SHALLOW, robbed of depth by the bluish circles under them. Sometimes they were overlaid with a film, which made me wonder if she had vision problems, or if a vitamin deficiency might be gradually destroying her sight. I wondered how she saw well enough to take her pictures and if their constant quality might be a repeated fluke, the result of her Konica's opening magically upon a person or an event at some moment of odd and startling revelation, so that it always seemed to capture, with a steady and efficient hunger, the truth of what was going on.

Her eyes had their milky look that Monday morning when I opened up my hotel-room door to go downstairs for coffee. She was crouched outside on the gallery rifling through her camera bag.

"The embassy won," she announced before she looked up.

"What?" I didn't understand. I was afraid I'd missed a story during my weekend at la Costa de Plata. She stood, shoved into my hands a bunch of glossy news photographs.

"Destroyed the press corps," she continued, moving past me into the room.

"Destroyed?" I was trying to imagine what had happened.

"In the softball game, dummy." She laughed. "The embassy staff beat us, twelve to three. You should have been there. It was great. Everybody got drunk afterward."

When I turned she was standing in the middle of the room squinting at the smoke wriggling up from her cigarette. She glanced around the room, spied an ashtray on the dresser, was stepping toward it when the ash dropped. She shrugged and grinned at me, maybe remembered our first encounter when she'd ground the ash into the carpet. She grabbed the ashtray, threw herself onto my bed, and snuffed out the cigarette.

"Where were you?"

Twin streams of smoke poured from her nostrils.

"Wait till you see what I have," I said, ignoring her question, heading for my desk to get the travel passes Rivas Valdez had signed for me.

"Wait till you see what I have," she mimicked. When I returned, she was stretched out on the bed, her arms beneath her head, her feet crossed at the ankles. I went to her, holding out the papers, touched her cheek with them before she finally took them.

"Why don't you look at what I gave you?" she said, gesturing to the pictures I'd dropped onto the bed.

By then I was accustomed to her habit of shooting, compulsively, anything that moved, scores more pictures than we ever needed, then developing, at her leisure and for her own amusement, the prints that didn't go out with the story.

The group she shoved at me were of the press conference, more than a month old. The print on top showed Rivas Valdez seated behind the dais in his uniform. I was sitting diagonally in front of him in a metal folding chair, surrounded by other reporters. The two of us were in such sharp focus the lines beneath our eyes were visible. Everyone else was blurry. Maybe he'd been answering a question, for his head was turned in my direction.

I brought the photograph to the window in my office for a better look. Sonia had managed to make it seem that we were gazing at one another intimately. Our looks somehow revealed memories of desire spent or renewed desire. I twisted the photograph so the sunlight bounded off it, drabbed out the tones of black and white, but our intense glances did not fade. Nor did his arrogance, which was defined by the angle of his head, the set of his mouth.

I put the photograph facedown on my desk, thinking it was a trick of some kind, more magic from her camera, because I knew we hadn't looked at each other that way. We'd hardly looked at each other at all.

"What's this? A new dress?" I heard her ask, saw her not far from me, though I hadn't heard her walk into the office. "You didn't have enough dresses?"

She grabbed the white dress, which I'd left in its box on an office chair. As she pulled it out and held it up, something shiny fell from the pocket, fell onto the floor, and she reached down to snatch it up.

"What's this?"

She was holding out her hand, and in it was another gem-studded chain, a bracelet. I stared at it dumbfounded, wondering how it had gotten there.

"I don't know."

"Well, don't look now, asshole, but it matches the one around your neck."

I couldn't stop my fingers from flying to my throat. I'd forgotten the chain was there.

"Who's your friend? Your rich friend?"

She was tossing the bracelet into the air, catching it in her palm, tossing it up again. Between the tosses she'd look into my eyes, and the film would clear from hers.

"Anybody I know?"

"What difference does it make?" I heard myself say, saw her proffering the bracelet. It dangled from the end of her index finger.

"Lots. Depending on who it is. I mean, Jack Travis, the poor sucker, has a thing for you. He can't stop talking about you. But obviously your material tastes run beyond the means of our illustrious little press corps."

She laughed, dropped the bracelet onto the table, reached up to touch my cheek.

"What happened to your face?"

"Nothing. Nothing happened to my face."

"What are the marks, then?"

She fingered the scratches, which I'd covered with liquid makeup and a concealing crayon. I brushed her hand away.

"It looks like you got mauled."

"That's ridiculous." I laughed. "It's nothing. Something must have bitten me when I was sleeping."

"Right," she said, shaking her head. "A mysterious creature with an eye for symmetry gets you while you're sleeping. Gives you a matching set of scratches, one on each cheek."

"No, it probably just bit me," I went on, knowing how stupid I sounded. "I did the scratching myself. In my sleep."

"Are all of these mysteries by any chance related?" she asked, pulling from her pocket the travel papers.

"Of course not," I said, and grabbed them from her hand.

"Why don't you wear the bracelet? It's a pretty bracelet."

She picked it up, turned to me, and smiled.

"You earned it, didn't you?"

"Why don't you mind your own business?"

"Bet you worked hard for it. On your back. Or maybe on your knees." She laughed. "The spoils of war."

I grabbed the bracelet, dropped it on top of the travel papers.

"What's your problem? What do you care?"

She shrugged. Again she picked up the photograph of Rivas Valdez. I expected her to ask if I was sleeping with him, but she didn't. She backed off just a little and engaged me in a minuet of glances. We kept looking at the picture and then at each other.

"You think you're peering into souls when you're only taking pictures," I said after a while.

"Not really." She turned the picture this way and that. "I'm only a technician. I just press the button that opens the shutter. It doesn't make judgments about what it sees, and neither do I."

"Well, this means absolutely nothing."

"Maybe not."

She dropped it onto the desk, walked into the other room, came back with her tobacco and rolling papers, sat in my desk chair. She poured a ridge of tobacco onto a square of paper, spun a cigarette, and tongued the gummed edge of the paper.

"But you know, Lizzie," she said at last, lighting up with her Bic, "I can't help being curious. Curious about the dress, the jewelry, the scratches, the travel papers. Curious about how you got them."

"As I said before, it's not your business. None of it concerns you."

She inhaled deeply, exhaled through her nostrils.

"Well, the travel papers are my business."

Again she picked them up.

"I'm curious about what you did to get them on a weekend when nobody knows where you were."

She waved the papers like a fan. Splotches of pink had appeared on her cheeks, and her eyes glistened.

"I asked for them. That's all I did."

She laughed, shook her head. "That must have been some question. Because I know at least a dozen reporters and photographers in this hotel alone who'd kill to get their hands on these."

"Killing wasn't necessary," I told her, but she interrupted, said, "You asked the man himself, didn't you, Vic the Prick?"

I turned away, because I had trouble lying outright. In the silence afterward, I remembered how, at some point during the weekend, we'd walked outside, across the lawn. It was night and we stood against the stone wall at the far edge of the property. He stood behind me, his hands on the wall on either side of me, and I remembered feeling safe, contained. I remembered looking down into the black water which heaved against the rocks below. I'm almost certain it was then that I'd asked him for the documents, although I don't remember exactly what he said, what I answered. My memories of that night were vivid but fragmented, like a slashed tapestry. The chauffeur had handed me an envelope containing the papers when he'd left me at the airport Sunday night.

"Do you want to go with me or not?"

I looked around, found Sonia back on my bed rolling yet another cigarette.

"Where? Where do you think you want to go?"

I told her of my half-formed plan to go back to the Rivera plantation, to the New Jerusalem Cooperative, for a follow-up on land reform. It was the excuse I'd used with Rivas Valdez, who had approved of the idea, had even given me the names of the agricultural advisers from the Agency for International Development.

"It ought to be fun to talk to these AID guys and meet the co-op leaders."

She shrugged, watched me through lowered lids.

"But where I really want to go is into the war zone. I know somebody who might be able to help us find a way there."

She sucked on her cigarette so its red eye glowed.

"The war zone," she said at last. "It's only sixty-five or seventy miles away, but it might as well be on the moon. Most of the bridges and train tracks have been blown up. And it's surrounded by military installations."

"Well, Mary Healy has a contract with a relief agency to run supplies and medicines up to Sangre de Cristo once a month. Which is close to the combat area. So it's got to be accessible. Somehow."

She shrugged, asked what I expected to find. I said I didn't know, then told her about the refugees at Nuestra Señora del Refugio.

"There are refugees all over the country," said Sonia. "What's the big deal?"

"Mary said she'd show me if I went there."

By then I was sitting on the bed beside her, holding a folded map of Bellavista. Through the haze of her cigarette smoke, I saw her finger find the Ixtapanga airport, then mark the route to Sangre de Cristo and the Rivera plantation.

"If we can get to Ixtapanga airport, it's not that far between any of these places," she said. "Maybe fifteen or twenty kilometers from Sangre to the plantation. But the area is probably crawling with armed types— *policía*, *guardia*, guerrillas."

"From what I can tell, we're not geographically restricted by these passes. So it wouldn't be illegal for us to move around."

"Yes, but do you want to get picked up in one of those remote hamlets? They'd pop your eyeballs out and shove them up your cunt before your almighty general had time to bail you out."

She grinned.

"That's if you're lucky. And what about me? I'm snack food for the vultures the minute I get picked up." Sonia dragged hard on the cigarette and pulled the map close for a better look. She smoked and looked for a long time. "You know, it's possible," she said at last, looking up and squinting. "The life I lose may be my own. But what the hell, Miss America? Why not?"

She stared until I looked away.

PRESIDENT: MORE AID FOR BELLAVISTA
from the Associated Press

WASHINGTON, D.C.—The President will ask Congressional leaders to give $55 million more in immediate military aid to Bellavista, a White House aide said yesterday.

The aide said the President will make his request at a breakfast meeting Friday before he leaves for Europe on a 10-day visit.

Congress recently approved an aid package of $200 million for the troubled Central American nation. The aide said the President was asking for more money in response to a recent terrorist incident in which the U.S. embassy in Libertad was fired upon and to a recent rebel attack upon an air base in which American aircraft were damaged.

If Congress rejects his plea, the President could redirect to Bellavista some foreign security assistance now earmarked for other countries, said the aide. This would permit him to bypass the full House and Senate and go only to their Appropriations subcommittees, where a supporting vote would be more likely.

"One way or another, the United States is going to put another $55 million into Bellavista," said the Secretary of Defense. "The sooner the better in my opinion."

PART TWO

La Zona de Combate

CHAPTER NINETEEN

*I*N THE MORNING, CIRCLES OF LIGHT WHIRLED OFF THE COCKPIT GLASS
and the wingtips of the Dragonflies as they swooped in pairs toward
the black slopes of the volcano. Dragonflies. Cessna A-37s. Slow,
low-flying planes designed for use on undefended targets. The planes
looked motionless. Then rags of orange flame burst from their bellies,
streaked the ice-blue sky, and evaporated. The sputter of the Gatling
guns echoed like an afterthought.

"Christ is with us," Mary Healy murmured as the Dragonflies disappeared into the dazzle on the far side of the volcano. Their drone stayed
with us for a long time. I wondered who she meant by "us," but could
not seem to ask her.

We were sitting on a stone ledge that edged the plateau of an adjacent mountain. Soon, with the help of two *sanitarios*, rural health-care workers, Mary would hold a clinic, examining pregnant women and ailing children, at the one-room adobe hospital across the dusty clearing from us.

"You'll see for yourself when the clinic opens," she promised.

Our distance from the aerial assault was impossible to judge. The tiny spotter plane had flown directly over us. It kept moving to the northeast, paused to drop incendiary rockets over the unseen target. Shimmering plumes of phosphorus cascaded through the sky. Then Dragonflies appeared and fired into them.

Beyond our ledge, the mountainside fell like a green curtain, sheer and gently rippled. A confusion of steep-angled slopes, black and darker shades of green, reached up to touch the curtain's hem, fell back into a twisting flume. The water of the flume was a white froth, distant as a childhood memory. It seemed as if we were at the world's edge, might float away at any moment.

"I'm so glad you came," Mary said, clasping my kneecap, anchoring me to the earth. Her fingers pressed the bone. My leg twitched against her touch. Her hand flew up, fell back into the space between her thighs. She watched it as though it might belong to someone else. The color deepened in her cheeks.

"Well, Lizzie, I am glad you risked coming up here," she repeated. Her hand took off again, banked in a wide arc toward the adobe huts, the ragged tents, and lean-tos made of sticks and plastic bags that huddled on the plateau in the protection of another rising slope. "It means a lot."

I didn't know what it meant, what it could possibly mean, my visit to the war zone, to the refugee camp called Mesa Verde, a place that defied meaning.

"Can you believe that Libertad is only, what? Seventy miles away?" Her voice droned like the Dragonflies, faraway yet insistent. "If we could fly, we'd be there in a few minutes."

The day before, Sonia and I had flown the other way, from Libertad to Sangre de Cristo, the first leg of our trip into the mountains, where the only flights were those of military aircraft. The six-seater had rattled when it lifted off, had dipped and skidded through the sky. Right away, the plane tilted sharply and I saw, thousands of feet below, green magma swirling in the mouth of an old volcano. Then it was gone; we were above the clouds. It felt as if we were breaking free, leaving everything behind.

"Seems like a lifetime since I've been there."

I didn't answer. Lack of sleep, the night-long climb, the thin air of those altitudes, had emptied out my head, made me feel weightless, unencumbered. It wasn't yet noon, but I'd already harvested material for several stories. I'd seen villages and granaries razed, cornfields and orchards burned to a black stubble by gasoline bombs and what the guerrillas would insist was napalm; wells poisoned with the carcasses of livestock shot by soldiers on foot patrol. I'd seen that the government was systematically destroying the food and water supply of thousands of noncombatants who still lived in the combat area.

Hordes of these ragged refugees had been our guides, leading me and Sonia along hidden paths to ruined wells, to high places where scorched acres stretched over slopes below like ragged cloths set in the sun to dry.

Among our guides had been a boy named Licho, maybe ten years old. His arms ended just below the shoulder. *"El fuego blanco,"* he'd announced when my glance caressed the grotesque stubs. White fire. White phosphorus. Death that billows from the bellies of airplanes, he'd said. Its glowing ash was strewn across the countryside, had marked our trail to Mesa Verde, glistening in the dark like frost. *Por un golpe de suerte*, by a stroke of good luck, Licho told me, I lost only my arms. Others had not been so lucky. The week before, a woman and her four children had been hit while picking corn in the tiny plot not far from their tent. The spotter plane had dropped its phosphorus, but no Dragonflies had followed. There had been no aerial assault. Only the woman and her children were incinerated. Licho brought us to the site, a patch of blackened earth laced with luminous ash, a *milpa* transformed into a graveyard. The crosses were woven from dried husks. *Por un golpe de suerte*, Licho repeated, I only lost my arms.

"Today's the first day of the rest of your life," Mary had hummed to me before dawn, shaking my hammock, tumbling me from an exhausting sleep in which I'd been climbing in the dark, stumbling up a steep path. With every step I took I thought I'd fall into a void. The sky had been spangled with the tracers and exploding shells of random fire, the earth glowing with phosphorescent residue. "Come on," she'd urged, pulling my arm. I let go of the dream. Sonia, who'd slept among children on the floor, was grumbling because Mary wouldn't let her light a cigarette. Then we were outside in the cool dark and a stolid woman gave us breakfast, a small sweet orange, a bitter drink made from chicory.

The sun was glimmering by the time we reached Mesa Verde, Distrito Uno, another camp perhaps two miles away. A Danish relief worker and a French priest were waiting for us, rushed us through the camp gathering up peasants—old men, mothers and children—who were waking to their morning chores. They swarmed around us, carried us off to the Río Luciente, the Shining River, one of Bellavista's borders. The camp went by in a blur, an endless grid of dark ramshackle tents, fetid even in the cool morning. Then we were at a bend in the shining river.

"Women and children were trying to make their way across into Costa Negra," said the relief worker, pointing to the rushing water. He was tall and gaunt. "The men had stretched a rope across, because nobody could swim. Dozens were clinging to this rope in the water. The gunships hovered right above them, firing. We could see the faces of the pilot and a North American adviser."

The crowd parted, and before us, at the water's edge, was a monument of stones adorned with flowers, wooden crosses.

"Maybe two thousand peasants, *campesinos* and their families, were caught in this hammer-and-anvil operation," said the young, bespectacled priest. His Roman collar was immaculate, his black clothes neatly pressed. "They were pushed from their own villages up here to the water. They were civilians, noncombatants. They had no defense."

Then he and an old man began removing stones. Neat stacks of skulls and bones filled the sepulcher. They were many shapes and sizes, placed according to their size. The smallest were in front, the skulls no bigger than my hand.

"That day so many vultures were picking at the bodies in the water, you could cross the river on their backs. . . ."

"The water looked like a black carpet. . . ."

"The river still spits bones. We gather them each morning. . . ."

By the time we left, we'd interviewed and photographed witnesses and survivors. I had everything I needed for a story—dates and times, a chronology, identified sources, pictures of the sepulcher, the river, even the identifying numbers on the helicopters. Gathering the facts had been simple, like picking up bones along the riverbank: I had the who, what, where, when, and how of the government's killing of civilians. I didn't have the why. I figured I could try for that from the ministry of defense, from the State Department, when I got back to Libertad.

"Sonia's just a little bit crazy, isn't she?"

Mary's low chuckle roused me, turned me to her. Her crucifix protruded from her fist. She tapped it against her chin.

"You mean the Huey?"

She nodded, grinning. One of the big gunships had shrieked out of the sky just before we'd reached the camp on our return. Its heraldic chop sent the children scattering and screaming, the adults off in a panicked effort to retrieve and protect them. The Huey laid a line of fire in the brush along our path, churning up a hysteria of dust and leaves as it scraped the tops of trees.

"She says the same thing about you," I went on, seeing Sonia standing with shells exploding all around to shoot her pictures. "Calls you a fucking crazy *gringa*."

"Fucking crazy, huh?"

I nodded, heard more of the low chuckle.

"But at least I don't chase after Hueys when their M-60s are blazing."

I laughed myself, remembering how Sonia had gone after the departing copter. "*¡Pavos!*" she'd shouted once it was clear nobody had been hit. Turkeys. "How could you miss us? Are you blind?"

They weren't trying to hit us, only to scare us, an old man had told her.

"Do you think you'll write the story?"

By then, half a dozen women, their bellies swollen in various stages of pregnancy, had gathered near the clinic door. They waved to Mary, called out greetings.

"Which one?"

"The slaughter at Río Luciente."

I nodded yes.

"Do you think they'll print it?"

"Sure. They can't not print it. It's a great story. My editors can't resist sources like the priest and that relief worker."

"It's gonna blow out the embassy. Whitaker will have a heart attack."

I shrugged.

"I'll have to talk to him. That's why I can't file till I get back to Libertad."

I imagined Whitaker's rosy complexion, his icy eyes, and wondered how and if they'd change when I questioned him.

"We'll have to make sure you make it back alive," I heard her say. Her burst of ragged laughter made me think of Gatling guns.

The rest of that day I wandered like the dispossessed, but Sonia seemed to be searching. The radiant mountain light stung my eyes, made me squint, made all boundaries and the horizon shimmer, but Sonia had abandoned her dark glasses. Whenever I looked at her, I saw her eyes instead of a distorted reflection of myself, and I saw how the light had changed them, making her black irises seem like wells that had no bottoms. All day her eyes would fasten onto mine and not let go, as if she might be trying to suck out my thoughts and feelings.

Mostly we stayed together, following the homeless peasants who'd appointed themselves to be our guides. But sometimes she'd go off, and then I'd track her through parched alleys, find her talking with someone or other, crouched against a tree, slouched in the shadow of a tent, sharing cigarettes and gum. "Sorry, Elizabeth," she'd call out with a wave, not being sorry. "These are my people, ¿entiendes?"

And I'd nod, yes, of course I knew, but in fact I didn't know I knew, had always known, not till later.

At some point, we stopped at the clinic, where Mary and the *sanitarios*, a middle-aged woman and a teenager who'd lost his left foot to a mine, tended patients with stethoscopes, thermometers, and folk wisdoms. They had no running water, virtually no medicines. Their limited resources were mobilized against a seemingly limitless variety of ailments —anemia, asthma, epilepsy, dysentery, parasites, arthritis, malnutrition, dehydration, malaria, dengue fever, bronchitis, strep throat, toothache.

Sonia and I were asked to stay outside, where the line of patients, at least one hundred of them, meandered far back, melting into sunlight. Dark gleaming women, their hair braided or pulled back into tight buns, sat bunched together on woven blankets for the long wait, bent over needlework or weaving. Children played around them and drowsed against their thighs; infants suckled their breasts. At the sight of us, the women began to laugh and preen, calling out, exuberantly competing to have themselves and their children consecrated by the camera. Sonia tried to oblige them.

Outside the clinic doorway, where a bright blue tarp had been stretched on poles for shade, the river of misery was dammed up. Why, I asked a group of women there, had they chosen to stay in the combat area after the government evacuations?

¿Evacuaciones? ¿Evacuaciones? ¿Cuáles evacuaciones? the women answered with a chorus of titters and guffaws.

My question and their response rippled like a crosscurrent through the river, where it turned into a joke about bowel movements.

"The only evacuations have been done by landowners," someone else cried. "Not surprising, since they're full of shit."

"There were no government evacuations," one woman said after the laughter. "The soldiers ran us off our land. They drove us from our homes. They pushed us into another line of soldiers who were waiting on a higher slope. They caught us in their fire."

Not long after that, the old man named Quique, who'd appointed himself our chief guide, brought us to the camp's *centro de comunicaciones*, the communications center, which turned out to be a field radio hidden in a thicket on a precariously steep slope. Its powerful antennas were positioned to pick up transmissions from the government's propaganda station, from the guerrillas' clandestine station, Radio Venceremos, and from the military encampments and guerrilla bases on the nearby slopes.

An adolescent girl, sitting with another old man close to the primitive-looking metal box, explained that she and others monitored the radio, in shifts of two, twenty-four hours every day. Radio Venceremos, she said, constantly switched frequencies in order to avoid detection, but offered vital information about all contacts between *el frente* and the government.

"*Si tenemos muy buena suerte, oyéramos a los yanquis,*" said Quique. If we are very lucky, we will hear the Yankees.

"*¿Eso se sucede frecuentemente?*" Does it happen often?

Quique shrugged and grinned. He had half a dozen teeth, all of them black stumps. "Once or twice we've heard the imperialist cowards when they are at their headquarters transmitting to soldiers in the field," he said.

Such a story, the story of Yankee soldiers transmitting to Bellavistan troops in the field, would elevate me in a single bound to the top tier of international journalists, an idea that released a surge of adrenaline, renewed my energy.

Sonia, however, had stretched out, was rolling herself a cigarette. "It's your watch, Lizzie," she murmured, stifling a yawn. She didn't seem to understand that if we heard North American officers involved in a Bellavistan military operation, the story would ignite a media conflagration.

"There's nothing visual about this, is there?" she asked, not looking for an answer. She tossed the papers and tobacco to Quique, settled herself into the grass. Soon all of them were smoking, lounging.

I remained hyperalert, sitting very close to the receiver with my pencil and notebook, my tape recorder ready. Then, in an exhausted stupor, I watched the sun move across the sky, watched shadows moving through our alcove. Sonia had fallen asleep. I tried not to think about fatigue or hunger, instead forced myself to concentrate on the babble of distant voices, the fragments of music, coming from the radio. They were confounded by the buzzing of nearby insects, the drone of distant aircraft.

After a couple of hours, with Sonia snoring nearby, my heart-quivering excitement relaxed into tense exhaustion. By then, my belly was so empty, it felt as if it were sticking to my back. I kept sucking on blades of grass to keep my mouth from drying up. I was thinking about moving on, about waking Sonia so we could work some other aspect of the story, when a single voice pushed through the babble, emerging from the electronic mists like a phantom from prehistory.

"Mesa Verde es un nido de subversivos."

The elegant voice sent an unruly impulse careening through my nerves. Its familiarity stunned me, even though I knew his was a voice I might expect to hear issuing important government propaganda: Mesa Verde is a nest of subversives.

"¡Oiga!"

Quique's urgent command to listen was superfluous. The radio's volume had increased until the phantom voice was booming.

"Vamos a destruir todo los nidos de los subversivos."

Sonia sat straight up, eyed me as if she wanted to dredge up the contents of my soul. I looked away, rubbed my neck. A weird current skittered up and down my spine.

We are going to destroy all the nests of the subversives.

"El general Víctor Rivas Valdez," Quique declared, grinning as though he'd discovered and produced the voice himself.

The general went on to say that the so-called refugee camps of Mesa Verde were no such thing, were, rather, base camps for *el frente*, training grounds for new guerrillas. A military victory would be within reach, he said, if guerrilla nests like Mesa Verde could be exterminated.

For that reason, he said, the army was now prepared to launch an offensive against rebel strongholds on Mesa Verde. Then his voice was hoarsened by more static, by an electrical disturbance. Frantically the old man and the girl spun the dials, repositioned the antennas, but the phantom had returned to the mists.

Yet his voice had changed them, replaced their quiet patience with tense fear.

"This is the first time that the government has dared to target our camps," said the girl. "So far they've made some show of respecting our status as refugees."

I'd just asked them how they'd protect themselves and when the offensive might begin when the monitors picked up Radio Venceremos and we all turned to listen.

The broadcast was dense with information about *el frente*'s activities, difficult to understand because of the speed with which the newscaster spoke. She gave the locations of military units operating in the area; said negotiations with international relief agencies were continuing in the effort to airlift food and medical supplies.

But her big news was that government troops were expected to move against Mesa Verde within forty-eight hours. Mesa Verde, Distrito Cuatro, was considered the most vulnerable, because it was farthest from the border, closest to government encampments. She said *correos*, runners from *el frente*, would be arriving soon with instructions for an evacuation. She urged residents of the camps to be ready when they came.

Then Quique, eager to pass this news on through the camp's internal communication system, led Sonia and me back to the main part of the camp. Along the way I suffered, painfully, the loss of my Yankee-voices story and the Pulitzer Prize I'd fantasized myself into winning. But I also knew that the story of the government offensive, if Sonia and I remained in Mesa Verde when it occurred, would be almost as good. We would be the first journalists to witness and report on the government's actions against civilians.

We'd almost reached the camp when the smell of frying tortillas overwhelmed my senses and reordered my priorities. I wanted food more than any story, and we picked up our pace, believing a meal was close at hand.

By then the sky was streaked orange and purple, shimmering with the light of the descending sun. Smoke from distant cooking fires wafted skyward. I ached to see how far away these fires were.

Then the sound of voices, hundreds of voices, reached us in a rolling surge and echoed in the cool mountain air.

"*Como un venado que ansia por a arroyos que corren, mi alma se ansia a ti, Dios mió.*"

Like a deer that longs for running streams, my soul longs for you, my God.

We saw them when we reached the ridge below, worshipers stretched from the clinic's blue tarpaulin to the stone ledge, streaming out on both sides, kneeling in the alleyways amid the tents, and on the stubble of surrounding slopes. The French priest was saying Mass.

"*¡Qué lindo!*" Sonia murmured, and I agreed that it was beautiful, not knowing if she meant the sound of all those voices or the panorama stretched out below us under the bejeweled sky. Sonia and Quique took off running, wanting to join the Mass. I took my time, then wandered the edges of the crowd in a kind of transcendental state. Later I saw Sonia receiving Communion, and saw Mary Healy giving out Communion with the priest.

We somehow found one another afterward. By then I was so hungry I felt translucent, and the sight and smell of other people's food made my fingers twitch. Mary led us through a horde to the cooking fire and hut of our hostess. We'd barely settled ourselves by the fire when our hostess handed us tortillas as thick and soft as a slice of homemade bread. The red beans on top were spiced with onions and tomato. I hadn't ever tasted anything so wonderful. I'd ravened my way through a second one when the sound of the helicopters reached us. I was certain the government offensive was beginning. Sonia and I jumped out, determined to record every detail. The children, too, ran off screaming, but most adults stayed and scanned the sky.

When the Hueys were almost over us, the refugees began shouting up at them:

"¡No tenemos miedo de usted! ¡Puedes arrojar bombas si te atreves!"

You don't scare us! Bomb us if you dare!

As the helicopters began to swoop and dive, Sonia and I chased them, hoping for a glimpse of whoever was inside, hoping for a glimpse of a Yankee, a Green Beret.

All around us, refugees were shaking their fists and chanting: *"¡El señor nos está mirando!"* The Lord is watching! *"¡Puedes arrojar bombas si te atreves!"*

Then, like a stricken bird, one of the choppers plummeted, sending all of us running. Its noise and wind were apocalyptic as it hovered, trembling, just above the ground. Finally I heard what must have been the grinding of the gears, and it began to rise. Countless white things burst from its doors. Through the twilight, as the chopper ascended, these white things soared over and around us. When one came close enough, I reached up, snatched it, a piece of paper.

"Premios para subversivos," it said in big black letters. *"¡$1,000 para compatriotas! ¡$2,000 para extranjeros!"* Below these words was a cartoon of an army officer handing a bag of cash to a grinning *campesino*.

The sound of laughter soon competed with the copters' chop. Throughout the camp, refugees were joining hands, linking arms, laughing as they danced around their fires under the rain of handbills. The flames shot higher as handbills fed those conflagrations.

"Premios para subversivos," the refugees were singing as they danced. Cash rewards for turning in subversives!

"A thousand bucks for a citizen, two thousand for a foreigner! Jesus!" cried Mary as we gathered up an armful. "That's a year's pay for about a dozen families. About ten years' pay for one." Then she laughed her hoarse laugh and joined the others in their dancing.

CHAPTER TWENTY

I ATE AN ORANGE JUST BEFORE WE WENT TO BED, FIRST SUCKING OUT the juice, then devouring the pulp. There was no water for washing, so the fruit's sticky scent stayed on my fingers. In the hammock, in the dark, I held them to my nose, thinking the tangy perfume might submerge the reek of too many unwashed bodies enclosed in too small a space.

The hammock swayed and wobbled, felt flimsy and precarious. I held one side, afraid the slightest move would flip me out onto those who were sleeping on the floor below. I lay on my side and Mary lay back to back with me. She'd dozed off right away.

Our hammock was suspended from rafters in the ceiling near an opening which served as a window. Mary had insisted I take the window side. Still the rancid human odor was almost overwhelming, and was overlaid with the smells of wood smoke, tortillas, and *frijoles*.

The hut was full of dark shapes, purple shadows, secrets. I was exhausted but still I couldn't sleep. Mosquitoes, moths, other insects thudded gently against the net which our hostess had unfurled around us, proudly, in apparent deference to our foreign nationality. Sonia, ensconced among countless children on the floor, had to do without. Even through its gauze, the moon was radiant, bright as a neon sign.

The moon reminded me of our trek to Mesa Verde, when it had been huge and very close, an orb of malachite suspended right in front of us. It lit the sweeping slopes, the shimmering puddles of phosphoric ash, the shadows of trees that moved with the wind or with our passage and seemed sometimes to be stalking us.

"*La luna es mi guía*," the moon is my guide, said our *correo*, Cobo, not long after we set out. He was pointing to it with his .357 Magnum. Cobo had insisted he was fourteen, but he didn't reach my shoulder. When I saw him for the first time, at our rendezvous point in the woods outside Sangre, the gun protruding from his waistband looked big enough to be a third arm.

Cobo thought of the moon as *un imán*, a magnet. He said he liked to imagine that it was pulling him up the trail, giving him energy, protecting him. For a while, I'd tried to do the same. I kept my eyes on the moon, let its cool rays pull me forward, and I wrapped myself in their shimmering protection. A dozen of us were walking at intervals of about thirty feet, because Cobo said the spaces would reduce casualties from possible sniper attacks, from the mines he said were buried on the trail. I didn't know, hadn't spoken to, most of the others, evidently Taupils, who were dressed like us in dark, sturdy clothing. They kept on going when Cobo left us at Mesa Verde Cuatro. Most carried bulky rucksacks, crates, or packages, and one balanced a wide, flat basket on her head. Before we left, two had set down their burdens before Cobo, unwrapped the cloths around them. When Cobo squatted to examine them, moon-light glimmered on the metal of a large machine gun, on the protective grease of a grenade launcher. Then the carriers rewrapped them, hefted them onto their shoulders, and we were on our way.

For most of the seventeen-mile trip, I seemed to be walking by myself, and my lunar protection quickly proved to be ephemeral. Like a silk shawl in a sudden gust, it blew away when the roaring spit of machine guns, the booms of unfamiliar armaments, exploded the cool silence, began to echo all around us. Red tracers arced through the sky. The ground trembled and the air vibrated. The barrage went on till my heart convulsed, shooting geysers of dark fluid up into my skull. I lost my balance but couldn't even see where I was falling. Then Sonia was beside me, pulling me up, clutching at my arm.

"I'm not getting fucking blown up or blown away all by myself," she cried. Fine tremors rippled through her body to mine. "If I'm going to die, I want company."

From a distance I heard Cobo urging us to keep on going, telling us we shouldn't be afraid. "Not of that, at least," he amended, gesturing toward the tracers. That, he said, was only harassing and interdiction fire, had no specific target.

Its only purpose, he explained, was to harass supporters of *el frente* in Sangre de Cristo and its environs, to interdict the possible movement of guerrillas and matériel from Costa Negra into Bellavista.

Just the month before, he said, the running dog infantry, and its fascist *gringo* advisers, had staked out positions in las Esmeraldas, had set up big guns there, 60mm machine guns, 90mm recoilless rifles, mortars, howitzers. The harassing and interdiction fire went on almost every night, he said.

Had it shown results? I asked, and he said what it had accomplished was to turn the population of Sangre de Cristo virulently against the pig government and its pig Yankee supporters. He spat onto the ground.

"Pero la comadrona," he said, waving the pistol at her tall, gawky form ahead of us. *"La comadrona es una santa. Lo que ella hace es milagrosa."*

She was hardly visible, just a dark form delineated by slivers of moonlight, but her brisk, determined walk made me think about what he'd said, that she was a saint, that her work was miraculous. Then the sight of her turned into a denunciation that slithered through my guts.

What I kept remembering, without wanting to, was how I'd gone to see her at the center, how I'd asked if she could arrange our trip into the combat zone, and how, when she'd hesitated, I'd told her how much I wanted to see the truth, to find it, and to tell it in my stories. What I kept remembering without wanting to was the way her cheek felt against mine when she'd embraced me, when she said she'd always known I'd tell their story.

The memory bound me, trapped me, but I couldn't grapple with its meaning. Instead I thought about how much I hated being with her in the hammock. Maybe I was afraid that my secrets would pass through me to her as I lay beside her in the dark; that our proximity would bring me face to face with something about myself I didn't want to see and didn't want to know.

In fact, the momentum of our journey kept pulling me forward, carrying me away from myself, from my secrets, and I wanted to keep going. When I closed my eyes, memories of the day and of our trip spun like handbills spilling out of Hueys. And my mind was running helter-skelter, trying to catch them in the dark. At one point—maybe I'd drifted close to sleep—Sonia was with me and we were chasing after the helicopters, hoping to sight Yankees. Wide awake again, I remembered we'd already found some, found them and lost them, on our flight to Sangre de Cristo. As the tiny aircraft trembled in its assault upon the sky, two husky North Americans had loomed like apparitions from seats across the aisle. One held aloft a paper sack emblazoned with the logo of McDonald's, waved it before us, and the scents of coffee and fast food quickly filled the cabin.

"Care for a cup of coffee or an Egg McMuffin?" he'd asked, his gravelly baritone soft and intimate, as if we were all old friends. He raised an eyebrow while waiting for an answer. He had the neck and shoulders of a bodybuilder, ruddy cheeks pitted with acne scars. I declined with a quick shake of my head, but Sonia's face was immediately crammed with the greasy sandwich. I tried shifting my focus to the partner but couldn't, saw him only peripherally. He seemed to be a double, scarred and hefty, with a military haircut and a pastel guayabera shirt.

The McDonald's man was garrulous, surprised, he said, to see "a pair of pretty girls" like us on a flight to Sangre de Cristo. As for them, well, they were headed for a couple of the strategic villages around Sangre de Cristo. I couldn't help wondering what they'd be doing there. But when I leaned toward him to ask, I inadvertently released, from the folds of my shirt, my press credentials, which were hanging from a ribbon on my neck.

"Jesus, Steve, a couple of reporters," whispered the partner, as if maybe we wouldn't hear him. He pointed to my IDs.

Sonia quickly corrected him. *"Estoy fotógrafo,"* she announced, holding up her camera to prove her point.

When the McDonald's man turned back to me, his eyes looked as though they'd just been sucked outside into the cold blue yonder. He looked away, disappeared us. He left us to wrap ourselves in the humming silence of the plane. I was drowsing into it when the word "phoenix" floated up from memory. Through images of ashes I remembered the Phoenix program in South Vietnam. I remembered how, as part of its pacification effort there, the United States sent CIA-hired assassins into scores of rural hamlets to "neutralize" the communists and their suspected sympathizers.

After the flight, after they'd left, Sonia and I joked that the pair must have been hallucinations, insubstantial, if stereotypical, images of American agents involved in covert Third World operations. Destabilization, not pacification, we figured, but couldn't decide what they were intent upon destabilizing: *el frente* or the junta, or only me and Sonia. For us, the plane ride and strange turf, on top of almost no sleep, had been enough to push us to the edge of stability.

By then, we were drinking warm Coca-Colas at a bleak refreshment stand outside the airport, where we'd gone hoping to find a taxi for the trip into Sangre de Cristo. It was a sagging lean-to with the word REFRESCOS painted on the outside. The pretty barefoot *moza* denied knowing any taxi drivers. She smiled, and the ruins of her teeth made her face look vandalized. A shirtless *muchacho* volunteered to search for one and ran out laughing. Then the girl handed us the Cokes, stepped back just a little, eyed us from an arm's length away. The *gringos* from the plane were *muchísimos*, joked Sonia. Much of a muchness, I responded, a surfeit of destabilization. Who needed them? we asked each other. We ran a pretty good do-it-yourself destabilization operation all by ourselves, we said, then laughed and laughed. The waitress stared as from a vast distance, apparently convinced, but also knowing it did not matter, that we were mad beyond salvation.

In the hut, a child was whimpering softly but incessantly, and someone else kept coughing, a deep catarrhal cough that seemed to signal a dangerous contagion present in the darkness. With my eyes closed, all the sounds got louder, and after a while I heard, soft as a whisper, unmistakable rhythmic rustlings. I listened, not wanting to, as they quickened, became more insistent, at last peaking with a single high-pitched cry that was quickly swallowed up or smothered. The feminine cry resonated in the dark until it turned into my own, a cry of shame and envy, rushing like water from a tunnel. Then Rivas Valdez was above me, in me, forcing the sound out of my throat. I was trapped in the mineral glow of his eyes while, like a priest, he whispered an incantation. His voice was gentle when he named me: *Periodista astuta*. Wise journalist.

Puta. Cunt. Whore. The names were pellets of hot liquid exploding in the bottom of my belly. They hurt and I could not resist them. He let me go just when I didn't want him to and I felt myself falling, falling back through endless space. But then I was again with Sonia and we were flying to Sangre de Cristo, not going down. The predawn air was still and balmy, but the plane shook as it banked out over the Pacific, turned toward las Esmeraldas. We were being buffeted by unseen currents, inexplicable shifts in airflow patterns. The pilot's blue-shirted back and muscular forearms were visible in the tiny cockpit. He assured us we'd reach Sangre de Cristo in *"veinte minutos, nada más."* But the plane tilted sharply and I was staring through the window into the mouth of the volcano. Then I was detached from everything. I must have screamed, because Sonia reached through the window and grabbed my fingertips to pull me back. But when I turned, it was Mary, not Sonia, who was holding me. "Poor baby," she crooned. "It's okay now." She pulled me closer to her on the hammock. I rolled onto my back, sweaty and breathless, panicked that Mary had seen Rivas Valdez. But of course she hadn't, because he wasn't there. She caressed my shoulder, and in minutes she fell back to sleep that way. Her fingers soon stopped moving, twitched once or twice, settled against my throat as if she were checking my pulse or about to strangle me. I moved her hand. It was warm and limp when I put it back against her side. Still I couldn't rest beside her and couldn't climb out without waking her, and stepping on someone underneath us.

Mary shifted in her sleep. The hammock rocked emphatically, then settled back into its gentle sway. The swaying made it seem as though we were drifting. My mind was drifting, too. I couldn't stop thinking, couldn't stop remembering, but I was not remembering the things I needed to remember, and I couldn't understand the things I did. Because next I found myself outside in the chill of the deserted airfield, where the grayish light made it seem like dusk instead of dawn.

"No sign," says Sonia, meaning the Americans. She shrugs and lights a cigarette as I join her in the gravel. I scan the airfield and the pines surrounding it. Beyond the landing strip is a row of Dragonflies, four helicopters, a couple of armored tanks. Sonia starts taking pictures.

"Didn't you see where they went? How could you miss them?"

"How could I miss them?" I see my reflection in her sunglasses when she turns to look at me. "Jesus."

She kicks the ground, and gray dust billows around our feet. The whine of the departing plane draws our attention. The plane takes off gracefully, effortlessly opposes gravity as it rises. I watch it go, feeling again a loss and the awful lightness of my being. As the plane disappears into the clouds, I wonder if I can go on without it, the lost thing I can't name.

But we do go on, Sonia and I. We walk to the refreshment stand, where we wait, drinking Cokes, until the taxi driver comes. He has a waxed handlebar mustache, a denim cap pulled low over one eye. A gallant, he holds open for us the back door to his two-tone '50s Chevy. But he cringes into the driver's seat when he sees our credentials, sees that we're *prensa internacional*—as though we carry trouble with us instead of just reporting it. To all of our inquiries he answers with the same guttural noise until we give up speaking, instead watch him watch the road, his head jerking from left to right as if he expected soldiers, or guerrillas, or maybe just *banditos*, to appear around each bend. A plastic Virgin, noosed with red yarn, swings from his rearview mirror. The Chevy grows hotter as the sun rises higher, but we keep all windows closed against billowing dust. The swaying Virgin hypnotizes. I'm in a heated trance when the woman runs into the road, her tangled hair flying behind her. The road slopes down and dense forest makes a mottled green wall on both sides, as if we were sliding through a chute. She stops us. The driver swerves when he brakes so he doesn't hit her. She is naked to her waist, waves her red blouse like a flag as she runs up to his window, presses her breasts against it. The driver looks away, tries accelerating slowly, but the woman clings to the car. *"Mira, mira,"* she is calling. *"Mira mis tetas grandes. Mira mis tetas grandes."* Her wild voice coils through the window, glittering and sharp like concertina wire. Running to keep up with the car, she moves to my window, bangs it with her hands, leans down to look inside, the tar pits of her eyes so close I could fall into them. *"Tengo tetas grandes,"* she cries, stops when she sees I'm a woman, and, being one, rob her of the only thing she has to sell. She leaps at the car, slams my window with both hands. *"Puta,"* she shrieks. *"Puta sucia."* Dirty whore. I hear something beside me, realize Sonia is in the open doorway, one foot wedged into the seat, one against the doorjamb. She leans across the roof to take some pictures. Again the driver brakes, the car jolts to a halt, and Sonia falls against the door. The woman screams, runs toward us, stops. Beyond her, at the road's edge, is an animal in a wooden cage, a monkey I think when it takes hold of the bars and shakes them. Bright patches of sunlight are stitched among the forest shadows. One of them drifts over the cage, turns the monkey into a child, a filthy toddler tied by its waist to the bars. I barely recognize it before we're sliding through the chute again. Through the back window I see the woman by the roadside watching. She holds a breast in each hand, looks down at them frowning, as if at bad fruit she is thinking of discarding.

Sonia curls into the corner, doesn't look at me. The driver picks up speed. I watch her, wondering who she is and how she does what she does. She lights a cigarette, exhales. "I got some great shots," she says after a while. She looks out her window. "It's what I do. I take pictures."

The car keeps going, but somehow I slip out of it. I watch it disappear down the chute. I find myself alone, in a tunnel where phosphorescent puddles glimmer. Far ahead, at its end, the woman of the roadside waits. The forest spreads out behind her, silent and umbrageous. Sunlight glistens on the tangled hair cascading around her shoulders. *"Mira mis tetas,"* she calls. Her voice is gentle and alluring. I can't help moving closer, but then see I've been mistaken. It is not the woman of the roadside, but a gringa whose hair is the color of the sun, whose eyes are pale as ice. I move closer, see chains of diamonds sparkling on her wrists and throat. Closer still, I see bruises, blurred hieroglyphs, across her breasts. I know they'd tell a story if I knew how to read them—but I don't know how to read them. Something in her hand is flashing like a heliograph: I glimpse my press ID. In the photo I am smiling. Look at my breasts, she repeats. Then another voice is overwhelming hers, a voice as sharp as wire as it coils through my skull.

"Mi hija y mi nieto se van a morir," a woman cries. *"¿Dónde está la comadrona? ¿La comadrona norteamericana?"* She is speaking Spanish, but I hear the words in English: My daughter and my grandchild are going to die. Where is the North American midwife? The abrupt motion of the hammock knocked me out of the tunnel, and I sat up in the hammock next to Mary.

"Estoy aquí," she called.

Estoy aquí. I am here.

CHAPTER
TWENTY-ONE

*T*HE TAUPIL MIDWIFE WAS TALL AND BROAD, MASSIVE AS SHE LEANED over the iron pots of steaming water. Orange flames danced under the pots, near the hemline of her long skirt, making it look as if she'd just risen from the flames.

"Todavía no," she announced when we reached the clearing outside the hut. Her voice was low, reverberant as far-off thunder. Not yet.

A straw hat with a black band was pulled low onto her forehead. Silver braids hung along the sides of her face, disappeared into strings of beads and feathers tangled around her neck. A crucifix glinted among them. She bowed her head over the pots.

We were breathless after running from the camp to this hut on a distant wooded slope. After Nilsa had awakened us with her terrible lament, we'd rushed behind her along a path into the woods, maybe a mile. She'd been carrying a flashlight, and it had swooped crazily over tents and rooftops, the scraggly tops of leafless trees.

The clearing was lit by the fire and the moon. The sky was full of stars. The green hands of my Timex read two fifty-five. Panting, grateful for the chance to catch my breath, I watched Mary looking at the other midwife. Nilsa was crying, tugging on Mary's arm, imploring her to help, but she stood there, pale and calm, her black medical bag clutched under one arm.

"*Todavía no,*" the Taupil repeated, her head still bowed. Steam wafted around her old face.

"*¿Todavía no qué?*" Mary cried. "*¿Nacido o muerto?*"

Not yet what? Birth or death?

Her words were taut with anger, with some other feeling I couldn't identify. She raked her free hand through her hair, and her own crucifix twitched against her shirt.

"*Ninguno,*" neither, the midwife answered and raised her head. She tilted it back on her thick neck until she'd fixed Mary with a black stare, a priestess unaccustomed to such queries.

"*Van a morir pronto,*" she said and lowered her head back to the steam. "*No podemos hacer nada.*"

They're going to die soon. We can't do anything.

Nilsa dropped to her knees beside the fire, blessed herself, began to pray.

"*Tal vez tú no puedes hacer nada,*" Mary said, stabbing the air with an index finger. Maybe you can't do anything. Her words snapped the Taupil's head back with such force the beads jiggled and clattered. "*Pero yo . . .*" Mary's voice trailed off. She lifted her satchel, shrugged. "*Vamos a ver.*" We'll see.

"*El bebé se enredó en el canal de nacimiento,*" the midwife intoned as she peered back into the steam. The baby is trapped in the birth canal. "*Se van a morir. Es la voluntad de Dios.*"

"The will of God?" Shaking her head, Mary turned to me and Sonia. "The will of God," she repeated. "Come on. Let's see what's going on."

The hut was warm, pitch-black, and absolutely quiet. The dark silence pulled us in, an inevitable force that made me want to flee, to hide outside in the vast chill, beneath the starry sky. But Mary's thumb and index finger had encircled my wrist and she squeezed to hold me there, just inside the doorway, where she paused to sniff the air.

"Doesn't smell like death," she whispered. She went on to say she could tell by the odor that the girl's membranes had not ruptured, that the amniotic sac was no doubt still intact. "Which means we have a little time. Not much. But some."

Sonia was pressing against my other side, holding my arm above the elbow. We were sniffing too. The scent was sweet and carnal, somehow familiar. A deep moan startled us, stopped before we'd found its source, seemed to resonate in the dark, anguished and profoundly sexual.

"She's alone," Mary declared, shaking her head in disgust or disbelief.

"*¿Quién?*"

The lilting word wisped like a note of music. The voice was young and insubstantial. I could not see anyone.

"*¿Quién?*"

The repeated note had force enough to prompt Mary's answer.

"*La comadrona norteamericana.*" The North American midwife.

Her brisk words contradicted the lilting voice, seemed alien in the intense, feminine darkness. "*¿Me conoces? Me llamo Mary Healy.*"

Mary headed toward the other voice, and we followed. She crouched over something in a corner, and we leaned over too, tried to see the swollen form on the pallet. I saw only subtle textures of skin and fabric until I found her face and the glitter of her eyes.

"*Sí, comprendo,*" the girl whispered, nodded until a contraction over-whelmed her. Mary had anticipated it, already held the girl's hands. Their palms were together, and Mary, on her knees near the girl's chest, turned over her forearms so the girl could pull against them as the pain swelled through her belly. Even in the lightless room I saw their vining forearms, twined fingers. Both quivered as the wild energy of the incipi-ent birth surged through the girl's womb, rippled out through Mary's hands.

A guttering candle descended near the girl's head. Just beyond its aqueous light the mother, Nilsa, melted into shadow. "Oh God," some-one whispered, calling my attention back to the girl, who seemed to be submerged, drowning, as if the weight of her great belly had forced her underwater. The jittery light played over her soaked dress and skin, her wet black hair. It was cut very short and sticking out in spikes. Perspira-tion trembled on her chin and under her eyes. She panted, and her lids fluttered against the light. Finally she focused on us, looked at each of us in turn, maybe, wondered which was the midwife. Her eyes were somber but not panicked, consenting but not submissive.

"*No me voy a morir,*" she said at last. "*Ni mi hijo tampoco.*"

Fatigue had robbed her voice—we could hardly hear her. But her statement was devoid of inquiry, of interrogation: I am not going to die. My child isn't either. Its certitude caressed my spine, the edges of my scalp.

Mary grunted, smiled.

"*Claro que no,*" she answered. Of course not. Her smile expanded into a soft chuckle as she asked the girl her name.

"*Claro que no, Rosa,*" Mary repeated. "*No te vas a morir, tu hijo tampoco.*"

Rosa was small-boned, very young, perhaps fifteen, and the angles of her face were muted by childhood fat. Mary had clasped her big belly as if to pull Rosa from a rushing current. Her reddened hands stroked its vast curves, slowed here and there to press. She lowered her head until her cheek rested against it. She closed her eyes, looked and listened with her fingers. One hand disappeared, reappeared with a small black fetalscope. She tapped the mountain of belly with it, her ear against the instrument as she roved its slopes. At last she stopped and frowned. She listened for a time but didn't speak. She offered me and Sonia each a turn. The baby's accelerated heartbeat, its echoes, were like the hoofbeats of a frantic horse trapped in a dark cavern.

"It's strong and steady, but much too fast, tachycardic," she murmured in English, translated for the girl just the first two facts. She caressed the girl's cheek, and the girl reached up to touch her.

"*¿Cuándo se nace mi bebé?*" she asked. When will my baby be born?

"*Muy pronto,*" Mary told her smiling. Very soon.

She took from her bag a surgical glove and covered her right hand, told the girl that she would examine her internally to see how much her cervix had dilated. She motioned to the Indian midwife who had soundlessly joined us, and the two of them moved Rosa to the bottom of the pallet, opened her legs so Mary could kneel between them. She rested one hand on the belly, inserted the other into the girl's vagina.

"*Dios mío,*" Nilsa cried as the midwife frowned at Mary, muttering something I didn't understand.

"*Está bien.*" It's all right, Rosa admonished them. The two of them looked away.

"They think vaginal examinations are harmful and shameful," Mary told us in English. "They're so superstitious it's impossible sometimes."

She glanced at Rosa, who nodded yes, told her to do whatever she needed to do.

"I'm pretty sure I'm touching the baby's fingers," Mary said after a moment. "It must be lying sideways. And it's managed to push its arm out."

"What does that mean?" I asked.

"Well, she's right," Mary answered, gesturing toward the Indian midwife. "The baby's trapped."

Mary pulled out her hand, removed the glove.

"Can you dislodge him?"

She shrugged, looked back at Rosa, who was writhing against a new contraction.

"A vaginal delivery is impossible. Hopeless."

Mary took my hands, placed them on either side of the belly. It rolled under my fingers like a wave sliding back into the ocean. Then the whole thing gradually hardened, like a muscle slowly flexing, only the movement was vaster, deeper, more intense, an awesome downward surge that turned Rosa's belly into stone and drove her from her senses. She howled at the peak of the contraction and the old midwife held a wet cloth to her mouth. The awful sound was smothered when Rosa's jaws clamped shut over the cloth. Then her belly softened.

"The force of these contractions is phenomenal," said Mary. "But they're futile. They'll never be strong enough to push the baby out. Because of its position. It's called a transverse lie. The chances of its happening are maybe one in a million."

"What does it mean?" Sonia asked as Mary placed her hands on Rosa's stomach.

"Sooner or later her uterus is going to explode."

"And then what?"

"She'll bleed to death. For starters. And while she's doing that, her baby's going to suffocate."

The sonorous voice of the Indian midwife interrupted us, and when I looked, she was grimacing ferociously, smoothing Rosa's hair back with her fingers. She said something I didn't understand, but Mary nodded.

"That's why the midwife says it's the will of God. That both of them will die. We should be preparing them for their journey."

Nilsa and the midwife continued to stare at Mary, at once suspicious and expectant. Maybe they still hoped she'd tell them Rosa and her child were not in any danger. She didn't. Instead, Rosa herself repeated that she wasn't going to die, and her baby wasn't either. She smiled, or tried to smile, at each of us.

"At home it's no big deal," Mary said in English, frowning at the girl. "They'd knock her out and section her. But here, I mean, Jesus."

She didn't complete her thought, instead tugged at her lips.

"You can do that, can't you?" I asked. "The cesarean?"

"Never have," she murmured. "I'm not a surgeon."

Then Rosa raised herself on an elbow, touched Mary's arm.

"Salve a mi hijo."

Her voice whispered but her eyes commanded: Save my baby.

"Por favor. Yo no tengo importancia, pero tienes que salvar a mi hijo." Please. I don't matter. But you must save my child. Even in the shadows, I could see the color flooding Mary's face. I glimpsed her distant, beatific look, but immediately she was nodding yes.

"They're doomed anyway, aren't they?" she muttered, gesturing for her black bag. I pushed it toward her, looked inside, saw for the first time the glittering, aseptic world of metal, plastic, and glass it enclosed, an organized world of instruments and medications that seemed absolutely foreign to the Mary Healy of the wild hair, ragged jeans, and crucifix; to Mary Healy, the zealot, the subversive.

She poked through the satchel, fingering this and that, mumbling something I couldn't understand, maybe a prayer, or an inventory of her instruments. At last she turned to the rest of us, looked over all of us, me and Sonia, Nilsa and the Indian midwife. Her uncombed hair fell to one side, a crown askew. Its tips shimmered in the light.

"Until the baby is born, I'm going to tell each of you exactly what to do," she told us in slow, careful Spanish. "If Rosa and her baby are to survive, you must do exactly as I say as quickly as you can."

The Indian midwife was to bring in at least two buckets of hot water, Nilsa was to gather as many clean cloths, sheets, and towels as she could find. Nilsa handed me the candle, and Mary told me to hold it close while she reached into her bag for an antiseptic solution and a syringe. She snapped open a vial of Demerol and filled the hypodermic. I moved the candle close to the girl as Mary pushed away her dress, swabbed her buttock with the antiseptic, and stabbed it with the needle. She gave the girl a second injection, and by then the buckets of water were steaming within Mary's reach. Sonia dropped the metal instruments into one of them, and Mary, on her knees, scrubbed in the other. I tied her hair back, pinned it up inside a cloth. Then Nilsa and the midwife hauled

Rosa up off the pallet and held her up in the shadows while I prepared what Mary called a sterile field, spreading across the pallet and onto the floor beside it the clean sheets and towels Nilsa had presented and on top of them draping sheets of sterile plastic from Mary Healy's bag. Even before I'd finished, Mary motioned back the others, and the moment I was done, they took off Rosa's dress, and she was naked in our midst. Her arms and legs looked frail, insufficient, behind her huge, glistening belly, which shifted and rippled as the baby it contained heaved and thrashed in its effort to be born. Rosa herself seemed to be sleeping. Her head had fallen to one side, and her open mouth was slack.

"She's floating on the moon," I heard Mary say, realized the girl was helpless. Sonia, wrapping her in a frayed flowered tablecloth, seemed to be enacting my urge to cover and protect her. Then all of them were lowering her onto the pallet, placing her so that her buttocks were at the end of it, her legs spread out to either side. The tablecloth covered her arms and chest but left exposed the great moon of her belly. Another contraction was in progress, and Mary, on her knees at the end of the pallet, told Sonia and me to wash our hands, rubbed her own in concentric circles over the hardening flesh. Once we'd scrubbed, we helped Mary on with another pair of gloves. Then she told me and Sonia to put gloves on too. "I know exactly what I need each of you to do," she said, somehow hearing my unasked question. "So put the goddamn gloves on, Lizzie. I don't have time to argue."

As we put our gloves on, she instructed Nilsa to straddle the pallet behind her daughter, where she could cradle Rosa's head, cool her face with damp cloths. The Indian midwife took her place where Mary pointed, on the right side of the pallet near the mother's knees, and she aimed a flashlight onto the girl's stomach.

"*¿Qué vas hacer?*" Nilsa asked. What are you going to do?

"*Voy a sacarlo,*" Mary answered softly, as though she did it every day. I'm going to take him out.

She didn't look at Nilsa, instead gestured to a plastic bag of IV fluids in her satchel, and I handed it to her as Sonia began arranging the instruments on the sterile sheet beside the pallet.

"What we're aiming for here, girls, is asepsis," Mary said, interrupting herself with a soft, giddy laugh. "It's what we all need in our lives, a little more asepsis."

She swabbed the vein inside Rosa's elbow, inserted the IV needle, and taped it down. I passed the bag up to the old midwife. Mary motioned for her to hold it higher, and the woman obeyed, but eyed her from beneath her hat brim. The thin, translucent tube of the IV fluids swung to and fro between them, a fragile connection.

"It might prevent her from seizing or dehydrating," Mary explained in Spanish, running her fingertips back and forth over the mound of belly.

She gestured for me to kneel very close to Rosa on her right side, told Sonia to stay put on her left where she would pass the instruments. She asked Sonia to put them in order, reviewed their names: scalpel, scissors, hemostats, which were small metal clamps like hairclips, and sutures and suturing needles. Sonia moved the candle closer to the instruments, squatted over them like a sidewalk peddler. Mary instructed me to scrub Rosa's belly with hot water and to cleanse it with the antiseptic.

Afterward, she held up another syringe, filled it with lidocaine, a local anesthetic. Again she ran her fingertips back and forth over the center of the belly, now only inches from my face. Faint rivulets of stretch marks curved from Rosa's navel to her pubis and its nest of dark hair. It was a mysterious and complex geography, one Mary knew very well. One I didn't know at all. She inserted the hypodermic laterally through layers of fat and muscle and released the anesthetic, and we saw it scurry through the tissues, a subterranean creature burrowing just below the surface of the earth. Mary rubbed her fingers along its path, did a second injection not far from the first.

"*Su marido es el comandante Ocho,*" Nilsa announced then. "*Es un gran guerrillero.*"

Sonia must have made a sound, or maybe she dropped an instrument, because I turned to look at her, found her standing, her face beyond the candlelight. Then she apologized, knelt back over the instruments, her face still hidden. I wondered what Nilsa's words meant to Sonia: Rosa's husband is Comandante Ocho, a great guerrilla.

"*Sus hijos serán la generación nueva, los hijos de la revolución,*" the midwife said, and Mary told her to be quiet.

Their children will be the new generation, the children of the revolution.

At last Mary asked if we were ready, and all of us said yes. Sonia held out her surgically gloved hand. The scalpel glittered in her palm. Mary looked at it for a long time. Her face contracted into a grimace. Filaments of sweat threaded their way through the creases. Slowly, she turned back to Rosa's belly, gazed at it, her eyes as pale as crystal. Her hands rested on its crest, but at last they lifted, floated above it, motionless as clouds on a windless day. Without taking her eyes off the belly, she reached for the scalpel, asked the old midwife to hold the light closer. Then, in one deliberate motion, as if she were drawing a line on paper, she cut Rosa open from just below her navel to just above her pubic bone. A red explosion gushed from the cut, and blood streamed down the slopes. Rosa did not make a sound, but her mother shrieked and the Indian midwife began muttering a prayer. Mary told both of them to hush. The mother's sobs remained insistent, metronomic.

"Open the incision, Lizzie," Mary ordered, but I didn't understand. "Move fast, retract it," she repeated, then called for clamps, which Sonia's nimble fingers offered while my own seemed frozen, paralyzed in front of me.

"Pull back the opening for me, the edges," she urged again. Then my gloved fingers tugged at the cut flesh, which, hot and slippery, kept sliding from my fingers.

"Oh shit, it's not deep enough," Mary cried as the sides of the incision resisted. Again she asked for the scalpel, hesitated for a heartbeat, then the blade disappeared into the bloody river, and Mary pulled her arm along its track. When she finished, my fingers sank into the opening, and I wedged and curled them below the layers of fat and muscle, heard Mary telling me to grab as if I were grabbing the edges of a cliff to keep myself from falling. Finally I had two fistfuls, and she told me to spread my fingers and squeeze to stop the bleeding, which I did, then pulled with all my strength. The incision began to open, and it wasn't at all like hanging at a cliff's edge; it was more like peeling tough rind off a fruit. I was crouched half under Mary, and Sonia's arms were entwined from the other side, so we'd become a single, six-armed creature. Through little geysers and eddies of blood, their queerly encased fingers clamped off veins and arteries, all the bleeding vessels, until the fruit itself emerged, the womb. It was bright pink, mottled, and intricately veined, a vibrant cosmos glistening in the shifting flashlight beam.

A heady, high-pitched hum, a chorus of oohs and aahs, seemed to come from Rosa's belly. Of course it was us, each of us, exclaiming at the sight of her full womb, and maybe the sound pleased Rosa, because she smiled as she floated in her lunar atmosphere. Then the old midwife leaned over for a better look, plunging Rosa into darkness.

Get back, Mary barked, motioned for her to aim the light right over the womb. The scalpel flashed again, like a small fish jumping out of water, and the bright pink fruit was split, was streaming blood and water. The harmonic chorus resounded, and through it Mary murmured, "Thank God the fluid's clear, see. It's clean. Beautiful. That means the baby's probably okay." And maybe it was, but I couldn't tell, because the fecund, oceanic smell blurred my vision, and when it cleared I saw something curled inside the tight, pulsing nest of flesh and blood, only inches from my fingers, a patch of a tiny arm, perhaps a rib cage or a thigh. Mary reached for it, grasping and tugging, grunting with her effort, and I kept open the feverish, wet edges of the nest. Rosa's triumphant but unconscious bellow of relief sounded before I saw Mary with the infant, standing, holding it up high so the silvery snake of the umbilical uncoiled and squirmed between them, and a warm rain of blood and amniotic water was falling over all of us.

CHAPTER
TWENTY-TWO

"**H**AY OTRO GRINGO AQUÍ, OTRO PERIODISTA," THE OLD MAN Quique told me sometime later that morning. I was sitting on the front stoop of our hostess's hut, meditating on the wonders of the universe, nearly overwhelmed by the wonders of the universe, when Quique sidled up to me, whispered that another Yankee reporter was there, somewhere in Mesa Verde. His face was very close to mine, and he grinned to show the glistening stumps of his black teeth.

"*¿Quieres hablar con el otro gringo?*" he asked.

By then the sun was high and very bright, and I was feeling transcendental, lost somewhere beyond hunger and fatigue.

"*¿Quieres hablar con el otro?*" Quique repeated. Want to talk to the other gringo?

He was pressing up against me, watching me with a gaze so rapt it felt as if he were stealing something from me. I ignored the stinking ruins of his mouth, remembered what Mary Healy had said before our trip: that Mesa Verde was a place of devastation and death, but also a place where anything could happen, a place of infinite possibility.

"*Por supuesto,*" I told him, smiling, but feeling my meditational condition recede like a tide. Of course I want to talk to the other Yankee reporter. Quique left in search of him.

Right away I knew this other Yankee reporter would be the free-lance photojournalist, the one who'd disappeared from the Hotel Lido's parking lot, the one whose rented Toyota had provided the only clue about his fate. It didn't occur to me that the other *gringo* could be anyone but him. I envisioned him, grizzled and ragged and smiling arrogantly, as he emerged from *la zona de combate*. I imagined the resulting front-page story: "Free-lance Photojournalist Found in War Zone, Alive and Well." I imagined the layout of his tale of life among the guerrillas, imagined Sonia's photographs, envisioned my byline above the text. I didn't, however, translate my imaginings into any kind of action, not even organizing my thoughts or jotting down any questions.

I don't know how long I sat immobilized, waiting for Quique to come back with him. Long enough to see two pairs of Dragonflies on strafing runs farther up the mountain. Long enough to see Mary leave for a clinic at the next camp. Long enough to wonder why Sonia hadn't returned from Rosa's.

At some point I began noticing the unfamiliar reek of my own sweat, the stink of blood and other birthing fluids that had splattered over my shirt and jeans. I'd washed my hands and face at Rosa's, but not the rest of my body. And though I had a clean shirt in my backpack, I couldn't put it on without bathing or showering. Even in Mesa Verde my mother's rule remained in force: you can't put clean clothes on a dirty body without risking cataclysm, maybe the world's end. I actually got up, compelled by an insane surge of hope, and tried to find a place to wash, a way to clean myself. Finding neither, I sat back on the stoop, in a small shady spot, my back propped against the adobe wall, wrapped in my own stink.

I began to think I ought to get out my notebook and organize my thoughts before Quique came back. Still I couldn't move—and I must have dozed off for a while. Because at some point I opened my eyes and saw Sonia sleeping in a nearby hammock. I reached for the hammock, thinking I'd shake her awake, ask her about Comandante Ocho and Rosa, about all her mysteries. I hesitated. The rise and fall of her chest promised to go on forever. Somehow I believed her mysteries would soon resolve themselves.

Again I closed my eyes, fantasized about cups of coffee, fried eggs, hot showers. Soon, however, big black flies, frenzied by the vinegary perfume of our sweat, by splatters of blood dried into our clothes, began buzzing around us. Their drone drilled through my skull. They also woke up Sonia, because I heard her cursing, *"Malditos moscones"*—damned flies—and when I looked, she was swatting at them. She began to smoke, one cigarette after the other, creating a little smudge fire that might protect her from the flies. She squinted through the smoke, dared the *malditos moscones* to bother her.

"Wasn't last night something?" I asked, feeling only half-coherent. "Some baby, huh?"

"God, yes, she's a beauty," Sonia answered. I waited for her to say more, but she didn't.

"Where did you learn to do that stitching?" I asked after a while. When Mary's fingers had begun to cramp, Sonia had taken over the suturing of Rosa's incisions. Like women sharing needlework, the two of them had labored over Rosa's belly, perfecting every stitch.

"Sewing hems." Sonia laughed, and I joined her. "Yeah, sewing hems on skirts."

"What will Rosa and her baby do during the evacuation? Can they travel?"

She shook her head and shrugged, exhaled smoke. I watched her, hoping she'd tell me more about them, Ocho and Rosa, about how she knew him, what he meant to her. But she just smoked and stared into the smoke. Finally I let my head drop forward to ease the muscles knotted in my shoulders. I closed my eyes and covered my face with my hands. Even so, the light hurt, as if my skull had cracked open and the mountain light were pouring through.

Maybe that's why, when I opened my eyes, looked up, and saw them coming toward us, they were chimerical in a ring of light that swallowed up their feet and made it seem they were floating: Quique, in his ragged clothes, like a scarecrow come to life; four younger men, all in T-shirts and jeans, several with thick beards. Three wore black berets, had belts of ammunition crisscrossed over their chests, grenades hanging from their hips, rifles in their hands. The last man was unarmed. He wore a khaki T-shirt and a camouflage hat, the kind worn by Bellavista's infantry. He was unmistakably North American.

I heard Sonia's gasp, the thud of her feet as she jumped out of the hammock. I remembered I hadn't told her about the other *gringo*. Still I was immobilized and sat thinking that my skull had broken open and my eyeballs were scorched beyond repair.

When at last I recognized him, which did not happen right away, I thought it was a trick, an elaborate and malevolent scheme by the *New York Herald-Sun* to expose me, to rob me of my job, my stories, my future. My impulse was to turn and run, but I had noplace to go, noplace except deeper into the free-fire zone, where I'd be endangered, lost. I had to stay to face him.

Finally I was standing, watching them float toward me in their ring of light. Sonia was close beside me, tense and alert. Her jagged exhalation gusted past my sweaty shoulder. I turned, saw her camera was already around her neck, the proper lens attached, but she wasn't touching it, instead began to comb her fingers through her hair. She stopped almost immediately, looked at the *gringo*, and he looked at her as he drifted toward us with the others. Their famished gazes connected like light beams in the dark. They didn't speak, offered no sign of recognition, but Sonia felt suddenly enkindled, and the flames began burning in her cheeks, reflecting in her eyes.

It was only then that Alan Hartwell, the *New York Herald-Sun*'s former correspondent in Bellavista, turned to me, held out his hand. "Elizabeth, I knew from the old man's description it must be you," he said. "But what in hell are you doing here?"

"Jesus, Alan, reporting, what else?" I must have said, or something like that, and I gripped his hand, released it, as my own questions flew past his, echoed them—What are you doing here? How did you get here? Weren't you supposed to be in San Diego?—and they might have been the last coherent sentences I spoke for some time. Because, as Hartwell and I spoke, one of the guerrillas, thin and wiry and somehow familiar, rushed up to Sonia and embraced her. She kissed him, crying, "Danny, Danny." He asked if she'd seen his *hijo*, his son, and she answered that she'd seen his *hija*, his daughter, not his son. Then this Danny took off down the path to the hut where Rosa and the baby were recovering, and Sonia watched him, laughing. It was a shrieky bird laugh stuck in a high pitch. She pointed to him with her thumb. "Comandante Ocho. My brother," she said.

*   *   *

I can't remember exactly what happened next. The five of us must have stood there in the clearing for a while. The rest of the camp was very quiet. Everyone was getting ready for the evacuation. If she'd known they were coming, Sonia joked, she'd at least have bathed and put on her best dress. Maybe she'd have baked a cake or bought champagne. She said she'd find cold drinks for all of us, and she left, running toward the clinic.

Hartwell watched her go, looking as if he'd lost something essential. When he finally turned to me, he smiled and shook his head, silently confessed his bewilderment.

"Well," he said, meeting my eyes. His were deep blue, the color of wild chicory.

"Well," I answered, unable to stop staring at him. I was trying to remember if I'd ever heard his voice before, trying to remember if we'd ever spoken to each other. I decided that we hadn't. I decided that although we'd worked out of the same newsroom, and I'd often seen him and watched him work, we'd been traveling in different orbits. His had moved much faster and had been closer to the sun.

"It's a long way from the South Bronx."

He smiled again, and his teeth flashed white and even between the fur of his mustache and beard.

"What do you mean?" I asked as his statement threshed my paranoia.

"I mean Mesa Verde's almost three thousand miles from the South Bronx, isn't it? Wasn't the South Bronx your last assignment?"

Quique's shout interrupted us, got us moving forward, and I didn't have to answer Hartwell's questions. He'd scouted out a shady spot on the far side of the hut and motioned for us to join him there. We went and huddled in the dust with Quique sitting much too close to me. Hartwell introduced the other two guerrillas as Ocho's bodyguards, said their names were Galgo and Gato. Greyhound and Cat. Galgo was clean-shaven and wore impenetrable dark glasses. Gato's long black hair was pulled into a ponytail. As the swarthy rebels sat side by side against a nearby tree stump, Hartwell told me Galgo had important contacts in the armed forces, would have some things to tell me later. But first, he said, we ought to talk, ought to get acquainted. Galgo and Gato pulled their berets over their faces for a nap, leaving Hartwell and me to face each other.

Which is what we did, faced each other, looking for a place to begin our conversation, our relationship, but not immediately finding it. Despite the glaring light, I couldn't see him very well. I seemed to see him through a sooty window, which must have been my many-layered grudge—my grudge against him because of his privileged education, his impeccable credentials, his meteoric rise at the newspaper, his status as Van Doorn's fair-haired boy, his Chosen One. Through this sooty window, the rugged, unkempt Alan Hartwell before me was overlain with remembered images of Alan Hartwell in New York, the Alan Hartwell whose uniform had been expensive loafers, button-down shirts, tweed jackets, and tortoiseshell eyeglasses. That Alan Hartwell had been a journalistic juggernaut, untouchable, and his passage through the newsroom had always left a turbulent wake of feelings, whorls of envy and admiration. I didn't know how to talk to him.

"So, Elizabeth, tell me, how did you get up here?" His voice was young and curious. "With the state of siege I thought journalists weren't allowed to travel."

So I explained, picking at the laces of my shoes, because his gaze distracted me, how I'd convinced the defense ministry that I should do a follow-up on the Cooperativo Nuevo de Jerusalem, and how, once I had permission to move about the countryside, I'd then persuaded a missionary I knew to help us make the contacts necessary to get into the war zone.

"It was so easy it was weird," I was telling my Reeboks when he interrupted.

"The missionary was North American?"

"She's with us here. Mary Healy." I said her name deliberately, saw him look away, and understood with a clarity as transparent as the light that she had been the missionary in his Aguas Oscuras story.

"She's the one who brought you to your witness, isn't she? Mary Healy was the missionary who helped you with your Aguas Oscuras story."

He didn't answer, rather watched a small red ant making its way up his pant leg. He put his finger in its path, and the ant crawled onto his finger, made its way toward his palm. I had an urge to shake him, to make him stop watching the ant, which was, by then, trapped and crazed by the curved slopes and crevices of his cupped hand. At last he held his hand out to one side, flicked away the ant. The tiny dot was airborne for an instant, then disappeared.

"You have your own massacre story now, don't you?" he asked. "Río

Luciente, right? You've got it sourced and verified half a dozen different ways. You don't need Aguas Oscuras."

"But you do." I wondered how he knew about my story, but couldn't seem to ask. "The truth demands to be told."

He shrugged, examined his palm where the ant had been. I watched him, remembering what my editor McManus had said: "Aguas Oscuras is a conundrum, a riddle with only conjectural answers." But I'd always known there was an answer, and I'd always known Hartwell had it. I had a crazy urge to shake him, to shake the answer out.

"The witness is an old woman." Hartwell spoke so softly I almost didn't hear him. "A wonderful old Taupil who lost almost everything during the war." When he turned to me, I saw his chicory eyes, the eyes of a teacher, a sage. "Her youngest daughter and her grandchild were murdered at Aguas Oscuras. She saw soldiers throw this infant into the air and catch it on a bayonet as it fell." His voice was low but urgent, and it cracked sometimes as he went on to explain that despite her faith, the witness was not immune to fear, that she'd been afraid for her own life. "I couldn't jeopardize her life to save my job. It didn't make sense to me. She'd already been victimized so many ways. I didn't need the job that badly. I figured I could always get another."

I think when Alan Hartwell said this, the soot fell off the window. Because afterward I seemed to see him very clearly: the journalistic juggernaut who'd fallen out of his trajectory and crashed to earth, disintegrated, was there in front of me, whole. And he was telling me, with absolute serenity, as though it had been his only possible course of action, that he'd relinquished his professional reputation, his career, to protect an anonymous old woman. At the murky bottom of the Aguas Oscuras conundrum was a reporter's moral choice.

Yet I was aware that he hadn't answered my question, hadn't confirmed that Mary Healy had been his missionary. He was still protecting sources.

"See, I never expected the government would try to deny it," he said before I'd had the chance to process his new image. "My mistake was thinking the government would admit the massacre and the United States would be outraged. Instead, the government of Bellavista lied. And the State Department colluded in the lie."

He leaned closer, enfolded me in his blue gaze, told me how Van Doorn had taken it personally—because the newspaper's reputation was also at stake—when he wouldn't go after the witness. "He not only believed that I'd fucked up, but also that I was fucking him over."

Through his words I saw the admonition old sad Liz had written on her Aguas Oscuras file: "The higher you fly, the harder you . . ."

"The craziest thing of all was that the paper had no commitment to the story. None. Now I think the truth was so grotesque that it undermined their most treasured assumptions about how power works in the world."

He paused, stretched a little, leaned back on his elbows. He turned tranquil, distant, as though he were relating a curious anecdote involving someone else.

"They decided that what I'd written couldn't be the truth. What I'd reported wasn't possible. So I became a liar or a fool."

Hartwell smiled his winning smile, and my heart nearly melted in its warmth. I realized that his serenity and confidence, whatever their source, must be a formidable news-gathering tool.

"Later, when the shit hit, Van Doorn pointed out that it was my word against the government's. And it wasn't just some disreputable Third World government whose word I was disputing. It was the word of a U.S. ally. Van Doorn said we had no way to independently verify what had happened."

Alan then reminded me how the governments of both countries had attacked his professionalism and his politics when the story broke. In fact, Hartwell and his reporting had become news, the subject of magazine features and op-ed columns.

"It was a classic instance of kill the messenger. Everybody was out for blood."

Again he held me with his unassailable blue eyes, and I nodded, like Quique, to encourage him. Even in his passion, Hartwell was serene, detached. His peaceful aura distinguished him from all the other reporters I'd known—news junkies like me, who lived in a perpetual state of jittery overstimulation, constantly high or looking to get high on gathering the news; forever craving the rush of a great breaking story.

"You know, I used to weekend at his summer house in Southampton. Van Doorn's." He took off his cap, rubbed his sweaty forehead, placed his hat on one knee. "I respected him so much. Then I found out the bastard was in Libertad. He was with Whitaker right before the report of the Aguas Oscuras investigation was made public." Hartwell laughed as if something in his throat had torn. "Van Doorn was actually in fucking Libertad. He managed to get in and out without me or anybody else knowing."

Hartwell grinned, glanced skyward. The two of them appeared there as if bidden, Whitaker, with his rosy skin and bulging eyes, and Van Doorn, his bald pate and his spectacles agleam. They stayed there, hovering above us in the bright light, distant as deities, as Hartwell went on to say the men had lunched alone, had kept no record of the meeting, not even in the ambassador's official journal, so nobody knew what they'd talked about, or even that they'd talked, until Hartwell found out through his sources. Again Hartwell smiled.

"Then I was called back to New York, reassigned to San Diego. Van Doorn said he was sending me there to season me and hone my skills. He said he wanted me to be a more fully trained journalist."

"Season you? Hone your skills?" I couldn't help laughing. "That's exactly what Van Doorn said about my extended stay in the South Bronx. He wanted to season me and hone my skills."

"At least you had a chance of learning something in the South Bronx." Instead, Hartwell had found himself working out of an office in a suburban shopping center in Southern California, a satellite of the San Diego bureau, where he'd found himself covering United Way fund-raising luncheons and meetings of the La Jolla Municipal Sewage Author-ity. "Talk about shit," he said. "It was pure shit. So I left."

He looked up, frowning deeply. Maybe then I should have asked him what he was doing in Mesa Verde, why he was back in Bellavista. But the question seemed too difficult, seemed clotted with too many other questions. He went on talking as I hesitated, and the question flew away like the ant he'd flicked off his palm.

"You know what it was like reporting here? It was like walking a wire without a net. Scary. I felt so precarious all the time. But it's what you have to do in a place like Bellavista to get anywhere near the truth. You have to risk everything. You have to put yourself in danger."

I began to hear a high-pitched keening in my skull—like a strong wind shrieking through. Through this wind shriek I saw him out there on the wire. Hartwell on a wire above a chasm, an aerialist, his arms outstretched. Then I glimpsed myself replacing him, glimpsed myself trembling on the wire, looking for the net, afraid to stand.

"Of course, when I fell, I got mangled because there was nothing under me," I heard him say. "No support." With the back of his hand, he slammed the ground, a simulation of his fall from the wire. "But it was okay. Because I had the truth. Which I never would have gotten if I'd been working with a net."

Again I glimpsed myself out there on the wire, trembling, looking for the net. Unwanted questions swarmed around this image like flies around spilled blood. What was Hartwell doing back in Bellavista? What was I doing there myself? Why had I been chosen to replace him? Why had I been sent? These questions were as unbearable as the light, something you must protect yourself against. I couldn't ask them. Instead my index finger drifted toward his face.

"What happened to your glasses? Tortoiseshell, weren't they?"

He threw his head back, laughing. Then he was unzipping an L.L. Bean waistpack and holding up the glasses. The right lens was a web of tiny cracks.

"I've come back to Bellavista searching for the truth behind the facts," he said, "and I can hardly see my hand in front of my face."

He laughed again, a deep easy laugh, and I should have laughed along with him. I should have laughed to realize that his intense, mesmerizing gaze was the result of faulty vision. Maybe if I'd laughed, we'd have become friends. Instead I found myself telling him about my interview with Whitaker, about what Whitaker had said about him, that he'd been swayed by the guerrillas.

" 'Flummoxed' is the word he used. He said you were doing advocacy journalism."

My tone was accusatory, but Hartwell found the words hilarious. His laughter seemed authentic, but he stopped abruptly, said that when you got close to the truth in a place like Bellavista, you couldn't be objective. Because it was so obviously a story of right and wrong. You had to pick a side.

"How can you be objective about torture and mass murder?" he asked, and the veins at his throat and temples seemed to swell as he waited for an answer. I found I had one ready.

"I'm professionally bound by the standards of the *Herald-Sun*. One of them is to tell both sides of the story."

"How can you tell both sides when one side, the most powerful side, is lying—and the other side is inaccessible? You can't. Besides, when you know they're lying, isn't it irresponsible, and immoral, to repeat their lies?"

"Who knows they're lying?"

My involuntary question loosed his plosive, disbelieving, "Don't you?"

I noticed that Galgo and Gato had awakened and were watching us. I couldn't answer Hartwell's question, so he himself responded. He responded with a lengthy list of my journalistic shortcomings, with all the evidence of why I should have recognized the lies. It seemed that he'd studied every word I'd written. The list, as he recited it, sounded like an incantation, fervid but barely comprehensible.

To begin with, I'd reported there would be water for Ciudad de Merced when there wasn't any water. And I'd hyped a massive program of agrarian reform that had stopped after the formation of one cooperative. In fact, I hadn't bothered to report that La Solucíon Pacífica existed only on paper, that it was nothing but an elaborate public relations scheme by the junta to appease the U.S. Congress. What's more, it apparently hadn't occurred to me to report that children were dying of hunger, and being brain-damaged by malnutrition, while humanitarian aid was left rotting at the docks. At the same time, lethal aid, guns and ammunition, kept pouring into the most remote areas of the countryside. As for the strategic villages, I'd reported they would make life better for peasants when any fool could see they were concentration camps where all civil rights were suspended. Where, at night, free-lance assassins, hired and trained by the CIA, prowled for suspected communist sympathizers.

There were my reports about the bombings for which Estrella Luminosa had allegedly taken responsibility. Had I even tried to verify the existence of Estrella Luminosa, let alone its responsibility for the bombings? So was I really telling both sides of the story?

What I wonder, now, is why I didn't try to stop him. What I wonder, now, is why I sat spellbound through his litany, which was offered in the gentlest of voices. I still don't have an answer. Galgo, Gato, and Quique were also mute, motionless, as they stared at us.

"What about those guerrillas at el Golfo de Virtud?"

This last question hit me before I had my bearings, and I tripped, fell backward into that balmy dawn when I'd knelt beside their stinking corpses.

"You know damned well those people were murdered," I heard him say, and she was back in my arms, the woman with the swelling like a fist above her ear, the woman whose skull contained a bullet fired at point-blank range. She felt fragile as I held her, and her earrings, tiny crosses, sparkled in the light. Again I saw the thing I didn't want to see, that she wore her blue jeans backward, a telling detail that had told me nothing. "Those so-called guerrillas, mostly teenagers, some of them just kids, were set up by the CIA and ambushed." His words came to me very slowly, but I felt them unlocking something, freeing me to know what I hadn't allowed myself to know before. The telling detail at last divulged its secret: the female guerrilla wasn't wearing her blue jeans backward. Her blue jeans had been put on backward by mistake. By the soldiers. After they had raped and killed her.

Then the swirling waters of the gulf washed over both of us, pulled her away, left me alone to fight a surging panic. What I wanted more than anything was to run away, to escape Alan Hartwell and his probing nearsighted eyes, his accusations and his judgments. But before I could, he asked another question, a question that breached my boundaries and sank into the bile at my core.

"Where is your outrage?"

He smiled when he said it. His tone implied that he might be inquiring after a notebook or a pen. "It's something I've wanted to ask you since I started reading your stuff."

"My what?"

"Where is your outrage?" he repeated, as though it were a technical matter, like my syntax; as though my outrage were in a category with dangling participles, split infinitives. My outrage.

"Where is my outrage?"

"Your outrage," he affirmed. "Your anger, Elizabeth. You've broken all these great stories but you don't take them anywhere. Every time you get your hands on something hot, you drop it."

"I'm a professional observer." My voice seemed to echo the shrill wail in my head. "I'm trained to be detached, impartial. I don't get emotionally involved."

"That's the trouble."

His voice was a whispered hiss, like the noise made by an inflatable device with a pinhole leak. It hissed relentlessly that my dispatches from Bellavista were nothing more than fragments, bits and pieces out of context. Sure, they were accurate, they seemed to tell a true story, but they revealed very little about the reality of Bellavista. Because I didn't dig deep enough. I left everybody with a bunch of broken pieces, a shattered lens through which nobody could see what was going on. I'd failed to paint a picture of reality.

At last he stopped talking. But when I looked up, Hartwell looked away—surprised, maybe, that he'd gone too far, said too much. His face was deeply flushed, and he began to finger the camouflage hat on his knee while I floundered in my swamp of shame.

Galgo, Gato, and Quique watched. I don't think they ever blinked. I was grateful that they did not understand English, grateful that Sonia hadn't yet returned. Because next I expected Hartwell to answer my unasked questions. I expected him to tell me that the *Herald-Sun* had sent me to Bellavista because I wasn't strong enough or brave enough to work without a net; because I wasn't skilled enough or aggressive enough to put the rest of the press corps on the run; because I wasn't good enough to dig up the truth behind the fabrications. Ever since I'd been assigned to Bellavista, this idea had been wriggling under everything else like a tiny restless worm: I'd been sent to Bellavista because I was not as good a journalist as Hartwell. I had been sent because I was only good enough to gather the most apparent facts, to take official assertions at face value, to process the prepackaged news doled out by the governments of the United States and Bellavista. I couldn't see the bigger picture. Hartwell was an aerialist, a juggernaut. I was a stenographer. I couldn't step out onto the wire.

Just then Sonia reappeared. She grinned and called out, "*¡Aquí están!*"—Here they are!—as she held up, between her fingers, half a dozen green bottles of Coca-Cola, which were dripping wet, miraculously cold. She walked around our little circle to distribute them, kicked Quique in the foot, told him to give Señorita Norteamerica some breathing space. He scuttled over to the tree stump with his Coke, and when she handed Hartwell his, his thumb grazed the inside of her wrist.

She'd combed her hair and washed her face when she'd gone after the Cokes. She'd also changed her shirt, and the shirt she wore was mine, a creamy blend of silk and linen, my only spare. She'd rolled up the sleeves, knotted the tails tightly at her slender waist. When she handed me my Coke, I sniffed an exotic but familiar blend of jasmine, rose, and spices. She'd helped herself to my perfume, Obsession. The scent was unmistakable.

"It's a risk you take when you bring your Obsession into liberated territory," she whispered, grinning at her wordplay. "I had to liberate some."

I could have corrected her right then, could have told her right then that she didn't have to liberate my stuff because she didn't have to primp for Alan Hartwell. Right then I could have told her that Hartwell's feeling for her had nothing to do with the way she looked or dressed. But I didn't tell her then, and later I forgot. It made me feel better anyway that there were cracks in Sonia's crust, too. In one of them was wedged the belief that her natural looks weren't good enough for Alan Hartwell. Which I already knew was not true even though she didn't know it.

CHAPTER
TWENTY-THREE

B Y THE TIME SONIA REAPPEARED, WEARING MY SHIRT AND PERFUME and carrying the icy bottles of Coca-Cola, I kept seeing, superimposed over everything, the wire stretched out over the chasm, the wire shimmering in the light—but it was empty, and I no longer knew where I was or how to find myself.

The moment Sonia reappeared, Hartwell began explaining how he'd ended up in Mesa Verde with Sonia's brother Daniel, whose *nombre de guerra* was Comandante Ocho. Hartwell, of course, was determined to write a book about Bellavista, a book that would contain difficult, complex truths, not the censored truths of daily journalism. Intent upon this mission, he had reentered the country by way of Costa Negra. He'd followed a circuitous route back into the country because he couldn't risk the State Department or the government of Bellavista discovering his plans. He'd spent weeks in Costa Negra attempting to make contact with *el frente*, specifically to make contact with Sonia's brother. Hartwell said he'd known that Daniel could and would help him get safely back into Bellavista.

"It was the least we, I mean my family, could do," Sonia interjected. Even then, her voice was different, more mature and resonant. "You see he, Alan, saved us, me and my mother."

"I didn't save you," he protested. "I performed a minor clerical chore."

The way Hartwell and Sonia went on to tell the story, the real Sonia Alvinas and her mother might have been killed during the earthquake. Or they might not ever have existed. They might have been born through a forger's pen just prior to their current engagements, and their only authentic existence might have been on paper. Neither Sonia nor Hartwell knew for sure. They agreed it didn't matter.

What mattered, Sonia continued, was that at a very dangerous point in her and her mother's lives, Hartwell had obtained for them all the necessary official documents, the identification papers, the mother-and-daughter birth certificates, that had enabled them to stay alive in Bellavista, to go on with their lives, or rather to start new lives.

"You can't imagine how desperate we were," said Sonia, taking out her tobacco and rolling papers. "I was thinking of taking up prostitution when I remembered my camera." She rolled herself a cigarette. "I figured I'd make more money that way than with my body." She laughed her wild bird laugh, and Hartwell's head snapped back. "You know the men in this country don't want a bag of bones like me." She lit the cigarette, exhaled a plume of smoke, laughed again. "I probably wouldn't have made a centavo."

At the smell of Sonia's cigarette, Galgo and Gato simultaneously sat up. She lobbed them the papers and tobacco pouch.

"Anyway," Sonia went on, "I ambushed him in the parking lot of the Hotel Lido one night, showed him some of my stuff. He didn't believe the pictures were mine. So we went out together and I shot more stuff, which he developed by himself." They laughed together. "Two weeks later, I was Sonia Alvinas, a stringer for the *New York Herald-Sun*."

"The rest is history," murmured Hartwell.

Sonia took something from her pocket, handed it to Hartwell. I couldn't see what it was, but remembered the day I'd met her when she'd rifled through my office at the hotel and taken something. Hartwell's chuckle coaxed me back to the present. He was holding by its neck chain his photo ID from la Oficina de la Prensa Internacional. He was clean-shaven and bespectacled in his picture, wore a jacket and a tie. Hartwell stared somberly into the camera as if penetrating all the ruses and subterfuges of Bellavista's byzantine government. Hartwell, the aerialist, the juggernaut.

"It's not like I was expecting to run into you," she went on, her eyes shiny as polished onyx. "But I figured what the hell. I'd keep it just in case."

It was quiet for a long time. Alan and Sonia stared off into the forest, trying not to look at each other. I watched them and thought there was an important question, one that needed asking. It kept darting through the air just beyond my reach. Quique had rolled and lit a cigarette before I managed to catch hold of it.

"Why?" I pointed with my thumb toward Sonia. "Who were?"

I kept trying to say more but discovered I was incoherent, incapable of forming a sentence. I could find words like "how" and "why" but couldn't make sentences stay together. The words kept flying apart, without the glue of meaning. I could see them swooping all around me, winged and filamented; not droning like Sonia's *malditos moscones* but flitting with antic energy.

"Why did?" I tried repeating, gratefully heard Hartwell finish for me. "Why did she need a new identity?"

I nodded, my head spinning. I almost missed his whispered explanation: That Sonia's real name, and her mother's real name, had appeared on the so-called death lists, those of Los Hijos Patrióticos de Bellavista, a clandestine association of oligarchs known to finance and direct the death squads.

"Why? Who?" I struggled.

"Do you remember anything about the closing of the university?"

Hartwell's question pushed me back into the *Herald-Sun*'s New York library, into its musty rows of clip files.

"Come on, Lizzie, you remember. The army rolled into the place in troop carriers, broke up a demonstration on the library steps with water cannons, tear gas. Afterward, they went inside the administration building and blew away a bunch of priests and professors, a cleaning woman, and the cleaning woman's daughter. Just to make sure no one missed their point. Then they locked the gates."

"The Reinaldo Rivas Library?"

My question seemed somehow crucial.

"Yes," he answered. "*El padre del general.* Well, one of the murder victims was a guy named Rubén Meza. He was a founder of the Democratic Socialist Party and head of the teachers' union. A big-shot leftist but a moderate, really, a reformer."

Sonia reached for me and squeezed my arm.

"He was my father."

Her radiant face and impassioned eyes were inches from my own. I couldn't take my eyes off her but couldn't get her into focus. She seemed to be emerging from a gauzy husk, and the husk was drifting upward. I think most of my bad feelings about Sonia went up with it, my anger and uneasiness about what had been her disguise: her grandiosity and volatility, her ragged clothes and funny hairdo.

Even as the gauzy husk was disappearing, taking with it my bad feelings, I remembered something else, something I didn't want to remember. It was that last night with Rivas Valdez when we were standing at the seawall, watching and listening to the ocean. He was kissing my shoulders, running his fingertips along my bare arms so gently that it made me shiver. "Who is she, your little friend Sonia Alvinas?" he'd asked, his voice as ineluctable as the ocean. I must have answered with my own question: "What do you mean, who is she? She's a photographer. She works for the *Herald-Sun.*" "But who is she?" he insisted, tracing the insides of my elbows. "She's highly skilled for a poor *mestiza.* The finest news photographer in Bellavista. So I can't help wondering about her. Who is her family?"

And leaning back against him, so the buttons of his shirt pressed along my spine, I told him everything I knew, which I didn't think was much: that my poor little half-breed photographer lived in *la colonia de los sobrevivientes* with her widowed mother; that maybe she had a brother; that she'd studied at a Florida university before the earthquake, during which her family had lost everything. And before we went inside, I might also have told him that she was a little crazy, paranoid; that she carried a gun in her camera bag, and was, frankly, a pain in the ass.

Sonia was speaking. Her words seemed to come from elsewhere, and they didn't signify much to me. At last I got her into focus, saw she was a different woman, slim and pretty, not unstylish, and I wondered why her slender fingers were encircling my arm.

"My father was Rubén Meza," this woman said. "My mother is Inocencia Quintero. My real name is Mariel. I'm really Mariel Meza Quintero."

Sonia's transfiguration happened very quickly, much too fast for me. Preceded by Hartwell's own metamorphosis, it left me feeling that I'd lost most of my senses. I'd retained only sight and hearing, and those I could not trust. Still Sonia and Alan kept talking, kept telling me things I did not want to know—that Sonia's oldest brother, Samuel, had already been disappeared by a death squad and was presumed to be dead; that the threats against Sonia and her mother had intensified once Daniel had emerged as a leader of the FMOLN. I think the two of them would have kept on forever, enchanted by their own voices, except that Galgo interrupted. Galgo said none of us had much time and it was his turn to talk to *la periodista norteamericana.*

As he moved toward me, he seemed suddenly to radiate ambivalence, a weird mix of eagerness and hostility. Sonia and Hartwell were already walking off somewhere with at least four feet between them—as though the intensity of their feelings for each other was crammed into that space and was keeping them apart. I watched them, hearing Galgo telling Gato and Quique to get lost, too, because what he had to say he'd say only to me. And I must have gone to get my tape recorder, a new one, purchased for the trip, because once Galgo began to speak, I saw it between us on the ground and its cassette was running in patient, soundless circles.

"Pues," he began, then hesitated. *"No hay Estrella Luminosa."*

I would have remembered his words exactly even if I did not have the tape: Well, followed by the hesitant pause, there is no Estrella Luminosa.

Galgo's voice was harsh and guttural, and he had trouble with his fricatives, an odd, lisplike defect of speech that made it difficult to understand him. I would have remembered them, too, his crude voice and flawed articulation, even if I did not have the tape.

No hay Estrella Luminosa.

There is no Shining Star.

"La Estrella Luminosa es la creación del ministro de la defensa. General Víctor Rivas Valdez."

As he spoke, Galgo eyed the recorder, examining it with his thick fingers now and then, gently, as though it might be an explosive, a detonation device.

Shining Star is the defense minister's creation, the work of General Víctor Rivas Valdez.

Galgo leaned toward me and frowned, maybe wondered if I'd understood him. Groups of short, straight scars covered his forehead, cheeks, and chin, as if something made of fragile glass had exploded in his face. A dragon tattoo covered one of his massive forearms.

"You mean Shining Star exists, but it's not leftist, don't you?" I asked in Spanish. "It acts on behalf of Rivas Valdez?"

He nodded very slowly. I wondered how he'd gotten his *nombre de guerra*, Greyhound—for he was neither slender nor graceful. I wondered if he ran swiftly or if he had extraordinary sight. I had an urge to take off his sunglasses, to look into his eyes. But his brooding tension stopped me. So I stared at the sunglasses, watched orange sunlight reflecting off the lenses like small explosions in a freeze frame.

How do you know? Who told you? I asked.

"Yo era un comando," Galgo answered. *"Ahora soy un desertor, un defector."*

I rechecked the recorder and jotted into my notebook. Later, if I hadn't had the tape, I would have thought I'd dreamed it, dreamed up this character named Galgo who said he was a deserter and a defector, a former military demolitions expert who'd been involved, under orders from Rivas Valdez, in many of the bombings blamed on Estrella Luminosa, and who offered convincing details of those incidents.

Galgo reached into his shirt, held out his hand. I picked up a small medal attached to a chain around his neck. It was the military identification tag of Corporal Juan Antonio Robles, who was born on September 7, 1953.

"Soy yo," he said. *"Es mi medalla. Soy Robles."*

It's my medal. I am Robles.

We'd arrived on earth the same year, not two months apart, but I wasn't thinking about that. Instead I was grappling with what Galgo was telling me. Because if it was true, then all of my dispatches had been part of an intricately layered lie. Which meant I had an obligation to expose the lie.

But I couldn't expose that lie, couldn't use anything Galgo told me, until I had verified his identity and confirmed the things he told me through at least one other source. No, I couldn't take his word. I had no idea who he was. But I also knew that any effort to verify Galgo's identity or to confirm the things he told me would put me there over the chasm, on the wire without a net.

I was imagining myself out there, clinging to the swaying wire, when this thought occurred to me: Galgo could be lying. Yes, Galgo could be lying. The idea rushed to me on such a wild surge of relief that it left me breathless: I did not have to believe him.

After that, when I looked across at him, he seemed to be an actor playing a guerrilla. With his scars and horrible tattoo, with the grenades hanging from his belt and the semiautomatic within his reach on the ground beside him, he didn't seem quite real. Rather, he seemed as if he'd been made up and costumed for a role.

And the odd, toneless way he spoke, with such a lack of expression, of irony, made him seem like an actor unfamiliar with his lines, an actor just beginning to learn his part.

I went on listening, and it was painless once I'd been relieved of the burden of belief. I heard him say how he'd been trained as a commando with an elite, ultrasecret unit that answered to a lieutenant colonel who spoke directly to the general. *Gringos*, mercenaries, former military men with links to the U.S. government, had trained him somewhere in the jungle near el Golfo de Virtud.

He'd been in it for the money, Galgo said. Yes, he'd been paid very well as a government terrorist. The turning point had come for him, he said, when he learned that his parents and a sister, poor farm workers, had been slaughtered in their rural village. After Christmas, he'd returned home, seen the ruins, and learned that his family had been killed and their homestead burned, by a marauding band of soldiers. He searched for the graves, but neighbors told him that their remains had been carted off for a mass burial at an undisclosed location.

It was then, said Galgo, that he'd disappeared himself, eventually making contact with *el frente*. He'd volunteered to use his skills against those who'd trained him. In recent weeks, he said, he'd firebombed two Hueys at a remote mountain base and ambushed, wiped out, a small elite unit, eight men, he figured.

He took off his sunglasses. His eyes were dull as stones, as though something vital had drained out of them.

How could I verify his existence? I asked those empty eyes. How could I confirm his allegations?

Talk to Hartwell, Galgo said. Hartwell knew everything about him. I tried explaining, but soon gave up, that Hartwell was useless to me as a source. Or rather that to use him would be to betray him. So I asked Galgo for details of his early life, facts I might be able to verify by tracking him through the military bureaucracy. But even as he answered, I realized that there was no freedom of information in Bellavista. Such records, even if they existed, would not be public anyway. Then he said the campaign of terror being blamed on ultraleftists was Rivas Valdez's strategy to mobilize the right, to reinforce the power of the military and to solidify his support from the U.S. government. The strategy was identical to that used by Ferdinand Marcos in the Philippines prior to his declaration of martial law—a move he'd made with the full support of the United States. But when Galgo first told me, the idea seemed insane, absurd.

"Why are you telling me these things?"

"Because there is a very large price on my head." He smiled. Several of his bottom teeth were missing. "The people here are very poor. . . . It's only a matter of time before . . ."

By then maybe I was fixated on his tattoo, the image of a clawed, scaly creature like the one I often thought lay coiled and submerged in the green slime at my core. My fingers began to trace its red eyes, its intricate limbs, the finned tail twisting up his biceps. Under it, Galgo's arm was hot and vibrant, like twined steel wrapped in a resilient thermal fabric.

Well, a *compañero* of his was still a member of the ultracovert unit, he went on, as if oblivious to my fingers on his arm. This friend informed to him from time to time. Was there any way for me to talk to him, the friend? I asked his arm. Because I knew he'd have some very interesting things to say. Not likely, Galgo answered. It would be too dangerous. For all of us. Because of Rivas Valdez. Rivas Valdez was a monster.

I became aware of the keening trill of birds in the trees and the drone of distant Dragonflies. Through this hum Galgo murmured that the land reform program would be the next target of Estrella Luminosa. This was the last thing his friend, the other commando, had told him. Estrella Luminosa planned to attack land reform.

And I remembered our appointment the next day, Sonia's and mine, at the New Jerusalem Cooperative.

Nuestra Señora del Refugio. Our Lady of Refuge. The name came to my mind when I saw Mary Healy in the yard outside Nilsa's hut when I arrived with Galgo. She was talking to Rosa and Ocho, explaining how to clean and care for Rosa's incision, when she turned and saw me.

"I see you've given up dressing for success." She pointed to my funky clothes and embraced me with a spurt of raucous laughter. "I didn't recognize you for a minute." I joined her laughter, grateful that she looked exactly the way she always had in her chambray shirt and jeans, grateful that she hadn't been transfigured, changed. The crucifix was in its proper place, and her crazy hair was spiraled all around her face. I hugged her briefly, reassured myself with her familiar antiseptic smell, the fragile feel of her skin. I gestured to Sonia, sleek and slender as a fashion model, who was standing nearby cuddling the baby. I couldn't seem to tell Mary what had happened, but she nodded gently, as though she already knew everything, understood everything. "I told you anything could happen here," she said.

Ocho took my hand, thanked me for my part in his daughter's birth. Right away I saw that the smudges under his eyes were identical to Sonia's, but the eyes themselves were softer, more compassionate. Rosa reached for my other hand from the pallet where she rested, expressed a gratitude that chastened and embarrassed me. I insisted I'd done nothing. Mary was the heroine.

"They named the baby María Elisabet. For you guys," Sonia interrupted. "But I'm the godmother." She preened a little with the baby, hugged her proprietarily. "*Pues*, they really wanted to name the baby for me, but they didn't know which name to use."

She laughed, and the others joined her, but I couldn't seem to. The light was fading quickly, but even in the dim light I sensed the depth of their connections—Rosa's, Ocho's, Sonia's, Alan's, Mary's—and my distance from all of them. While they talked, intensely, joyfully, it seemed, snatching an unexpected interlude from the catastrophe around them, I kept thinking about Galgo's story and what I'd have to do in order to report it. When the rest of them were eating soup, I sat by Ocho and asked him for a statement about the war, a statement I could use for publication.

"*La violencia es siempre repugnante,*" he answered.

Violence is always repugnant.

His answer caught me unprepared, and before I had another question ready, he went on that his own father was his hero.

"Truly he was a great man. He was a pacifist. He believed in evolution, peaceful change. He never carried arms. He did not know how to use a gun. But he was gunned down at the university. Eight bullets in his skull. The military did not like his ideas, so they blew his brains out."

"And now you are a killer." I gestured to the gun on the ground by Ocho, to the ammunition and grenades draped around his body.

"Yes," he answered, nodding as if he'd been long aware of the irony. "Now I'm a guerrilla, a murderer."

Los correos, the boy runners, interrupted us, showing up suddenly and soundlessly like ghosts.

"Ya empieza la evacuación," said one of them. His child's voice was incongruous with his solemnity: The evacuation is beginning. I leaned toward him through the shadows, took in his odd silhouette. He was Licho, the boy who'd lost his arms to *el fuego blanco. Por un golpe de suerte,* just his arms. His partner was our escort Cobo.

"Tenemos que salir de Mesa Verde ahora mismo," Cobo said, peering into my eyes, making sure I understood. We must leave right now. I responded with a brief nod.

What about Estrella Luminosa? I asked Ocho as everyone began dispersing. The Mateo Omaño National Liberation Front had no relationship with it, he insisted. All he knew about Estrella Luminosa was what Galgo had told him. He offered an expressive smile that was very much like Sonia's. "We do not engage in acts of terrorism," he said. "We are morally opposed to the use of violence against noncombatants. This is how we distinguish ourselves from those we fight against."

The camp was dark and absolutely silent by the time we left. It was impossible to imagine that hundreds of refugees were departing for the long journey up steep slopes, along paths that wove perilously close to government encampments. To impassive mothers and grandmothers, Mary had distributed her supplies of Valium, Xanax, and Benadryl. These medications would induce torpid sleeps in infants and toddlers, whose involuntary cries might betray the refugees. The women had strapped babies to their backs and bellies, carried toddlers in makeshift gurneys. Rosa, too, cradling Maria Elisabet, was carried on a stretcher the men had fashioned from her pallet. Quique, her mother, and some older children would be taking turns.

In darkness they would make their way along narrow ledges giving way to sheer drops and across flimsy footbridges that swayed—like my high wire—above deep flumes. If they succeeded, Mesa Verde would be empty when the aerial bombardment began at first light. No one said what would happen if they failed.

We headed out at more or less the same time, Sonia first, behind Cobo, her own dark shirt over my creamy one to make her less visible in the dark. Mariel Meza Quintero. I wasn't used to her, didn't know how to act around her. Close by, Mary Healy strode ahead, full of energy, her face limpid in the moonlight. The three of us followed Cobo into the wilderness. We immediately began our descent, scrambling down a stony slope so steep we stumbled and slid. Right away I lost all sense of time. The vast, empty sky turned purple, luminous. The terrain grew lustrous with puddles of phosphorescent ash. Once I turned around, but nightfall, like an abrupt awakening that hides a dream, had hidden Mesa Verde. I could not see anything at all.

CHAPTER
TWENTY-FOUR

*A*FTER OUR RESPITE AT THE CONVENT IN SANGRE DE CRISTO—
where Mary left Sonia and me—the early-morning trip to the
Cooperativo Nuevo de Jerusalem was something like a free-
fall. We covered the same turf we'd covered just two days before, before
going to Mesa Verde, but covered it much faster, going down instead
of up, hurtling along at about fifty, heedless of ancient autobuses and
ox-drawn carts, of dogs, chickens, and children on the road.

El chofer—I'd paid him two hundred U.S. dollars to take us all the
way—drove so fast that the villages and the golden swaths of drying
corn between them were blurred and unfamiliar. Sonia and I drowsed
against each other, slept, rousing but not really waking at the checkpoints
of *las villas estratégicas*, where the driver gave more of my cash to *las
patrullas de defensa civil* to wave us on our way.

The explosion that destroyed the Cooperativo Nuevo de Jerusalem went off within an hour of our arrival, just minutes after we'd toured its glistening tiers of dark green coffee plants, talked to and photographed the smiling *campesinos*. We were drinking warm Coca-Colas with an American agricultural adviser, a former Midwestern farm boy, when the warm air quaked, gusted, slid away. Orange flames, flecked with dark fragments of debris, billowed over the blackened barn, high above the melting trees, up into a cobalt sky. The sound came afterward, a reverberant sky-ripping boom that slammed us to the ground, and even as I sucked earth I thought the shattering noise irrelevant. Because by then I knew I was witnessing the fulfillment of Corporal Robles's prophecy. Cheek to the ground, I saw farm workers, detached from gravity, floating free, and flocks of squawking wild birds reel up into the sky. I saw farm machinery, trees, small buildings blown apart, on fire, and everything began falling into place for me. I knew at once that Corporal Robles— the tattooed Galgo—had not been lying: Estrella Luminosa was *la creación del ministro de la defensa*, General Víctor Rivas Valdez.

I knew why Sonia and I had been allowed to keep on going after being stopped so many times by soldiers. And I understood why Rivas Valdez had given us the travel documents in the first place: so that Sonia and I could provide a firsthand account of an act of "leftist" terrorism, an account that, within minutes of its occurrence, would be transmitted all around the world.

The screams of the injured, the panicked shouts of their coworkers, cut through my grotesque jubilation at my own survival. And even as I scrambled to my feet to join other survivors in a helter-skelter triage effort, it occurred to me that the general's margin for error had been very, very narrow.

---

11 FARM WORKERS KILLED
IN LEFTIST BLAST
Future of Land Reform in Doubt

by Elizabeth M. Guerrera
Herald-Sun Staff Writer

IXTAPANGA, BELLAVISTA—Eleven farm workers were killed and 13 others, including an American agricultural adviser, were injured in an early-morning explosion here that left in ruins this country's first worker-owned coffee plantation and throws into doubt the future of its sweeping land reform program.

According to government officials here and at the U.S. embassy, leftist terrorists of the Shining Star Brigade have claimed responsibility for the Wednesday bombing, which occurred in a large barn as workers, just beginning the day's work, were picking up equipment.

The conflagration immediately spread to the slopes of the 2,700-acre cooperative. It destroyed most of the coffee crop as well as other outbuildings and equipment before burning itself out.

Everyone in the barn at the time of the blast was killed. Most of the injured were those just arriving at the farm or those leaving the barn on their way into the fields. The cooperative, called New Jerusalem, employs hundreds of day laborers.

U.S. Ambassador Richard M. Whitaker called the explosion "a catastrophe" that may strike a death blow to the beleaguered land reform plan through which half of this troubled country's farmland was to be deeded to peasant farmers.

According to officials, Shining Star's communiqués to the United States embassy and to Bellavista's press ministry stated that the organization placed plastic explosives in the barn, which the American advisers used as an office, to protest the United States' extensive involvement in the agrarian reform program. Neither communiqué was immediately available to reporters.

The United States has put more than $60 million into the program. In addition, a score of agricultural advisers have been sent here through the American Institute for Free Labor Development (AIFLD), a private labor organization funded in part by the State Department's Agency for International Development.

The agrarian reform plan, the most extensive yet attempted in Latin America, was designed by American experts and initiated at the behest of Congress, which vowed to withhold from Bellavista all military aid, currently pegged at $1.5 million a day, until efforts were made to more equitably distribute the nation's resources.

AIFLD's Frederick Simpson and his partner, Daniel T. Browne, live and work at the remote cooperative. Browne suffered a broken ankle in the blast. Simpson was unharmed.

In an interview moments before the explosion, Simpson called American involvement "an instance of pure, benevolent cooperation between Uncle Sam and a Third World country that's stumbling toward democracy."

Control of the nation's rich farmlands, its only natural resource, has been a major point of conflict in a four-year-old civil war which has claimed some 43,000 lives.

Defense Minister Víctor Rivas Valdez called the bombing "a disturbing escalation" of Shining Star's terrorism. Though a recent spate of bombings in and around the capital city, Libertad, has been attributed to Shining Star, there have been no other civilian casualties.

"Nothing is sacred to these terrorists," said Whitaker of the bombing. "We're talking about Khmer Rouge–type communists here. The lives of their countrymen mean nothing to them."

The Khmer Rouge, under the leadership of Pol Pot, is believed responsible for the deaths of some 1.5 million Cambodians during a four-year reign of terror that began in 1975.

Officials here describe Shining Star as the radical left-wing fringe of the Mateo Omaño National Liberation Front (FMOLN), the Marxist guerrilla army. No members of Shining Star have yet publicly declared themselves. The media, hampered by stringent state-of-siege laws, have been unsuccessful in their efforts to locate and meet with them.

Whitaker has previously likened the shadowy organization to Peru's fanatical Shining Path, or Sendero Luminoso, which has waged a campaign of terror in Peru's rural countryside for many years.

In recent interviews, FMOLN guerrillas denied all associations with Estrella Luminosa. They stated that their organization does not engage in acts of terrorism and is morally opposed to violence against noncombatants.

Representatives of the FMOLN were not available for comment on yesterday's bombing.

Rivas Valdez said yesterday that trouble had not been unexpected at New Jerusalem, a plantation formerly owned by the Rivera family, prominent members of the oligarchy.

"We were prepared for violence from the right, from those who were forced to give up their land," said the general. He termed it ironic that the violence had come instead from the left. "We created these cooperatives to pacify the leftists. This is what they asked for."

CHAPTER
TWENTY-FIVE

*I*N PRINT, THE NEW JERUSALEM BOMBING STORY LOOKED EXACTLY LIKE the truth. In print, the New Jerusalem bombing story not only looked exactly like the truth but it was also displayed the way I'd always wanted my work to be displayed. And when I finally saw it, downstairs at the Hotel Lido Sunday night, I was giddy and breathless as if I'd reached a pinnacle after a long, hard climb.

The 24-point headline, two lines, ran across three columns, and my name was there in boldface type beneath it: Elizabeth M. Guerrera, *Herald-Sun* Staff Writer. Sonia's stunning photographs were laid out above the story, but I hardly noticed them. I couldn't help staring at my own name there on the front page, at my byline on the front page of a fat Sunday edition.

Of course, mine was not the lead story. The lead story was a national budget story out of Washington. But my story ran just below the fold, in the right-hand columns, where it demanded immediate attention. I saw it even before the deliveryman had split the cord that held the bale of papers. As I bent to grab the top one, I heard the envious and congratulatory murmurs of my colleagues, who'd been waiting for the paper too. I straightened up, ran my hand across my story, absorbed it through my fingertips.

They were ineffable pleasures, the texture and scent of newsprint, the heft of a newspaper when you held it. Mine was the kind of work that gave you something to hold on to—and if you held on tight enough, nobody could take it from you. For a few moments I stood there, in the honeyed light of the lobby, holding the newspaper. I accepted the compliments of my colleagues, and actually believed, for those few moments, I deserved them.

The congratulatory murmurs, however, subsided too soon, and my colleagues departed. I carried the heavy newspaper to a table at the far edge of the terrace, near the pots of fiery poincianas. I seemed to be carrying something else, a jagged blade wedged somewhere in my chest, and I ordered Wild Turkey. I drank the first drink very quickly, to make the feeling go away. In fact, I didn't really want to read my story. I didn't want to see what my editors had done to it. Most of all I didn't want to think.

All day I'd worked on the story of the Río Luciente massacre, and I'd worked very hard, because it helped me not to think. In the morning I'd called my mother to ask how she was, to find out if she'd seen my story. The *Herald-Sun*'s Sunday edition would have hit the streets late Saturday—and I wanted a firsthand account, a witness to my history. But Mum was confused, distant. She hadn't seen the newspaper. I hung up, broke our connection, but her whisper-soft voice released a depth charge. Memories of all the other times she'd been confused and distant exploded in my face. I tried ignoring them. I hid myself in work, but the evanescent memories congealed and turned corrosive anyway.

I filed the story of the Río Luciente massacre before I went downstairs for the newspaper. And though I thought it was good work, one of the most powerful stories I'd yet written, I felt restless and uneasy—and the uneasiness only increased after I picked up the newspaper and walked out to the terrace. I didn't want to think about the New Jerusalem bombing story in print. I didn't want to think about the past or where

I'd come from. I ordered another drink, watched the pastel lights reflecting off the pool, smelled the heady scent of roses.

The candle on my table was contained inside a globe of delicate pink glass. Its light flickered on the newspaper, my hands. Behind me, as from a vast distance, I heard the clatter of expensive meals being served to others, the murmur of many voices. At last I looked back at the headline—"11 Farm Workers Killed in Leftist Blast—Future of Land Reform in Doubt"—and I could not help seeing what I'd been trying not to see: that I'd produced a journalistic aberration, a mutation, a story that was absolutely accurate and yet devoid of truth.

With it, I'd proved Hartwell's theory: that you can't tell both sides of a story when one side, the most powerful side, is lying and the other side is inaccessible. What was worse, my story seemed to answer, to affirm, the rhetorical question he'd asked in the blinding light of Mesa Verde: When you know they're lying, isn't it irresponsible and immoral to repeat their lies?

Of course, by the time I sat on the hotel terrace trying to melt the jagged blade with Wild Turkey, the story of the New Jerusalem bombing no longer belonged to me. By then it had escaped my control and taken on its own life. There had been accounts on the government-owned radio and television stations, and countless secondhand accounts by the wire services, by independent Latin American media, by other North American dailies. Every account had blamed leftist terrorists of Estrella Luminosa for the deaths and devastation. With every repetition, the lie turned glossier, gained more of the patina of truth.

But as I sat there with the bourbon and the newspaper, I couldn't help wrestling with one immutable fact. Before the story of the New Jerusalem bombing had escaped into its own life, I had reported lies as if they were the truth. Even as I'd dictated my story into the telephone, enunciating carefully for the recording device at the other end of the wire, I'd been colluding in the lie.

I tried to remember mitigating circumstances, tried to remember that I hadn't had much choice. I'd only quoted sources, reported the statements of government officials. Anyway, my editors never would have taken Galgo's word about Estrella Luminosa. I couldn't take his word myself. Yet if I'd withheld the story while attempting to verify his allegations, I would have been beaten on the story. In fact, no editors had been available when I'd filed the bombing story, by telephone from the airfield at Ixtapanga. All that day, as Sonia and I traveled back to

Libertad, I'd been frantic to talk with them, with McManus, frantic to tell them everything I knew. I planned to write them a long memo, a synopsis of my reporting that would detail not only Galgo's charges about Estrella Luminosa, but also the Río Luciente massacre and the government's apparent policy of total war against civilians in the Mesa Verde region.

"Great stuff, Lizzie, great story," is what McManus said when I finally reached him in New York later that Saturday. "The pictures are sensational. We're gonna blow everybody away. It's a fucking miracle you and Sonia weren't killed."

Even as his praise warmed and buoyed me, I tried to say there were problems with the story. But before I could, McManus was telling me he'd made some minor changes. In the interest of fairness and accuracy, he said, he'd moved the FMOLN's repudiation of terrorism down lower into the story.

I remembered the paragraph exactly: "In recent interviews, FMOLN guerrillas denied all associations with Estrella Luminosa. They stated that their organization does not engage in acts of terrorism and is morally opposed to violence against noncombatants."

Despite its circumspection, the paragraph was crucial to any representation of reality. I'd placed it near the top. It had been my fourth or fifth paragraph.

"I'd consider this a pro forma disavowal," said McManus. "Isn't this exactly what we ought to expect to hear from them?"

He didn't wait for an answer, went on to point out that the FMOLN had made no specific comment vis-à-vis the New Jerusalem bombing.

"They didn't address this particular incident," he said. "We can't imply that they denied the bombing when they didn't even make themselves available to answer any questions."

Not until I sat drinking bourbon on the terrace did I see that McManus had moved the paragraph almost to the bottom of my story. It was, to be exact, the sixteenth paragraph. It ran below my explanations of the Khmer Rouge and Sendero Luminoso. Implicitly it linked el frente with Pol Pot's bloodthirsty army and the incomprehensibly violent Peruvian Maoists.

Comandante Ocho's repudiation of terrorism and of violence against noncombatants did not appear on the front page but rather on a jump page—a page deep inside the newspaper where front-page stories are continued. From marketing studies on the subject, and from my own experience, I knew most people wouldn't read it. Or, if they did, they would be convinced by then that Estrella Luminosa was the terrorist arm of the FMOLN; that it was guilty beyond any shadow of a doubt.

"Who are these people anyway, these FMOLN guerrillas you talked to?" McManus went on to ask—and I tried to tell him without giving anyone away. I began to say their *nombres de guerra* were Comandante Ocho and Galgo, realized immediately how fantastic it sounded.

"Well, they're not part of *el frente*'s high command, are they?" he asked, and I said Ocho might be but that I honestly didn't know.

"Where did you meet with them? Why didn't you get back in touch with them, nail down some answers?"

His questions struck like sharp stones, and I tried to fend them off, tried to explain that I'd met with them near the refugee camp called Mesa Verde, a place off-limits to reporters, where a full-scale war was going on. My interview had been cut short by an evacuation of the area. But that was another story, I said, the intensity of the air war in that area, and the question of Mesa Verde's status as a refugee camp.

It must have been then that McManus interrupted, said in an unmistakably accusatory tone that I'd been "out of contact" for at least three days, and that in New York they'd been "more than a little concerned" about my whereabouts.

"My whereabouts?"

"We didn't know where in hell you were until you filed the bombing story. Now it turns out you were at this refugee camp. Wherever the hell it is."

His tone demanded an explanation, and I gave one, said I'd sent him a letter through the Mexico City bureau. I said I'd thought it was a safer route, considering the state of siege and the dangers involved in my unauthorized travel. McManus had not received my letter.

"The thing is, Lizzie," he said, "we never discussed the possibility of you deliberately violating Bellavista's regulations on the foreign press."

It was, he went on, one of those "sticky ethical questions" that had "to go through channels," that had to be approved by many editors. It was the only way the *Herald-Sun* could support reporters in those situations, in the event that something went wrong.

"We never cleared that kind of travel for you. And certainly not for Sonia."

"Look, I saw the chance, I grabbed it." I was trying not to let his patronizing tone cow me into silence. "I'm back now. Everybody's safe and sound." I took a few deep breaths, abandoned the idea of giving him a written synopsis of my reporting. Instead I heard myself divulging Galgo's secrets.

"Jim, I have sources telling me not only that Estrella Luminosa isn't associated with *el frente*, but that it's Rivas Valdez's baby. That he's mounted this campaign of terror to gain sympathy from Congress, to galvanize the right and consolidate his own power. It's exactly what Marcos did in the Philippines."

I heard his quick intake of breath, thought I recognized the sound, the sound of a news junkie confronted with the possibility of some really great stuff.

"You know, Lizzie," he said after a minute, "we really can't afford to have you running around half-cocked down there."

"Half-cocked?"

"Oh, shit, Lizzie, I didn't mean that the way it sounded. But this is crazy. Not a month ago we profiled the guy in the magazine. Made him a fucking hero."

I heard what must have been his queer, apologetic laugh. I imagined him there in the newsroom, his glasses pushed up to his forehead, so he could rub his scaly eyelids.

"Look, you're doing a terrific job. We have total faith in your work. But the general feeling here is that you were irresponsible disappearing like that. Now you show up and tell me your own front-page story might be part of an elaborate hoax."

Through my office window I had a panoramic view of the ruins of Libertad in the valley below. I could also see the sparkling towers of *la comandancia*, the crucifix on top of Nuestra Señora del Refugio. They seemed to be opposing poles between which I was reeling.

"You know," McManus went on, "I was sending Joe Soza from the Mexico City bureau over to find out what was going on. I had him booked on a flight early tomorrow morning."

McManus's voice seemed to come from far away, as if it might be blowing out of the clouds on the far side of Nuestra Señora del Refugio.

"My source is a defector," I said as if I hadn't heard him. "He claims he was a commando in the unit that did the bombings. He told me a lot of stuff about the bombings, about his training by North American mercenaries."

McManus was silent long enough for me to wonder about the integrity of our telephone connection. In the echoing quiet I suddenly wondered how many other ears were listening, where and how we were being taped.

"Rivas Valdez?" he asked then, as if we'd only just begun to talk, as if he'd only, just then, begun to listen.

"Rivas Valdez," I repeated, and the words made my guts churn. I felt him in the room with me, felt him with such a heated panic that I turned around to make sure no one was there. I was turning back when a curious dazzle shot up from the floor and caught my eye. It was the diamond bracelet, curled like a tiny snake, in the carpet by the corner of my desk. I wondered what it was doing there, why the maid had touched it, how she'd found where I'd hidden it in a drawer.

"This is potentially more explosive than the bomb that killed those farm workers. The junta and the state department will be screaming bloody murder. The ramifications are . . ." His voice trailed off. I held the phone looking alternately at the bracelet on the floor and the distant ruins out my window.

"But you think I ought to try to track it down, don't you? I know . . ." I was about to tell him Galgo's name, but stopped myself. "I might be able to track this defector through the military bureaucracy."

"Of course I think you ought to track it down—but I'm doubting, even if it's true, that you'll find much of a trail." I picked up the bracelet, dropped it into a file drawer, closed the drawer. "Anyway, we'd need more than one source. And our sources will have to be unassailable."

I saw Galgo with the facial scars like something made of fragile glass had exploded in his face. I saw the dragon tattoo on the arm that felt like twined steel, heard his guttural voice. He was not, in any way, the kind of source the *Herald-Sun* would consider reliable. "Unassailable," McManus repeated, and I remembered Hartwell's eyes, bright blue flecked with lavender. He was a perfect source, but I could not say anything about him.

"Look, Lizzie, I'm going to tell Joe Soza to go ahead. He's one of our best, and it won't hurt to have him with you for a few days."

I didn't know Joe Soza, but whoever he was, I didn't want him with me for a few days. I didn't want Joe Soza on my turf, in my territory. I didn't want him messing with my stories, my babies. But I didn't know how to tell McManus. I couldn't tell McManus. I told him, instead, about the Río Luciente massacre, and about the government's apparent scorched-earth policy in Mesa Verde, its apparent use of napalm to destroy the crops and livestock of peasants. It all sounded somehow banal compared with Estrella Luminosa, but he told me to go ahead and file the story, that he'd take a look at it, that we'd "go with it" as long as what I wrote was fair and accurate. By the time our conversation ended, I felt I'd lost something important. I had no idea what it was, or where I stood, or even what I was trying to accomplish. All I knew was that when Joe Soza, whoever he was, showed up, he'd take everything away from me.

"Remember," warned McManus just before he hung up, "our commitment as journalists is to be scrupulously fair and accurate." Scrupulously fair and accurate.

I don't know how long I sat there on the terrace. I don't know how many trips the mute, white-jacketed waiter made between the bar and my isolated table. The candle flame kept flickering inside the pink globe, but the clatter of dinners being served eventually subsided along with the hum of diners' voices. Then a silvery moth, its antennae like tiny iridescent feathers, zoomed in from the dark, and found, unerringly, the hot mouth of the candle's globe, flew into it. Immediately the moth began its struggle for release, and I watched its struggle but kept seeing something else: the empty wire shimmering over the chasm. I pulled the candle closer, tried to lift the globe. The pink glass seared my fingertips, but the globe wouldn't budge. The moth spun crazily inside, thudded against the glass, at last fell into the flame. The incendiary light burst brighter for an instant and then the pink globe went black.

It was like walking through a velvet tunnel, walking upstairs in the dark. The lights were out on the gallery leading to my room, but it happened often, so often I had no curiosity about the cause. The moon sent shafts of light onto the walkway in front me, and I took in, with a somnolent sense of wonder, the hard white stars in the black sky, the fragrance of frangipani and bougainvillea. I was drunk enough to have misplaced my boundaries, to wonder where I left off and the rest of the world began, but not too drunk to see the lanky shadow on the railing outside my room. An irregular inky shape slouched against the vine-covered supporting beam there. I paused not far away, wishing I weren't drunk. As I hesitated there in the dark, I realized it was a man and thought he must be one of Rivas Valdez's thugs. I had time to wonder what he wanted, how I could escape. Right away I realized that from where the thug was sitting, he'd been able to see me downstairs on the terrace, and that he'd probably been watching me for some time. Rage and a turbulent sense of violation surged through me. Then the shadow was standing right in front of me and another musk overwhelmed the perfume of frangipani and bougainvillea. It was the scent of autumn flowers and of the cold, rooty earth that holds them.

"Elisabet," he said. The hot pellet spiraled through my skull and chest, liquidized in the bottom of my belly. Somehow it released my newspaper and a sudden gust or my panic sent it flying all around me. A myriad of sections blew against my ankles, flew up against the railings. Even in the confusion of his touching me, taking my arms, I turned to find my story. I struggled to retrieve my front-page story.

"You've been traveling," I heard him say from somewhere behind me, and as he pulled me closer, I couldn't help seeing his eyes, shallow golden pools, adapted for night vision in the jungle. "You like to go to forbidden places. *Pues*, come with me, *mi amor*. There is one more place I want to take you."

CHAPTER
TWENTY-SIX

I WALKED BAREFOOT ACROSS THE GREAT LAWN, THROUGH THE SEAWALL gate, down broken stone steps to the water. The sky was overcast, and it made the water darker. I walked along the edge of it, lifting my long skirt, draping it over my arm. The skirt was white, soft as a bandage, flimsy as a veil. The water was aching cold. It frothed around my ankles, tugging at my feet, trying to pull me deeper. Even as I resisted, stepping out onto the black sand of the beach, I imagined going under, being pulled away.

I found a smooth ledge of rock and sat on it. Black sand speckled my feet. When I tried to brush it off, the sand stuck to my fingertips. There was a purple bruise above my ankle. It hurt when I tried to wipe off the sand. I remembered myself in the morning, standing in the bathroom, naked by the mirror. All the little cuts and bruises showed up in the light. I read them with great care, the runic poems that told of our attachment.

I wiped my fingers on the dress. The specks of black sand stuck to it. There were blisters, translucent bubbles, on three fingertips. I didn't remember how I got them. The surf kept splashing against the rocks below where I was sitting. It eddied in the pits and crevasses around me, dissolved back into the ocean. I didn't know what time it was. I thought the tide was coming in.

When I woke up, the dress was laid out on a chair beside the bed. There was no underwear, just the dress. The fabric was some kind of gauze, pervious as broken skin. My own clothes had somehow disappeared. In the night I cried for them, the carpet pressed like moss against my cheeks and lips. Where did you put my clothes? I cried, a prisoner desperate to escape, and unable to move.

"*Era la criada,*" I heard him say from somewhere in the room. It was the maid.

I don't want to be your prisoner, I told him then, and he answered that I wasn't. You're free to leave anytime you wish, he said. You don't have to do anything you don't want to do.

His voice hovered above me, though he was sitting in a chair on the far side of the room. The chair was gilt, ornately carved, with an elaborate high back. Its legs ended in clawed feet and his bare feet rested precisely in between them. The feet were all I saw from my place down in the moss.

Yes, I was a prisoner, but not his prisoner, he amended a little later. His voice was gentle, ruminative. I was a prisoner of myself, of my own fears and weaknesses, of my desires, he said. Then his feet began to move and he was above me, lifting me out of the moss. He kissed me, held me naked, cradled and caressed me until I cried some more. "*Mi amor, mi vida, mi muñeca bonita,*" he whispered, and every time he named me I felt myself reborn. Finally, all the tears were gone.

It was after all the tears were gone that he promised me it wouldn't hurt. It didn't. The blade was thin and sharp. It flashed out like a serpent's tongue and red milk spurted from my breast. Fear is faith in evil. When he held the blade, I was not afraid.

What he found when he opened me were all the hungry places, all the empty, echoing places, and when he'd found them all, I learned that he could fill me up, and keep me from falling off the earth.

* * *

The thin strip of beach wound out on either side of me. Rising up behind me were the rocky slope, the seawall. In front of me the ocean was churning metal, glittering far out before mist blurred the horizon. Not far from where I sat, a broken sign had washed up on the rocks. In black letters, it read *"eligro!"* and I wondered what it meant, this sign, if it was a misspelling of *alegre*—merry, cheerful, happy. I got up, made my way closer to it. Right away I understood my mistake. What was missing was an inverted exclamation point and an uppercase *p*. The sign was saying *"¡Peligro!"* Danger! It warned of riptides a short way down the beach.

I went back to my place on the volcanic ledge. The world looked flat and empty. I was at the edge of it, wondered how I got here. I remembered walking with him through a gate at the Hotel Lido, a back gate hidden in the vines that I hadn't known existed. I think he was dressed in black, and he held open for me the door of a black Jaguar that was crouched in the shadows of the hotel's service driveway. I remembered climbing into the Jaguar as though I had no choice and thinking, as I did, that I was stepping out of my own life, couldn't ever go back.

Our takeoff was so fast and powerful it seemed not to be happening at all. The speedometer's green needle arced past 100, glowed some distance beyond without a tremor. Then the window near me opened and the wind reached in, roughly massaged my scalp.

"I want you to remember," he said as I fumbled for the button that would close the window. I couldn't find it, or I found it but couldn't make it work. He drove and drove. All the roads were dark and empty.

Sitting on the ledge with the waves breaking just below me, I thought of something from my other life, something Mary Healy had said during our trip down from Mesa Verde. "Aren't you afraid?" Sonia had asked her, and Mary had answered with her nervous laugh. "I guess it was a moment of surrender, my decision to come back," she said. We were walking arm in arm behind Cobo, trying to keep each other from falling in the dark. "I felt I didn't have a choice." She paused, glanced up at the stars, laughed again. "But ever since, I've sensed this radical union. I mean with Him. And no, I'm not afraid."

"You're not radical," joked Sonia. "You're totally subversive." But Sonia had not understood. By radical Mary meant fundamental, not extreme; radical as in root or growing from a root.

Yelping dogs distracted me. On a bluff above the rocks, a soldier held a pair of sleek black Dobermans. He was one of the soldiers who incessantly patrolled the estate, walking its perimeters with the dogs, sentineling with automatic rifles the high walls in the front. The leather of his high boots gleamed. Like a cowboy, he carried a six-shooter in a holster on his hip. The frantic dogs danced against the chains he held in his gloved fist. The chains were taut, trembling. The soldier raised his arm, a show of strength, and stood there for a while, looking me over or looking out over the water, I couldn't tell. Like the maids and the chauffeur, like all the other Rivas servants, he had a way of looking but not seeing. All of them had this way of looking me over but not seeing me. They helped me to believe I was a figment of my own imagination. The soldier moved on.

My mind was racing, and I tried to slow it down, tried to think back, tried to remember how, the night before, after everything we'd done, I'd fallen into a deep, helpless sleep. I was dreaming that I had melted into the earth, a peaceful lightless place, by the time the quake began. It was a slow, languorous tremor that rolled up from deep inside the earth, rolled over me. I understood it as a metaphor, the cataclysm, the objective correlative of a profound loss, the loss of something I couldn't name. I was buffeted, shaken, and the pitiless motion woke me up. I thought he must have shaken me awake, harshly, urgently.

I saw him in his silk robe, standing by the open French doors, on the far side of the room. A gust of air blew in, lifted the curtains. The huge house shuddered and creaked. The bed slid from its place, and I reached for the bedpost, thinking the old house was about to collapse, the earth to open. Glass shattered somewhere. Outside the dogs were howling. The next jolt bored right through me, an insistent warning.

"You've felt tremors like this before, haven't you?" I heard him ask, and I remembered that I had, now and then, at the hotel. "Really, it's nothing." He turned toward me. "A minor diastrophism. A slight tectonic adjustment."

The shaking stopped before he finished speaking. I heard the ticking of the clock on the gilded table by the bed. The small gold clock was facing backward, precariously near the table's edge. I couldn't see what time it was, couldn't seem to reach the clock to turn it. He was walking toward the bed, and I wondered if he ever slept, if he'd been watching me as I did. He sat beside me, fixed the pillows for me, smoothed the comforter around me. "There is nothing to be afraid of. It's over. Now go back to sleep."

His soothing voice turned me into a child. But when I closed my eyes, I was thinking of tsunamis, walls of water. I was thinking they were set in motion by such tremors—jitters around the Ring of Fire, missteps in the tense grinding dance of crustal plates, the Cocos and American, miles under the Pacific.

I stood up and walked along the beach, looked carefully for anything I might have found, as though searching for clues to my own existence. In its way the beach was pristine. There were no signs of the minor diastrophism, of the tectonic adjustment. Nor were there any plastic diapers, Styrofoam cups, straws, tampons, condoms, plastic milk jugs, fast-food containers. I walked and walked but didn't find anything at all.

The water surged up around my calves, caught my hem even though I held the skirt up high. It occurred to me that the tide was rushing in and I ought to hurry back or there wouldn't be any beach left for me to walk on. When I was halfway there, I saw him standing on my ledge. Inside me something jumped, and it felt almost like hope: he was looking for me or watching me. He was barefoot and his white pants were rolled at the ankle. His white shirt was unbuttoned and the soft breeze lifted its tails like wings. He stood there motionless. I was afraid he'd disappear. I walked faster. When I was closer to him, I had the thought that we should be in an advertisement, a print ad for a glossy magazine. Because we were so good-looking in our white clothes on the silver beach. I imagined what we could sell: perfume, liqueur, automobiles, watches, maybe a life-style. He did not disappear. When I was within his reach, he took one of my hands, held it as I climbed over the rocks. We sat down side by side, and he put my hand on his thigh beneath one of his own. His hand was very warm, and it covered mine completely. I leaned against him, my head against his chest, where I felt the beating of his heart. I reached up and touched his throat. My fingertips reached the pulse point below the corner of his jaw. The blood jumped against my fingers, as certain and relentless as the waves. I closed my eyes, listened to the beating of his heart, felt his pulse against my blistered fingertips. We stayed that way for a long time. Then he helped me up and we walked back to the house.

The water was full and hard, stinging hot, and I turned around and around inside it, glimpsing, from different angles, my naked self in the steamy mirrors around the shower, a woman in mist, haze-hidden. A piano concerto, something by Mendelssohn, I thought, made its way through the pelting water, and it was so beautiful that I wished I could stay there forever, inside the rushing water, the lilting music. I was probably obsessed with the music, rich and complex music by Mozart, Haydn, Vivaldi, Ravel, Telemann, Stravinsky, Bartók. I was probably obsessed with the music, for it had been incessant during those days with him. The music had filled up my empty head and expressed all the feelings I couldn't or didn't dare to feel. Of course, I didn't choose the music and I knew I didn't choose the music. But I kept telling myself, those days with him, that if I'd chosen, I would have chosen this one or that one, the same things that he'd chosen, because whatever I was listening to seemed always to be exactly what I wanted to hear. I was shampooing my hair when the piano concerto stopped abruptly. Right away I heard the other voices. They were a distant babble, incomprehensible, and I turned off the water, afraid some other men had come into the room.

"*Pues, no hay Estrella Luminosa.*"

In the sudden silence, the guttural voice and slurred fricatives were unmistakable. They transformed my bones into rubber, and I felt suspended there, by the glass door of the shower.

"*La estrella Luminosa es la creación del ministro de la defensa, el general Víctor Rivas Valdez.*"

Swaying on rubber legs, I wondered what Galgo was doing there and why he was saying such things to the general. I grabbed the mirrored wall to keep myself from toppling, but it was slick with shower steam, and I couldn't get a grip. Through the opened bathroom door, in a wedge of darkened bedroom, I saw him on his claw-footed throne. He seemed to be alone.

"How could you make bombs with hands like that?"

It was the thin, high voice of an American girl.

"How could you make bombs with hands like that?"

Her words seemed freighted with suppressed laughter, with sexual innuendo or invitation. I saw myself reaching for Galgo's calloused hands, touching his fingertips. Of course, the voice was mine. He was playing my audiotape from Mesa Verde.

"*Soy Robles,*" Galgo declared then. "*Yo era un comando. Ahora soy un defector. . . . Rivas Valdez es un monstruo.*"

I heard the click of a button, the whir of tape rewinding. The sounds were crazily amplified. Then Galgo repeated his hoarse warning: *Rivas Valdez es un monstruo.*

Swaying very slowly closer to the doorway, pressed flat against the mirrored wall, I saw he held my tape recorder. He was turning it over in his hands, pressing all its buttons. The sound was too clear and loud, too pure, to be coming from my little tape recorder. And the interview was out of sequence—the things Galgo and I were saying to each other didn't follow, made very little sense. I realized he must have spliced and dubbed the tape, and was playing it on another system, the one he used for the music. The tape recorder in his hands was a stage prop, a distraction.

"You mean Estrella Luminosa exists, but it's not leftist. Hmmm? Is that what you mean?"

My questions echoed eerily as I hovered by the doorway, looking through it, maybe thinking I could find a way out. He didn't look up, didn't look at me. There was no way to get past him. I thought I'd close the door, close the door and lock him out, but right away I saw there was no door lock. After that I couldn't seem to move.

"Toda mi familia son campesinos. Mi papá, mi abuelito." Galgo's excruciating voice went on without making any sense. *"Trabajamos tanto pero somos pobres. . . . Somos indios."*

The bathroom was vast and glimmering, full of mirrors, pink marble, golden fixtures. It was lit by sconces on the walls. I wanted to disappear, but I saw myself everywhere, even when I wasn't looking, and I saw that I was drenched and shivering, frozen in a puddle.

"El supuesto terrorismo izquierdista es un parte de la estratégia de Rivas Valdez para movilizar los derechistas, la derecha extrema," Galgo said. The alleged leftist terrorism is part of Rivas Valdez's strategy to mobilize the right wing, the extreme right. I couldn't remember that he'd said that.

"El apoyo de los yanquis es la cosa más clave y fundamental de todos sus planes."

Support from the Yankee government is the key to all his plans.

It occurred to me that I should get a towel, wrap myself in a towel. Then I saw that all the gleaming towel bars were empty. A marble counter was lined with glistening jars of creams and perfumes, shining bowls of soap, cosmetics, flowers. But there weren't any towels. The desire for a towel released me from paralysis. I began to pace the mirrored cage, searching, trying not to see myself.

"Is there any way for me to contact him, this other commando? I would really love to talk to him."

My Spanish was slow and heavily accented, but my voice was breathy, promising. "I would really love to talk to him. . . . You know . . . I bet he has some really interesting things to say."

My breathy declaration was followed by a throaty sound, a hum. Maybe I'd said "Hmmm?" or "Auhh?" But the tape somehow amplified this interrogative into an enticement, a lure. "Hmmm?" The repeated sound threw me off balance, and when I looked into the mirror, I saw myself spinning, lost in a multitude of naked selves. I held on to the marble counter, tried to stop the spinning, tried to think. If I could only get a towel, I thought, I could escape the bathroom, and somehow get away from him. I spied some cabinets beneath the counter, thought they must contain the towels. I'd bent, was reaching for a golden latch, when I glimpsed him in the mirrors, watching me from the bedroom. His eyes glowed, hot and dangerous. His tension skittered toward me, entwined me. I let go of the latch, straightened up. I tried to ask him for the towel, but couldn't get the words out. I opened my mouth, but the words were stuck inside. "Víctor," was what I said as I stood there, trying not to see my own fear in the mirror.

"*Mentirosita.*"

Little liar.

His whispered hiss reached me at the same time he did. I lunged away from him, looking at the cord he held like a lasso or a noose. I slipped in the puddle, and my face slammed against the marble wall. Through glowing sparks, he caught me, pulled my arms up behind me, slipped the cord, the sash of his robe, around my wrists. I tried to pull my arms away, but he yanked them higher until the pain snatched away my breath.

"If you North Americans understood the true nature of Bellavista's government," Galgo declared, "you would refuse to support the war."

I saw Galgo very clearly, the orange sunlight like explosions reflecting off the lenses of his glasses. But I had trouble understanding him, trouble translating his Spanish. By the time I did, the cord had slithered up around my throat, and in the mirror I saw it loop around my elbow on the other side.

"Oh, you've been talking to Alan Hartwell, haven't you?" the girl's voice asked. The silky question was followed by a kind of sigh, a little throaty hum. Through it came Galgo's laughter, his grudging confession that he had talked to Alan Hartwell, but his insistence that the ideas were his own. There was a gap on the tape then, a deliberate moment of silence that gave us both a chance to absorb the meaning of what had been said, the multiple betrayals. And I absorbed them, gasping on the cord, skidding toward a black hole, wishing it would open and swallow me.

"¿Dónde está Robles? ¿Hmm?" Rivas Valdez asked, and his voice seemed to come from far away. *"¿Dónde está el otro, Hartwell? ¿Hmmm?"* He was mimicking my throaty hum, the verbal tic I hadn't known was mine. Our eyes met in the mirror. "No, Víctor, please," I whispered.

"Where is Robles? Who helped you to find him?"

His voice was toneless, and the questions were somehow banal, but he squeezed the cord after he asked them, and black snow blurred my vision. He loosened his grip and I whirled back, saw how my pupils were dilated, how my chest was heaving. I recognized the fear, but didn't recognize myself. My lip was already swollen, but all I felt was an icy numbness at my edges and inside something hot and roiling like magma almost ready to erupt.

"You mean Estrella Luminosa exists, but it's not leftist, don't you?" My *gringa* voice curled around us, warm, and elastic with promises. "It acts on behalf of Rivas Valdez? Hmmm? Is that what you mean?"

"Trampista, mentirosa," he muttered, and again our eyes met for a moment. His moved on, and I watched him in the mirror as he examined, without curiosity, my armless body, my breasts, ribs, hips, thighs, and the bruises that marked them. He shifted the cord in his hands, tugged it till I moaned. "Where is Robles?"

"I didn't say I made the bombs," Galgo answered. "I placed them. . . ."

"¿Dónde está Robles? Who helped you to find him?"

"No," I answered, and he struck my face. Flames licked my cheeks and mouth.

"Where are they? How did you find them?"

His robe had fallen open, and the skin of his chest and belly smoldered along my back, my buttocks. I felt how hard he was against me.

"Me vine de nada," Galgo declared, then laughed. *"Lo hice por el dinero."* I came from nothing. I was in it for the money.

Again he jerked the cord, and my arms were snapping from their sockets, my windpipe closing off. The fingers of his other hand wound through my hair.

"Maybe I was lucky," Galgo confided. "I found out I was fighting for the wrong side."

"Where is Hartwell?" He yanked my hair. "How did you find him?"

When I didn't answer, he jerked the cord and the black snow began to gust. I slid closer to the hole, saw it opening in front of me.

"Elisabet, Elisabet," he called from far away. *"Engañadora, mentirosa."* He hit my face to bring me back. "You talked to Hartwell, too. Where is he?"

When I didn't answer, he struck me again, and through black snow, I slid into the hole, a lightless tunnel. "Who brought you to him? Who brought you to them, Elisabet? Was it that other *gringa, la comadrona?*"

Then I saw her, Mary Healy, her face limpid in the fading light as we left Mesa Verde. I remembered what she'd said about surrender, and not being afraid. The jumbled cycle of questions and blows continued. I don't remember many of the words. I only remember the black snow, my long slides down the tunnel, how he always called me back— *trampista, mentirosita,* and how the questions began again. I told him nothing, yet through it all, I heard myself and Galgo.

"You say it was North American mercenaries who trained you as commandos?"

"Yes. Somewhere in the jungle near el Golfo de Virtud."

"What were their names? Do you remember any of their names?"

"No. They used war names like mine, Galgo."

"I would really love to talk to him . . . that other commando. . . . I bet he has some really interesting things to say."

"Soldiers killed my parents and my sister. I never found their graves."

"Oh, you've been talking to Alan Hartwell, haven't you?"

"Hartwell is dead," Rivas Valdez said sometime or other. "Hartwell is a dead man." He listened to my howl of outrage with meditational tranquillity, calmly watched the thrashing protest that seemed to separate my arms from their sockets. Then I understood that Hartwell wasn't actually dead, but would be if Rivas Valdez found him. Hartwell was as good as dead—that's what Rivas Valdez meant. Hartwell and Robles, Ocho—all of them—would be dead when and if Rivas Valdez or his men found them.

I believed that I was too. I was sure that he intended to kill me right there before the mirror so I could witness my own murder. I believed that he would kill me without the grace of passion. Because I was aware of his not feeling anything at all. And sometimes, when I saw him hit me, or when I felt him take away my breath, my consciousness, I wondered how he could without feeling anything at all.

But then he hit me again, and I seemed to know exactly where I was. Suddenly it was all so familiar that it felt almost like home—the place of boiling pain and awful voices, the place of pinkish light as if something in my brain were bleeding. I knew its breadth and depth, recognized all of its dimensions, and the moment that I recognized them, I stopped being afraid. When I looked again into the mirror, saw his savage eyes and his serenity, I knew, without surprise or fear, that he didn't care at all about my answers. He could get the information elsewhere. All he cared about was hurting me. He only wanted to hurt me, not kill me. It wasn't that he felt nothing, but rather that his feelings were dangerously constricted. They'd been honed to a vicious point, were as hard and durable as a piton. I understood I was their object, the object of their merciless attack, but the moment I understood this, another thought occurred to me: that he must love me. The idea glistened before me, a vast hot refuge whose boundaries I couldn't see. He had to love me to be hurting me so much.

Right after that the black snow started to fall, and I began to slide away. Then both of us were falling, falling down the mirrored wall, and I glimpsed us as we fell, two radiant images on a silver screen. After a long time we stopped falling, landed on cold ground where there was no light at all. He heaved himself against me, pushed into me, proving that I'd lost my skin, my boundaries. My strangled cry seemed to vibrate for a long time. Through it he whispered liar, cheater, whore. And I knew the words were true. Everything he said was true. Please, Víctor, please, no, I begged, and I saw him ignore me, saw him over me, overpowering me in the shimmering mirrors all around us, and I felt him deep inside me. Then I was shaking with involuntary spasms that felt like diastrophisms, tectonic adjustments. "Did you fuck him, too, Elisabet?" he asked me while I came. His voice was low but urgent, rage-driven, not like when he'd asked the other questions. "Did he make you come, Elisabet? Did you fuck Robles? Did you fuck him? Tell me if you did." The question metamorphosed into a raging chant. Did you fuck him, Elisabet? Did you? Gradually the chant crescendoed—Did you fuck Robles? Tell me. Was it his tattoo? Elisabet? Did you like his tattoo?—and then it fell away into something else, and I heard it as it fell, and what I heard was plaintive, sad—Did you fuck him, Elisabet? Did he make you come? At last the chant was ending, the black snow gusted, and he was collapsing over me when I heard its alien punctuation, a raw, inchoate sound. A scavenger in the dark, I grasped this unintended gift, his involuntary cry, before I slid away.

It sounded like rain, the running shower, and when I woke up or came to, the light was dull and silvery as during a spring storm. I saw myself, curled up on the cold floor, as though inside a womb. I sat up, hurting inside and out, and felt myself unbound. My arms had been untied but they were quivering, steadily vibrating, as with some mechanical malfunction. I couldn't stop them or control them. Yet it was not my arms but my throbbing left knee that demanded my immediate attention. Because a pain stabbed through it and a worm of blood was curled over the pain. It kept growing as I watched. Nearby I saw a shattered jar, some kind of lotion splattered over the floor. A small piece of the broken glass was embedded in my knee. But I couldn't move my arms to get it out, felt hypnotized watching the red worm grow. Then he was beside me, glistening from his shower, murmuring over my cut, the unintended injury, the wound that could be dealt with, healed.

Whispering *pobrecita*, poor thing, he lifted me, carried me to the bed, where he held my knee between his hands. He kissed my knee, moved his fingers over it, retrieved a bloody shard of glass. He held it out, and it sparkled on his finger before he flicked it away. He wiped the blood off with a towel, kissed the cut, rubbed it with his thumb. Then he massaged my wrists and arms and shoulders. And he held me, covered me with kisses. *Pobrecita*, he whispered as he kissed my face, my wet hair, my tears. Poor little thing. I'm sorry, so sorry. His exhalations were like feathers on my throbbing skin. I wondered, but only vaguely, what he meant, if he was sorry for what he'd done or only sorry about my knee. When it was time he moved my legs apart, kissed me there. I swelled, softening against him. My legs were trembling like my arms, the vibrations rippling all through me. At last I held him in my recovered hands and both of us were saying yes. Then there were no other voices, just ours, against the hushing white noise of the empty tape.

CHAPTER
TWENTY-SEVEN

THE ROOM THEY BROUGHT ME TO WAS BIG AND EMPTY, MAUVE with ivory trim. Its windows looked out over las Esmeraldas. When they brought me there, early in the morning, the mountains shimmered in the light. All of the windows were open and a fragrant breeze was drifting through. We could hear the squawks and caws of birds. McManus was drinking beer. A ragged wedge of lime had sunk to the bottom of his pilsner glass. A waiter poured coffee for me, and as I lifted the cup to drink, one of the men from the embassy gestured for him to leave. Then it was just the four of us, sitting in the big mauve room, at a table covered with ivory damask, looking out the window, or at our drinks or fingers, without anything to say. The birds were very loud.

"You know, Lizzie," said McManus after a while, "for the last week or so, the rumors have been burning like a prairie fire up through the Latin bureaus to El Paso, San Diego, Washington."

His voice was low and uninflected, as if our conversation were continuing, not beginning.

"I don't actually know how they got started. Somebody in Mexico City had apparently been tipped." He took a swallow of his beer, looked into the distance just above my head. "Now a sudden sense of self-preservation has shut everyone up."

Still he didn't look at me, instead gazed at his hands or into his glass. The men from the embassy did not share his difficulty. They watched me steadily, with antagonism and aversion, the way Bronx cops look at "perps," the despised perpetrators of mundane crimes. One of them was tall and burly with an emptily aggressive mien. The other was thin and scholarly, edgy and alert. He wore aviator glasses and held in both hands a manila envelope, the kind with numbered black stripes used for interoffice mail. He was vaguely familiar. I wondered if I hadn't seen him from time to time on the terrace of the Hotel Lido. Or maybe at an embassy news conference.

When I saw how they kept looking at me, the men from the embassy, like Bronx cops staring down a perp, I wanted to tell them both to fuck off. Or to take a picture, it would last longer. But I couldn't seem to speak, couldn't tell them anything. I couldn't even meet their eyes. Instead I found myself looking around and through them, the way the Rivas servants had always looked at me.

"After all, it is the kind of thing you hear from time to time. Especially when female reporters are involved. It almost always turns out to be vicious gossip, dirty talk." McManus's voice was hoarse and distant, as when we talked on the phone. I could almost hear the hums and echoes of the long-distance wires in the silences between his words. "But then the ambassador, um, Whitaker, Whitaker called Van Doorn. I suppose it was a courtesy. Of sorts."

I'd been sleeping when they came for me, still felt dopey, half awake. I couldn't understand what McManus was telling me, couldn't assimilate the reality that he was there, in flesh and blood, and not attached to a receiver at the end of several thousand miles of wire.

"And, uh, Whitaker," he continued, "that is, the ambassador, uh, he's promised that nothing's coming from the embassy. As long as you cooperate."

"Cooperate?"

My voice sounded peculiar, my involuntary question odd.

"We'll be leaving tomorrow night. On a corporate jet."

It occurred to me then, on an evanescent rush of hope, that I must still be sleeping, lost in one of my awful, vivid dreams.

"We've come to take you home, Lizzie. As soon as we tie up some loose ends here."

The word "home" somehow demolished hope. It evoked images of my mother's apartment in the Bronx, not my own place in Morningside Heights. I stumbled past them, onto the phrase "loose ends," and though I wondered what it meant, I again found myself mute.

"In case you haven't figured it out, Lizzie," I heard McManus continue, his voice finally textured by some feeling, "this is a fucking international incident, potentially explosive, with a lot of possible ramifications that none of us can even see yet."

His passion pulled our eyes together for an instant. His were bloodshot, crusted near the lashes. He needed a shave, a fresh shirt.

"What are you talking about?"

My question seemed to provoke a vehement chorus of tongue-clicks, nods, and sighs. Yet it demanded to be asked and answered. I thought I ought to make them spell it out. I wanted to know what they knew and how they knew it. Or at least I thought I did. The three men looked at one another. Aviator Glasses unwound the red string of the envelope's tab closure. He pulled out a plastic resealable bag. Inside were the diamond necklace and bracelet. They were clearly visible, but he opened the bag anyway. They slid out onto the table, where the diamonds dazzled blue and red and orange, as if each contained a tiny fire. The sight of them seemed to ignite a blaze of humiliation around me. I felt it burning up around my face and eyes, making it hard to see.

"These were in your room. Hidden in your room." A bony finger pointed to the diamonds. It belonged to Aviator Glasses. His voice was thin and high. I couldn't place his accent.

"Well, in fact, Lizzie," McManus interrupted, "it's not your room, but the *Herald-Sun*'s room. It's also the *Herald-Sun*'s office equipment. That's why we were within our legal rights, and I'd say our moral rights, to enter them and look around. And, after all, you weren't there. Again you'd disappeared."

I kept looking at the diamonds, thinking I ought to say something, but I couldn't think of anything. During this silence, it occurred to me that McManus must have arrived from New York while I was still at la Costa de Plata; that he'd been at the hotel, and gone through my rooms, with the others, while I was with Rivas Valdez in the peacock-colored room. The blaze around me burned hotter, and within it glowed a white-hot rage that strangers had gone into my space and searched through my belongings. Aviator Glasses' voice whined on.

"We've found and spoken with the jeweler who made them. General Víctor Rivas Valdez, the commander-in-chief of Bellavista's armed forces, paid cash for them. They cost more than four thousand dollars."

"Four thousand dollars?" A spurt of hysterical laughter escaped with my exclamation.

"You accepted gifts, very expensive gifts, from a news source, a government official." McManus spoke in tones of wonder and bewilderment, his statement so erroneous, so absurd, that it demanded immediate correction.

"You think I give a shit about those things?" I was pointing to the diamonds, and if I could have reached them, I would have brushed them to the floor. "I don't know what they are and I don't care what they're worth. I didn't want them. And I never wore them. So I definitely wouldn't say that I accepted them."

"But you didn't give them back. They were in your possession. And you hadn't told anyone about them, not anyone in the newspaper's chain of command."

"What does that mean? What do you think that means?"

My spontaneous questions vibrated in the balmy air, and as I looked from one man to the next I wished I hadn't asked them.

"For a time, for some time," McManus began, and then abruptly stopped. The color in his face changed from grayish-white to fuchsia. He lifted up his glass to drink and found it empty. He put it down, peered into it.

"You've had a . . . you've been having . . ." Again he stopped and shook his head, looked at me.

I suppose, if I'd ever had a father, he might have looked at me like that, at one point or other in my life, with sorrow and profound dismay and a feeling of ambivalent attachment. But I'd never had a father, so I couldn't say for sure. "You know, Van Doorn is with Whitaker right now," McManus finished, as though he'd explained everything. He looked frantically around the room. Bodyguard got up, went to the door, and several minutes later the waiter returned with another beer and a pack of cigarettes for McManus. My eyes fastened onto Bodyguard, but I was thinking about Van Doorn. Somehow it terrified me, the idea that Van Doorn, like a divinity incarnate, had come to Bellavista because of me; that he was, at that moment, talking with the U.S. envoy about me, about my sex life. It was my first inkling of the magnitude of my transgression.

Bodyguard had returned to his seat, and Aviator Glasses was fingering the interoffice envelope, which was bulky and misshapen, and was telling me as he did that "everything" about my relationship with General Rivas Valdez had already been documented; that the nature of my relationship with Bellavista's defense minister had been established beyond any doubt; that it was "incontrovertible." His lips were thin and wet, and sometimes he stopped fingering the envelope to push back his glasses with his middle finger. The State Department, he went on to say, was aware of "virtually everything" that Víctor Rivas Valdez and Elizabeth Marie Guerrera had ever done together. It would be, therefore, pointless, he said, for me to try to deny any of it.

I wanted to ask him what he meant by "everything"—if he meant simply all the times and places we had been together. Or if he meant the things we'd actually done when we were alone. The question— "What do you mean by 'everything'?"—struck me as very funny, and I almost laughed when I thought of it. The arrival of the waiter with the beer and cigarettes gave me time to realize the answer would not be funny, and so I didn't ask it.

Instead, struck by Aviator Glasses' vehemence, I began to wonder what political machinations had led up to the knocking on my door that morning, to our meeting in the mauve-and-ivory room. I wondered how the State Department had discovered our affair and why it had chosen this particular time to reveal what it had discovered. I wondered if Rivas Valdez hadn't betrayed me himself because I'd gotten too close to the truth. Or if the State Department was blackmailing him, coercing him into carrying out its policies. But my ideas were only half-formed, the most apparent angles in a complex geometry of possibilities. I'd hardly begun to consider them when I heard Aviator Glasses, leaning toward McManus, softly asking if he wanted "further clarification" of the "sensitive nature" of the situation. Without waiting for a response, Aviator Glasses murmured something about the Republic of Bellavista being at a crucial juncture in its painful history; something about Rivas Valdez being a married public official in a Roman Catholic country; something about fornication and disgrace. He went on to say something about me, about what I was, but McManus stopped him. He raised his hands and held them out as if staving off blows. McManus began mumbling something about nightmares, and someone else—it must have been Bodyguard—remarked that the general's wife and children were returning to Libertad from Miami that very day; that the general's wife and children were expected at Cauchimpca within the hour. I heard myself declare as though it mattered, "Well, they're not really children, you know. The youngest is sixteen." All of them ignored me.

"I'd like your credentials now, Lizzie," said McManus next, and again the hums and echoes of the long-distance wires seemed to muffle his words. "As I think I've already said, I've been asked to retrieve all of your credentials."

Retrieve. The word didn't seem quite right to me, and McManus, like all good editors, was always particular about his choice of words. "Retrieve" means to get back, to salvage, or to rescue, and I didn't understand how McManus could get back something that belonged to me; how he could rescue or salvage what essentially was mine. Yet I couldn't seem to ask him, couldn't formulate the question. I dropped one hand into my lap, felt the ID cards in my pocket. McManus had told me to bring them all when they'd come for me. Without wanting to know why, refusing to think about it, I'd gathered them all up, pocketed them. I'd felt their weight throughout our conversation, necessary and reassuring. I didn't want to give them up. I knew I'd never get them back.

"Why?" I finally asked.

"It's critical . . ." McManus paused, then looked around the table. I expected him to tell me that I had no right to ask, that he wouldn't answer. Instead, after his pause, he seemed only too glad to tell me. "Van Doorn and others feel it's crucial that you be stripped immediately of your press papers. That you understand with absolute clarity that you are no longer a *Herald-Sun* correspondent. That you are no longer to consider yourself a working journalist."

McManus drank from his beer, lit a cigarette.

"You've compromised yourself beyond any . . ." He couldn't seem to finish the thought, and he gave up, began another, which also wandered off. "You've compromised the *Herald-Sun* in a . . ." He looked around the room, then into his beer and at his fingertips, before he spoke again.

"Should any of this be made public, uh, that is, should any of this reach the, uh, the media . . ." He said "media" without any trace of irony, as though it were a dreaded virus, and then he paused, inhaled deeply. "Well, if any of the media get hold of this, it's of overriding importance that the *Herald-Sun* be seen as having acted swiftly and with resolve."

"If it's so fucking important, why didn't Van Doorn tell me himself?"

A stream of smoke escaped McManus's throat along with a rag of laughter.

"You know, Lizzie, if he were in the room with you, I don't think he could restrain himself."

A frisson of perverse pleasure told me I was glad to have provoked such a strong reaction in Van Doorn, the potentate. I noticed Bodyguard chuckling, and he didn't stop until Aviator Glasses turned to him. "The way Van sees it," McManus went on, looking at the glowing tip of his cigarette, "the paper's two centuries of unquestioned integrity may be down the tubes because some overly ambitious girl reporter got hot pants for a head of state."

McManus was thin and gray, desiccated. His sudden descent into slang was ridiculous. Moreover, I could have argued that Rivas Valdez was not a head of state; that he was, in fact, just one member of a junta. I could also have argued with McManus's use of the expression "hot pants" and with his characterization of me as overly ambitious. But what came out instead was another involuntary question. "Girl reporter?"

"Well, okay, a woman . . . a female reporter." He took a long swallow of his beer, put the glass down, dragged on his cigarette. "Lizzie, you've taken expensive gifts from this man, a high government official, a primary news source. With all the discretion of a, uh, a mynah bird, you've stayed for days at his estate. You've been having all kinds of sex with him. It says here that he liked to . . ." McManus was pointing to the envelope, but he stopped abruptly, drank some beer, shook his head, and grimaced. "Never mind," he muttered. "It's sordid. Truly sordid."

Of course, I wanted more than anything to ask McManus what it said Rivas Valdez liked to do. I couldn't help being curious about what it said he liked to do. I couldn't help being curious, either, about the contents of the envelope, maybe tapes and photographs, maybe just notes and speculations, and the difference mattered greatly. But by then the three of them were staring at me in a way that fed the flames of ignominy around me, and I felt naked in the flames. The men stared and stared, and I couldn't get away from them, realized they must be imagining whatever it was that Rivas Valdez liked to do, wondering about it. I could not help thinking, from the way they looked at me, that they knew something about me that I didn't know myself. And though the flames kept burning hotter, I sat up very tall and looked from one man to the other as though none of it mattered. I remembered my coffee, picked up the cup to drink, put it back down when my arms began vibrating with another mechanical malfunction. Finally I heard myself ask, my voice soft and girlish, as on the tape from Mesa Verde, "What about him? What's going to happen to him?"

The question evoked no response at all, just more stares and silence.

"What about him?" I repeated, my voice tinged with a hysteria I didn't feel.

"Him?" McManus raised an eyebrow, looked mystified.

"Víctor." His first name echoed in the quiet, a betrayal of our intimacy. "I mean, Rivas Valdez. What's going to happen to General Rivas Valdez?"

The question seemed to confound them. At last Aviator Glasses turned to McManus, deliberately ignored me.

"The point is, Jim, peccadilloes aside, the future belongs to Rivas Valdez." He smiled and nodded, as though offering a warranty. "This country has a chance now."

I glimpsed the future then, saw Rivas Valdez resigning from the military and running for president, as a civilian, in the U.S.-supervised general election. The glimpse struck me as authentic, and I wanted to see more, but the voice of Bodyguard blinded me.

"I suppose a man in his position is allowed a peccadillo or two, huh?" he asked with his obnoxious chuckle. "I don't suppose anybody could fault him."

Peccadillo. Like "retrieve," the word detached itself from its companions and demanded swift consideration. I thought it meant a slight transgression, a minor offense. I realized I was the peccadillo, the offense. But I wondered why they hadn't simply said this, instead of using an obscure and possibly misleading word. I was still wondering when McManus repeated his request for my credentials. I looked at him, unable to move. I wondered where his eyeglasses were, wondered how long it had been since he'd slept. Then I spied the glasses poking out of his shirt pocket. "Come on, Lizzie," I heard him coax. "You've got to give them up."

When I reached for them in my pocket, I remembered how, not long before, I'd cried for my lost clothes as if they were limbs or organs, vital and irreplaceable. Then all my laminated ID cards were arrayed in front of me on the table, and I felt my self being looted, ransacked. I saw them all, my identification cards from the *Herald-Sun*, from Bellavista's foreign press office, from the State Department, sundry others. Most displayed the ambiguously smiling face of a woman I hardly recognized. I studied the variations of this ambiguously smiling woman, but she yielded nothing to me. I noticed the brass chain attached to the *Herald-Sun* ID and the pink ribbon attached to the one from the foreign press ministry—for I'd worn both of them around my neck. While the men watched, I took back these IDs to remove the chain and ribbon. I put the IDs back onto the pile, put the chain and ribbon into my pocket. Because, though they probably seemed worthless, they were mine. The ribbon and the chain belonged to me. And the moment I put the IDs back onto the pile, Aviator Glasses swept them all into his envelope, and I couldn't help thinking, ironically, as I watched him, that my career had just been swept into the great dust heap called history.

McManus watched him, nodding yes, and his mouth twitched into a blank smile, as if everything were right and just, the way it was supposed to be. The embassy men muttered something to McManus. Finally, the two of them were standing and Aviator Glasses was shaking McManus's hand. "I don't think there's any reason for us to stick around for the rest of this," I heard him say, and McManus smiled, assured him that there was no reason for them to stick around. So Aviator Glasses and Bodyguard left, walking together, with the envelope, out of the mauve-and-ivory room. The waiter reappeared, and when McManus ordered beer, I ordered Wild Turkey, a double, without ice.

The knocking on the door had not surprised me. Even in my sleep I'd been waiting for it. Even in my sleep I'd known that it would come. I'm still not certain exactly when I knew. At least since the previous afternoon when Rivas Valdez's driver had taken me back to the hotel and left me at the front door amid a flurry of brightly liveried hotelmen. As though discretion, secrecy, no longer mattered. But I think I probably knew before that. I think I knew, without wanting to, when I'd gotten up and he was gone. I'd gotten up and he was gone and my own clothing had been laid out there for me, cleaned and pressed. It was a favored and indispensable part of my foreign correspondent's wardrobe, an olive-drab shirt and pants from Banana Republic, clothes Sonia invariably ridiculed. Rivas Valdez despised them, too, but for completely different reasons. When I saw them, laid out and ready for me, I couldn't help decoding the sign. It was a dismissal, final and irrevocable. On the terrace outside the peacock-colored room, the ocean glistened, soft turquoise. There were yellow roses on my breakfast tray. The papaya was sweet and ripe, bright orange. Maybe I would have cried, except the maid's scarab eyes never stopped scurrying over me. And when the driver finally came for me, he, too, looked at me in a way he'd never looked at me before, his eyes resting lazily on my mouth, my breasts, my hips. I could tell, from the way the driver looked at me, that I was no longer Rivas Valdez's exclusive property, his whore. I was fair game.

But even though I knew, I couldn't think about it, could not feel anything about it. Not even when I stepped out of the big sedan in front of the hotel and all the liveried hotelmen fell still when they saw me, then parted like the waters of the Red Sea to make way for me. As I stepped out of his car, I remembered how I'd stepped out of my own life several nights before when I'd gone with him, Rivas Valdez, and how I'd known, even then, that I couldn't ever go back. Yet there I was, trying to go back, passing through the Red Sea, through the silent phalanxes of hotelmen, into an altered place, a perilous and alien place. Right away, in the lobby, I ran into someone from Reuters or Agence France-Press. I asked at once about Jack Travis. I was thinking that if I could talk to Jack, if the two of us sat down and had a drink, I might be able to figure out what was going on. I wanted to get my bearings, to salvage something, before I met Joe Soza, the correspondent who'd been flown in from Mexico City. I knew Joe Soza must have been at the hotel for at least a day. I knew our meeting was inevitable, no matter how much I dreaded it. The journalist from Reuters or Agence France-Press or whoever it had been asked me, Where had I been? Didn't I know his visa, Jack Travis's visa, had been revoked the week before, and that he'd already left the country? That basically he'd been kicked out of the country, though nobody knew why? Where had I been? And how could I not know that? the correspondent had asked, laughing with disbelief, and I had turned and walked away.

Sonia and I had been away—in Sangre de Cristo and Mesa Verde—for about five days. That's where I had been. But I didn't bother trying to explain to the journalist from Reuters or Agence France-Press or whoever it had been. Instead, I calculated that Travis must have been asked to leave immediately after Sonia and I had flown to Ixtapanga. I also remembered wondering where Travis was the Sunday when I'd picked up my New Jerusalem bombing story. But that night I was distracted. I'd spoken at length to no one and no one had volunteered the information. And so I'd missed the news of his departure.

Then I turned and saw the headlines of that day's *Las Noticias*, the government-owned newspaper. I'd also missed a story, an important follow-up to the story of the bombing at New Jerusalem. For the junta had announced that the land reform program would be suspended until the farm cooperatives could be better protected. There were many more details about the bombing itself and about the alleged workings of Estrella Luminosa. As I read this propaganda piece, I knew Joe Soza must already have filed a more objective version of it for the *Herald-Sun*. Finally, I understood that I'd lost everything, that everything important had somehow gotten away from me.

Maybe because I needed to keep functioning, or because I wanted to convince myself that I still occupied my own life, I'd driven down to Libertad. I'd parked beside the plaza, and taken a taxi to *la colonia de los sobrevivientes*, where I'd gone looking for Sonia. I thought I ought to warn her, to tell her that she and her mother were almost certainly in danger. Only I couldn't find them. Not even when I gave up the taxi, got out, and walked through all the dusty, unnamed lanes and alleys, where countless survivors lived in the rubble of old buildings. I don't know how many I talked to, how many I asked, families eating rice and beans in the shadows of their shacks, barefoot children playing with sticks and cans, lovers hiding in dark corners, men sharing bottles on broken steps and benches. Nobody knew Sonia Alvinas or her mother. And though everyone claimed not to know them, I told them all, if they should find them, or meet them, to tell them to go right away to Nuestra Señora del Refugio.

I went there afterward myself, in the glowing dark, when kerosene torches lit the plaza and shabby local troubadours had begun to sing and strum their guitars. I could not actually ignore *la comandancia*, radiant with nocturnal power, or the soldiers teeming on the plaza. But they seemed like vestiges of a previous existence, no longer relevant to me or to my situation. I hurried across the plaza, saw that el Centro de Cambio y Creatividad remained unlit, that Mary Healy's van wasn't parked out front. And once I'd climbed the steps, I also saw that its carefully hand-painted sign was gone. Spray-painted in its place were the words *putas* and *subversivas*. I knocked and knocked, was about to leave when Alba, the young Taupil midwife, Mary's protégée, opened the door. For a moment her beauty silenced me, the way it had the first time I'd seen her, when she was birthing Silvia's baby boy.

"Mary no está aquí," she whispered. *"No se cuando regresará."*

Mary wasn't there, and Alba didn't know when she'd return. I explained about Sonia and her mother, that I'd left messages for them to go to the church, to wait for me at the church, and I asked Alba to call me if they came. They would probably be safer at home than at Nuestra Señora del Refugio, Alba said. But of course, they were welcome, and if they showed up, she would get in touch with me. She shut the door and I drove back to the hotel, speeding in the dark, not feeling anything at all.

Falling into sleep had been something like falling into the black hole, a quiet, dark place where I was lost to myself for a little while. But early in the morning, sometime before they came for me, the ringing telephone awakened me. The sound was high and sharp, two short bursts, a pause, then two bursts more, over and over again, an alarm with an obscure meaning, an alarm I knew was going off too late. When I got up to answer it, there was just a click and a buzz of disconnection.

After all of that, the knocking on my door came as no surprise. The surprise was McManus and the others. Because Soza was the one I had expected, the one I'd known would come. Joe Soza, who was going to take everything away from me. Or who already had. So at first, when I'd seen the three of them standing in the gallery shade, backlit by the morning sun, I thought one of them must be Soza and that McManus had brought him by to introduce us. By the time I realized that this made no sense, McManus was saying in his curiously flat voice, "Get dressed quickly, Lizzie. We'll wait here for you. Bring along all of your credentials. And the keys to the Volvo." I'd dressed in the olive-drab shirt and pants from Banana Republic, which were crumpled on the floor. I'd gathered up my keys and credentials and put them in a pocket. When I'd opened up the door, the three of them were still there, leaning against the railing, waiting.

I couldn't stop my arms from vibrating. I held them close to my body, held on to my glass with both hands so McManus couldn't see. It was very quiet, with just the two of us in the big room, which was a banquet room or a ballroom. Maybe the birds had flown away. Or maybe I just couldn't hear them anymore. I looked up at the gleaming chandeliers wondering who, in Bellavista, gave balls or banquets. I also wondered what we were doing there, in that particular room. I wondered how it had been selected and by whom. It must have been an attempt to avoid all other members of the press corps—an attempt, I thought, that was bound eventually to fail.

McManus coughed, cleared his throat, giving me a signal I could not ignore. I turned to him, saw that his editorial eyes had finally attached themselves to my face. Sometime or other he'd put on his glasses, and he wore them low on his nose. He gazed at me through their glittering half-lenses. The lenses magnified his eyes, maybe endowed them with visionary powers. I looked back, wondering if it was the beer or the departure of the others that had enabled him to look at me. Then, more than anything, I wanted to leave, to get up and run, but I was somehow bound there with him—not God Himself, but a messenger from God. Or the father I had never had. I was bound there with him in a state of excruciating intimacy, an intimacy that pulsed with his contempt. From time to time he shook his head no and muttered, "Jesus." Or he said my name, "Lizzie." But I couldn't tell if these were questions, inchoate demands for an explanation, or merely expressions of loathing and disbelief.

It must have been during the silences between his exclamations, while he watched me with his editorial eyes, that more of my past pushed its way back into my memory, pushed me closer to knowing things about myself that I didn't want to know. Maybe his palpable disgust galvanized my own self-disgust. For I found myself back in the Bronx, at the Galaxy Motel, with its working girls, its garish lights and scummy rugs. On this unexpected trip, its aura of sad dilapidation and the desperation of the diseased and drug-addicted whores sickened me. The sex crimes detective was with me, and for a time we played the games we'd played there, games I'd always told myself were just harmless diversions. I watched with nausea, maybe terror, but even in the pristine light of the hotel's empty ballroom, I couldn't tell what any of it meant.

"You know, the revelation of truth is the reporter's primary task and his moral obligation," McManus suddenly intoned. It sounded like a speech he had prepared. "Our work is implicitly moral. Ours is one of the few moral professions left in the world."

He drained his glass and lit another cigarette. The little crystal ashtray was already overflowing.

"Therefore we must be, above all, honorable men and women. This kind of impropriety, or maybe I should say turpitude, is, uh, it's inimical to our task."

Of course, I knew it wasn't true that journalism was one of the few moral professions left in the world. It wasn't true at all, but only should be true, that ours was one of the few moral professions. But I couldn't seem to argue.

"I mean, you really blew it, Lizzie. You fucked up in the worst possible way."

I know I should have answered, somehow defended myself, but no words came to my mind. Instead, McManus and his magnified eyes were triggering a memory more urgent than our conversation. I was remembering how McManus had taken me up to Van Doorn's cloud-swept office the day I'd been assigned to Bellavista. With a brief, piercing pain, I recalled how I'd expected to be fired that day. How I'd expected to be thrust into the abyss for my transgressions, the secrets I kept hidden even from myself. I'd expected to be fired, not promoted, and when it hadn't happened that day, I'd erased from consciousness the possibility that it ever could. I'd forgotten all about my past.

"You know, there's an ineluctability to history, to the history of nations," his voice droned on. "That's why Bellavista's story will continue. And Rivas Valdez's story, for better or worse, will continue, too. But your story, Lizzie, well, I'm afraid your story's over. At least as far as the news business is concerned."

McManus's lips curled into a smile shape, and I recognized his pleasure at the idea that my story was over.

"Unless you fail to cooperate," McManus went on. His voice seemed to be coming from a gently roaring place beyond me. "In which case the details of your situation might hit the media. In which case, we, the *Herald-Sun*, would be required to do a story. We would have to put our cards on the table. Every last one of our cards."

I understood his threat, but my anger remained dormant beneath layers of detachment. I listened with curious disinterest as he added that my story would then continue, perhaps spectacularly, but briefly, and in a way that no woman in her right mind could possibly want. "You'll have your fifteen minutes," he concluded. "But then what?"

My urge to argue over the word "spectacular" immediately subsided. I couldn't imagine who would bother with the story. Except maybe some esoteric professional journal. I couldn't imagine the *Herald-Sun* not doing its best to bury the story—in the back of the last section or at the bottom of the Metro Briefs in some Monday early edition.

"What I'd like to know, though, is how this thing got started." Again McManus cleared his throat, blew smoke out through his nostrils. His head was cocked toward me. He appeared objective and detached, a newsman trying to shape a narrative that made sense. "That's the thing I'd really like to know. How he got to you. Can you tell me, Lizzie?"

But with telepathic proficiency, our waiter then appeared, offering fresh drinks, a clean ashtray. I was grateful for his interruption, watched his skillful work, realizing that the bourbon must have already broken down my boundaries. For McManus's question breached the layers of detachment and found its target deep inside me, the feverish swamp which was my shame. The flames of ignominy blazed around me once more. Through wavering fire, I saw him, Víctor, standing near the grotto of the Virgin watching me. Again I felt overpowered, the way I'd felt that day at Aguas Oscuras. I'd wanted him so much. It was a fierce and reckless wanting, irrational and carnal. I'd wanted him to touch me—as if, when he did so, he would give me some of his power. Once he had, I would have given anything to have him touch me again. I would have given anything. I'd given everything.

"I feel sorry for you, Lizzie."

McManus's voice rumbled from a space beyond the flames. I glanced at him, believing, for an instant, that his magical eyes had seen what I'd been thinking. Immediately I looked away, looked into my glass. Because Rivas Valdez was still with me and I needed him to stay. I conjured until I saw him as he was and had been, sinister and irresistible. I saw him as I'd first seen him, standing on the terrace, while I swam in the pool. He'd been holding something in his hand, something I'd mistaken for a weapon. The hidden thing flashed in the sunlight like a heliograph—and I'd understood his signal perfectly without knowing that I had. I remembered how he'd looked, and what it had felt like, when he'd pulled me back from the precipice at El Purgatorio. Afterward, I'd believed he could keep me from falling off the earth. I saw myself always dressing and undressing for him; saw how I let him turn me into whatever he wanted me to be. At last I saw him in the mirror beating me, saw his feral eyes and his tranquillity, saw how, even then, I'd failed to recognize or to experience my own degradation.

"You've destroyed yourself. And for what? Huh?"

I could see McManus right in front of me, could see his moving mouth, but superimposed over him was Rivas Valdez. I glimpsed him in his white clothes standing on the ledge above the beach, watching for me, looking for me. And when I saw him, I felt myself opening, reflexively, with hunger and longing, and the opening was like the gulf, dark, and treacherous with swirling currents.

"Because you wanted to get laid?"

McManus was leaning toward me, and his words arrived on a fetid cloud of beer and tobacco fumes. They brought me back into the present, where I found myself exposed, stripped of my personal context, my private history. He'd thrust me into his context, the context of my profession, of international politics, of a very public life where I was a pariah and a fool.

"I mean, this guy, Rivas Valdez, he's the kind of man who uses women like, well, like tissues, for God's sake. Places for the deposit of certain bodily fluids. He goes through them one after another. That's how much value they have for him. I figured you were smarter, Lizzie. Jesus. That you had more pride." He made a noise, some kind of snort or chuckle. "You didn't ever think it was going to mean anything, did you?"

"Mean anything?"

"You didn't ever expect this to be a significant relationship, did you? You knew it was just fucking around, didn't you?"

"It's irrelevant, isn't it, what I expected?"

The power of my own voice surprised me. Against McManus's cruelties, against all of my own expectations, my boundaries had been restored. I was no longer experiencing a breakdown. I was sitting there with my drink, politely sipping my drink, looking at McManus as if I felt nothing, knew nothing.

"You know, Jim, he didn't coerce me," I heard myself say. It seemed important to clarify the point. "It wouldn't be at all accurate to say that he got to me. I exercised my own free will. All God's children are endowed with it, aren't they? The ability to choose?"

"But why?"

McManus tilted his head so he could see me through his half-glasses. He waited for an answer, a newsman determined to shape a narrative that made sense.

I shrugged, thwarted him, because I didn't have an answer. Or rather, I thought, the answer must be swirling in the currents of the gulf, inaccessible. Maybe for a time I searched the opaque waters for it, because I almost didn't hear him when he spoke again.

"You know, Lizzie, we're praying to God this thing doesn't break." His head was bowed over his beer, and a fresh cigarette smoldered between his fingers. "The entire editorial staff, management, the board of directors. We're on our knees praying this thing doesn't break. Because if it does, if somebody gets it, the wires, or the newsweeklies, or the networks, the harm will be irreparable."

I tried to imagine the harm, but couldn't, couldn't imagine anything at all.

"We're in damage control," he droned on. "The *Herald-Sun* and the embassy are working together in the damage-control mode. We've already gotten Whitaker's word that nobody's going to find out anything from the embassy. As long as you cooperate. That means the rest is pretty much up to you."

"Up to me?"

"Well, we're hoping that you'll leave without any hassles. If you come back with us, cooperatively, we're willing to put you on some kind of leave. Hell, Lizzie, we'll pay you to stay out of the newsroom. And maybe, if you're discreet, and if everything goes the way we want, you might be able to work again someday. Certainly not for us. But maybe you can work at something, earn a living."

"What about Río Luciente?" I must have asked McManus then. "What about the massacre?"

"What about what?"

My question, I could see, had drawn a blank.

"What about my story on the massacre at Río Luciente?"

He nodded, very slowly, as though trying to remember a bit of trivia from ancient history. I'd filed the story only three or four days before. I watched him struggling to remember, myself remembering the lead exactly.

The Río Luciente cuts a shimmering blue swath through remote northeastern Bellavista, a vital resource for poor Indians who have lived here since before the time of Christ. The Río Luciente, or Shining River, has provided not only fish, but also water for drinking, bathing, and washing clothes.

In recent years, since the eruption of a bloody civil war that has so far claimed 43,000 lives, the river has provided something else—an escape route for refugees, a way to get to neighboring Costa Negra.

"Didn't you see the story? Didn't you ever see my story?" I seemed to be stuck on this question, and maybe I was standing because I saw the story disintegrating with a rage and panic I couldn't feel about myself.

"It was a great story. There were no holes. I answered all the questions."

"Anything could have happened to it," McManus muttered before I went on, reciting for him, like a crazy person, the rest of my lead:

" 'Reports of the army's deliberate killing of groups of civilians have been frequent during Bellavista's civil war, particularly in areas like Río Luciente, where there is no electrical power, no contact with the outside world. Yet evidence regarding specific incidents has usually proved elusive. Often there is no one left to tell the story.

" 'Not so in Río Luciente, where the slaughter of perhaps three hundred women and children took place in the presence of international relief workers and clergymen. According to witnesses, most of the murders occurred as mothers and children tried to cross the river by holding on to a rope that had been strung across it because none of them could swim.' "

"Calm down, Lizzie. Sit down," he commanded, holding out both hands, but I couldn't stop.

" ' "The gunships hovered right above them firing," said a French priest who lives here with the refugees. "We could see the faces of the pilots. Afterward, so many vultures were picking at the bodies in the water you could have crossed the river on their backs." ' "

Then I stopped, because my throat was closing up and I didn't want to cry.

"The nature of Bellavista's military isn't exactly the issue here."

McManus had pushed out his chair, was leaning back in it. He'd lit a cigarette and he smoked, watching me as if I were an actress in a TV melodrama.

"Rivas Valdez is a fascist, an autocrat," I told him. I blew my nose into a napkin. "He's a very dangerous man."

He nodded, smiled.

"What are you going to tell me next, Lizzie, that you worked on your back for the greater glory of American journalism? That you're still objective and detached? That kinky sex is a new investigative technique? Jesus."

He laughed.

"Don't use my byline. Run the story without a byline. But for God's sake use the story."

"I don't care how good the fucking story is. Van Doorn would never consent. Not under the circumstances."

Another spurt of fury escaped.

"You never wanted that story. You don't care about the truth. You never did."

Still McManus calmly watched, and I could tell I no longer existed for him, that my opinions didn't matter.

"If you cared so much, Lizzie, you could have kept your pants on." At first I wasn't sure I'd heard him. "Okay, that was a low blow," he went on. "But I guess what I expected, what I was hoping for, was some expression of remorse, maybe some shame."

Shame. I almost laughed. Because my life was saturated with it: shame over my circumstances, our poverty, my crazy mother, my absent father. Shame over myself—that a woman I repudiated was me; shame that, though I didn't understand her and could not control her, I had to claim her. I'd been born into shame the way some people are born into money. It had marked me indelibly, the way wealth marked Mary Healy. And there was McManus, examining me with his editorial eyes, hoping for an expression of remorse or shame. I almost laughed.

"How could you sabotage yourself like this, Lizzie? Your career— down the tubes because you fucked around. Everything you've worked for. . . ." His voice was gentle and it trailed off, but his swollen eyes stayed locked on mine. I couldn't look away. "You were a damned fine newswoman." Even through the roar, he sounded like he meant it. "One of the best. You had everything. And now you're done, finished."

My eyes escaped, discovered pots of lustrous flowers bobbing in the breeze from the open windows. I watched them, wondering if, after all, Van Doorn and McManus hadn't thought I was a good reporter; if, after all, I hadn't gotten my promotion just because I'd earned it. Then I watched the flowers dance, thinking that if I burned long enough I'd simply turn to ash and blow away.

CHAPTER
TWENTY-EIGHT

*T*HE PHONE WAS RINGING WHEN I GOT BACK TO MY ROOM, AND I rushed inside to answer it. I grabbed it as if it were a flotation device, something to keep me from going under.

"I'm having a Big Mac attack." I didn't recognize her voice until she laughed, Mary Healy. "Meet me at McDonald's, my treat. I've got a surprise for you."

I hung up, filled with crazy jubilation, because my life was going to continue after all. My life wasn't over—no matter what McManus said.

I took a taxi, waited for Mary near the flags outside the restaurant. There were three of them—the Stars and Stripes; the green-black-and-yellow banner of Bellavista; the smiling red face of Ronald McDonald on a field of butter yellow. The restaurant occupied a new shopping strip adjacent to the ruins. Its golden arches sparkled in the midday sun. Madonna's "Like a Prayer" blared from the speakers of a nearby record store. Except for the military jeeps that seemed to use it as a shortcut, the parking lot was empty. The ruins just beyond looked prehistoric. Or maybe they looked more like a movie set, not real. I wondered where Sonia could be. It seemed like centuries since I'd looked for her. Only it had been the afternoon before. Then Mary's van entered from the direction of the ruins, zoomed straight toward me, screeched to a halt inches from the flagpoles.

"The hamburger that ate the world," she declared as she bounded out of the van. She squeezed me roughly, and I looked away. She let go, pretended she hadn't smelled the bourbon. "It's what the United States is down here fighting for, you know," she went on. "To make the world safe for Big Macs."

Soon we were inside, sitting at an orange Formica table, surrounded by plastic philodendrons, with heaps of greasy fast food arrayed before us. She lifted her burger from its Styrofoam box with both hands, examined it instead of me. She looked thinner, more translucent than before.

"You can have Aguas Oscuras. I mean the story. Everything is all set." She nodded sagely, took a dainty nibble, quickly licked a bit of sauce that had squirted onto her lip. Again I glimpsed the Connecticut debutante.

"Well, what do you think? Are you ecstatic?" She looked up, smiling, and shrugged when I failed to respond. "Okay, you're stunned into silence. But eat, at least." She pointed to the untouched food on my tray. I squeezed some ketchup over the french fries. "It's a great story. Your editors will be blown away."

I know I should have told her right then that I was no longer a credentialed journalist, that I no longer worked for the *Herald-Sun*. I should have told her right then that I could not do the story for the *New York Herald-Sun*. But I couldn't get the words out.

"We'll get Sonia and go up there this afternoon."

"Sonia?" I asked, grateful for the recovery of my voice. She took her time chewing and swallowing that mouthful, went on to a sip of chocolate shake.

"She's with us at the center. She and her mother showed up last night. Maybe around nine. Just before curfew."

"She didn't call. I told Alba to have her call."

"She called. I called. We all called." She laughed, a hard bright sound. Her eyes seemed full of light. "You didn't answer."

Her fingers poked through the fries, pushed them this way and that. She finally pincered one, brought it to her mouth, chewed it carefully. Twenty times, I thought.

"See, what's happened," she continued softly once the potato was safely on its way through her gastrointestinal tract, "is that some people who live near there, near the shrine, found a body dump. A pit filled with skeletons. It confirms the witness's story. That's why she's agreed to come forward. I mean, she's agreed to talk to you. And to be photographed."

Again she smiled, and I smiled back.

"But I've been reassigned," I heard myself say, my words as unreal as the plastic philodendrons. "I'm flying out of here tomorrow night."

I was breathless as my words hovered there between us, amid the stifling odors of grilled beef and tallow-fried potatoes. They were the closest I could get to the truth. Still, I was terrified that she would ask me why, why I'd been reassigned. Even through her smile, I kept seeing my ID cards as they were swept away, into the interoffice envelope. I didn't want her to know that my identity had been looted, an essential part confiscated. I couldn't bear to tell her why, to have her know who I really was.

"Oh, Lizzie," she exclaimed, shaking her head. "You know how to free-lance stories, don't you? For God's sake! Do the piece for someone else." She laughed. "Who needs the *Herald-Sun*?" She took another bite of her burger.

When her words registered, I understood that I was still a professional journalist even if I no longer worked for the *Herald-Sun*. Even if I no longer had credentials. What I understood as I gazed back into her eyes was that it didn't matter if I no longer worked for the *Herald-Sun*. Because I was still a reporter, and I could sell the story anyplace. To any of our rivals, the big-city dailies. To the *Village Voice*. Or to a magazine. *Vanity Fair. Rolling Stone. Esquire*. It was a great story and I could sell it anyplace.

"So fuck the *Herald-Sun* and all its editors," I said, and burst out laughing.

"Yes, fuck 'em," she replied and joined me in my laughter. And to myself I said fuck Rivas Valdez, too. Fuck the U.S. embassy, the State Department, and the entire government of Bellavista. It was a great story and it was mine. The story of Aguas Oscuras belonged to me.

Mary and I sat there, hunched over Big Macs, giggling and planning how to do the story. We made our plan, and as we made it, it seemed perfect, simple. She, Mary, had some last-minute business to attend to at OPEN which involved the witness. She would head up there, get the witness, go on to Aguas Oscuras, where she would pick up Luz and her daughters, who would be returning to OPEN for a while. I would meet them there late in the afternoon, after renting a car at the airport and picking up Sonia and Alba at Nuestra Señora del Refugio. Mary said the rented car, a car nobody could identify with either one of us, would be safer anyway. If we met at Aguas Oscuras before dark, we would have plenty of time to take photographs and interview the witness before returning to OPEN—Ciudad de Merced—by curfew. We agreed that if anything went wrong for either one of us we would meet back at the clinic at OPEN.

I rediscovered my appetite while we planned, had no trouble at all finishing the messy burger, a mountain of fries, two cups of coffee. The synergism of adrenaline, caffeine, and Wild Turkey created a wondrous high, a feeling of well-being and power. I realized as we talked that I'd finally be able to tell the truth, the whole truth, and that, by doing so, I could salvage my career. Not only was Aguas Oscuras a great story in and of itself, it was also a chance for me to save myself.

Was she afraid? I must have asked her then.

She was nibbling a fry, but her free hand moved to the crucifix, enclosed it.

"Not for myself," she said. "But you know, these other women who've come so far with me, these women I love—yes, I am afraid for them. They're not safe anymore, and I'm responsible." She squeezed the cross inside her fist. "That's why we've been in the process of disappearing them. In our own way. We're closing the center and the OPEN clinic, which have been the target of so much hatred."

"Where will everyone go?"

"Here and there in Libertad, Ciudad de Merced, the countryside. Everywhere, really. The center won't be a center anymore, but we'll continue with our work. . . ."

"What about you?"

She shrugged. "I'll find a place. I always do."

She let the cross go, went back to her food, and I watched her, thinking she was a crazy *gringa*, and that I loved her craziness.

I hardly noticed the soldiers who came in behind us and took seats across the aisle. I suppose they registered their message subliminally.

Because later, in an obsessive effort to remember everything, I saw them at their table drinking coffee, wrapped in ammunition belts, their M-16s across their laps. In my memory, I saw them exactly as they had been, those young soldiers. Not talking, but watching us, their black eyes like bullets in dead faces. At the time I paid them no attention. When we'd looked out the plate-glass window and seen more soldiers outside, eating burgers in a jeep, Mary had joked about Bellavista's goon squad, its only growing employment sector, and we'd laughed and gone on with our plans. I'm sure there were two more of them, lounging against the glass on the far side of the front door, when we finally left. Passionate with our scheme, and full of laughter, we managed to ignore them.

"The vision still has its time," Mary said once she'd climbed into the van. She reached out through the open window for my hand, smiled her beatific smile. It no longer scared me, that smile, and I met, without flinching, her odd, translucent gaze. It seemed perfectly appropriate that she was quoting Scripture.

"Whatever else might happen, don't forget it, Lizzie. The vision is pressing on toward its fulfillment, and will not disappoint."

Looking at her then, absorbing her confidence and faith, I remembered the first part of the quotation: "Write the vision clearly upon the tablets so everyone can read it."

She nodded, grinned at my erudition.

"That's your job, the writing. Just make sure you get it right."

Again she smiled, squeezed my hand tighter. Then, with a yelp of ironic laughter, she let me go, jerked the van into reverse. She swerved in a wide arc toward the exit. Once she waved, stretching her arm straight out the window, as if she were still trying to reach me.

Jeans. Jeans. Blue jeans. What the soldiers wanted was blue jeans, stone-washed denim blue jeans. They stood outside the Cherokee, pointing through the window at the ones I happened to be wearing. Calvin Kleins. At first I thought they wanted mine. At first I thought they wanted me to take mine off, right there at the airport checkpoint, and give them up. The two of them laughed when I suggested this. No, no, no. They didn't actually want my jeans, but instead wanted me to buy them each a pair. I looked at the dashboard clock. I was running late and hadn't yet left the airport. It had taken nearly two hours to rent the four-wheel-drive car—the rental desk had been closed for siesta. Then they'd had to check and clean my vehicle. I insisted that they not bother, I'd take it as it was, but then I wasted fifteen minutes figuring out how to drive it.

The problem at the checkpoint was my lack of proper documents. *"Documentos, por favor,"* the first young soldier had asked me, the ubiquitous command in Bellavista, the one I had been dreading. I smiled back at him with nothing to offer but my New York driver's license. Without papers that permitted me to travel, the second soldier informed me, I had no right to be driving out of the airport in the rented Cherokee. Why, I asked the pair of them, who kept grinning at me, why had I been rented the Cherokee if I had no right to drive it? They didn't know, shrugged helplessly and grinned some more. Then, in an accent I had trouble understanding, they started talking about jeans. Jeans. Jeans. Blue jeans. What if I just give you the money and you go buy the jeans yourself? I asked, wondering how much cash I had, realizing it probably was not enough. They laughed together, happily it seemed, but shook their heads no. They wouldn't let me through. There was nothing sinister about them, just an innocent determination. They were doing business. So I turned around and drove back to the main terminal building. Where, the boys had assured me, a boutique sold genuine Calvin Kleins for about eighty-five U.S. dollars a pair. I found the boutique, went inside, bought the jeans in the sizes they had told me. While there, I selected several more pairs, in more or less the same sizes, charged them on my American Express card—five hundred dollars for stone-washed denim blue jeans. I signed the charge slip, figuring I could argue with the tax man that the jeans were a legitimate business expense.

Afterward I went and cashed a check, asked for U.S. currency, tens and twenties, guessing they were the best denominations for bribes. The checkpoint boys were ecstatic with their blue jeans and hastened to lift the electronic gates for me. Yet I wanted something else, a piece of paper from them stating that I was allowed to travel. Or at least a piece of paper that looked like an official travel document, something with big stamps on it. The soldiers chatted in their little booth for several minutes, finally shrugged to indicate their helplessness. I held two twenties out my window. The bills were brand-new, smooth and shiny. After a moment, the bills had disappeared and I was holding a sheet of blue paper with black stamps. The soldiers waved me on my way.

It was this officially stamped sheet of blue paper, with another pair of twenties folded up inside, that bought my freedom from the next checkpoint three miles away, that permitted me to drive on into Libertad, to El Centro de Cambio y Creatividad, where Alba and Sonia were waiting.

But the traffic at this checkpoint, outside the U.S. embassy, was backed up like at the Lincoln Tunnel at rush hour, and the two-lane road had swollen into six or seven. The stinking lines of buses, pickup trucks, and taxis inched along so slowly that the Cherokee kept stalling and the air conditioner exuded puffs of warm, moist air. Some time passed before I glimpsed, in the glittering distance, what must have been a motorcade into the embassy compound and the military roadblocks holding back the traffic. I remembered that a Congressional delegation had been scheduled to arrive from the United States that very day. This Congressional delegation was to be fêted at the embassy, along with members of the junta and other political and military leaders.

Stalled there in traffic, I couldn't help imagining Rivas Valdez and his wife at the embassy party with Whitaker and all the others. Of course, she didn't have a face, his wife, though all the others did. I imagined that Van Doorn and Joe Soza would be there, too, and I couldn't help wondering if they'd meet the general and his faceless spouse; wondering what all of them would talk about if they chatted over drinks. When I was close enough to see the gleaming limos entering the embassy compound, I remembered what McManus had said about the ineluctability of history. I also remembered what he'd said about me, about my professional history, and his queer smile when he'd said it. Even then, sweating in the Cherokee, going noplace fast, I believed I'd prove him wrong. I believed it all the more when the soldiers at the checkpoint took my money, gave me back the blue paper, waved me on my way.

"I don't understand why she left this," Alba said in Spanish, holding up Mary's satchel. We were standing in Mary's office just inside the front door of El Centro de Cambio y Creatividad. "Maybe she's coming back here."

"No, no," I insisted. "We're supposed to meet her at Aguas Oscuras. She's picking up Luz and then meeting us there. I'm positive."

Alba nodded without speaking. She was holding the satchel in both arms, like a baby. I, too, wondered why Mary had left her bag behind— I'd never seen her travel without it. But it didn't seem important enough to spend time talking about.

"Bring it along. Just bring it," I urged, trying not to sound impatient. "Give it to her when you see her."

Again Alba nodded, chewing on her lip.

"Let's go," said Sonia through a cloud of cigarette smoke. Even in the shadows of El Centro de Cambio y Creatividad, she was wearing her dark glasses. "It's giving me the creeps hanging around here, waiting. We'll be lucky if we make it up there before curfew."

It occurred to me then that Sonia was also crazy, reckless, to be going with us. Because she was very vulnerable, much more vulnerable than I was.

"Give me your cameras, if you want," I suggested. "I'll take the pictures."

"Greedy bitch," she replied, then laughed. "You couldn't pay me to give up this chance. Not even if my life depended on it." She snorted at her morbid joke, shoved back her glasses, raked me with her somber eyes. I looked away, realizing she knew everything, that she somehow knew everything about me.

Maybe because Sonia had unnerved me, or maybe because of all the dusky shadows, I took a wrong turn just outside Libertad. None of us realized it for quite a while. Not until we found ourselves, or, rather, found ourselves lost, in a mountainside shantytown on the far side of the city. We were retracing our route when a tire blew and the Cherokee skidded across the rutted roadway, stopping inches from a precipice.

"Look," Sonia commanded once we'd stopped and gotten out. She was gesturing to the crosses that marked the slope below. "We almost landed in a body dump."

I opened up the back, discovered that the jack was missing. "Shitsville," I corrected her, remembering how, at the airport, I hadn't let them clean or check the car. "Shitsville is where we landed."

The pickup truck was driving very slowly with its lights out. We'd been walking maybe fifteen minutes and it was the first sign of human activity we'd seen.

"Fucking death squad," muttered Sonia. "Just our luck."

The truck stopped, trapped us in its high beams, blinding us momentarily. I fought the urge to run. "Need help?" a man's voice called in Spanish, and we stood there in the light yelling out our tale of woe. In minutes we were sitting in the back of the pickup on our way back to the Cherokee. There were five of them, two in the cab, three with us. All were armed with shotguns and machetes, but I don't remember any of their faces, don't think I ever saw them clearly.

They said they were members of a *patrulla de defensa civil*—a civilian defense patrol—the men who provided the jack and helped us change the tire. But it wasn't until we'd finished with the tire that one of them thought to ask where we were going, to ask us for our documents.

"*¿Tienen documentos? ¿Dónde están sus documentos?*" he asked, suddenly frowning, examining each of us carefully, as though suspecting us of subversion, other heinous crimes.

Documentos. Documentos. Not one of us had *documentos*.

But we're only returning to Libertad, I said, attempting a soft smile. They moved away, talked quietly among themselves. I heard them say something about *la prensa internacional*; something about all three of us violating the state of siege, other laws regarding *la prensa*. It didn't occur to us to question their authority. Suddenly I felt precarious, as if I'd just stepped through a hole in the earth. Then I heard Alba's voice. Aren't these nice jeans? she called out. I bought them for my brother. The members of the civil defense patrol moved closer to the Cherokee. Oh, yes, they're very nice jeans, the youngest answered. He had always wanted jeans like that. I glanced into the car, saw that Sonia and Alba had taken the jeans out of the bag, were displaying them across the backseat. With the car door open, the interior light was on. A fresh ten-dollar bill protruded from the coin pocket of each.

The clinic at Ciudad de Merced was dark and empty when we got there. The rooms were not quite ransacked, but the furniture had been pushed around, the contents of drawers and cabinets spilled out or thrown around. Two of us played flashlights over the walls and floors. The empty rooms, the mess, gave nothing away.

It wasn't quite curfew, so we went back out, drove through the darkened streets, thinking we might be able to escape OPEN and go on to Aguas Oscuras. But the dusty lanes were full of people, hurrying, on foot, back to their dwellings. Jeeps full of *policía* roved through them warning that curfew approached. I had no more jeans, and hardly any cash, nothing else with which to buy our way past checkpoints, roadblocks.

"I guess this is it," muttered Sonia when I turned, headed back to the clinic. "This is fucking it."

Alba said nothing. She just clutched Mary's bag and stared out into the night. We stayed in the clinic at OPEN, lying on pallets on the floor. We didn't really sleep, just dozed off sometimes, waiting irrationally for the sound of Mary's van, her footsteps. At first we talked, theorizing that she must be staying with Luz in the little village outside Aguas Oscuras. And once, well after curfew, we called El Centro de Cambio y Creatividad, but Milagros said Mary had not called and no one there could guess where she might be. After that we stopped talking.

Now it seems inevitable that we ended up there, helpless in the dark, separated from Mary Healy and our grand scheme of revelation. Looking back, it seems that we should have been able to foresee that long, lightless night in the clinic at OPEN. But of course we had not foreseen it, nor anything like it. So we lay there, gasping on the musty smell of the earthen floor, stunned and disbelieving.

"You know, I met Joe Soza," Sonia whispered to me shortly after I lay down. I turned to her, saw her in the shadows, holding a lighted cigarette, blowing smoke rings.

"Well?" I said at last. "So?"

"So you fucked up in a big way, Miss America." She made a throaty noise, waited for the response I didn't give her. "I suppose you know it, huh?"

"What did Joe Soza have to say?"

"That he was replacing you as the *Herald-Sun*'s Bellavista correspondent. Temporarily. Until a new reporter could be assigned."

"That's all?"

"It was enough. I'm pretty good at math. I added it all up." She stopped and I hoped she was finished, but she wasn't. "I knew before we went to Mesa Verde, anyway. I knew I was right."

"Then what are you doing here? Why did you come?"

She didn't answer for a time, and I watched her smoke, her face hidden.

"Because of Mary. Because of her faith. She's a crazy *gringa*, one of the craziest. But she has faith."

Of course, Sonia didn't mean Mary's religious faith, nor did she specifically mean her faith in the revolution. What she admired, I think, was Mary's belief in justice and the courage of her absolute commitment to fight for it.

"Does she know?" I asked after a while. "I mean about me?"

"We talked about you. Just a little. Last night." Sonia shrugged, blew more smoke rings. "We didn't come up with any answers. But she wanted you to have this story. She said it was yours, that you needed it. She said it was going to help you."

Again the flames of ignominy burned painfully around me, and everything flickered in their reddish light. I wondered exactly what she knew, wondered how I was going to face her.

"And by the way," Sonia said, diverting me, "thanks for looking for me and my mother. Thanks for trying to help us."

The sun had not yet pushed its way through the morning haze. Shimmering high grass, dawn-wet, swayed like curtains all around us, tall enough in places to glisten near our eyes. The air was moist and still, acrid with the smell of smoke. Overhead, the birds wheeled and glided. Not far away, the Virgin stood placid in her grotto. She had been there, impassive through it all.

Some time before, once we'd learned what had happened, we had all stopped talking. Only the cicadas kept up their high-pitched chir, like a panicked ringing in my ears that might not ever stop. We had worked for several hours, and when at last we'd finished, and the rest of them had knelt to pray, I heard the other sound, the noise that might have been a bird's cry, or the whimper of a wounded animal. Because I couldn't pray, and couldn't stand there thinking about what the red earth held, I began to search, following the sound. I found her several hundred yards across the trackless golden meadow, curled up in the grass, where she'd fallen, hidden, slept. She was about two years old, covered with cuts and bruises. Her cotton dress was torn in several places. "Mama," she kept saying. She stopped the moment she saw me, began to sob instead. I reached through the high grass to pick her up. She was almost weightless in my arms. I held her close, held her while she cried. Because by then I knew who she must be as well as what she'd lost.

We'd scuttled with our lights out past the OPEN checkpoint and its sleeping guards before the end of curfew, before dawn. Somehow we found our way along the darkened roads until I recognized the dense green tunnel that opened onto Aguas Oscuras. The dawn light, majestic even through the clouds, snatched away our voices. I slowed, pushing my way through the swaying high grass toward the Virgin's shrine. There was no transfiguration, not even the illusion, but Alba was out and running anyway. I parked, got out, followed at a distance.

When Alba finished praying, we left the shrine, walked along the water's edge, then through shimmering high grass. Except for the cicadas, everything was quiet. Sweat tickled my temples, my upper lip and chin.

The smell of smoke oppressed us. It made me think of the massacre and wonder if the earth hadn't opened in the heat to give it up. Finally we reached the ruts of the old road that twisted like twin serpents through the meadow. We walked along these ruts as they rose and curved toward the forest. When we reached the highest point we paused, surveyed the golden flatland which had once held the village of Aguas Oscuras.

Mary's van, its blackened shell, was like a sunspot in this meadow. We saw it, lying on its side, in a shallow gully near the entrance to the forest. Its windows were shattered—from the heat of the fire or the energy of an explosion. A ring of blackened grass surrounded it. Wisps of smoke curled up from it, disappeared into the air.

Nobody moved for several minutes. We stood, watched smoke wisping from the ashes of our hope, and then tried walking toward the van. We swerved away before we reached it, repelled by the scorched disintegration. Instead we walked around and through the meadow, circling and circling the scorched earth, but unable to approach the fatal umbra.

We came across a woman's sandal, a pair of bloodied underpants, a baby doll with one eye, a girl's flowered dress, a red barrette, a soldier's camouflage cap, a hank of black hair shining on a branch like the feather of an exotic bird, and finally Mary's copper crucifix on its broken leather cord.

We probably could have stopped then, once we'd found the crucifix. Because we all understood, without having to say it, that finding the crucifix beyond the charred shell of the van marked an end, the absolute end. Yet we could not stop. We could not stop walking, could not stop searching.

Sooner or later, at Alba's insistence, we did approach the sunspot. Sonia helped to brace me and Alba climbed onto my shoulders. She scaled the hot metal, managed to open one of the doors.

"¡Está desocupada!" It's empty, she called out just before my heart exploded. But Alba did not come back empty-handed. She retrieved, from beneath the driver's seat, the fireproof box of consecrated hosts.

We kept circling in wider circles, pushed outward by the centrifuge of violence, not knowing exactly who or what we were looking for. We followed patterns of crushed grass, broken vines and flowers. We found blood puddles, spent shells, places where someone must have run and where someone must have fallen. We didn't speak, but I think all of us were trying to do the same thing, trying to put something back together, something that might make a meaning. What we got were fragmented signs of merciless pursuit, fatal struggles, and a terrible vision of our own fate, the murders from which we'd been saved by the wrong turn outside Libertad.

We'd worked our way back to the shrine when we saw the Taupils, two of them, eerie shadows in a stand of junipers behind the grotto. We assumed they were the murderers, and Sonia took out her gun. But as we approached, the old man and the teenage boy dropped to their knees and blessed themselves. *"¡No dispare!"* Don't shoot! the old man cried.

"¡No tienen que disparar!"

We saw the women when we reached the Taupils. They were face-down in the grass beyond the shrine, half hidden by a hillock and more trees. There were four of them: Mary Healy. Tía Amparo, the silver-haired Taupil from OPEN. The *sanitaria* named Luz. Her daughter Esperanza, who was ten years old. They were lying close together, their arms flung around one another, as though they'd died that way, embracing. But we'd already gathered up the evidence. We knew they had not died that way, embracing. They had died one by one. Alone. Pursued.

The moment I saw them, I understood that the witness, the witness to the atrocities at Aguas Oscuras, had been Tía Amparo, the clinic manager at OPEN, the Taupil with the silver braids. She was the one I would have interviewed, the one who was to have divulged her secrets, the secrets that were to have redeemed me. Tía Amparo. I'd met her my first week in Bellavista. But she had died with and for her secrets.

Then, in a voice that was no more than a whisper, the old man began to explain. The night before had been warm and very quiet, almost supernaturally still, he said. He and his son were sleeping in their hut nearby in the forest when the cries awakened them. Women's cries from far away. Terrible cries, like those of women giving birth. He paused, and I saw he and the boy were covered with dirt and blood. I saw the pit they had been digging, a grave.

Did you hear anything else? The old man turned toward my voice. Racing motors. Screeching tires. Men's voices. Loud music. Then more cries, women's cries. We walked to the edge of the forest, but we saw nothing. It was too dark. Even the moon was hidden. We were so afraid. We had nothing, no weapons. We heard the gunshots. Many gunshots. An explosion. Again the sounds of motors, screeching tires. Afterward the silence.

So you began to look for them?

We began to look. We found them one by one. We brought them here. So the vultures wouldn't get them.

The old man covered his face with his hands and began to sob.

Don't cry. You could not have saved them, Alba told him. You would have been killed too.

"*Pero la gringa es la santa, Sor María, ¿verdad?*" he asked.

"*Sí,*" Alba answered. The *gringa* was the saint, Sister Mary.

If it had not been for the birds, we all would have stood there paralyzed. Maybe if the birds had not been wheeling and gliding overhead we would have been unable to keep going. But the birds were calling out to one another, gathering and waiting. So we climbed into the pit with the old man and the boy. The world turned hushed and distant as we began using our hands, flat stones, a tire iron from the Cherokee, the peasants' spade and shovel. At last the hole was large enough, and we beat the vultures. We moved them from their place in the high grass to the place in the earth. Afterward we stood or knelt at the edge with the clumps of rusty earth exploding in wild sprays from our hands and shovels until all of them were blanketed.

The whole time we worked, I heard the famished click and whir of Sonia's camera, almost as incessant as the cicadas. But quite a while would pass before I was able to look at Sonia's photographs. A long time would pass before I was able to see, in Sonia's photographs, certain objective facts that I could not acknowledge or absorb that day. That the women were mostly naked, were dressed only in the ragged bits the Indians had found for them. That rifle shots at close range had shattered their skulls, destroyed their faces. That Mary Healy's hands had also been shot off. As though she'd put up her hands to shield her face, and they'd taken the full impact of the blast. Even then I could not imagine that they'd shot off her hands, her strong and skillful hands, before they'd raped and killed her.

The little girl's legs were wrapped tightly around my waist and her arms were knotted at my shoulders. Her fingers, hooks of fear, dug into my neck and back. The way she held me made me think of drowning victims. Of how, in panic, they could lock their arms and legs on you and pull you under. As we walked through the high grass back to the others, I knew that I was stronger, that she wouldn't pull me under, even if she never let me go.

The sky was vast and glimmering behind its silver nimbus, gravid with its secrets. Beyond where the others were praying, the big cedars swayed and the mountains faded like a dream into the sky. Dying you destroyed our deaths. Rising you restored our life. Lord Jesus come in glory. Their words came to me as an undulant murmur. Alba held the ciborium. It was made of pottery, lined with gold. The gold gave off slivers of light. Then they turned and saw the child.

Nobody knew her name. Nobody remembered the little girl's name, and she herself wasn't talking. Of course, we knew who she was, knew right away that she was Luz's daughter, Luz's youngest child. But none of us could remember what her name was. We theorized that she'd been somehow overlooked when the others were taken from the van. That she'd then saved herself by going off and looking for her mother. The fact of her survival had almost overwhelmed me. Just as her voice, calling Mama, like a fragment from a dream, had almost overwhelmed me. When I'd first seen her, curled up there in the grass, terrified and helpless, she seemed to be a hallucination. Until I touched her, felt her need.

The loss of her mother, and whatever else she had experienced, turned her mute after I found her, and nearly a year would pass before she spoke again. When she finally spoke, she talked, the way very young children often do, only of the present. Of the pigeons cooing on the window ledge outside my apartment; of the lights and buttons on the elevator, and the way the door slid shut like magic. Neither the future nor the past seemed to exist for her. In fact, the events of that night in Aguas Oscuras were permanently lost to her memory. As if she'd been reborn when I found her in the high grass. As if she'd been flung out of the centrifuge of violence and reborn into my arms.

That morning, as she trembled, grasping me, and I rubbed her back, whispering senseless words I don't remember, no one knew her name. For the others, the urgency to go subsumed the miracle of her survival. We were swept away in it, a current so swiftly moving that my memories are confused, insubstantial. I see the old man and his boy melting back into the forest. Alba urging me to drive her to another place, higher up into the mountains. Alba speaking with such self-containment she seems to be looking out at me from someplace far away.

I see myself pulling over onto the dusty shoulder of a remote road, see a panorama of trees, steepening slopes. "I know where I am going," Alba says, and it occurs to me that her tranquillity was the kind Mary longed for but never quite achieved.

We get out, and Alba looks into the front where the child is almost hidden in the seat. The child has black hair, black eyes, caramel-colored skin. She watches us with ancient eyes, eyes that seem to know what she cannot possibly know. Alba leans through the open window, looks at her for a while. I see that they are sisters in gender, race, and grief. The thought makes me hope that Alba will relent and take her, relieving me of all responsibility.

I hear the whir of film rewinding and Sonia is shoving the small film canister into my hand, rifling through her camera bag, giving me several more. "I have to go. I can't go back."

She smiles, squeezes my arm. "You've got to go tell my mother, okay? Her English is lousy. So you've got to speak Spanish. *¿Comprendes?*"

"I'll speak Spanish," I tell her.

"You've got to make her understand." She squeezes harder.

"She'll understand." I can't help but smile, because we both know she will.

"Tell her to get ready. To be ready. Because somebody will come for her. I don't know when but very soon. Because she belongs with us. With the family."

She lets go of my arm. The three of us look at one another. Our faces, hands, and clothes are smudged with earth and soot and blood. *"El crucifijo,"* Alba says then. After a minute, I understand. I open up the back, where Mary's cross lies among the bloody clothes, the doll, the soldier's hat, the red barrette, the sandal. I pick up Mary's crucifix, hand it to Alba. We hold hands for a minute, the cross between our palms. She opens Mary's satchel, a place to hold the crucifix. I glimpse the organized, antiseptic world of instruments and medications. Among them is a folded piece of paper. Alba takes it out, shrugs at the incomprehensible English, hands it to me.

"Stuff to get, things to do," it says in Mary's flamboyant scrawl. It lists sutures, penicillin, brandy. Then it says, "Call Mom and Dad, AeroVista." The paper was ringed with doodles, as though she'd been talking on the phone, or waiting for something while making it. Among the doodles she had written, "I believe in the Resurrection!!!"

I try to translate for her, have trouble, so Sonia finishes the job. Then we run out of words. At last I see the two of them heading for the trees, Alba with the satchel and the metal box, Sonia with her camera bag. The green place closes over them before I feel the note still in my hand.

On the way back down the mountain, there were no more cicadas, just the ringing in my ears, and I turned on the radio to try and make it go away.

"A cache of weapons and revolutionary propaganda has been found at health clinics operated by a North American subversive named Mary Healy."

The words, in the rapid-fire Spanish of a government news broadcast, spewed from the radio with such energy and conviction they sounded like the truth.

"Healy, who gained access to our country by pretending to be a Roman Catholic missionary, has long been suspected of terrorist activities. Her links to *el frente* are well known. She is now considered a fugitive from justice. . . .

"Government forces have beaten back communist rebels in the disputed northern territory called Mesa Verde. At least four hundred communists are among the dead. . . .

"Citing a resurgence of communist activity in the countryside as well as the atmosphere of lawlessness in the cities, Defense Minister Víctor Rivas Valdez has taken control of the junta and declared martial law. Rivas Valdez calls it a distressing but necessary interlude in the nation's march toward democracy. He promises, however, that a presidential election will be held in the spring. . . ."

I turned off the radio, slowed down, not knowing where to go or what to do. The narrative was breaking apart, though the story was not over. The child kept looking at me with her ancient eyes, and I had trouble looking back.

In the gullies by the road, I could see little crosses, some with nameplates flashing in the light. They signified the efforts of *las madres de los desaparecidos* to memorialize the missing and the dead, their children. *Las madres de los desaparecidos*. The mothers of the disappeared. Among the disappeared, I knew, were many mothers, like the mother of the nameless child beside me. Mothers of the disappeared. Disappeared mothers.

I pulled over and got out, stood against the car. Through the windshield I could see her with her bruises, her torn dress, the huge eyes in which I read her loss and fear. I didn't know what to do with her, didn't know what I could give to her, or any way I could help her. I decided then to take her back, take her back to where I'd found her. To leave her with the Taupils. Because I didn't know what to do with her, and had nothing to give her. And I knew somehow that if I took her with me that day, I would always have her. So I decided I would turn around and take her back to them, to the Taupils, to somebody, so she could be brought up in the language and culture of her ancestors, connected to her past, and the history of her people.

I was moving toward the car door when she climbed out of the other side. On tiny legs she waddled like a beast, rushed away from my rejection. She fell when she reached the bottom of the gully. She didn't bother to get up, just lay there curled over her sorrow. I watched her, remembering her mother at the prayer meeting when she'd told the story of her rescue by Mary Healy. I remembered that her mother's name was Luz, which meant light. Then I remembered Aurora, the murdered girl in the South Bronx. I remembered her mother's grief in the awful homeless shelter and how I'd walked away from her; how I hadn't told their story.

Again I looked at the crosses, the small white crosses, some with nameplates, some without. The child lay among them, at the bottom of the gully, collapsed over her losses, sobbing. I thought about her mother, Luz, and about other mothers, about Aurora's mother and my own. I thought about mothers of the disappeared and disappeared mothers, all of them.

Then Mary came back to me. I saw her clearly, as through an open window, with the night sky glowing all around her. "Love and faith pull you out of all your hiding places," she told me. Her eyes were curious, her grin ironic. She was as she had been, strung taut between rage and compassion. "They take you places you don't want to go." Then she laughed her odd laugh, disappeared.

Again I saw the child, collapsed among the crosses. Between us stretched a puddle of doubt as dark and viscous as spilled blood. But another feeling had begun to overwhelm my doubt, my sorrow, and I knew it was not true that I had nothing to give her. Finally I was walking to her, and I found her, turned her, held her face between my hands. Her hot cheeks seemed to melt my fingers.

"No tenga miedo." Don't be afraid, I told her in the language that was not my own.

Her terror seemed to subside, or maybe I just imagined it. I reached through doubt and picked her up. She reached back, clasping me. Her hair smelled like grass and smoke. I did not know what to do with her, not even what to call her. But someday I would tell her that her mother's name was Luz, which meant light. I would tell her, someday, about her mother and her sister. I would tell her about Mary Healy and Tía Amparo, about all the things they had done. Someday I would tell her that all of them were called women of light. I would also tell her that there were no children of light in Bellavista.

We got back into the car, and she settled in beside me, her head pillowed on my leg, where she soon fell asleep. The engine squawked when I turned on the ignition, released the brake. Below, along the downward slope, I could see the twisting highway, the tentacular subsidiary roads curling off into the jungle, all the routes of sorrow. I knew I might be lost, because there were no signs, but it didn't seem to matter. I kept on driving anyway, maybe or not toward Libertad. As I drove, I listened—to the humming of the tires on the gravel and the rise and fall of her breath, ephemeral as grace.